W9-BCM-652

Praise for
DECEPTION & DESIRE

"Seductive, dreamlike . . . A racy, mystical story where no conclusion is foregone."
—*The Times* (London)

"Hugely entertaining."
—*Daily Express*

"A pacy, well-written blockbuster . . . For those hooked by Beauman's previous two romantic thrillers, this last in the sequence is a must."
—*Good Housekeeping*

"An accomplished thriller . . . A chilling conclusion."
—*Woman & Home*

By Sally Beauman:

DESTINY
DARK ANGEL
LOVERS AND LIARS*
DANGER ZONES*
DECEPTION AND DESIRE*

*Published by Fawcett Books

Books published by The Ballantine Publishing Group
are available at quantity discounts on bulk purchases
for premium, educational, fund-raising, and special
sales use. For details, please call 1-800-733-3000.

DECEPTION
&
DESIRE

Sally Beauman

FAWCETT GOLD MEDAL • NEW YORK

Sale of this book without a front cover may be unauthorized. If this book is coverless, it may have been reported to the publisher as "unsold or destroyed" and neither the author nor the publisher may have received payment for it.

A Fawcett Gold Medal Book
Published by The Ballantine Publishing Group
Copyright © 1997, 1998 by Sally Beauman

All rights reserved under International and Pan-American Copyright Conventions. Published in the United States by The Ballantine Publishing Group, a division of Random House, Inc., New York, and simultaneously in Canada by Random House of Canada Limited, Toronto. Originally published in somewhat different form in Great Britain by Transworld Publishers Ltd., in 1997.

All of the characters in this book are fictitious. Any resemblance to actual persons, living or dead, is purely coincidental.

http://www.randomhouse.com

Library of Congress Catalog Card Number: 98-96112

ISBN 0-449-00248-9

Manufactured in the United States of America

First American Edition: June 1998

10   9   8   7   6   5   4   3   2   1

For Alexander Mackinnon
fear ioúil gasda, caraid
gasda, agus duine gasda.

There are terrible spirits, ghosts, in the air of America.

D. H. LAWRENCE, *Edgar Allan Poe*, 1924

HIPPOLYTA: 'Tis strange, my Theseus, that these lovers speak of.

THESEUS: More strange than true: I never may believe
These antique fables, nor these fairy toys,
Lovers and madmen have such seething brains,
Such shaping fantasies, that apprehend
More than cool reason ever comprehends . . .
Such tricks hath strong imagination,
That if it would but apprehend some joy,
It comprehends some bringer of that joy;
Or in the night, imagining some fear,
How easy is a bush suppos'd a bear.

SHAKESPEARE, *A Midsummer Night's Dream*

DECEPTION
&
DESIRE

Part One

INTERVIEW

Chapter 1

Was she afraid or not afraid? The interview was drawing to a close; from outside the theater dressing room, where it was taking place, came the murmur of traffic and the wash of rain; it was early afternoon, yet the light was already beginning to fade.

Across the room from her interviewer, both women seated on hard upright chairs, the actress Natasha Lawrence was positioned with her back to her dressing table and its mirrors, which reflected her in triplicate. She was leaning forward a little, hands clasped in her lap, answering a question about her work. She did so in a low, somewhat hesitant voice, which, mingling with the sound of rain and the faint purr of a humidifier, had a lulling effect. Was she afraid? This question, and most of the other questions her interviewer, Gini Hunter, would have liked to ask, had not been, and apparently could not be, voiced.

This interview, like many Gini had conducted in the past, had been loaded with restrictions. For the past year, Natasha Lawrence had been playing the title role in *Estella*, a musical by a celebrated English composer that had been a *succès fou* in London, and was now a *succès fou* in New York. The musical was based on Dickens's *Great Expectations*, and adjustments had been made to the novel. The part of Estella, that lovely poisonous child, trained by mad Miss Havisham to break men's hearts, was given greater prominence in the musical than in the book. There had been surprise when Natasha Lawrence took this role—her first singing role—for her fame was as a movie actress. Confounding the critics, however, she had proved to have a powerful, true, sweet singing voice. This, combined with her acting ability, never in doubt, had helped to turn *Estella* into a triumph. Gini Hunter, an agnostic where musicals were concerned, admired Lawrence's performance, but retained a strong preference for the original novel; this preference, obviously, she had been careful not to express.

Now, after nearly a year of eight performances a week at the Minskoff Theater, an exhausting and demanding schedule, Natasha Lawrence was leaving the show. She was being replaced by a slightly less famous name, and the rumor was that ticket sales were beginning to fall off. Natasha Lawrence was returning to film work, specifically to a movie directed by her former husband, Tomas Court; this movie, Gini gathered, was to be shot in England—and beyond that would not be discussed. She was here, for the *New York Times*, at the behest of an editor to interview Natasha Lawrence as she prepared to leave the cast of *Estella*. That, at least, was the reason for the interview given to the collection of press agents, PR representatives, secretaries, and aides who stood between Natasha Lawrence and the outside world; the true reason was different—as, in Gini's experience, was usually the case.

"I hear *talk*," said Gini's editor friend, a young man who was rising fast. He was playing with rubber bands, a quirk of his.

"Talk, talk, talk," he amplified, flicking a band and catching it. "Talk about the ex-husband, for a start, white hope of American movies et cetera et cetera—but a strange man, by all accounts. Why the divorce? They still work together. I find that weird. Don't you find that weird? I can tell you, I wouldn't get on the same *airplane* as my ex-wife."

He paused; he toyed with deflecting to the subject of his own marital sufferings—a favored topic—eyed Gini, and changed his mind.

"Talk about the *bodyguards*," he continued, putting a bracelet of rubber bands around his wrist. "Never moves a step without them, *I* hear. Why? Your common or garden variety Hollywood paranoia, d'you think, or more than that? Is she afraid? If so, of whom? Of what?"

Gini sighed. "I'll ask," she said. "I don't expect an answer. Do you?"

"You never know." He gave her an evasive look. "The *Conrad*," he said, surprising Gini. "*I* hear she's after an apartment in the Conrad. Why? Prestige? Security? She won't get it, of course. She has about as much chance of moving in there as I have of moving into the White House. . . ." He paused. "Less."

Gini agreed. The Conrad building, once described as the East Side's answer to the Dakota—a description that applied to its architecture, not its residents—was well known as one of the most desirable, conservative strongholds in New York. Gini could not pass it without imagining fortifications: castellated walls, a drawbridge. The Conrad, a bastion, was not the kind of building that admitted actresses, particularly beautiful, still-young, divorced actresses with a child—Natasha Lawrence had a boy, aged six or seven, she would have to check, from her marriage to Tomas Court.

"You want me to ask her about the Conrad?" Gini said. "She's even *less* likely to discuss that. Anything else?"

"A little glimpse of her soul." The young editor was not without wit or charm; he smiled. "Come on, Gini, you know. Insights. Insights. Who she truly is. What makes her tick . . ."

Gini gave him a look. She rose. "How many words?"

"Thirteen hundred." He removed the rubber wristbands, tossed them up, and caught them—a neat trick.

"Fine. You want the glimpse of soul in my lead paragraph, or can I save it for the close? Thirteen hundred words gives me a whole lot of choice."

"Now, Gini, don't be humorous," the young man said.

"Why not? This is a farce."

"True. True. How long have you got with her?"

"One hour. In her dressing room."

"Ah, well." The editor shrugged. "Maybe she'll open her heart to you. . . ."

"And if she doesn't? Which she won't."

"Then we run the picture bigger," he replied.

In the quiet of the dressing room now, the actress was continuing to speak in that low, lulling voice. The humidifier purred; every so often, its machinery underwent some minor galvanic disturbance; it would whirr and click, send out a sudden puff of water vapor, then revert to its steady background steaming. The actress was answering a question Gini had asked her about the most famous of the movies she had made with her husband, *Dead Heat*. That movie had been controversial, to say the least; Natasha Lawrence spoke of it in a measured, intelligent, but impersonal way, as if it had been directed by a stranger and the leading part had been played not by herself but by someone else. Gini glanced toward her tape recorder, which was patiently recording this answer; most of the answer was unusable for journalistic purposes, and Gini suspected Natasha Lawrence knew that. She glanced at her watch; she had less than ten minutes left. It occurred to her that Lawrence, who had controlled the circumstances of this interview from the first, was still controlling it.

"No personal questions," the press agent handling all publicity for *Estella* had said. That stricture had been repeated by the others who formed a protective shield around Lawrence as, over the weeks leading up to the interview, its date, time, and location had constantly been unpicked and restitched. It had been reiterated finally, the previous day, by a deep-voiced and heavily accented woman named Angelica, the dragon woman who was Natasha Lawrence's chief guardian.

Angelica's role was part domestic, part managerial, part protective, said sources, advising Gini to stay out of her way. Angelica, officially, was nanny and caretaker to the actress's son; unofficially, she was caretaker also to the actress herself.

"No personal questions," she had rasped down the telephone to Gini. "You've got that? No questions about her son, or her marriage, or her divorce, or Tomas Court. And don't think you'll be able to wait awhile and then feed them in when your tape's switched off. You have one hour. In that hour, you can ask her about her movies, or her stage work, or *Estella*; she's there to talk about her *work* and nothing else. She has to conserve her energy, and her voice. It's demanding, playing an eight-performance week. You're lucky to be seeing her at all—and if I had my way, you wouldn't be. So those are the terms, and don't imagine you can ingratiate yourself and alter them once you're in there. She won't fall for *that*."

Indeed she would not, Gini thought, looking at the actress, who, gentle in appearance, and gentle-voiced, conveyed nonetheless a certain steeliness Gini did not altogether like.

She had been expecting that Lawrence would eventually drop her guard, at least enough to become expansive, and her own questions had been designed to provoke expansiveness. Gini had tried the technique of leaving a silence at the end of the actress's answers—a silence most interviewees felt a compulsion to fill. Neither angled questions nor silences were effective; Natasha Lawrence said what she had to say, then stopped. She was adept at putting the onus on the interviewer; she did not belittle the questions asked exactly and she showed no signs of impatience, yet however much Gini crafted the questions, she answered as if she found them predictable, as if she were now speaking from a prepared script.

She was better at evasion, diversion, and deflection than most politicians. Gini resigned herself to the fact that there would be no breakthrough here. She angled another question at her, to which the actress began a patient reply. She addressed this reply, as she had done most of the others, to the floor; Gini, free to look away, searched the room for something, anything, that would lend color to an article she could already see would be workmanlike at best.

This dressing room—and she was sure Lawrence had chosen it as the location for the interview for that reason—was an anonymous place. The dressing table behind Lawrence was bare of telegrams, cards, or photographs. It resembled a table in an operating theater; instead of gauzes, clamps, and knives, there lay the instruments of Lawrence's profession—soft sable brushes, little pots, tubes and sticks of color, a huge crystal jar of pinkish powder, on which nestled an unlikely thistledowny pink powder puff.

Across the room, lined up on a shelf, was a lustrous row of *Estella* wigs. Next to them, hanging from a rack and protected by a white sheet, were the various costumes Lawrence wore as Estella, including that cruel child's first-act white dress, a slippery white organdy like a chrysalis, waiting for the lovely poisonous butterfly Estella to hatch.

Could you play a character like Estella, Gini wondered, a woman trained from her earliest youth to break men's hearts, unless somewhere within you, you had the germ of such characteristics yourself? Estella, after all, was the embodiment of poor, mad, jilted Miss Havisham's revenge on the male sex, and spiritual murder was her intent. Could you play such a woman, or indeed the strange ambivalent women Lawrence had played in her former husband's movies, without being able to imagine them? And could you imagine them if you did not, inside the psyche, contain some little seed that, given the right soil, water, and nutrients, might have made you into such a woman yourself?

She did not know the answer to that question, which applied, she supposed in passing, to other women besides actresses. She would have liked to ask it, but could think of no way of posing it that would not sound banal or trite.

She had less than five minutes left. She turned back to the actress and looked at her carefully as she continued to speak. Famous though she was, a physical description of her would be necessary for this article, and Lawrence was not easy to describe: beauty never was. She was wearing a very plain dark dress; the three mirrors behind her on the dressing table framed her lovely head. The two outer mirrors of this triptych were angled; all three were lit with bare, glowing bulbs, which created a halo, a fizz of light, around her dark, heavy hair, and her pale face and neck. The effect was to suggest that there was more than one woman seated opposite her; as Lawrence moved, or gestured, her other ghostly selves in the mirrors did also.

The length and weight of her hair was apparent only in the mirrors, for she wore it drawn back from her face and gathered in heavy coils at the nape of her neck. Was she beautiful? Yes, she was surely very beautiful, Gini thought, but the grammar of beauty was hard to convey. Did it consist in those dark straight brows, in the etch of the cheekbones, or did it reside in those astonishing inky blue-black eyes, which could convey on-screen, or in the huge spaces of a theater, the tiniest nuance of emotion, the smallest flicker of thought?

It was perhaps in its mobility that the beauty of this face lay, for Natasha Lawrence's features were expressive, even when her words were not. She looked wary and tense, also fatigued; whatever else she was afraid, or not afraid of, she was certainly fearful of questions, Gini saw. She glanced at her watch; the actress was already rising to her feet. She had two minutes left.

"Do you mind having to live with bodyguards?" Gini said.

The question took the actress by surprise, as she had hoped it would. She covered that surprise quickly.

"Of course. But—it's necessary. In my position . . ." She gave a small shrug. "I've lived with them for years now. You get used to it."

"I heard—" Gini began, reaching across to switch off her tape.

"I'm sure you heard a lot of things." The actress gave a slight smile; she began to move toward the door.

"Is it worse when you're appearing in a theater? You must feel more protected on a movie set. . . ."

"Not really. You feel protected nowhere. Is your tape recorder off? I don't want to discuss this."

Gini put the tape recorder in her bag and rose. Suddenly, she found she was tired of this; she could not wait for this meeting to be over, to leave the theater. After an hour's conversation, she had obtained perhaps three or four remarks that she could weave into her profile of the actress; the resulting article would tell readers something and nothing, she thought.

She looked at the actress, who was about to open the dressing-room door, and tossed in one final question, expecting no reply.

"Is it true you're considering moving to the Conrad building?" she said.

To her astonishment, the actress showed greater animation at this than she had done throughout the interview. She smiled, then laughed.

"How do these stories start?" she said. "The Conrad? I don't think they'd welcome me with open arms, do you? No, I'm moving back to California. I've bought a house in the hills outside Hollywood. It's being decorated for me by . . ." And she mentioned a fashionable West Coast name; she gave a small sigh. "It's due to be finished this week, so as soon as I finish in *Estella* . . ."

"Can I use that?"

"Yes. It's no secret I'm going back to California. I'm sorry, but the hour *is* up. . . ."

She held out her hand and took Gini's briefly in her own. Some polite farewell was expressed; Gini was reminded of the final prearranged conditions of this interview: that a copy of the article should be made available in advance of publication, so that the accuracy of the facts—and *only* the facts, the actress said with another smile—could be checked. Then she found herself outside in the corridor with the door firmly shut.

Gini negotiated the labyrinthine backstage corridors, faint with a residual scent of makeup, hair spray, disinfectant, and sweat. She emerged into the alleyway that led down to the stage door; it was still raining, and Manhattan had not yet emerged from the day's permanent dusk. She was taking the shuttle back to Washington, D.C., where her husband Pascal and their baby son awaited her. It was Halloween, and—the interview already receding from her mind—she was anxious to be back. She walked toward Times Square, the bluish exhaust-heavy air pungent with the smells of a city winter, of pretzels and of chestnuts roasting at some corner ahead. She tried to hold on to her interview as she hailed a yellow cab.

In the cab, she flicked open her notebook, where, during the course of the interview, she had jotted down a few comments. She closed it again, leaned back. Her mind curled away from the dressing room and the interview to the journey ahead: the shuttle, then another taxi, the familiar streets of Georgetown, brick pavements, decorum, and her husband and son waiting for her in her dead father's house.

It curled back, back like a wave, to her father's funeral a month before; to the visits to the last of the clinics that had preceded that funeral; to the stations on the way to the end—and the end, inevitable for all men, had been hastened in his case. Two bottles of bourbon a day for twenty years; promise and talent allowed to leach out; none of the scenes of reconciliation that she had believed must surely happen in those final weeks. Her father had lived angrily and died angrily, and now all that remained, in every sense, was to clean up.

She could feel it mounting, block by block, as they drove, some strange female need to dust, scrub, polish, sweep; some need to spring-clean a house that was about to be sold, and clean away the thirty-one years of her accumulated memories. Then she, Pascal, and their beautiful son, whom she loved with a painful intensity, would be free to leave. The whole of America lay before them: east, west, north, south. Should they begin with the clean bracing air of the eastern seaboard, or head for the plantations, the Spanish moss, of an imagined but never visited Deep South?

She looked forward to an hour, two hours, with her son when she returned. He was still too young to understand Halloween, but the previous evening, she and Pascal had hollowed out a fat orange globe of a pumpkin. They had given it round eyes, a triangular nose, and a wide, smiling, unthreatening mouth. This pumpkin, lit from inside by a candle, would be placed in the window to welcome her home; it would greet the children who came to the door for trick or treat. Thus far, and no further, would she go to acknowledge the date; she wanted to begin giving her son Lucien the childhood she had never had, but she was too recently bereaved—if bereaved was the term—to wish to celebrate more fully the night of the dead.

So the pumpkin would glow, her son would be persuaded eventually that the purpose of lying down in his little red cot was to sleep, then there was the long tranquillity of an evening with her husband to look forward to. They would make their plans for Thanksgiving—her friend Lindsay Drummond would be coming from England to celebrate it with them—and they would make their plans for their American itinerary, for the book Pascal would photograph and she would write. They would sit by the fireside and consult yet more guides, yet more maps.

The journey ahead opened up in her mind and the highways of America beckoned. She had forgotten Natasha Lawrence and all those unanswered questions long before the cab driver, recalcitrant, twitching, and fuming with some unspecified rage, was paid off.

Natasha Lawrence, who had intended to answer no questions of any import, forgot the interview even more quickly. She regarded interviews as a necessary evil. Once they were over she wiped them out of her memory. She had learned years before—and she was a woman of great self-discipline—that to worry about interviews encouraged vanity and self-doubt, also, lately, fear—so *click:* gone from the screen, gone from the memory bank. On this occasion, the only question that had caused her any disturbance was the one about the Conrad—

and she had dealt with that. *Click,* and the past hour was gone; she felt reinvigorated at once.

Her life, organized by others, was well organized. Within five minutes of Gini Hunter's departure, she was in the back of her dark limousine, with its dimmed windows, being carried north through the darkening streets of New York. Within half an hour, she was back in her apartment at the Carlyle Hotel, where she could be with her son for at least two hours before her return to the theater. Those hours, which nothing was allowed to interrupt, were the only point in her day when she felt that, unwatched, private, and secure, she need no longer act, but could simply be herself.

Today, however, she had one small extra anxiety.

"Has the package come from Tomas?" she said to Angelica as she entered the apartment, pulling off her coat.

"No, but he called. He's sending it to the theater by courier; it'll be there when you go in tonight."

"Ah," Natasha said, looking at Angelica and taking the pile of letters and packages she held out. She looked down at these in a nervous way; Angelica sighed.

"It's all right," she said. "Nothing from *him.* I checked. And no calls either . . ."

Faint color rose in Natasha's cheeks; hope lit in her eyes. She glanced over her shoulder at her son, who had looked up from his book. He knew better than to ask questions, or greet his mother at this point; he bent to the pages of *Treasure Island* again. Angelica lowered her voice.

"It's been four months now. Nothing for four months."

"I know."

"He's never been silent for this long before."

"I know."

"Maybe he's dead." Angelica lowered her voice still further. "Could be. Hit by a truck, jumped off a bridge . . . It happens all the time. . . ."

"To other people, yes."

"I dreamed he died. I told you. I dreamed it just the other night."

"Ah, Angelica."

Angelica placed great faith in her dreams, which were often dark and occasionally malevolent. Natasha Lawrence might have liked to place equal faith in her dreams, but she had learned from experience, and now did not. Angelica's dreams often inverted or reversed truths, and sometimes—like most dreamers—she allowed her own desires to write her dream scripts. The actress looked at her harsh lined face, at the two wings of gray in her short black hair. In the gentle light of the room, Angelica's eyes were small, black, and glittery as jet. She was of Sicilian descent; she loved and hated with a resolve and implacability the actress often envied; she also claimed to know how to curse. Perhaps, Natasha thought, and her heart lifted, perhaps Angelica's knotty, intricate curses had finally taken effect. She leaned across and kissed her cheek.

"What time did Tomas call?" she said.

"About an hour ago. He's sending the book to the theater, like I said. And something with it—a surprise, he said. Some kind of present. Small. Don't miss it, he said, it'll be inside the book. . . ."

"A present? It's not my birthday. It's not our anniversary. Inside the book?"

"He said it was the best present he could give you. . . ." Angelica's face hardened; she did not like, and had never liked, Tomas Court. "Whatever *that* means. You'll understand when you see it, he said." She paused, giving the rest of her message with reluctance. "He sent his love. Talked to Jonathan for a bit . . ."

Natasha Lawrence crossed to her son and kissed his forehead.

"You talked to Daddy, darling? Was he in Montana? Was he at the ranch?"

"I guess he was; I forgot to ask. He's bought two new horses: a gray one for you, she's called Misty, and a little one for me—Diamond. He's got a white blaze on his nose and four white socks."

"Oh, how lovely." His mother kissed him again. "So, he was at the ranch?"

"Maybe." Her son's small features composed themselves in a frown. "I meant to ask, but we got talking about my book." He held up the copy of *Treasure Island*. "I told him all about Blind Pew and the Black Spot. Blind Pew's kind of scary. He has this stick, and even though he's blind, he finds these people out; he tracks them down, and you can hear him coming with his stick, tap, tap, tap. . . ."

His mother straightened up a little hastily and made a small sign to Angelica. "I'm sure I remember," she said. "Blind Pew comes to a nasty end. He gets his just deserts. . . ."

"That's what Daddy said."

She glanced at her watch. "It's time to put on your Halloween costume and show me. And Angelica's found a special Halloween cake. . . ."

The cake was in the shape of a witch; she was mounted on a broomstick, flying over a white-icing moon, through a milky chocolate sky. Jonathan's excitement at this, and at dressing up in his Halloween costume, touched his mother deeply. She looked at her son, who was small for his age, and who had a small, somewhat melancholy face—an expressive face, a little clown's face—and his innocence pained her. At seven, carefully protected and nurtured, Jonathan still did not understand how unusual this Halloween was. He would not, like other children, be going out to trick-or-treat. His one excursion, watched over by Angelica, would be down the hall to an elderly guest at the Carlyle who had grown fond of him and who was known to be safe. He would return here, have his costume admired by Maria, the masseuse who would arrive shortly, and then, when his mother left for the theater, would watch a Disney video with Angelica, while a bodyguard, as always, stayed within reach. Her son was a prisoner of her fame and his father's fame, and a prisoner of those people, and those forces, that such fame could attract.

This thought, as always, she tried to push aside. Four months of silence, she said to herself. She tried hard to concentrate on the details of a day to which she had looked forward—the witchy cake, Jonathan's magician costume, the wand he had made, and the magic stars on his cape. She could see how proud he was of this costume. She gave the requisite cry of fear when he embarked on a spell, and she shrank back and screamed obligingly when Angelica made her entrance as a burly and convincing witch. But she found she could not concentrate; her mind was running ahead to the theater and the mysterious present from her husband. Tomas, a man of few words, a man who used words with care, would not promise her the best present he could give her, unless he meant what he said.

"You're tense," Maria said to her a little later, in Natasha's bedroom, as she began her massage. She scooped some of her herbal oils into her palm and began a slow rhythmic kneading of Natasha's back. The room filled with the smell of lavender and rosemary; Maria, a plain woman, had magical hands—but not tonight.

"Feel that—all that tension," she said, her hands easing and pressing at the back of Natasha's neck. "Try to relax it or you won't sing well tonight. What are you worrying about? You're worrying about something—I can feel it right here."

"Nothing. Everything. The Conrad, an interview I did, the performance tonight, Tomas, Jonathan, life, why I've been left in peace for four months . . . I don't *know*, Maria."

"You're lovely," Maria said, with a sigh. Her capable magic hands moved gently down Natasha's spine. "You're the most beautiful thing I've ever seen in my life. Just lie still. You've been working too hard. Relax. I can get rid of all your problems—you know that."

Her therapy, usually effective, was without effect that night; Natasha Lawrence remained tense when the massage was completed. One and a half hours before curtain up, she was back in her dressing room, and there waiting for her, as promised—but Tomas Court always kept his promises—was the package her former husband had sent.

It was contained inside a padded envelope, then wrapped again in thick brown paper, on which, in Tomas's cursive script, was the name "Helen." She turned it this way and that, then unsealed the wrappings. Inside, as she had expected, was a copy of a novel, and inside the leaves of the book was her surprise—a tiny clipping from a Montana newspaper, dated earlier that week.

Her hands began to shake; the print blurred before her eyes. She read the story, which concerned the discovery of a body in Glacier National Park, three times. Indeed, Tomas could have given her no better present than this. Nevertheless, lighting a match and watching the scrap of newsprint flare, she destroyed her present at once. She crumbled the dust in her fingers, then washed her hands and began the process of making up her Estella face.

It was agreed by the entire cast, and all the stagehands, that for some reason, Natasha Lawrence's performance was especially electrifying that night.

Part Two

HALLOWEEN

Chapter 2

The party was being held on Halloween to celebrate a film; possibly the completion of a film, or its launch, possibly the clinching of some deal in connection with a film. The photographer, Steve Markov, who wangled the invitation for Lindsay Drummond, was inclined to the latter view. "Money," he said, holding up the invitation hand-delivered to Lindsay's London apartment. He sniffed it in a theatrical manner. "I smell money. A coproduction deal? Subsidiary rights? Video release in Venezuela?"

He smiled one of his fugitive mocking smiles. Lindsay regarded him warily. Markov was one of her oldest friends, but his superabundant energy tended at times to swamp her. In the past, other friends, in particular Gini Hunter, had mitigated Markov's influence. But Gini's departure to Washington, D.C., had left her unprotected, fighting some lonely rearguard action. Markov was currently conducting an energetic campaign to alter her life—he described it as *sad*; she suspected the invitation was part of these maneuverings. Having smiled, adjusted the dark glasses he permanently wore, and stretched back against the cushions of her sofa, he confirmed this.

"You have to go, Lindy," he went on, more firmly. "I'm going. Jippy's going. You should go. *'Nel mezzo del cammin,'* my best beloved. Get a life."

"I detest that phrase," Lindsay replied, turning the invitation this way and that. "That phrase is glib. That phrase is cant."

"Which? The Dante?"

"*Not* the Dante, and stop showing off. Stop calling me Lindy. How do you read this damn thing anyway?"

"You hold it up to a mirror, I think."

19

Lindsay did so. The card, which was shocking pink and had appeared to be printed in Arabic, Sanskrit, or hieroglyphs, at once became readable, if less than informative.

Diablo!!!, it read. Beneath that, in a smaller typeface, was a brief command: "Lulu Says Come to Celebrate All Night on All Souls' Night." Appended, in a very small typeface, was an address in London's Docklands, three fax numbers, and the Halloween date.

"Who's Lulu?" Lindsay asked.

"Lulu Sabatier. You must know her; she's a legend. Everyone does."

"Do *you* know her, Markov?"

"Not exactly." His tone became evasive. "I know *of* her; she knows *of* me. Now she knows of you, so she's invited you to her party. Except it won't be her party, not really. Her place, but she'll just be fronting it. Welcome to Wonderland, Lindy. You know movie people. You know how they operate, yes?"

"She's in PR, in other words." Lindsay gave him a cold look. "This is a PR party. Give me strength."

"PR? PR? I'm seriously wounded by that accusation. . . ."

"And *Diablo*? Who's Diablo? What's Diablo? Where's Diablo?"

"You mean you don't *know*?" Markov removed the dark glasses, the better to give her a pitying look. "Lindy, where have you been this last month? *Pluto,* perhaps? Diablo, sweetheart, is the name of Tomas Court's new production company, and Tomas Court, white hope of American movies, is going to be *at* this party, Lindy, my dear. In person. Himself. Or so Lulu claims, Lulu not being one thousand percent reliable, of course."

Lindsay digested this information. She had her pride.

"Markov," she said firmly. "I have no intention of going to this party."

"You're intrigued; admit you're intrigued."

"Markov, I don't go to this kind of party on principle. Life's too short."

This remark, as Lindsay instantly realized, was a mistake. A smile curled around Markov's lips. He finished his postlunch coffee, then made his conversational pounce.

"Do you want to change your life, or not?" he began. "Because

I seem to remember, honeychild, that last month, or like the month before *that*, you said—"

"I can remember what I said."

Lindsay hastily rose to her feet. She edged across to the window and looked down at her familiar London street. Leaves whirled in an autumnal wind; the sun shone; the weather had an optimistic look. Backing away from the window, she thumped a cushion into place, tidied up the already tidy pile of Sunday newspapers, surveyed the detritus of the lunch table, fetched the coffeepot, and poured herself another cup of coffee she would not drink.

She had hoped that one of these aimless activities might deflect Markov; none did. With buzz-saw determination, he stuck to the point.

"*Age* was mentioned," he was continuing, still with that maddening smile on his face. "*Career* was mentioned. *Domicile* was mentioned. I suspect the term 'empty-nest syndrome' came up. . . ."

Lindsay gave a groan. One of Markov's least pleasant traits was his perfect recall of past conversations. Could she actually have used that trite phrase "empty nest?" Surely she had not sunk as low as "syndrome?"

"I was drunk," she said. "*If* I said that, which I doubt, I must have been drunk. It doesn't count."

"Bad news, sweetheart. You were stone-cold sober. . . ." Markov paused. "Angry, though. Fierce. You positively *trembled* with resolution. I was moved, Lindy. I was impressed. . . ."

"Will you stop this?"

" 'I am sick of being a fashion editor'—that's what you said. 'I am sick of the fashion world.' You were going to talk to that editor of yours. Have you talked to that editor of yours?"

"What, Max? No, not yet."

"Fresh woods and pastures new—you quoted that."

Markov gave a theatrical sigh. "Darling, you were having lunch with some publisher. A *contract* was being dangled. This publisher—a *very* big wheel—wanted a book on Coco Chanel. You, Lindy, were going to write that book. It was going to be definitive. It was going to make you poor, but never mind that. Has this lunch with the big cheese of British publishing actually happened?"

"No, I postponed it. I need time to think."

"And then there was the real-estate agent. . . ." The buzz saw hit a higher pitch. "This guy had two firm potential buyers for this apartment. He was promising a bidding war. He pointed out that this is now a highly desirable area of London, so *if* you sold, you'd make a profit. Not a large profit, I admit, but just enough to buy, or rent, a small hovel somewhere outside London, in the sticks. In this hovel, you, Lindy, were going to commune with nature. A dog was mentioned, and a cat. Ducks featured, as, I'm afraid, did chickens. . . ."

"Will you stop this? Markov, that's *enough*. . . ."

Lindsay sank her head in her hands. She was beginning to regret, deeply regret, having asked Markov and his lover Jippy to Sunday lunch. She had done so partly because she was fond of them both, partly because they happened to be in London, and mainly because Sunday, that family day, was now the hardest, the loneliest, the most interminable day of the week.

With a sigh, she raised her head and inspected her pleasant and familiar living room. This apartment had been her home for eighteen years; formerly, it had been occupied by Lindsay, her son Tom, and her difficult mother, Louise. Now difficult Louise, astonishingly, had remarried and moved out; Tom was in his second year reading modern history at Oxford. Thanks to their absence, the room was depressingly tidy. Markov and his friend Jippy, who was sitting beside him, but remaining silent as always, would soon be leaving; then the apartment would also be depressingly quiet. Lindsay feared this.

Even that quietness, however, might be preferable to Markov's present unrelenting assault, now moving in a most unwelcome direction. In a moment, Lindsay thought, a name— a forbidden name—would be mentioned. She embarked on a few more displacement activities, caught the glint of Markov's pretentious dark glasses, and sat down. She glared at the glasses, which Markov rarely removed; maybe he would be merciful, she thought. He was not.

"Rowland," he said. "The name Rowland McGuire was mentioned; several times, sweetheart—which was progress. Which was honest, at least. Because let's face facts, honeybunch—that man is at the back of this."

"I never mentioned Rowland," Lindsay cried, hearing a

familiar defensive note enter her voice. "Well, maybe once or twice, in passing. Can we stop this conversation? All right, I said I intended to make some changes in my life. I'm *making* them, Markov. In my own way, at my own pace."

"*Pace?*" Markov gave a snort of derision. He looked at his watch and rose to his feet. "*Pace?* Lindy, we are talking sluggish here. We are talking *snail*. We are talking chronic inertia and galloping indecision. We are talking one millimeter every other century. . . ."

"Give it a *rest*, Markov."

"And why? Because of a man. Because of *that* man. Lindy, you have to cure yourself of that man, and do it fast. As far as that man is concerned, you, Lindy, are *invisible*. You are less than a speck on the very distant horizon. When are you going to accept that?"

"I have accepted it. I've *nearly* accepted it."

"Lindy, I'm now going to be brutally honest." Markov drew himself up. "You, Lindy, are *not his type*. Now, God knows what his type *is*, but it isn't you. I think he's a fool, Jippy thinks he's a fool, but there you are. Three years ago, I thought we could bring him around, make him see sense. I put a lot of time and energy into that project, Lindy, if you remember. . . ."

"I do remember. Much good it did."

"Precisely. *Nada.* Zilch. So the time has come, Lindy, my love, to cut your losses. You have to hitch a ride, darling, to a different city on the highway of life. . . ."

"Markov, *please*. Give me a *break*."

"And you have to leave that son of a bitch behind in the parking lot. Am I right or am I right?"

"You're right, and he isn't a son of a bitch; he's good, he's kind, he's clever, he's handsome, he's nice."

"He's *blind*." Markov became stern. "What you need, Lindy, is some McGuire antibiotic. . . ."

"I *know* that. I'm administering it. I'm in midcure right now. . . ."

"You are? And when does this cure cease?"

"The end of the month. This month. I've set myself a deadline, Markov. Truly . . ."

This reply, forced out of her, was another mistake—as Lindsay almost immediately realized. A crafty little smile curled about Markov's lips. Next to him, the silent and gentle Jippy gave a sigh. His eyes fell on the pink mirror-writing invitation card, abandoned on a table. Markov at once picked it up.

"This party," he said, with emphasis, "takes place on the last day of this month. All the more reason to go. You can celebrate your new-won freedom, for a start. You can meet new people, make new friends, and kick-start your new improved McGuireless life."

"Thanks, but no thanks."

Lindsay took the proffered card and tucked it back in the pocket of Markov's chartreuse-colored jacket. Then, since she knew that beneath Markov's affectations of speech and dress, his intentions were kindly, she patted the pocket and gave him an affectionate kiss on the cheek.

"Really, Markov, I know you meant well, but I wouldn't enjoy it. I wouldn't know anyone there. . . ."

"That's the entire point."

"You go, then you and Jippy can tell me all about it. It's the day before you go off to Greece, isn't it? You can tell me all about it when you get back. That gives you plenty of time to work out a good story—who was there, what I missed. . . ."

Markov, who rarely hesitated, hesitated then. He shifted from his right foot to his left.

"Jippy thinks you ought to go," he announced. "In fact, this was all Jippy's idea. You suggested it, didn't you, Jippy?"

It was Jippy's main characteristic to speak only when it was unavoidable. Now, directly appealed to for confirmation, he rose to his feet. Jippy had a very bad stammer.

"I d-d-did," he said.

This unexpected endorsement made Lindsay pause. At her first meeting with Jippy, two years before, she had assumed that his reluctance to speak was caused by the stammer; further acquaintance with Jippy had taught her that the reason for those silences lay deeper.

Jippy was a rare being: he spoke only when he had something of import to say; when he did so, his remarks, although sometimes difficult to interpret, were usually unequivocal, generally wise, and invariably brief. Lindsay looked at him with affection and with sudden doubt. Jippy was a small, squarely built man, with neat dark hair, gentle eyes, and a childlike demeanor. Lindsay herself was not tall, but Jippy was shorter still, and could have been, she calculated, little over five feet. He might have been thirty-five, or much younger, but in certain lights he could look older, considerably older—as if he had been around for centuries, Markov said.

Unlike Markov, who was flamboyant, Jippy cultivated anonymity of dress. Today, as usual, he was wearing clean, pressed blue jeans, a navy blue sweater that a schoolboy might have worn, and a white shirt. His old-fashioned lace-up shoes were smartly polished, and, in a way Lindsay found heartbreakingly sad, he always looked spruced up, as if for a job interview—his expression, shy and somewhat hopeful, dogged but melancholy, suggesting it was a job Jippy was never going to get. He would have passed in a crowd without anyone's giving him a second glance—indeed, Lindsay suspected that he preferred and intended this—but on closer inspection, he conveyed a powerful and disconcerting benevolence. Quite how he did this, Lindsay could not have said, since the benevolence seemed to radiate from him, without visible source, unless it be his eyes, the gaze of which was steady, as if expecting the best in others, and yet sorrowful—or so Lindsay thought.

Jippy's origins were in many ways obscure: Lindsay had never discovered his true name, where he lived or what he did before meeting Markov, or indeed how they had met. His ancestry, however, was for some reason elaborately exact. He was one half Belorussian, one quarter Armenian, one eighth British, and one eighth Greek—on this issue, Jippy was emphatic, even pedantic. He was Markov's photographic assistant as well as his lover, and according to Markov, he was a genius of the darkroom, indispensable to Markov's latest experiments with silver and platinum prints. Lindsay knew virtually nothing else about him, except for one key piece of information, which, true, or untrue, Markov always stressed. He claimed that, from the Armenian grandmother, Jippy had inherited second sight.

He was a gifted astrological interpreter, Markov said; he could read palms and sense auras, and was, at unexpected moments, afforded views of the future. This clairvoyance, whether a blessing or a curse, Jippy was said to treat with fortitude and circumspection, never discussing the ability himself.

"Pay attention to Jippy," Markov liked to say. "He's the seventh son of a seventh son, and believe me, you don't argue with that."

Lindsay, who was more credulous and superstitious than she might have liked, was not disposed to argue in any case. From first meeting and first handshake, Jippy had impressed her. She liked his appearance, his reticence, and his stammer; she liked *him*. Markov loved him, of course.

When, therefore, she learned that it was Jippy who had suggested procuring the invitation to this ludicrous party, and that it was not one of Markov's devious, harebrained schemes, she began to see that mirror-writing invitation in a new light. Was it possible, could it be that . . . did Jippy see something fateful here, to which she was blind? She looked closely at Jippy, whose steady, liquid, brown-eyed gaze held hers. Perhaps she had been hasty; what harm could it do to go, after all? Was it not tempting to believe that, at last, she might be finding new purpose and direction to her life?

At worst she risked being bored; escape would be easy; she would be free that night. Had she not, as Markov had just annoyingly reminded her, resolved to break out of the indecision and inertia that had comprised the last three years of her life? On the other hand, of course, Jippy was a social innocent; it was bound to be an appalling party, filled with people she neither knew, nor wished to know. Yes, it might have been intriguing to meet Tomas Court, whose movies she greatly admired, but a glimpse of the man, or one brief handshake, was the best she could expect, and that, she thought, she could well live without.

And then there was the location: the party was to be held in some Docklands loft. It was miles from where she lived, in Notting Hill Gate; she was sure to get lost in those eerie ill-lit riverside streets. It would be dark; it would be Halloween; she would almost certainly have to park miles away and then venture past gloomy wharves, threatening alleyways, at the end of which, by mud and slippery, weedy steps, the Thames sucked and washed. . . . She gave a small involuntary shiver. "I know you both mean well," she began, "but I *really* don't want to go. I have to go to Oxford to see Tom that weekend. It's just before the New York collections, so I'll be getting ready for New York and I'll have a mountain of work. . . ."

Jippy made a gesture, a tiny, quick motion of the hand. He patted her arm and smiled, and began to lead Markov toward the door.

"S-see how you feel," he said, "on the n-night."

"Oh, all right, I'll think about it," Lindsay conceded, "if you both promise to go to it too. Markov, you might as well leave the invitation. . . ."

Jippy smiled broadly. Markov smiled broadly.

"In your left pocket, I think you'll find, Lindy," Markov said, opening her front door, exiting fast, and shutting it with a smart click.

Lindsay had forgotten Jippy's other skills: his sleight of hand, his conjuring tricks, his ability to convey solid matter from that place of concealment to this. She put her hand disbelievingly into the pocket of her jacket. It closed over the pink, mirror-writing invitation to a party. She still had no intention of going, she told herself. Over the next two weeks she constantly reminded herself of this.

Yet, when it finally came to Halloween, and the last day of her spiritual antibiotic course, Lindsay weakened. Invitations to Lulu's parties, she had heard, were much in demand. Lulu was *famous* for her parties. Lindsay, a social cynic, placed little faith in such claims, or in parties. On the evening in question, however, she discovered she had decided to go after all; a mysterious process. In the shower, she was still undecided; wrapped in a towel five minutes later, her mind was made up.

She threw on a red partyish dress, hated it, pulled it off, kicked it across the room, and donned a black one. She screwed into place the prettiest earrings she possessed, which had been given to her by Gini as a parting gift: two teardrops of pale jade that seemed to have been imbued with an animation of their own, so that they shimmered or trembled before she made the least gesture or the slightest turn of her head.

She ran up- and downstairs in stockinged feet as darkness fell and her front doorbell kept ringing. She gave a bar of chocolate to a diminutive witch and her brother the hangman. She gave a tube of sweets to a werewolf, and some Turkish delight to a covey of skeletons from next door, escorted by a lugubrious father with an ax through his head. She was fore-stalled by a gorilla and a ghoul when finally leaving, and lacking sweets or small change, thrust a five-pound note into the startled gorilla's fur paw. The gorilla and the ghoul, she noted, fought a brief battle for possession of this prize in the middle of the street.

Then, over an hour and a half late, and thoroughly rattled, she set off. Lindsay was a bad driver, and her sense of direction was dysfunctional. This fact had often been remarked upon, amiably and laconically, by Rowland McGuire. Even in his absence, Lindsay was determined to prove him wrong. She failed; as he had predicted, she lost herself in the dark streets of the Docklands almost at once.

Chapter 3

"... the Thames," Lindsay said, raising her voice and peering upward at the white, bloodless face of a complete stranger, an exceedingly tall vampiric and emaciated man, whose features she could only just see through candle smoke, cigarette smoke, and some peculiar foggy density that hovered in the air.

"What? What did you say?"

Another piece of human driftwood hit Lindsay hard from behind. She stumbled, then righted herself. She had arrived late; most of the other party guests appeared to have arrived early and were already wrecked. She gazed helplessly around her. If this room was like an aircraft carrier—and it was; several planes could have been parked in this space—its decks were awash. Waves of random conversations kept breaking over her; people surged on all sides; she could not even see properly, since it seemed Lulu Sabatier eschewed electric light. This entire, huge, confusing loft space, with a bewilderment of metal stairways; jutting, galleried upper decks; dark archways that might lead somewhere or nowhere, was lit by candles. In the center of the deck, or floor, was a lipstick-red-colored couch, to which partygoers clung like a life raft, and thrumming up through her feet, she could sense some mysterious energy, like the power of a whirring turbine, buried deep in the bowels of a ship. The throb and pulse of this power source had a propulsive effect. Lindsay felt it was propelling her through the dark and the smoke to some vital but as yet undisclosed destination. She felt she would surely arrive somewhere eventually, but meanwhile she felt unstable, not too sure of her balance, and faintly seasick.

She peered up at the landmark of the tall Dracula man. He

had just avoided being speared by his fat neighbor's cocktail stick and was looking down at Lindsay with a mad desperation.

"I can't *hear*," he shouted. "You cannot hear a goddamn thing in here. . . ."

"The *Thames*," Lindsay yelled, with equal desperation. "I said, this place is very hard to find, isn't it? I nearly drove into the Thames twice. . . ."

The pale man, she perceived, was not interested in this. He was not interested in Lindsay either, but—hedging his bets—he was not yet prepared to be uninterested. She could already see that he had an acute case of party squint, partly caused by alcohol, she suspected, but also caused by visual dilemmas.

It was not easy to keep one eye perpetually on the entrance doors, in case *someone* came in, while keeping the other eye on two hundred guests, all of whom kept milling back and forth, and any one of whom might be (several certainly were) *someone* as well. Nor was he prepared to cast off Lindsay yet; she too, after all, might turn out to be *someone*, though he seemed to find that possibility unlikely. He performed another periscopic maneuver, then, with an irritable frantic air, bent one eye upon her from a great height.

"Fog," he shouted. "This room is full of fucking *fog*. Why has Lulu opened the fucking windows? I mean, it's *October*. It's *Halloween*, for fuck's sake. What kind of maniac opens the windows in October? The fog comes in off the river. It mists the whole place up. . . ."

"If Lulu didn't open the windows," Lindsay yelled, "it would be impossible to breathe. . . ."

"Ahhh . . ." Momentary hope dawned in his eyes. "You know Lulu then?"

"Intimately," replied Lindsay, who had still to identify her hostess, let alone be introduced to her. "Lulu and I go way back."

This statement, designed to annoy, had an arresting effect. The pale man clasped Lindsay's arm in a demented grip, and said something frantic and inaudible, something washed away by the incoming tide of adjacent conversations.

". . . Is he here?" Lindsay heard, as the conversations ebbed. "Because fucking Lulu *swore* he was coming. . . . Only reason

I'm here . . . Have to speak to . . . Urgent . . . Project . . . Script. This man is my *god*. I mean no exaggeration, my *god*."

"Is who here?" Lindsay shouted back, decoding this.

"Court. Tomas Court."

"Where? Where?" cried the ponytailed neighbor as this magic name was uttered. He spun round, grabbed the pale man with one hand and Lindsay with the other, spilling champagne down her dress.

"He's here? Did you say Tomas was here?"

"No, I said *maybe* he was here." The pale man swayed. "I said Lulu *said* he'd be here. Look, d'you mind fucking letting go of me?"

"Apologies, my friend." The ponytail stepped back half an inch, and with difficulty focused upon Lindsay.

"And this is?"

"I don't *know* who this is," the pale man replied in an aggrieved tone. "She knows Lulu. She *says* she knows Lulu. . . ." He paused. "Whereas I've never fucking *met* Lulu. I've been here eight times and I've never met her yet."

This surprising information seemed to forge an instant bond. The two men embraced.

"Shake, pal." They shook. "I'm beginning to wonder, my friend," the ponytail remarked, in Jacobean tones, "whether Lulu exists."

"She says she does." The pale man turned accusingly to Lindsay. "Knows her intimately. Friends from way back . . ."

Fixing her with his eyes, insofar as he was able, the ponytail demanded to know where, in that case, Lulu was. "Because," he said, swaying like a yachtsman, "I've been promised an introduction to Tomas. I spoke to a very very close aide of Lulu's called Pat."

The two men eyed each other.

"Pat? Pat?" The pale man sighed. "That rings a bell. But there's a lot of aides. Lulu has a *confusing* number of aides. . . ."

"True. Here tonight, though. Definitely here—somewhere. I have assurances. Lulu's here—and so is Tomas Court."

Lindsay, growing anxious to escape, attempted to edge away, but the group behind her pushed her back. Oblivious to her presence, an expression of demented reverence came upon the pale man's face.

"Tomas Court!" he cried. "I worship that man. I bow down before him. I say—and I don't fucking care who hears me say it—I say: that man is my god."

"A director of genius, my friend. No argument. *Dead Heat*?"

"Incandescent. I've seen it fifteen times. A masterpiece. I fucking wept."

"Pure film, my friend. In a class of its own. Except . . ."

"The spider sequence?"

"Cheap. I would have to say that. Edging toward the cheap."

"Vulgar?"

"My friend, I'd have to agree. Seriously vulgar. Even jejune. You could say—a mistake."

"He makes mistakes!" Here, the pale man became very animated. "Okay, it's heresy, but I'll say it: Tomas Court makes mistakes, misjudgments. And *Dead Heat* is riddled with them."

"He's sold out, in my view. He's peaked, let's face it. He peaked a while ago. He was a flash in the pan. He . . ."

"Actually, he's over there," said Lindsay, who had now decided that she disliked these two very much. "He's over there by the door," she continued, giving them both the sweetest smile she possessed.

"Don't you see him? By the door, with Lulu."

She pointed across the room. There, in a thick cluster by the entrance, stood a tall and dramatically dressed woman of a certain age, who jutted up from the heaving crowd like a gaunt, weather-beaten lighthouse. None of her companions was Tomas Court, now so famous that Lindsay would have recognized him, and the tall woman was not Lulu Sabatier, but paleface and ponytail deserved punishment, and this woman was, without a doubt, the most terminally boring woman Lindsay had ever met in her life. Grasping Lindsay as she entered, she had pinned her to the wall and gone through her last screenplay scene by scene and comma by comma. Emma was mad about it, she said; Michelle had read it—it was female, female, female—and Michelle had flipped.

"That woman there." Lindsay pointed again. "The one in the burnoose. That's Lulu. She's been waiting there for Tomas

Court all evening. He just came in, a second ago. Sharon Stone
was with him, I think. . . ."

"Christ . . ." Paleface and ponytail convulsed. Parting the
waters, they hit the waves at speed; as some wind in the room
took up the cry "Tomas Court, Tomas Court" a host of backup
vessels surged in their wake. A social tide turned; two, four,
ten, fifteen, thirty others caught the prevailing current and
made for the beachhead of the burnoose. Lindsay watched this
armada with delight. The burnoose woman, used to being
avoided, greeted her newfound popularity with stupefaction.
Lindsay slipped her moorings, shifted behind the now-vacant
pillar, and resolved to lie low.

She had been at the party less than an hour; it felt like a week.
It was certainly a mistake in these circumstances to be drinking
prudent Perrier and ice. What she needed was a triple brandy,
or intravenous vodka perhaps. Since she was driving, the best
she could risk was a glass of champagne. If she drank it
extremely fast, however, having eaten nothing sinch lunch,
perhaps all these frogs would turn into princes; perhaps all
these basilisk women would turn and welcome her; perhaps
the air would begin to ring with good fellowship and wit. And
if that transformation failed to occur, as seemed likely, she
would find Markov and Jippy and insist on escape.

Confidence, confidence, she muttered to herself, easing
between knotty groups of people who showed no inclination to
admit her. She grabbed a glass of champagne from a scurrying
waiter and found a haven of relative quiet and space in an
embrasure by the windows. She drank half of the champagne
with medicinal speed. Here, she was able to conceal herself
from paleface and ponytail and any revenge they might seek.
She moved back behind a huge and magnificent swagged curtain, constructed from plebeian sailcloth, but fringed with pa-
trician silks, and, watching the ceaseless ebb and flow, waited
for the magic potion—it was Krug—to take effect.

Here, with a view down through wisps and drifts of mist to
the sleek black curve of the river, she became calmer. Below
her, she discovered, lay a garden, a garden that was subtly and
theatrically lit, with a dark central fish pool, clipped topiary

shapes, and some pale statuary. She could see a goddess or two, one lacking arms, a lovely blind Nereid, and a nymph on a pedestal, who appeared to ward off the attentions of a nearby god. It was an enchanting garden, made the more beautiful by the flow of the river beyond, and she found that the garden—or the champagne—was soothing her. The throb of those mysterious party turbines seemed quieter. Leaning against the iron balustrade across the open window, she inhaled damp, foggy city air. Was she in London? She felt she might have been elsewhere, anywhere. She was beginning to feel like Alice, made tiny enough to enter Wonderland by swallowing the contents of a bottle labeled "Drink me," and then made absurdly tall by nibbling a cake.

She thought of Alice, swimming in a lake of her own tears. She thought of Alice, a most sensible girl, stabilizing her size fluctuations by—how had she done it exactly? Lindsay frowned down at the imperceptible flow of the river below, trying to remember—by eating from alternate sides of a mushroom, she thought—and a vivid image came to her of reading this story aloud to Tom when he was seven, perhaps eight. It was a period, she knew, of some background pain, one of the last occasions when her ex-husband, down on his luck and thrown out by the latest girl, had attempted to come back.

It was probably the time, if she was accurate, when she finally realized, five years after her divorce, that she neither loved nor needed him anymore. She could remember looking at him, as he stood in the doorway; she could remember the faint surprise she had felt as she realized that she had loved, married, divorced, and agonized over a man whom she neither liked nor respected; a man who had wasted too much of her time. How *stupid* I was, she had thought, closing the door.

Yes, all of that had been happening; yet now, looking back, she found that those incidents had drifted away, and in their place, anchoring her, distinct as the links of a chain, were her evenings with her son; evening after blessed evening, hour after peaceful hour, in which they shared the fantastic adventures of a Victorian child, encircled by lamplight, absorbed in a story, both of them contented and wanting nothing more.

Over a decade ago, those evenings, now. Sharp as a *poignard*, Lindsay felt the familiar stab of regret. Such states of grace did not, and could not, endure; childish things, and even the most adult of children's books, were put away. Children grew up, and now her son's need for her company was diminished and infrequent—as she had always accepted it would one day be.

It would have been consoling, she thought, watching the river flow, to know that someone else did still retain a need for her; the kind of need that accompanies love: a husband, an enduring partner. It would have been easier and less painful, Lindsay sometimes believed, to adjust to her present state had she not had to do so alone. However, alone she was and alone she was likely to remain, and the worst possible way of dealing with that was to indulge in this kind of melancholy introspection. Lindsay pinched herself viciously—one of her cures— and read herself a few bracing lectures. She turned her back firmly on the river and the lovely shadowy garden below; such views encouraged nostalgia and self-pity, she feared.

She eddied out into the party again, trying to convince herself that she was glad to be there.

After a while, she managed to accost a tiny waiter, bearing a huge platter aloft. He presented her with tiny but delectable offerings: a wren's egg with a paring of black truffle; a tadpole-shaped blini glistening with caviar—real caviar, as it proved. She forced a conversation with some mad-hatter movie journalist about something; she talked to Tweedledum and Tweedle-dee who, in her experience, were always present at all parties. She was addressed by a dozy dormouse; by a duchess—and she actually was a duchess, or so some unctuous caterpillar of a man confirmed. There were a number of queens here, of course—in fact, queens were particularly thick on the ground. She looked desperately around and behind and beside them for Markov, certain to be queening it on an occasion such as this. But she could find no sign of him, or of silent Jippy, and after a while the utter randomness of these unlikely conversations began to tell. Lindsay felt afflicted with egos: me, me, me, cried her interlocutors—my screenplay, my company, my role, my percentage, my agent, my image. . . . Lindsay fled.

It occurred to her—she had seen a flight of steps—that somewhere there must be a way down to that tempting garden below, perhaps via one of the archways, or one of the corridors that seemed to lead off this aircraft-carrier deck. Carefully, she navigated in what seemed to be approximately the right direction. She was a little delayed, *en route,* first by the famous and poisonous actor Nic Hicks, who mistook her for someone else, and then by a man who claimed she was his third wife and the love of his life. She was further held up by an impetuous man who grabbed her arm, waved a bottle of pills, and announced he was about to commit suicide; on Lindsay's informing him that, in these circumstances his decision was perfectly understandable, he had a change of heart and decided to have another drink instead.

At last, still nursing a few dregs of champagne, she found herself alone in a corridor, a long white corridor, lined with posters for, and stills from, famous movies: *Casablanca, Persona, Citizen Kane, Gone with the Wind, La règle du jeu, Pulp Fiction, Jules et Jim, Dead Heat, Bicycle Thieves, The Virgin Spring.* . . . Lindsay had seen all of these films, many with Tom, who was a film buff and movie addict. She passed along the display, slowing first at one, then another. She came to a halt in front of the celebrated poster for Tomas Court's third and breakthrough movie, *Dead Heat,* the film paleface and ponytail had been lauding and denigrating earlier.

It showed a still from that movie that had now become so famous it was part of the collective consciousness, imprinted on the minds of almost everyone, whether they had seen the actual movie or not. This image, reproduced on a million T-shirts, had first been seen by Lindsay some eighteen months before in New York; it had been blown up thirty feet high, and had been fronting the facade of a movie theater on Broadway. A marriage of beauty and menace, she had thought then; she had found it disturbing, and still did.

It was a cunningly lit, rear-view shot of Natasha Lawrence, still Tomas Court's wife when the movie was shot, but divorced from him shortly after its premiere. Her back was bare, and she was framed by a suggestion of a white curtain to her left, and by a blank white wall in front and to the right of her. Lawrence's singularly beautiful face could not be seen; her dark hair was cropped as short as a boy's; her right arm was lifted and pressed against the wall; her left arm was pressed against her side; a shaft of light slanted against the curve of her spine, below which the picture was cropped.

This image might have been, and in some senses was, an Ingres-like tribute to the beauty and allure of a woman's back, though Lawrence was thinner than any of Ingres's odalisques. The eye was drawn by the exquisite pallor of the skin, by the arch of the slender neck, by the line of the spine; it suggested the skeletal, while celebrating the voluptuousness of flesh. Then, gradually, the eye was drawn by what appeared, at a casual glance, to be some small birthmark or blemish, a small dark patch high on the left scapula. On closer examination, this dark area proved to be neither a blemish, nor a tattoo—most people's second assumption—but a spider, an actual spider, a real spider, of modest dimensions, with delicate legs and black skin. Discovering this, women had been known to shriek and shrink back; Lindsay herself, who could deal with spiders, had felt a certain revulsion. A Freudian revulsion, Tom had later annoyingly claimed; a revulsion Court no doubt intended, Rowland McGuire had remarked, since Court was the most manipulative of directors—and the most manipulative of men, or so it was said.

Looking at this image now, Lindsay felt she saw elements in it that she had missed before; the image, and the very violent sequence from which it was taken—a sequence she had never watched in its entirety, because she always covered her eyes— seemed to her to have a riddling multiplicity of meanings. It could be read both ways, she felt: from the right and from the left.

She was about to pass on toward the stairs, which she could now see at the end of this corridor, and which she hoped, if her navigation was accurate, might lead down to the garden below, when a small accident occurred. Stepping back, eyes still on that poster for *Dead Heat*, she collided with a woman, and— apologizing—swung around. The woman, equally startled it seemed, almost dropped the four laden plates she was balancing, and gave a cry of alarm.

Lindsay, guiltily aware that she might now be trespassing, looked the woman up and down. She was tall and gaunt, with a large nose, rabbity teeth, small round granny glasses, and an arresting head of long, thick, near-white hair. Despite the hair color, she was, Lindsay realized, around forty years old, no more. She was wearing what might have been a uniform: a neat black dress with white collar and cuffs, but no apron. Was she a waitress? Lindsay looked at the woman, and then at the plates she was somewhat furtively carrying.

"Goodies," said the woman, following the direction of Lindsay's glance.

The woman appeared to have raided the sumptuous buffet table Lindsay had glimpsed earlier, through the crowds. Heaped on the plates were cheeses and grapes; there was a large wedge of some spectacular gilded pastry pie, some of the wrens' eggs, a glistening pyramid of caviar. There might have been some lobster—Lindsay thought she glimpsed a claw—and on the largest of the plates was a cornucopia arrangement of little tarts and cakes and miniaturized meringues, spun-sugar confections, and tiny chocolate petits fours. Balanced on top of them was a marzipan apple, tinted pink and green, with a clove for a stem; a pretty conceit. This, to Lindsay's surprise, the gaunt woman suddenly passed to her.

"Delicious, yeah?" It *was* delicious. "Mrs. Sabatier is really pleased with these caterers. She says they're a find."

"I expect I shouldn't be here," Lindsay said, extracting the clove, and, for want of anywhere else, putting it in her pocket. "I hope this isn't out of bounds. . . ."

"No worries." The woman smiled, showing even more rabbity teeth, then began to move off, and Lindsay trotted after her. "I was just wondering—I wanted to see the garden. . . ."

"The garden?" The woman came to a halt.

"Would Mrs. Sabatier mind? I could see it from above. It looked so beautiful. There's all these marvelous statues, a goddess, a nymph. . . ."

The woman hesitated, then shrugged.

"I guess it's all right. Mrs. Sabatier's gone to bed anyway. She avoids these parties of hers like the plague. And you are?"

"My name's Lindsay Drummond. I work at the *Correspondent.* . . ." The woman looked her up and down.

"Right. Mrs. Sabatier probably wouldn't mind. It's those

stairs over there. If you get stopped, if anyone objects, just say Pat gave you the Okay. . . ."

"Pat?"

"That's me. Really." She made an encouraging gesture. "It's fine. The doors are open. You don't need a key."

As she made this remark, Pat was moving off rapidly again. With Lindsay at her heels, she approached a wall of bookshelves at the head of the stairs. Without further speech, she opened an invisible door in these bookshelves and disappeared. What a cunning piece of *trompe l'oeil*, Lindsay thought, pausing to examine it; why, even the hinges were well-nigh undetectable. She examined the false book spines, amused; then she began to descend the stairs. There, at a turn on a lower landing, she ran into Markov and Jippy at last. They turned back with her and accompanied her to the garden below, where, Markov claimed, they had been lurking for a while.

"Smart move, huh?" he said. "It was purgatory up there. Wall-to-wall jerks. No sign of Tomas Court. We saw you skulking at the window. We waved. . . ."

Lindsay was not listening. She was looking around her, entranced. A secret garden, she thought, invisible from the street, invisible from any other building except the one she had just left. Mist drifted across the symmetry of the hedges and settled above the still surface of the pool. It was as quiet as any country garden; she could hear, just, the tidal slap against stone of the river beyond; from above, like the murmur of bees, came muted sounds from the party; no traffic was audible and no roads were visible; across on the far bank of the river, she could just see the outline of some industrial building, bulking as large as a cathedral in the dark. Markov and Jippy had taken her arms; now, Lindsay disengaged herself. She wandered away, touching the stone goddess's crumbling hem, then the base of her ardent god's pedestal. She reached up and touched the Nereid's sightless eyes.

"Look, Markov, Jippy," she said. "Isn't she lovely? In daylight, I'm sure she's meant to be blind, but the moon gives her eyes. She's looking across the river. . . . What time is it, Markov?"

"Nearly midnight."

Lindsay had moved off again. She trailed her hand dreamily

over the crisp crests of the topiary hedges and made her way along a path, the river flowing ahead of her, and Markov and Jippy somewhere behind her in the shadows. Perhaps Jippy brought me here for the garden, Lindsay thought; perhaps it was Jippy's companionship that made her feel truly at peace for the first time that evening, for Jippy's presence always calmed.

She stepped through a gap in the hedges and approached a wooden balustrade. She leaned over it, wisps of mist drifting, then clearing, and looked down at the flow of the tide. The river was smooth and dark, a liquid looking glass; reflected in it, bending gently then reassembling as the currents moved beneath, she could see the moon, lights like orbs, and an Ophelia-woman, pale and poised on the tide, who looked up at her, half drowned, from some water world beneath.

In the distance, a church clock chimed, then another, then a third. The last minute of the last hour of the last day of deadline month. Lindsay thought of Rowland McGuire, who had felt close, very close, the instant she came out here. She would summon him up, Lindsay decided, before, as she had resolved she would, she said her final and irrevocable good-bye.

Rowland McGuire, this week, was away. Taking his first vacation in a year from the newspaper he edited, he was climbing with friends on the Isle of Skye, or possibly—for his plans were subject to change—he had moved on to join another old friend from his Oxford days, a man who, as far as Lindsay could gather, was associated with the film industry in some way. This man had wanted Rowland to join him in Yorkshire, where he was engaged on some hush-hush project that— for unspecified reasons—required unspecified assistance from Rowland McGuire.

Scotland, Yorkshire. Lindsay closed her eyes, spinning together these inconclusive strands in her mind. Behind her somewhere, Markov was talking about nothing as usual, and Jippy was walking up and down in a somewhat anxious way. She concentrated: *Yorkshire,* she felt sure and, since her imagination was on such occasions busy, detailed, and compliant, Rowland rose up before her with a visionary speed.

There he was, in some remote place—Rowland liked remote places, and liked to be alone in them. Lindsay discovered he had spent the day on some Brontë-esque moor. She could see its crags and its heathers; she could hear a lapwing's cry. She could watch Rowland stride across these wuthering heights: this she did for a while, and very dark, handsome, and desirable he looked. Then Lindsay settled him down in an inn by a blazing log fire, an inn delightfully unencumbered by the friend or other inconvenient occupants. Rowland, she found, was reading—well, he usually was. Yes, he was definitely reading, and he was wearing the green sweater Lindsay had given him the previous Christmas, a sweater that was almost exactly the same green as his eyes. She could not quite see the title of his book, a pity that, but she could read Rowland's mind. He was thinking about her; he had just decided that before he turned in, he would give Lindsay a quick call.

"Correct me if I'm wrong," Markov said, on a plaintive note, "but is it suddenly arctic out here? Jippy, can you feel the wind getting up? It's *Siberian*. Brrr . . ."

"Oh, for God's sake, Markov, shut *up*," Lindsay cried, and concentrated again.

It might have been pleasant had Rowland begun that telephone call with some momentous word—"darling," for instance, would have done very nicely indeed. Lindsay's imagination, however, had its dry, its legalistic side; it was a stickler for accuracy. Rowland, therefore, did not use this, or any other inflammatory term, he simply addressed her, as he always did, by name.

And then—she could hear his voice distinctly—he told her in a friendly, fraternal way what he had been up to this past week. He inquired as to her own recent activities and announced he'd be returning to London soon. He recommended a book for Tom's Oxford history course. He passed on his best wishes to Tom; then, with less obvious warmth, but a politeness characteristic of him, he sent his regards to Lindsay's difficult mother, whom he disliked, not unreasonably, and to her mother's new husband, disliked by both Lindsay *and* Rowland, who disparaged him with enjoyment and accord.

These formalities over, he said, as he often did, that it was good to hear her voice, hoped she was well, and looked forward to seeing her again soon.

Lindsay disconnected. It was a conversation of a kind she

had had with Rowland a hundred times: amusing, polite, concerned, dispassionate, brotherly; these conversations broke her heart. Rowland, of course, did not know that; at least Lindsay hoped he did not, for she kept her own feelings well concealed, and had done so now for a long time—almost three years.

Lindsay opened her eyes; the moment felt auspicious. She looked down at her own wavering Ophelia-woman reflection, and wished Rowland a long good-bye. She said her farewell, her final farewell, to the other Rowland, the Rowland she wanted but could not have, the Rowland who inhabited a future that was never going to happen. Let him *go*, oh let him *go*, she said to herself, and then, since she wished him nothing but well, she added a rider: that Rowland might find a woman who would bring him the happiness he deserved, and that he would do so yesterday, tomorrow, at once, very soon.

This was a spell, as Lindsay was aware. She could sense its power in the air, but it was important, indeed vital, that effective spells be correctly wound up. Accordingly, she touched wood three times; she crossed and uncrossed her fingers three times, but these actions seemed insufficiently solemn—she felt, obscurely, that some offering or sacrifice needed to be made. And so, hoping neither Markov nor Jippy could see her actions, she opened her small evening bag. Inside it, folded small, was a note written by Rowland McGuire. It was not a long note, nor were it contents—they concerned work—of any great significance, but it was the only specimen of Rowland's handwriting she possessed, and she had been carrying it around like a talisman for nearly three years. A small square of paper: "Dear Lindsay," this note began. If she read it, she knew she would weaken, so she did not read it—anyway, she knew its four-line contents by heart. Leaning over the balustrade, she let this charmed piece of paper fall. It eddied toward her, then away; a current of air caught it, and it settled on the water like a pale moth; she watched it be carried away by the tide.

The gesture made her sad, but she also felt immeasurably lighter, she found. She floated back up the path, arm in arm with Markov and Jippy, Markov grumbling about the cold and Jippy's quiet gaze resting on the flagstones ahead. It was at this point in the evening, perhaps a little belatedly, that Lindsay, glancing at Jippy, wondered if he might have been influencing her once more. It was Jippy, after all, who had suggested Markov procure her the invitation to this party; it was at Jippy's urging that she had kept that invitation, and she began to suspect now that it was Jippy's influence that had weighed with her when she finally decided to come. It was odd, was it not, she thought, that he and Markov had been in the garden all evening, as if they had been waiting for her there. With Jippy, mainly because his presence was so silent and unobtrusive, it was always easy to forget he was there; it was only after her meetings with him were over that Lindsay sometimes suspected he had *influenced* her in some shadowy way, with some invisible sleight of hand.

Now, drifting back through the garden to the stairs, she had, strongly, the sensation that Jippy had possibly been guiding her, and that he was certainly guiding her now. This was superstition on her part, she told herself; Jippy did not *do* anything to which she could have pointed in evidence—at least not for a little while. Even so, the impression grew; it was imprecise and hazy, yet it was strong. Jippy's grip on her arm was light; he guided her back along that white corridor, Markov forging ahead of them both now, and he guided her back through the tides of that party crowd. Lindsay could sense both that he wished to speak and was as yet unable to do so, and that he had a destination in view for her; looking at his pale, set face, she felt sure this destination was close, perhaps just the other side of those entrance doors.

Their passage through the party was not the easiest of odysseys. Caught up in the swirling currents, they were buffeted toward that lipstick-red couch with its limpet men and siren girls; negotiating that, they were accosted, several times, by various ancient mariners wishing to tell various tales. Jippy guided them past these hazards; he paused briefly as paleface and ponytail hove into view, lamenting the latest news, which was that treacherous Lulu Sabatier had organized simultaneous Halloween parties in New York and Los Angeles to celebrate Diablo, and that—ultimate treachery!—Tomas Court was now rumored to be at one or the other of these.

"But *which*, my friend, *which*?" ponytail cried.

"I don't *know*," paleface responded. "I don't fucking well *know*."

"If I find Lulu, my friend, I won't be responsible for my actions. . . ."

"I'll fucking well *kill* her," cried paleface, diving into some murky confluence by the doors.

Jippy gave a small gentle smile at this and touched Lindsay's arms. The crowds parted like the Red Sea before Moses, and she and Jippy surged through. Outside, in the peace and darkness of the streets, Jippy and Markov escorted Lindsay back to her car. They walked, footsteps echoing, along narrow cobbled streets, with the dark walls, the rusting winches and traps of abandoned warehouse machinery, rising up on either side. Just audible on the breeze came the slithering sound of river water against mud; Lindsay could sense that Jippy still wished to speak and was still struggling to voice words.

Nearly half a mile from Lulu's loft palace, they finally found Lindsay's little car, parked outside a ruinous, boarded-up church, with one of its wheels—Lindsay was impetuous at parking—on the pavement. From the deserted streets, from nowhere, the taxi Markov had been demanding of the air some seconds earlier, now appeared. No one was too surprised by this phenomenon; such things tended to happen when Jippy was around.

"Greece, tomorrow." Markov kissed Lindsay. "Blue skies, sun, pagan temples, *divine* hotels. Enjoy Oxford. Enjoy New York. See you when we get back, my dearest. We leave at dawn!"

He then began to argue with the taxi driver—he always argued with taxi drivers on principle—about the route he should take to Markov's London apartment, which, like the other bolt-holes Markov maintained around the world, was enviably situated, utterly practical, and very small.

"Good-bye, Jippy," Lindsay said, kissing him. "I hope you have a wonderful holiday. Send me a card. . . ."

"I w-w-will. I . . ." There came a lengthy, choking pause. Knowing that Jippy was finally about to volunteer the statement she had sensed was imminent when they were in the garden, Lindsay waited quietly while he fought consonants.

"Y-y-y-yaw . . ." Jippy stuck painfully; his brown eyes

beseeched her. Lindsay did not prompt, for she knew that could make him seize up completely; she shivered as the wind gusted.

"Y-y-y-York . . ." he managed finally. Lindsay stared at him. Drops of sweat now beaded his forehead; his face was pale. Gently, she took his hand.

"*York*? Do you mean Yorkshire, Jippy? I was thinking of Yorkshire, earlier. When we were in that garden. Did you know?"

Jippy nodded, then shook his head. He gripped her hand tightly; his own felt deathly cold.

"Ch-ch . . ." This word, also, would not be said. Lindsay glanced over her shoulder at the desolate, semiruined building, with its forlorn boarded eyes. Church? Was Jippy trying to say "church"?

"Are you all right, Jippy?" she began. "You look . . ." She hesitated; "afraid" was the word that sprang to mind, but she was reluctant to use it. She could sense some alarm, some skin-chilling anxiety; it was being communicated to her from Jippy's cold hand. His lips were now trembling with the effort of words; his eyes rested on hers with a doglike fidelity; she could not tell for sure, she realized, whether his expression was happy or sad. He gave a small convulsive jerk of the head and suddenly the word, the phrase, burst through its restrictions.

"Ch-check your machine."

Lindsay looked at him blankly. She had been expecting a less mundane statement; according to Markov, Jippy's words often carried a secondary, hidden meaning, but this suggestion seemed to defy all but the most obvious of interpretations.

"My machine, Jippy? You mean my answering machine? When? Tonight? But I always check it anyway. . . ."

Jippy's burst of eloquence was over. This time, he did not shake his head or nod; he bestowed on her instead one of his heartening, benevolent smiles—a smile Lindsay would remember, many months later, when she came to consider the results of this evening, and of Jippy's advice. He pressed her hand, then climbed into the cab beside Markov. As it drove away, both men waved. Curiouser and curiouser, Lindsay thought, driving home.

Mindful of Jippy's words, and still haunted by his expression, she checked her fax and her answering machine immediately upon entering her apartment. Her hopes, which had risen high on the drive back here, now fell. No faxes, no messages; the machine's unwinking red light mocked her. During her absence, no one had called her—from Yorkshire, or from anywhere else.

Chapter 4

Toward midnight, the same night, Rowland McGuire put down the book he had been reading, rose, and threw another log on the fire. He pulled on the green sweater Lindsay had given him the previous Christmas, and moved quietly past the table where his friend Colin Lascelles was contriving to smoke two cigarettes at once and exude desperation. He opened the door.

This rented cottage was set high on the north Yorkshire moors. Until his eyes grew accustomed to the darkness beyond, Rowland could see nothing. He drew the door half shut behind him, looked out, and waited. After a while, he began to see the tussocky shapes of heather and gorse, the broken suggestions of crags on the horizon and, thrown out across the blackness above him, a glittering profusion of stars.

"Don't tell me you're going out *now*?" Colin called. "You're mad. It's All Souls' Night—the night of the dead. The hobgoblins will get you. I'll find you in the morning, stretched out, stone cold, with your teeth bared in a vampiric smile. . . ."

"I'll risk it; just for a while. I like walking at night. It would be quite pleasant to breathe. You've smoked two hundred cigarettes this evening. . . ."

"Two hundred and *two*." Colin's voice rose in a wail. "I need your advice, Rowland. I'm going insane. . . ."

"You've had my advice. I've been giving you advice for three days."

"I need *counseling*. I need therapy. Jungian analysis might help. . . ."

"You have a point there."

"Rowland, I'm having communication difficulties, severe ones. That bloody man's unavailable; he's not taking calls. And

47

my fax machine won't *feed*; it's making these puking noises,
Rowland, every time I redial. . . ."

"Tough," said Rowland, and closed the door.

Ignoring the primal, plaintive cries this action provoked,
Rowland crossed the cottage's small untended garden, opened
its reluctant gate, breathed in the freshness of the air, and began
to walk up the steep track beyond.

Somewhere below him, hidden by the curvature of the hills,
lay the cluster of church and farms that comprised the only
settlement resembling a village for many miles. From that
hamlet, as he walked, came the sound of a church bell tolling
midnight. An infinitesimal pause on each stroke, before the
clapper struck bronze; the turning of a day, the turning of a
month; not a night of ill omen, Rowland thought, increasing
his pace, but, rightly, a night when the dead were remembered
or placated, and prayers were said for the salvation of their
souls.

It was not the dead, but the living who were on his mind as
he walked. As soon as he was alone, he felt the touch of a hand,
heard the whisper of a voice; since the hand and the voice
belonged to a woman now the wife of another man, and mother
to that man's child, he tried at once to push her away and
drown all remembrance of her. He had tactics for this process;
sooner or later, they usually succeeded. It was harder here, in
this isolated place, than it was in London, where he could be
distracted by the hurly-burly of work, but even so the exorcism
could be achieved.

Facts, and the contemplation of facts, helped; it was also
useful to have problems that needed solving. Lacking now the
enjoyable immediate difficulties he could rely on in London—
investigations, deadlines, departmental politicking, the constant pursuit of news—he turned his mind instead to his friend
Colin Lascelles's current difficulties, which were now reaching
crisis point. These difficulties Rowland had been co-opted to
solve. Colin, as he noisily insisted, was suffering; his sufferings emanated from his current employer, the "bloody man,"
not taking his calls that evening, the American film director,
Tomas Court.

Quite how he had been cast in the Sherlock Holmes role in
this saga, Rowland was unsure. Colin's techniques, as usual,

had involved emotional blackmail, hysteria, genuine pathos, and winning charm; Rowland had found himself shifted by millimeters from the role of spectator to the role of participant. Now, apparently, he was on the case and expected to solve it by means of his intellectual and deductive powers. Colin had a touching faith in these powers; Rowland had rather less faith, but he was fond of Colin and anxious to help him, so now, walking on, he set his mind to his task.

In Colin's view, canvassed with great frequency, all his current difficulties could be overcome, and the looming crisis averted, if only they could, together, decode Court's perplexing character.

"If we could just figure him out, Rowland," he had announced earlier that day, "my problems would be over. I'm not *reading* him, that's the trouble. He's like a bloody anagram—and it's an anagram I can't solve on my own."

Rowland, who was gifted at anagrams, indeed at verbal puzzles of all kinds, now set himself the task of rearranging the vowels and consonants that comprised what he knew of this famous man. It interested him to do so, since Court was a director Rowland admired, though he was sometimes repelled by the darkness and chilly precision of his films. These films, it seemed to Rowland, set a series of cinematic traps for their audience; they were orchestrated with great care, although that care was often well disguised. Certain critics, and they tended to be aging and male, missed the shape and purpose of Court's movies, unable to see beyond their genre disguise. Younger critics, and Rowland agreed with them, could see the use Court made of cinematic conventions. To Rowland, Court's movies had an inexorable logic; frame by frame, they bore the stamp of his vision; they were conceived, shot, and edited by a cunning and well-disciplined directorial hand.

The movies then, Rowland thought, were his best clue to Court's character; beyond them, the facts were few. Court rarely gave interviews, and any biographical evidence was minimal. He was of Czech descent, and as far as Rowland could remember, had grown up poor in the Midwest, at some point anglicizing his original family name. He was now in his forties, and had come to movies unusually late for an American new-wave director. He was not some Hollywood wunderkind, but had studied movies as a mature student, after several years in the military, in—as far as Rowland could recall—the marines. His early work as a director attracted an art-house following; it was only after his marriage to the already famous Natasha Lawrence that his career took off. With their third film together, *Dead Heat,* the Court cult truly began. Now Tomas Court was divorced, some parties claiming the divorce was bitter, others amicable; whatever the truth, Court and his former wife continued to work together, and were about to do so again, as Colin confirmed. According to Colin, Tomas Court had loved and lost—in which case, Rowland thought dourly, Court's circumstances mirrored his own.

Still intent on releasing memory's grip, the last clinging grasp of its small, cold-fingered hand, Rowland turned his mind from such considerations. The track forked here, and he decided to head off to his left, making for the shadowy outcrop of rocks high above him. He began to consider his richest source of information, his friend Colin. Colin was scarcely the most reliable of witnesses, but he was an entertaining one. With a sense of growing relief and amusement, walking on, Rowland considered Tomas Court the professional, who had erupted into Colin Lascelles's life, via a two A.M. telephone call from America eight months before.

At that time, Tomas Court had been riding high on the critical and commercial success of *Dead Heat* (Genre: thriller. Setting: an unidentified American city). There was advance-word praise for his then soon-to-be-released movie, *Willow Song* (Genre: *film noir.* Setting: a Paris populated by American émigrés; according to Lindsay's son, Tom, subsequently: "A cross between Tarantino and Henry James").

In that telephone call, Court had informed Colin that he was now planning to make his first movie in England, and that it was to be an adaptation of a nineteenth-century novel. It would star, as most of Court's movies did, his former wife, Natasha Lawrence; it would be produced and scripted, as were all his movies, by Court himself. Colin had been surprised by this information, since the subject matter represented a departure from Court's previous movies. Later, on reflection, he was less surprised. Court's work had always been eclectic, and he liked to experiment with different genres; if a director such as

Scorsese could move from mafiosi to Edith Wharton's *of Innocence*, why shouldn't Court decide to take a s_ _ _ course?

Colin, who had been fast asleep when the call came through, and who discovered he had a blinding hangover when awakened, realized, at some point in the conversation—it dawned on him slowly—that Court was virtually offering him the job of this movie's location manager. At which point, fumbling for light switch and cigarettes in the dark, he requested further details. When? He was told. Studio, backers? He was told that too. Financing, budget? A stream of precise and impressive figures flowed down the phone. By that time, Colin had the light on; he was holding a pad and pencil in his right hand and juggling two lighted cigarettes in his left. Elation was taking hold. He had just agreed to meet Court in Prague, two days later, and Court was about to hang up, when it occurred to Colin, through qualms of residual intoxication and mounting excitement, that there were other rather more vital questions he should have asked.

He duly asked them. In particular, he asked which nineteenth-century novel Court meant to film. To his surprise, Court then became evasive. The name of the novel was not given over the telephone, nor was it given at the subsequent first meeting in Prague; a meeting that took place in a huge, shuttered, dimly lit hotel suite, and that lasted precisely one hour. During that hour, the tall, soft-spoken Court asked questions, and Colin, who was nervous, talked a great deal. He was not allowed to smoke— Court claimed to suffer from asthma, and indeed several asthma inhalers were in prominent view. By the time he left, Colin felt he had overcome this disadvantage, that he had talked good sense and acquitted himself reasonably well.

It was only later, as he went over and over the interview in his mind, that he realized how inconclusive, how puzzling, it had been. Recollecting it, it became disorderly; a dusty imprecision now clouded his view. He realized he could not recall exactly what Tomas Court had said, and that he had spoken very little. He realized that, having expected to acquire information, he had acquired virtually none—meanwhile he himself had given too much away.

"I *talked*," he had told Rowland, over a drink a few days later. "I damn well never drew breath, God knows why. Something came over me. He just sat there; he wasn't even asking questions by then, and I suddenly felt this *compulsion*. It was like the confessional. Worse. I just gabbled away. . . ."

"What about?"

"I don't *know*." He sank his head in his hands. "My father, my brother's funeral, my American great-aunt . . ."

"Never mind. . . ." Rowland tried to sound encouraging. "Things must have improved. What about work? Did you tell him—"

"Work?" Colin gave a bitter mirthless cry. "I never *mentioned* work. I meant to, obviously. I was going to tell him my Visconti anecdote. I thought that might go down well. But I didn't. I just talked about feelings. I could die of embarrassment. He'll never use me now. I told him things I didn't even *know* until that exact moment. I wasn't even looking at him; I was too intimidated. I was just staring at those blasted asthma inhalers and spilling out my soul."

Colin's Sophoclean gloom proved unfounded, and his predictions were not fulfilled. Court subsequently offered him the job of location manager, but several more weeks, another meeting, and innumerable telephone calls later, he still had not seen a script, even a draft script, even an outline, and he still did not know the name of the nineteenth-century novel Court intended to film.

Others, he discovered, on making delicate inquiries, were similarly in the dark. Court, it seemed, was hard to pin down, but had been flitting in and out of London over the past months and *seeing* people. He had approached the doyenne of British casting directors; he might have secured the services of a legendary, autocratic, and inspirational designer; he had had talks with technicians and SFX specialists; agents had been lunched; certain actors had been wooed—even the name of Nic Hicks had been mentioned—and now gusts of rumor, counterrumor, expectation, and surmise had begun to waft around London's fashionable watering holes. A tremendous, inchoate energy had been released, but just as, on each of these flitting visits, it swirled up into a dust storm of excitement and activity, Tomas Court would depart.

He would depart to a film festival in Berlin, or to Lo..
for postproduction work, then sneak previews of *Willow*..
He would swoop off to Reykjavik for two days, or Oslo for
three, or Athens for an hour and a half. Alternatively—and as
Rowland understood it, this was the present situation—he
would be holed up in the ranch he had recently bought in
northern Montana, situated near Glacier National Park, and
consisting of ten thousand acres of rock, river, and trees—this
according to Colin, who had never been there.

These absences, as far as Rowland could understand, made
little difference since, wherever he was, whether in a limousine, or midair, or holed up in his wilderness stronghold,
Tomas Court *communicated*. From him, or from one of his
numerous aides, assistants, and sidekicks, issued a daily, sometimes an hourly, flow of letters, faxes, and calls. The tenor of
these, Rowland gathered, was terse. In person and on paper,
Tomas Court seemed a man of few words. Of the few words
employed, his favorite was "no."

Extracting information from him, Colin had rapidly discovered, was as difficult as finding a vein to extract blood from in
a sinewy arm; when the vein *was* located, the blood refused to
flow. Nor was he alone in this difficulty, Colin found, encoun-
tering the famous actor Nic Hicks one evening in a theater bar.

"Don't ask *me*," Hicks said languidly, eyeing Colin and
affecting indifference—Hicks was currently very hot indeed,
and liked to emphasize this; but Colin, who had known him
virtually since birth, was not deceived. Neither man liked the
other. "He's talked to my agent, obviously," Nic Hicks went
on. "Played his cards *very* close to his chest. I get so sick of
those power games, don't you? I said to her, Yawn, yawn—just
tell him to send the script and I'll read it. Meantime, darling, he
can join the queue."

"Quite right," Colin replied, stoutly and vengefully. "I fear
he's after Ralph, anyway. . . ." Nic Hicks paled. "So I wouldn't
fret if I were you."

Colin renewed his inquiries elsewhere and was similarly
thwarted. Everyone caught up in the Court operation, it
seemed—the technicians, the agents, the casting directors—
felt that they knew what was going on until, like Colin, they
analyzed the situation later and discovered they had been fed

mere droplets of sustenance, just enough to keep them engaged, but no more.

It had taken Colin over a month to discover that the movie Court planned was based (loosely, Court stressed) on the last novel by the least known, and least admired, of the three Brontës; it was *The Tenant of Wildfell Hall*. Colin was not a great reader of fiction, and he was suspicious of female novelists; he had managed to avoid ever reading a single work by any of the Brontë sisters. He was proud of this feat and in another situation might have boasted of it; confronted by Tomas Court, he immediately lied.

"Yes, yes, yes, yes, of course!" he cried. "Fascinating. Timely. Brilliant. Mind you, it's years since I read it. I'll reread it at once. Tonight. Can't wait . . . What, er, what made you decide on that novel, Tomas?"

Tomas Court, as Colin had noticed by then, had remarkable eyes. He now turned those eyes upon Colin and bestowed upon him one of his long, silent, disconcerting stares.

Court's eyes, narrow, somewhat catlike, and not without beauty, were of a pale, watery, greenish hazel hue. Colin found it impossible to read their expression, and could never say why he found their inspection such an unpleasant experience. Court always appeared well mannered, patient, and calm; nothing in his gaze suggested disapproval or distrust or dislike, yet Colin at once felt deeply uneasy, as if Court possessed some alien vision, X-ray eyes, Martian eyes, that enabled him to see through Colin's body to inspect the back of his skull. Lies, evasions, boasts, and untruths, Colin feared, lay naked before the gaze of this soft-spoken man. He squirmed in his chair (they were meeting in New York, this time, in yet another dimly lit, anonymous hotel).

Colin's question he felt, was like most of his questions, not going to be answered. Rebelling, and summoning some residue of spirit, he repeated it. Court sighed and looked away.

"The heroine interested me, I guess," he replied. "She's the tenant of the title, you see."

Colin did *not* see. He assumed illumination would come when—as he later put it to Rowland—he actually read the blasted novel. Tomas Court now provided him with a copy of it, and of his draft script; with alacrity Colin read both. Having done so, he was none the wiser. He liked the script, which seemed to him to depart from the original novel quite rapidly, but he found the novel itself very heavy going indeed.

"I ploughed through," he reported to Rowland. "I ploughed through *religiously*. . . ."

"And?"

"It's all very well for you to smile; you already know it. You never damn well stop reading; it's a disease with you. You *like* things like that—God knows why."

"You didn't enjoy it then?"

"Enjoy it? I was *crucified* with boredom. The beginning's okay. This mystery woman arrives; she's called Helen. I like that bit, but after that it's downhill all the way."

From this robust, if possibly simplistic view, Colin could not be dissuaded. Rowland wasted no time on arguments; Colin, armed with Court's script and abandoning all thoughts of the novel, began work. He was very experienced and very good at his work, and initially the location scouting went well. Several months passed, during which Rowland occasionally received progress reports. These, at first, were very upbeat, then a detectable note of doubt began to creep in.

Initially, Tomas Court was a marvel, and Colin worshiped at his shrine. He lauded his attention to detail, his perfectionism, the constant fertile flood of his ideas. Then, it seemed, Court could be inspired, certainly, but was also somewhat *changeable*. A week later, the word "indecision" was used; a week after that the charge had hardened—"willful perversity" was now the term. Spoken of as "Tomas," and with considerable warmth, when this saga began, this modulated to a curt "Court," then a period when he was known, in a jocular, defensive tone as "the evil genius"; for the past month he had been simply "that bloody man." These were the staging posts whereby Colin's initial enthusiasm and admiration dwindled to uncertainty, then irritation, then irascibility, then resentment, and finally—this was his present state—despair.

This journey of Colin's toward the crisis he had now reached had been watched by Rowland from the sidelines. It had amused him at the time, and it amused him now, but beneath the amusement he felt a certain unease. He paused, having finally reached the vantage point on the hills to which he had been walking. He looked back the way he had come, bracing himself against the wind, which at this height was strong. It gusted, then insinuated, this wind, buffeting him, then channeling itself through the crevices in the outcrop of rocks against which he leaned. In doing so, it acquired a voice, a thin note of eerie lamentation, which seemed to emanate from the rock, or from the air itself. It chilled Rowland and threatened the equanimity he had been working hard to achieve. Realizing that he had remained out far longer than he had intended, and walked farther, he moved away from the plaintive rocks, turned back toward the cottage, and began to descend.

The wind hit him hard between the shoulder blades; it sang out its ghostly protest as it whistled between stones and tugged at the heather. This was a bleak place. Rowland paused, fighting the past, then turned up the collar of his jacket and continued on. He would have liked to return with some useful advice for Colin, but could think of none. He could tell him, of course, to stop worrying over whether or not Tomas Court was now playing games with him; he could tell him to soldier on. Colin would do that in any case, though, for he was tenacious. His present fear, of course, which he could not bring himself to name, was *failure*; Colin, deeply insecure, always feared failure, and yet ran to greet it, to anticipate it; there were reasons for this, as Rowland, his friend for many years, was well aware.

All of these events, Rowland realized, told him more about Colin's character than Tomas Court's. Colin had always been precipitate, rushing in where angels feared to tread, and Rowland, who usually fought his own impulsiveness more successfully, had always liked, even admired him for this. Colin was also passionate, a man of extremes, as Rowland knew he too could be, on occasion; but Colin was less measured and lived in a world of violent opposites—there was tragedy or comedy, triumph or disaster, with no gray, indeterminate area in between.

This characteristic of Colin's did not make it any easier to help him now, and it did not help Rowland in his attempts to read the character of Tomas Court through the curlicues of Colin's style. Colin, utterly thwarted, fearful of failing and being rejected by a man he had placed high on a pedestal, was now busy dismantling that pedestal. He had spent the last three days here in Yorkshire oscillating wildly from optimism to pessimism, attacking as vices the very qualities he had seen as Court's virtues before. Court's perfectionism had become perversity, or pedantry; when Colin was at his lowest point, bumping along the riverbed of pessimism and paranoia, he had begun to claim that Court was intent on destruction. "I know what that bloody man is after!" he had cried that morning. "He wants me *destroyed*."

The reason for this assertion was, on the surface of it, simple enough. For *Wildfell*, as he now termed it, Colin had, as his first task, to find, confirm, set up, cost, and work out the logistics for a total of 123 locations. Some were exteriors, some interiors; some would be used for several lengthy scenes, others for only a few seconds.

Over the past months, sometimes traveling in the company of Court himself, or one of his assistant directors, or alone, Colin had found, and had confirmed by Court, all but one of these locations. This process had gone well—suspiciously well, Colin now said. One problem—there remained that last, key, still-unfound location: the exterior of the Wildfell Hall of the novel's title. In his opinion, Colin had found at least thirteen potential Wildfell Halls, thirteen *perfect* Wildfell Halls.

Tomas Court, formerly the perfectionist, now the pedantic nitpicker, had liked none of them. In fact, he had hated them, and had reiterated his hatred, his dissatisfaction and disappointment in a stream of wounding, cold faxes and calls. Colin, stung, had continued his search—was still continuing his search. He had traveled the length and breadth of England; he had made desperate forays into Scotland, and even more desperate forays into Wales. Returning, he dispatched batches of photographs, videos, diagrams, maps, and notes around the globe to the peripatetic Tomas Court. Time would pass—Court liked to keep him on tenterhooks, Colin claimed—then back would come word from Montana, or Berlin, or Los Angeles. "No" was the word, it was always the word, and so often and so unkindly had that word "No" been said that it had precipitated in Colin a profound confidence crisis. "It's not just my reputation that's at stake here," he had said three weeks previously, in London, having inveigled Rowland into joining him for dinner after work, "it's my *sanity*. I want you to understand—that bloody man is sucking the marrow out of my bones, Rowland. I'm at my wit's end. I don't know where to turn, so I'm turning to you. Help me out here, Rowland. Just *advise* me, that's all I ask."

Rowland had resisted this plea. Once or twice in the past he had been sucked into Colin's dramas via the advice route, and it was not an experience he had enjoyed.

"Listen . . ." Colin went on, "you know the blasted novel. There's a description of Wildfell Hall in chapter two—you remember? Now, you're interested in architecture. In fact, you know quite an impressive amount. Not as much as I do, obviously, but enough. You spend half your life climbing or walking in godforsaken places. . . ."

"That isn't true. I wish it were."

". . . So you have the right background knowledge. You must have some ideas. Think, Rowland. I need somewhere remote. An old house, large, ideally Jacobean, untouched and unrestored—and gloomy, Rowland; it has to look dark, threatening, even haunted. Large, spooky, remote and 1610, that's what he wants. At least, I think that's what he wants."

"You don't sound too certain. Why? You must have a brief."

"Of course I have a brief. And I've fulfilled it, to the letter, thirteen times."

"Then there must be some requirement you're missing."

"Well, I don't know what it is. Atmosphere, he said. What's that supposed to mean? It means anything you damn well want it to mean, which is why he uses it. I'm telling you, Rowland, that bloody man is devious, perverse. And for some reason I don't understand, he's hanging me out to dry."

"Perhaps," Rowland suggested as gently as he could, "perhaps it would help if you read the original novel again." Colin shuddered. He drank a glass of red wine very fast. "This is ridiculous, Colin. You've worked with some of the best directors in the world. Houses? You've got an encyclopedic memory for houses. . . ."

"Have I?" Colin gave him a humble look. "I don't feel as if I have—not anymore. I've had confidence suction. Rowland, please help. Don't turn me down."

Rowland hesitated. He always found it difficult to be sure when Colin genuinely needed help, and he was aware he could be manipulative. His friend had always lacked confidence in his own abilities; a legacy from his childhood, Rowland suspected, for he had grown up in the shadow of his elder brother, killed in a car accident when Colin was in his last year at school. On the other hand, Colin thrived on crises, and if none existed, was capable of creating some of his own. On balance, Rowland thought then, he believed Colin was truly in need of some help and moral support; there was now genuine panic and bewilderment in his manner, and it alarmed Rowland, since it reminded him of Colin as he had been when he first encountered him, in Oxford, eighteen years before.

That meeting had taken place late at night, in the quad at Balliol College, where they were both undergraduates, although they had then moved in very different social spheres. Colin, who could be heard yodeling before he was seen, was wearing white tie and tails, and was accompanied, or propped up, by a clutch of cronies from some ancient, snobbish, august Oxford club whose members devoted themselves to getting drunk fast. Colin had just won a competition that involved drinking straight down as many bottles of vintage claret as was feasible in five minutes. He was already celebrated throughout Oxford for his feats in this respect, which had won him the nickname Deep Throat. On that occasion, he had consumed two and a half bottles of Chateau Margaux 1959, and was, astonishingly, still vertical. Rowland had not come from the kind of school, or the kind of background, essential for membership in such clubs; upper-class louts were not his favorite companions, and—given to puritanism then—he had looked at this rowdy group of Etonians with distaste.

He had been about to pass by when something in Deep Throat's expression caught his eye. He was regarding Rowland with a flushed, kindly innocence, this red-haired young man, who was the heir to twelve thousand acres, who had just consumed wine which cost more than Rowland could afford to spend in ten weeks. His expression conveyed precarious dignity, absurd pride, and incipient distress. He made a hiccuping sound and fixed Rowland with blue, alarmed eyes. "Help," he said, with surprising distinctness, as he began slowly, like a felled tree, to topple forward toward the flagstones of the quad. Rowland, in a better state of alertness than the friends were, found he had moved forward, held out his arms, and caught him. They then scattered, and Deep Throat was sick—ignominiously, understandably, and *accurately*, as he remarked the next morning when Rowland called in to check on him.

"I missed my shoes!" he said, bright faced. "I missed yours as well. Here, have some champagne. Childe Roland to the dark quad came. I'm going on the wagon tomorrow, so shall we celebrate now?"

They celebrated, at nine in the morning, with a bottle of Dom Pérignon. Rowland missed two lectures and made two discoveries: he was less of a puritan than he had thought, and he liked Colin Lascelles, who, it seemed, was even more appalled at the prospect of inheriting twelve thousand acres and the minor title that went with them than Rowland McGuire was.

The next week, hungover again, he drove Rowland out into the countryside north of Oxford and stopped the car on the edge of a beech wood. He pointed; below them, in a valley enfolded by gentle Cotswold hills, was one of the most beautiful houses Rowland had ever seen.

"That's Shute," Colin said. "It will be mine one day. It should have been my brother's, only he died." Then he let in the clutch, drove them back to Oxford, and started drinking again.

From that moment on, Colin attached himself to Rowland, and Rowland, often exasperated by him, grew fond of him. In the eighteen years since, their relationship had changed little. Although Colin had learned to control his drinking, indulging in binges only occasionally, and was now highly successful, he remained incorrigible, and he still treated Rowland as a surrogate brother. He still asked Rowland's assistance from time to time, and when pressured, Rowland grumbled, then, often against his better judgment, gave way.

So, on the occasion of that dinner, he had agreed to help. He promised to mull the matter over, consult some friends, and see what he could come up with. He suggested Colin meet him in his editorial office at the *Sunday Correspondent* the next day; there, Rowland would join him as soon as he could escape from a round of meetings.

He found Colin ensconced in his office, propositioning his secretary. Having extricated her from a situation she appeared to be enjoying—Colin was good-looking and had undeniable charm—Rowland gave him a brief and, he hoped, helpful lecture on Anne Brontë's Wildfell Hall.

"Think about this house, Colin," he said. "Think about the mystery woman you like so much at the beginning of the book. She's taken refuge in Wildfell Hall, hasn't she?"

"Ye-es," said Colin, eyes beginning to glaze.

"It's not her permanent home. She doesn't *own* it; she's renting it, from a man."

"I don't really see," Colin began mutinously, "that it makes the least bit of difference *who* she's renting it from. It could just as well be some mad old grandmother—so what?"

"No, Colin. *Think.* This woman is young, she's beautiful, she has a son—and she's lied about her past. She's living under a false name and she's in *hiding* at Wildfell Hall. What happens almost immediately after she's moved in there?"

"Oh, I don't know. All these bitchy women in the neighborhood start gossiping about her. Gilbert Markham meets her and falls in love with her. Then they all find out she's having a secret affair with the owner of Wildfell Hall, who's this tall, dark, brooding man. Then we get this flashback bit, and it goes on and on and on. . . ."

"Dear God." Rowland buried his head in his hands. "Colin, think. Use your *brain.* Forget all this gobbledygook; you're getting the plot wrong. Think about property, and *sex*, Colin, and the connections between the two. . . ."

At the mention of sex, Colin's face brightened. "I don't quite follow you, Rowland. . . ."

"Listen, Colin, it may have escaped your notice, but for much of the novel, all the *property* is owned by men. The question Anne Brontë raises—one of the questions—is whether the men own the women as well."

"Oh Lord—it's *feminist*, you mean?" Colin blinked. "I must have missed that. No wonder I didn't like it; I can't stand that sort of thing. It's so *unnecessary*, don't you find? Look, Rowland, this is all very interesting, but I have to find a *house*. . . ."

"I know that, but this house symbolizes something, Colin."

"Not to me it doesn't. A house is a house. It has four walls, a roof, and a door. Come on, Rowland, you said you'd give me some suggestions. . . ."

Rowland gave up. He passed Colin a list. Of the four houses on it, it turned out, three had already been suggested by Colin and rejected by Tomas Court, a fact he had neglected to mention. This did not appear to demoralize Colin; on the contrary, he assumed a businesslike demeanor, produced numerous dog-eared maps and notebooks, and showed signs of cheering up.

"I knew I could rely on you!" He beamed at Rowland. "We think alike. We're getting somewhere now."

Pointedly, Rowland looked at his watch.

"There's just one leetle problem, Rowland. This fourth place you suggest . . . it's, well, it's a bit too remote. It's a hundred miles from all my other locations, there's no road to it, no hotel nearby. . . ."

Rowland controlled his temper. "You didn't mention roads or hotels."

"Well, I thought you'd *realize*. I have to house a crew, the cast, Natasha Lawrence. I have to consider costs: transport, caravans, limousines, generators, computer links, catering, security. Stars don't *walk* to location, Rowland, and they're kind of fussy about hotels. I can't put Natasha Lawrence up in some boardinghouse, now can I?"

"Why not? She's there to work. I imagine she'd survive."

"Don't be naive, Rowland. You know perfectly well it doesn't work like that. We're talking suites, twenty-four-hour room service, a pool, a gym. She has a bodyguard, and she works out with him every morning. . . ."

"You said *remote*, dammit. . . ."

"I know, but there's remote and remote. Now don't get testy, Rowland, and don't give up on me. . . ."

"Give up on you? I wouldn't dream of it. After all, apart from the small matter of getting out a Sunday newspaper, I have nothing else to do. My calls are being *held*. I'll just tell them to hold them for the next hour, shall I? Or would two suit you better?"

"Now, Rowland, don't be sarcastic. I can't take it, not just now. Please, Rowland," Colin said, in a very small, pathetic voice. "*Please*. I'm begging you now. I've helped you in the past. You remember that time at Oxford when I lent you my lecture notes?"

"No, I don't."

"What about all those Oxford girls? I was useful to you then, Rowland. When you broke their hearts, who consoled them? I did. Max occasionally, I admit, but I was the chief consoler, Rowland, remember that."

"You're confusing consolation and opportunism, I think."

Colin waved this objection aside. "Rowland, let us not argue about ancient history. . . ."

"Argue about it? You can't even *remember* it. You were drunk, Colin. Perpetually drunk. You were drunk for three whole *years*. . . ."

"You're right. You're right." Colin sank his head in his hands. "I was an irresponsible wastrel. A ne'er-do-well. The Lascelles black sheep. But you set me on the straight and narrow, Rowland. You got me through my exams. I'll never forget that. None of my family ever forgets it. . . ."

Rowland tensed.

"So I know I have no right to ask for your help again, but you did mention you were going on holiday next week. . . ."

"What's that got to do with it?"

"Nothing. There's no need to look so suspicious. I just thought, since you'll be going north anyway . . ."

"Colin, I'm going climbing. It's the first holiday I've taken in over a year."

"Of course. And you need that break, Rowland, you deserve it. You're looking tired, tense. Which is why I thought you might like to spend a few days in Yorkshire on your way back from Scotland. I'm renting a cottage up there as my base. It's on your route back, Rowland, and that bloody man will still be bombarding me with faxes and calls. By then, I'll be on my eighteenth perfect house, I expect, and ready to shoot myself. So it just occurred to me, maybe, out of the goodness of your heart, and because you once loved my sister, Rowland, years ago . . ."

"I did not love your sister."

"Well, she loved you, which is much the same thing, and despite your failure to respond, she still speaks fondly of you. She's recovered, of course; she has four children now. Even so, every time your name comes up, I catch this little gleam in her eye. . . ."

Rowland sighed. "Dear God. What have I done to deserve this? All right. Okay, you win. Give me the damn address and I'll look in on my way back. . . ."

Colin had taken this capitulation generously. Having got his way, at which he was skilled, he skedaddled. And now, here Rowland was, in a cold leaky cottage in the back of beyond, in the company of a man who, like himself, could not cook. For three days, subsisting on lumpen cheese sandwiches and cans of soup, he had endured Colin's plaints and joined him on fruitless searches for a place that Rowland too was beginning to believe did not exist.

It was a chimera, he told himself, opening that reluctant creaking gate and approaching the cottage. When he had first been drawn into this ridiculous quest, he had seen Wildfell Hall clearly in his mind; now it had receded. The more he listened to Colin, the less he saw.

It was diverting, this search, up to a point. It had the advantage of distracting him, but he now intended to return to London and work, and the real world. He would leave in the morning; he would be back in his own house by tomorrow afternoon. He might telephone Lindsay perhaps. . . . It was morning now, he realized, looking at his watch. He would grab a few hours' sleep and leave immediately after an early breakfast. . . . And he entered the cottage intending to firmly inform Colin of this.

"Well, well, well, well, *well*," Colin said.

Rowland stopped in the doorway. It was at once apparent to him that Colin, noisily suicidal when he left, was now drunk. It was one-thirty in the morning; during an absence of one and a half hours, Colin had contrived to become merry. His long thin limbs were stretched out on the sofa; his auburn hair was disheveled; he had his feet to the fire, a large tumbler of Scotch in his hand, and a Cheshire Cat grin on his face.

"Aha!" he said indistinctly. "Good news! *Doubly* good news! What a dark horse you are, Rowland. What a very *nice* world this is."

Rowland took this announcement with equanimity. He removed his wet boots and poured himself a Scotch from a near-empty bottle. He sat down in a squashed, comfortable armchair on the other side of the fire. Colin watched him beatifically as he did this.

"Well now, let me guess," Rowland said eventually, when Colin seemed about to achieve nirvana or fall asleep. "You've had a call from Tomas Court? A fax? He actually likes one of the houses?"

"He does. The first one we saw; the one you suggested; the one near the sea. He's just got the videos."

"Well, now that is good news. Your problems are over. Great."

"You're a true friend, Rowland; that's what you are. A friend in need, indeed." Colin paused and showed signs of becoming emotional.

"Think nothing of it," Rowland said. "I wouldn't cry about it, if I were you, Colin. Are you sure you really want that whiskey?"

It seemed Colin did want the whiskey. It seemed that he might resent being deprived of the whiskey. It seemed he was prepared to put up a fight about the whiskey. In fact, he would fight any man who came between him and the whiskey; fight him to the death. Rowland agreed that this was a very reasonable point of view.

Colin, who had risen uncertainly during this recital of his rights, sat down again uncertainly. He looked at Rowland and, at length, appearing to recognize him, reiterated his opinion that Rowland was a dark horse, a very dark horse indeed. He tapped his nose as he said this.

Rowland found this statement, and the reasons for it, rather harder to unravel. After ten minutes of obfuscation, he had the gist. Awhile after the good news from Court, which Colin had immediately begun celebrating, a woman had called, wishing to speak to Rowland. This woman, whose name was Lynne, or Linda, or possibly Lynette, had a voice and a manner Colin instantly liked. Or, another way of putting it, he and Lynne, or Lisa, had hit it off. They had, it seemed, chatted away as if they were old friends; they had chatted away for *hours*, about Yorkshire, and men who liked walking in the dark, and life, and this and that.

"This and that?" Rowland said, when this account rambled to a conclusion. "And her name's Lindsay, by the way."

"Lindsay! The fair Lindsay! I salute her!" Colin drank.

"She's dark, not fair," Rowland said, his manner slightly irritable.

"Dark *and* fair. With a voice. With a *magical* voice. It has a catch in it." Colin seemed to be sobering up rapidly. "I could have listened to that voice all night. She liked my voice too; she said so. She said I sounded very *merry*. I cheered her up."

"I'm delighted to hear it." Rowland rose. "Did she leave a message for me or was she too busy complimenting you?"

"Can't remember."

"Try. She must have had a reason for calling."

"She sent her love."

"Not that. A proper reason. What did she want?"

Colin was relapsing again; the angelic smile had reappeared on his face. "We came to an understanding," he announced.

"I doubt that."

"We did. We *communicated*. Arrangements were made! I remember! I remember!" Colin flailed, then subsided. "It was a friendly call, she said. She wondered when you might be getting back. You're *friends*. Friendly friends. That's what she said. And after that . . ."

"After that, what?"

"I proposed. I proposed marriage."

"I see." Rowland gave Colin a long, cool, green-eyed look. "And did my friend accept?"

"I think she did."

"Well, accept my congratulations," Rowland said evenly. "And now I'm going to bed."

Chapter 5

At ten that same morning, Lindsay's son Tom was calm. He was in the large bedsitting room of his lodgings in a tall, dilapidated but pleasant north Oxford house; from upstairs and from below, where other undergraduates had rooms, came the sounds of music: Mozart from the north side, Dire Straits from the south. He was stretched full length on a sofa with an unfortunate cerise slipcover, a sofa that even his landlady, the *distrait* widow of a physics professor, admitted had seen better days. As much of the cerise as possible was disguised by an Indian cotton throw found by Tom's girlfriend, Katya. Tom had managed to position himself so that he avoided the jab and prod of springs.

On his chest was balanced the third bowl of cornflakes he had eaten that morning, this one moistened with water, as he and Katya had forgotten to buy milk the previous day. He munched a spoonful experimentally; they tasted edible. He turned a page of the large book propped on his knees, which detailed the economic consequences upon Germany of the Treaty of Versailles.

Across the room from him, Katya, who ostensibly lived in her college, but spent little time there, was pecking away at the keys of her word processor with two fingers. She was wearing a white nightdress and woolly socks; her auburn hair was wound up in a bundle on top of her head, from which precarious tendrils escaped. Every so often, she would stop pecking at the keys, push these tendrils aside impatiently, lean forward, adjust her large working spectacles, and glare at the screen. Her essay, on George Eliot's *Middlemarch*, was due to be delivered to her tutor, the terrifying Dr. Stark. It should have been completed the evening before, and would have been, had she and Tom not decided that a late-night six-hour Halloween retrospective of classic vampire movies was more urgent than a nineteenth-century novel, or inexorable inflation in 1930s Germany. Then they had had to eat, then Cressida-from-upstairs had arrived with some red wine and Algerian grass; then they had had to sleep—well, go to bed anyway; then . . . Tom considered the subsequent events with pleasure. Two hours of actual sleep? One and a half? He abandoned the corn-flakes and half closed his eyes; the tome on his knees slid to the floor. Ten, ten, ten. Oxford had so many churches, and none of their clocks synchronized. The chiming of an hour could last five minutes or more, and Tom, loving the city, loved it especially for this stretching of time.

Peck, peck, peck went Katya's fingers on the keys. Katya, expected to get a first, as was Tom, was fierce in her typing, fierce in her opinions, this being one of the reasons why Tom had now loved her for two years. No, more than two years, he thought, lazily, stretching out his legs and wriggling his toes. Two years, two months, a week and two days. The length of this period of fierce fidelity pleased Tom; it reassured him that he had not inherited his father's genes; his father, whom he scarcely knew and now never saw, being, as Tom sometimes contemptuously said, a fickle weakling of a man. Two years, two months, a week, two days and—he paused to calculate—twelve and a half hours.

It was at this point, very suddenly, that Tom ceased to be calm. He leaped to his feet as if electrocuted, and stared wildly around the room. The room, he now saw, was a slum, a pigsty. How had this escaped his notice before? The bed in the alcove was unmade; there were T-shirts and socks strewn across the floor; on the table was a stack of last night's dirty plates and unwashed wineglasses; there were cigarette papers and obvious roaches in the ashtray. He sniffed; did the room smell of grass? He thought it might smell of grass. He plunged across the room and opened the window wide.

"Oh my God. Oh my God," he said. "It's today. It's today *now*."

"So?" Katya did not look up; she pecked even faster at the keys.

"Mum's coming. She'll be here any minute. She'll be here in less than half an hour."

Katya glanced at her watch. "She'll be late; she's always late. She'll get lost. You know how she drives. . . ."

"Shit, shit, double shit." Tom was leaping crazily about, stuffing socks under pillows. "What if she *isn't* late? What if she's on time?"

"Stay calm. Just give me two minutes; I'm almost finished. I just have to be really savage about Will Ladislaw. . . ."

"Who?"

"He's the love interest. In here." Katya indicated a fat paperback copy of *Middlemarch* from which protruded slips of white place marks, like a porcupine's spines. "*Not* one of Eliot's successes. An apology for a man."

Tom moaned. He emptied the telltale ashtray, picked up the dirty plates and glasses, and shoved them into a cupboard. He closed the door, straightened the duvet, punched the pillows, then stood looking around him with an expression of wild surmise.

"What else? What else? There's bound to be something else. Mum has X-ray eyes; she doesn't miss *anything*. What about the dust? There's all this *dust*. Where does all this dust come from?"

"Lindsay's seen dust before. She won't mind. I can't think why you're fussing. Lindsay's cool."

"Cool? She's my *mother*."

"I expect she'll understand. I wish you'd shut up. I just have to skewer this love scene. How can you be a genius and write a love scene like this one? It creaks. There's a ridiculous storm. She can't do storms. She's pinched the storm from one of the Brontës. Charlotte, I think. Where's my *Jane Eyre*?"

"Under that coffee mug, next to the ashtray. Christ—quick, give me that ashtray. . . ." In the act of reaching for it, Tom paused. He could now read the words on Katya's computer screen; they were not kind words—Katya was young, as well as fierce—and they caused Tom some alarm.

"Shit, Katya—you've really . . . You don't mince your words. Castrated? Epicene? Poor Will what's-his-name . . ." He bent more closely and read the next paragraph. Unconcerned, concentrated, Katya continued to peck away.

"Bloody hell." Tom gave a sigh. "Is this guy Will supposed to be the hero?"

"Sort of. Maybe. I can't make up my mind. Neither could Eliot, unfortunately, and it shows."

"You say—this guy Will Whatsit isn't erotic then?"

"He's handsome." Katya shrugged. "Passionate. He obeys some of the conventions. But not erotic—no."

"Do heroes have to be erotic?"

"Sure, heroes ought to exude sex. They have to have sexual power."

This statement alarmed Tom. "Sexual power?" he said. "Come on, Katya—that's a nineteenth-century novel. Closed bedroom doors."

"No one screws, you mean?" Katya, still concentrated, typed a final blistering sentence. She leaned back in her chair, removed her spectacles, and smiled. "*That* doesn't matter. In fact, it helps. The reader's vile imagination does all the work. . . . You want to know what makes a man erotic in a novel?"

"I already know: money and looks. I've read *Pride and Prejudice*. Hell."

"You're wrong. It's silence: a capacity for silence. Obviously, money helps—or did. Social status. Dark eyes and dark hair . . ."

"Shit, shit, shit," said Tom, whose hair was fair.

"But silence is vital. If a hero is a man of few words, he remains mysterious, and mystery in a man is *always* erotic. . . ."

Tom felt humbled. He made a private vow to be as Trappist as possible from then on. Perhaps it had been a mistake to be so open with Katya? Perhaps, in revealing his heart to her, he had disarmed himself and unwisely divested himself of a vital weapon in the male armory. Enigma. Mystery. Silence. Erotic power.

"Shit," he said miserably. "I'm a failure as a man. I see it now. I'm like Will Whatsit. I'm an eunuch, a castrate. I'm epicene."

That, at last, attracted Katya's attention.

"Are you?" she asked, leaning forward and touching him in a way, and with an immediate result, that gave the lie to this statement. Tom forgot about novels and heroes, and also about the time. Ten pleasurable minutes later, he remembered clocks; he leaped out of bed with a panic-stricken howl.

"Shit. Double shit. Where's the duvet?"

"On the floor. Pass me my jeans."

"This is terrible. This is appalling. I love you, Katya."

"I love you too. Comb your hair."

Tom combed his hair, which was now rather longer than when his mother had last seen it. He felt his chin, decided to shave, decided not to shave; he found a clean shirt and rushed about the room. While he rushed, Katya put things in order. She achieved this, it seemed to Tom, in about fifteen seconds. The dust disappeared; the fluff on the carpet was sucked away; papers lay down in piles; books stacked themselves on shelves. A quick, fierce burst of female efficiency; suddenly chaos no longer threatened and the detritus was gone.

Fifteen seconds after that, Tom was posed on the sofa, surrounded by suitable evidence of undergraduate industry; Katya, also posed with book in hand, was seated opposite, smelling of rose-petal soap, demure in an armchair. For five minutes, all the church bells of Oxford chimed the half hour. Both waited expectantly.

"I *told* you she'd be late," Katya said a short while later.

"I *told* you we had time. We could have . . ."

Tom, intent on a heroic, erotic silence, ignored this prompt. He gave Katya a volcanic look; Katya giggled; Tom persevered. Katya's amusement died away; she shifted in her seat, lowered her eyes, and, to Tom's triumph, blushed rosily. Tom was just congratulating himself on the ease with which he had mastered this effective new technique—nothing to it, much easier than actually speaking, a cinch—when the telephone rang. Both Tom and Katya expected it to be Lindsay, calling with some excuse for her delay. It was not Lindsay, however, but her friend, and Tom's friend, Rowland McGuire. Rowland, it emerged, was trying to track down Lindsay.

They spoke for some while, then Tom replaced the receiver.

"Great," he said. "Rowland's going to join us for lunch. He's going to drop in on his way back to London. He's got some friend with him. . . ."

"A woman friend?"

"No. Some man who was up at Oxford with him. Works in films."

"Interesting." Katya gave Tom a sidelong glance. "Lindsay will be pleased. You don't think . . ."

"No, I don't," Tom said, in a very certain tone. "Katya, I've told you a billion times, they're *friends*. . . ."

"He might fancy her. I think it's on the cards, and you'd be the last person to notice if he did."

"My mother? You must be mad. She's thirty-five. She's been thirty-five for quite a while."

"She's Rowland's age, or thereabouts."

"That's different. Get it into your head—my mother is not Rowland's type."

"Why not? She's pretty; she's nice." Katya paused; she gave a small frown. "What is Rowland's type?"

"Damsels," Tom replied darkly, "or so I've heard. Beautiful women. *Difficult* women. Women who need rescuing. Rowland's gallant, or so people say."

"Do they indeed?" Katya's frown deepened.

"People gossip about Rowland." Tom shrugged. "It's probably all lies. They say he breaks hearts. In the nicest possible way, of course."

"He's arrogant," Katya said, thoughtfully, after a further pause. "He's one of the most arrogant men I've ever met, but some women—*older* women—like that kind of thing. Lindsay might like it, for one. . . ."

"She doesn't. They're friends; that's it, nothing more. Why can't you accept that? As far as Rowland's concerned, my mother's an honorary man. . . ."

"An enviable fate."

"Katya, I've *told* you, Lindsay's given up on men in the romantic sense. She gave up years ago. She's not interested and she doesn't need them. She has a good job, a good salary, lots of friends, her own apartment. She's got shot of my grandmother, which is nothing short of a miracle. I'm not there, messing the place up. She's her own woman. Why would she need a man?"

Katya could think of several answers to that question, not all of them polite. In different circumstances, she would have voiced them, but now, merciful to Tom and condescending to the blindnesses of man and son, she remained silent. One day, she thought, when the moment was more propitious, she might have to explain to Tom, that he, like most sons and daughters, chose to neuter his mother. She herself avoided this error only because her own mother flaunted her sexuality with an abandon Katya both envied and loathed. This ambivalence Katya also wished to confess to Tom, but the moment had not yet come. She hesitated, then rose and crossed to the only mirror the room possessed—a small one, with a crack in the glass.

Like her mother, Katya was tall; unlike her mother, Katya was not thin. She examined her own reflection censoriously; it suddenly occurred to her that her hair might look better down.

"Maybe I should change," she began. "I'm not sure about this sweater. . . ."

"Change? Why?"

"Oh, I don't know. For lunch, I suppose. If all these people are coming . . ."

"Don't." Tom also rose. He kissed the back of her creamy neck. He wound one of the auburn tendrils around his finger. "Don't, you look lovely just the way you are. You . . ."

He stopped, remembering the Trappist vow; a screeching of brakes was heard, then a few swearwords as Lindsay attempted to park outside.

Tom clattered down the stairs to let his mother in; Katya remained, gazing moodily at her own reflection. Eventually, after many toings and froings, much unloading and dropping of packages, a laden Tom and a laden Lindsay finally arrived in the room, talking rapidly, and breathing fast.

Tom had been up at Oxford only a few weeks for this, the first term of his second year; this was Lindsay's first sight of his new lodgings. Being optimistic and loyal by nature, she began admiring things at once. It was a wonderful house in a romantic street; she loved the trees outside and the leafy view of roofs and dreaming spires. The room was really spacious; you scarcely noticed the pattern on the carpet once you were inside, and as for that cerise sofa, well, it looked very comfortable, and the Indian throw was marvelous, how clever of Katya to find it. . . . What, the kitchen was just across the landing, and shared? How convenient; what fun. No, of course she didn't need to see it, but she had brought this huge casserole thing that Tom and Katya might find useful, oh, and some sweaters Tom had left behind—it might turn cold at any moment—and somewhere there was a poster she'd found, in case the walls were bare, and somewhere, somewhere, damn these wretched carrier bags, there was a bottle of that scent Katya had said she liked. . . .

Throughout the confusions of this speech, Lindsay, who could never bear to arrive anywhere empty-handed, delved into bags and tossed wrapping paper around. The gifts, apart from the sweaters, were well received. The walls here *were* bare, and Tom was delighted with the spider poster from *Dead Heat*. Katya opened a large flagon of scent called L'Aurore and dabbed some behind her ears. Into the autumnal sunlight of the room came a burst of spring, the scent of hyacinths and narcissus.

Katya kissed Lindsay, then reminding herself, as she sometimes did, that she was going to be a novelist and as such should *observe*, she drew back and watched. She liked Lindsay, and now that she knew her better, she was beginning to see that Lindsay was adept at a variety of actressy tricks. Lindsay rarely entered a room, she *erupted* into it, chattering away, beginning on one sentence, and then, before it was completed, beginning on the next. She might look boyish, with her slim build and her crop of short, curly, dark hair; she might be inches shorter than statuesque Katya; and she might, like a small boy, possess a great deal of engaging and disruptive energy—but to a degree, Katya suspected, she cultivated this. Lindsay's energy, Katya felt, was channeled in a protective way. The chatter, the hand gestures, the insouciance were a form of disguise—they distracted attention, and Lindsay intended them to do so, from what she might actually be thinking or feeling; and Lindsay, in a muddled, loving, well-intentioned way, was afraid of revealing her true feelings above all; or so Katya thought.

Watching her now, Katya suspected that Lindsay missed

Tom desperately, and was desperately afraid he might sense that. For this reason, intent on freeing Tom, she put on an act of loving dissimulation: possibly lonely, she stressed how busy she was; perhaps yearning to stay, she emphasized that this visit was a kind of flyover, and that she would have to rush back to London immediately after lunch.

Katya was touched by this and by Tom's blindness to the deception. Tom loved his mother and was, in many ways, very close to her, yet he was blind in this respect. This interested Katya, the future novelist. She made herself some crisp, pitying mental notes on the insights and sightlessness of love.

Lindsay's acting ability, she noted, came under further strain when Tom announced that Rowland McGuire and some friend of his from Yorkshire would be joining them for lunch. It is difficult, perhaps impossible, to disguise immediate delight—and Lindsay, Katya saw, could not do so. Her eyes lit; faint color appeared in her cheeks; when she spoke, there was joy in her voice.

"Rowland called? He called here? Which friend? Oh, Colin? Heavens, I spoke to him last night, when I was trying to get Rowland. He was terribly drunk. . . ."

At this point, breaking off, Lindsay suddenly remembered that she had brought with her some champagne, to celebrate the new lodgings; it was really for Tom and Katya, but perhaps one bottle might be opened up.

One was opened, which provided Lindsay with more opportunities for distraction and conversational feints. Fiddling with the foil, as Tom and Katya fetched and washed various glasses, Lindsay gave them an animated, but edited, account of her telephone call to Yorkshire, and its results.

She did not mention—she was too reticent, and too ashamed—the minutes she had spent staring at the unwinking red light of her answering machine. After all, to call Rowland—who had left the number in case of emergencies, he said—was an inexcusable weakness. Shortly before, she had vowed to exorcise his influence, to abandon her hopes. . . . Yet working against that solemn resolve was a deep residual unease, the result of her final conversation with Jippy.

Jippy had mentioned "York," which must surely mean "Yorkshire." He had advised her to check her machine, yet there was no message on that machine. Perhaps then, the absence of messages *was* the message . . . at which point, Lindsay's nimble treacherous heart gave a lurch. Something was wrong, that was why Jippy had seemed so alarmed. Could Rowland be ill, or—and here Lindsay's quick-start imagination kicked in—or worse, could there have been some accident? A climbing accident? A car accident? Frayed ropes? Failing brakes? One second Lindsay saw Rowland lying injured somewhere, the next second, he was deep in a gully, pale, dying, with her telephone number on his lips. She hesitated no longer; with a sweet sense of full justification for this recidivism, she had dialed the Yorkshire number.

"And I got Colin," she said, pouring champagne. "He was celebrating. Apparently, Tomas Court is about to make a film in England, and Colin's the location manager. . . ."

"Tomas Court? Wow!" Her son gave a low whistle.

"Court's been giving him a very hard time, but thanks to Rowland, Colin has finally found him some house he needs. We had a long talk. He told me all about Court and that strange ex-wife of his—she was being stalked, he said, for years, and she nearly had a breakdown, and it led to their divorce. . . . Colin was *not* discreet. And then . . ." She paused. "Then, he started flirting with me. Rather well, considering I've never met him."

Tom sighed and gave his mother a censorious look.

"And *very* well considering how drunk he was. We were talking for ages. Rowland was out on one of his strange night walks and Colin kept saying he'd be back at any moment— only he wasn't. And then . . ." She glanced at her son with a smile. "And then, this was the best bit, Colin proposed."

"Proposed?" Tom's face was now very censorious indeed. "And he's never met you? He must have been pissed."

"He fell in love with my voice," Lindsay said, with dignity. "We'd been talking about obsession—obsession was in the air, like a germ, and I think Colin caught it. We discussed love, at length, then he proposed. I accepted, of course."

"I don't *believe* this. Mum, listen . . ."

"We've decided on a spring wedding. Then we're going to spend the rest of our lives together, in contentment and decorum, after some initial years of heady romance." She paused.

"So, you're about to meet your future stepfather, Tom. I hope you're looking forward to that. . . ."

"One question. One little question." Tom groaned as he refilled their glasses. "Why didn't you hang up?"

"Certainly not," Lindsay replied with spirit. "It's time I remarried and Colin is the man for me. He is very charming. I think I've done well for myself."

"This lunatic," said Tom, in a gruff tone, "is arriving here any minute—with Rowland. Now, I'm praying he was so pissed that he's not going to remember any of this. . . ."

"In that case, I shall remind him—at once. I don't intend to be jilted, Tom, I can assure you of that."

Tom sank his head in his hands. His capacity to be embarrassed by his mother was well developed—indeed, he could be embarrassed by her breathing, or so Lindsay said. He gave a deep sigh.

"Mum, you remember the time you turned up at school prize-giving in that micro-skirt?"

"The Donna Karan? Yes."

"And you remember that cricket match, when you argued with the umpire?"

"That umpire was blind as a bat."

". . . And then you chatted up the headmaster over tea in the pavilion?"

"Of course I remember. He was a widower. That was such a brilliant move."

". . . And then he invited you to lunch?"

"A very *useful* lunch. Consider the consequences."

The consequences had been that, several months later, the headmaster had been snapped up by Lindsay's svelte but difficult mother, Louise. He was now, therefore, married to Tom's grandmother. Fortunately, this appalling event, which Tom could never have lived down, had happened after he left school. Lindsay, unrepentant, regarded this as one of her greatest *coups*; her son did not.

"*All* of those occasions, Mum, every single one of them, were embarrassing. They caused me suffering—trauma, I expect. Well, the embarrassment quotient now is even higher. When this Colin maniac arrives, Rowland's *also* going to be here, and Rowland can be unpredictable. He might not like this. . . ."

"Too bad."

"He'll think you're making fun of his friend. . . ."

"Make fun of my future husband? I wouldn't dream of it."

"Mum, I'm warning you, and I mean it. *Don't*. You'll be making a mistake."

Tom rose. He had spoken quietly, but there was suddenly no doubt that he was in earnest. Lindsay, who had been about to reply, stopped short. There was a silence. Consternation came into Lindsay's face.

"Do you mean that, Tom?"

"Yes, I do. Sometimes—I guess you just push too hard, all right?"

"Tom, wait a second now," Katya began. "Lindsay was teasing you. She didn't mean . . ."

"No, no, Katya—he's right."

For one painful, peculiar moment, Katya thought Lindsay was about to cry. She realized that the act Lindsay put on was far more effective than she had conceived, and that for some reason Lindsay was under strain and deeply upset. She regained control very quickly, however. Looking at Tom, she made a face that was wry and contrite.

"I know, I know." She gave a sigh. "I push too hard and I talk too much, and perhaps—it's not very restful. I do understand that, but I was only teasing you, Tom—Katya's right. I liked Colin, and I wouldn't embarrass him. I didn't really intend to say anything. . . ."

Tom smiled. "Admit you were tempted."

"Yes, I was." Lindsay returned the smile. "But I won't say a word. He's bound to have forgotten, and I won't remind him. I promise to behave *impeccably*, all right?"

It was very rare for Lindsay to break a promise to anyone; with her son, every promise made was religiously kept. Tom, knowing this, at once relaxed; Katya, who had suddenly sniffed the cordite of trouble ahead, assumed that trouble had been avoided. Lindsay became quieter and was perhaps tense, but the next half hour passed pleasurably.

Everything was fine, fine, fine, Katya would later tell

herself—until the moment when they heard the roar of an engine, and Katya, looking out of the window, saw a long, sleek monster of a sports car pull up.

Chapter 6

"It's an Aston Martin," Tom said, awe in his voice. "Oh my God, it's a DB5. *Classic*—I'm not missing this. I'll let them in. . . ."

The door slammed shut behind him.

"I didn't know Rowland drove an Aston," Katya said.

"He doesn't."

"Well, he's driving one now. It must be your fiancé's, I guess."

"Don't, Katya." Lindsay gave a wan smile. She joined her at the window. Both women watched the tall, dark-haired figure of Rowland McGuire extricate himself from the low-slung driver's seat. He was wearing aged clothes, as he had been on most of the occasions Katya had met him; in this case an antique tweed jacket, a dark green sweater, and ancient corduroys. Clothes clearly did not interest Rowland McGuire in the least; Katya had decided that this was because Rowland tried to make no impression, and cared neither to please nor attract. When Rowland entered a room, he did so as himself, arrogantly indifferent as to whether he was approved, liked, sought after, or dismissed. Sometimes Katya admired, and sometimes she resented this.

Rowland did not appear to be in the best of tempers, however. He looked impatiently up and down the street, then glanced up at the house; Lindsay moved away from the window at once.

Rowland, with Tom's assistance, then proceeded to lever and yank the Aston's passenger from his seat. He protested volubly; his face had a greenish pallor and the thin November sunlight seemed to be paining his eyes, for he donned a pair of dark glasses at once. He walked with exaggerated care toward the door of the house, wincing as Rowland banged the car doors shut.

"Your fiancé has a hangover," Katya said.

"What does he look like, my fiancé?"

"Well, he's not as tall as Rowland, but who is? He's about six feet, maybe six one or two. . . . Even shabbier clothes than Rowland. Thin, quite elegant . . . Oh, he's sitting down on the garden wall. . . . No, he's standing up again. He's talking to the privet hedge."

"Just my luck. Not just a maniac, a dipsomaniac. Hair? Does my fiancé have hair? Black? Brown? White? Bald? Katya, tell me he isn't bald. I don't think I'm ready for a bald fiancé. . . ."

"No, no, he has rather wonderful hair. Auburn. Byronic if you're being charitable; in need of a barber, if you're not. Hang on. Oh, he has excellent eyebrows—diabolic eyebrows; they go up in peaks. . . ."

"Don't be absurd. You can't see his eyebrows from there."

"I can. He just looked up. Oh—he's smiling. He's shaking hands with Tom. He has a very good smile. An angelic smile . . . Terribly *pale* though. Alabaster. I think he's about to pass out. What's he doing *now*? Oh, he's sitting on the doorstep. I think he's gone to sleep. Rowland *not* amused. Face like thunder . . . Riot act being read . . ."

Lindsay made a moaning sound. "Oh, not one of Rowland's lectures. Katya, I'm not looking forward to this."

"What a brave man. He's just told Rowland to piss off. Rowland not too amused by that either. Wait a second—yes, he's vertical again. They're coming in. Brace yourself. . . ."

Lindsay had ceased to listen, Katya realized. Turning, she watched Lindsay arrange herself, first on a chair, then opt for standing up. She was wearing very understated clothes, as she usually did, despite Tom's allegations. Fashion-pack black, Katya thought, examining Lindsay's flat black pumps, black tights, short, pleated, black skirt, and black polo-neck sweater. Katya felt envious, as she always did, of Lindsay's boyish build; she herself was too curvaceous, or—as Katya put it in her more self-critical moments—Junoesque. She pulled down the baggy sweater she was wearing and crossed her arms over

her breasts. The eyes of the two women met in mutual understanding; Lindsay's hands flew to her earrings, two delicate,
pale jade teardrops.

"Why did I wear this today? I look as if I'm going to a
funeral. . . ."

"You look fine, Lindsay. You look great. Those earrings are
really pretty. Are those the ones Genevieve gave you?"

"Yes. Gini's good-bye present when she left for Washington.
I—they're hurting my ears; I think I'll take them off. . . ."

To Katya's surprise, Lindsay did so—and in an odd, furtive,
hurried way too. As footsteps could be heard mounting the
stairs, she thrust them into her pocket. She again sat down, then
again stood up.

"I hate meeting people I don't know. It makes me so nervous. Shall we open some more champagne, Katya? Yes, let's.
I'll replace it another time. . . ."

Thus Lindsay created yet another of her diversions, Katya
thought. It was not the arrival of a stranger, but of Rowland,
that was making her nervous, Katya decided, watching her
with amusement and some pity. By the time the door was
finally opened and introductions were being made, Lindsay
was again suffering a useful female difficulty with a champagne cork. This ensured that, within seconds of entering,
Rowland McGuire and this Colin Lascelles were both caught
up in an argument, Colin advocating shaking the bottle, Tom
intervening to protest that wasted half the champagne, and
Rowland quietly taking the bottle from Lindsay, kissing her on
the cheek, greeting Katya, and opening the champagne without
the least difficulty or fuss.

"Coffee might have been a wiser idea," Rowland said, with
a glance in Colin's direction. "And strong black coffee, at
that."

"No, no, no. The worst possible thing." Colin was already
ensconced on the sofa; the dark glasses had been removed and
he was beaming at everyone with a genial delight that suggested he had known them all for most of his life.

"Do you get hangovers, Tom? Katya? I had a hangover for
three *years* when I was here. Alka-Seltzer; prairie oysters—
none of that works. The best cure of all is a pink gin—but a
glass of champagne is also excellent. Thank you, Lindsay. It

settles the stomach, soothes the brain, reminds the legs how to walk. . . ." He looked at Lindsay in a considering way, over the rim of his champagne glass; he hesitated.

"We did speak on the telephone yesterday, didn't we?"

"Last night, yes. But only very briefly . . ."

"Oh good, I thought we did. It's just—well, I was celebrating. A bit of a bender. Then Rowland was up at dawn, as usual, banging on the door, hauled me out of bed, made me pack—I kept asking him, what's the hurry? Another couple of years and I'd have slept it off. Now, I'm still feeling the aftereffects: head a bit woozy, memory on the blink. . . . So I wasn't sure—" His brow crinkled; he turned a pair of blue, innocent eyes on Lindsay and gave her an anxious look. "I hope I made some sort of sense when we spoke? Rowland nagged—he does that. Why did you call? What did you want? Was there a message? He kept it up in the car, for hundreds of miles—I had to go to sleep. . . ."

"There wasn't really a message. Nothing important. I just wondered when Rowland was getting back. Don't worry about it. I'd been at a party and I know how it is. . . ."

"A party?" Rowland handed Lindsay some champagne. "And was it good?"

"No, horrible. Something to do with a movie company called Diablo. Tomas Court's new production company, oddly enough, Colin. In fact . . ."

"Did you go on your own?"

"No, Rowland, I went with Markov and Jippy. I talked to two homunculi, a man called me 'babe,' and then I left."

This précis, or the champagne, which she drank a little too fast, gave Lindsay courage. With a small glance in Rowland's direction, she sat down on the cerise sofa next to Colin and began asking him about Yorkshire. Within minutes, Colin, visibly recovering, was launched on a saga only too familiar to Rowland. "That bloody, *bloody* man," Colin began, and Rowland moved off.

Lindsay listened with excessive attention; Tom and Katya were drawn into a discussion of Court's movies and psychopathology. After pacing backward and forward in an unsettled way for a while, Rowland stationed himself near the shelves at

the far end of the room where, with close and apparently pleasurable attention, he began to examine the books.

Rowland often absented himself in this way on such occasions, so no one took much notice of this. When the discussion
moved on to the subject of *The Tenant of Wildfell Hall*, Katya
rose to fetch the book in question. She found Rowland was
holding her copy and examining it—presumably not reading
it, since the book was upside down, she noted. As she approached, he corrected this and turned the pages, the margins
of which were filled with vituperative comments from Katya.

"Don't read those," said Katya, blushing scarlet. "Rubbish.
Childish stuff. I wrote those a year ago, at least. . . ."

The remark seemed to amuse Rowland. One of the most disconcerting aspects of the man, Katya thought crossly, was his
unreadability. Impossible to tell now if he was amused by
something she had written, or by her, or by himself. Rowland
McGuire's intelligence always piqued her, and his proximity
always made her physically self-conscious. When he was
nearby her hands felt clumsy, she felt overburdened with
breasts and hips. Was it the contrast between her figure (womanly) and the adjective "childish," that amused him? Or had
she written something very stupid? Katya snatched at the book.

"Are you always that unforgiving?" Rowland remarked,
relinquishing it.

"I don't forgive bad writing, no," Katya snapped.

Another assessing, glinting, green glance was his only reply
to this. Katya could not decide whether to withdraw or attack.

"Don't tell me you like it," she said, half turning, and thus
retaining the option of retreat.

"I like certain aspects of it, very much."

Rowland appeared to have no interest in being challenged
further. He took down another book from the shelves—
Coleridge, Katya saw—and began reading. His other ability, to
make her feel invisible, Katya had noticed before. She gave
him a cutting look, returned to Tom, put her arm around him,
and sat down on the floor next to him. There she remained,
seething and smiling, until Lindsay, stopping Lascelles in midsentence, rose and announced with tense animation that if they
didn't leave immediately—*immediately*—they would miss the
table she had booked for lunch.

* * *

The restaurant Lindsay had chosen was called Tennyson's. It was a large brasserie, much favored by undergraduates, serving good, inexpensive Italian wines and the best hamburgers in Oxford. It was very crowded. Approaching their table, in an alcove flanked by potted palms, Lindsay noticed that the floor was oddly unsteady. It occurred to her that she had eaten no dinner the night before and no breakfast that morning; she had just consumed four glasses of champagne on an empty stomach, and this was disastrous. She had something she needed to say to Rowland, a confession that grew more urgent by the second. This confession, which she might have made on the telephone the night before, had she reached him, had to be made before Rowland returned to London and spoke to her editor, his old friend and colleague, Max Flanders. She began to see that this confession could be made now, over lunch, and in front of the others. There were several advantages to that somewhat cowardly approach, not least that, if Rowland were angry—and he might well be angry—he would be constrained by their presence, and would have to keep his anger to himself.

Sober up, sober up, she muttered under her breath, looking at a wavering table, as waiters fussed with extra chairs. Important, she felt, to get the seating right . . .

Unfortunately, Colin Lascelles also had ideas about the seating; while Lindsay was still arguing silently with a potted palm, he put them into effect. Tom sat at the head of the table, with Katya next to him and Rowland beside her; Lindsay was seated opposite Rowland and next to Colin Lascelles. Rowland seemed indifferent to these arrangements, and preoccupied, but every time Lindsay looked up, she met his gaze. She would have to meet his gaze when she made the confession. She would do it soon, she promised herself. Maybe she should do it when the first course arrived, or perhaps the second; no, at the dessert stage, that would be the moment. Meanwhile, no wine, no wine at all, and masses of starch to soak up the champagne . . .

"And so," Colin was saying, "Court hired a team of private investigators because the police were getting nowhere, and the man was smart; he always called from phone booths, and he always called from out of state. . . ."

"Weird," said Tom. "And this was going on when they made *Dead Heat*? That puts a whole new construction on that movie. . . ."

"Before, during, and after." Colin nodded. "It started around two years after their son was born, and I believe it's been continuing ever since."

"Horrible." Katya gave a small shiver. "And he threatened them?"

"So I gather. Not Court himself, but Natasha Lawrence, yes. Also the son. So you can imagine . . ."

"Did he use a name? Why couldn't they trace him?"

"He moved around too fast, I think. And he did use a name—a false one, presumably. What was it? What was it? Something very ordinary—King, I think. That's it, King. Jack? John? No. *Joseph,* that was it."

"Joseph?" Rowland said, speaking for the first time, and so suddenly that Lindsay jumped. "Joseph King? You're sure that was the name?"

"Yes. Definitely."

"Joseph," Rowland said, "or Joe? As in Joe King. As in Joking?"

"Good God." Colin blinked. "You're right—I was told Joseph, but there could be a pun. Joking. Joe King. I never thought of that."

"Why did you never mention this to me, Colin?" Rowland gave him a sharp glance. "I've had months from you on the subject of Tomas Court and you never said a word about stalkers, or threats."

"I know," Colin blushed, "and I should have kept my mouth shut now. It's the hangover—my tongue runs away with me. Forget I said any of this, all of you; it's probably all gossip, anyway. Tomas Court never said a word about it, needless to say. One of his assistant directors told me. . . . Ah, food! I'm the prawns, I think. Rowland, were you soup or salad? Lindsay, you were definitely salad. . . ."

"Spaghetti. I was spaghetti."

"No, no. Salad. A small green salad, wasn't she, Rowland?"

"Yes."

Lindsay accepted the salad meekly. She pronged a lettuce leaf with her fork and moved it around in a puddle of vinaigrette. She nibbled the leaf and wolfed some more bread. She gulped the rest of her Perrier and then, as the conversation resumed, decided that perhaps, since Colin had already poured it, a little wine might be risked. She drank a glass of something red, which Colin instantly refilled. Lindsay, joining in a conversation about Oxford, talking fast, did not notice this.

Suddenly a hamburger had arrived; she had no recollection of ordering a hamburger—Lindsay felt courage flow back. Colin had just finished a long disquisition on the subject of Balliol College; there was a lull in the conversation—the perfect moment to spring her surprise. In fact, she had several surprises to spring, but the others could wait for another occasion. Now, she had to make her main confession; she fixed her eyes firmly on Rowland's green Christmas sweater.

"I've resigned," she said, in a very small voice.

Either no one heard this remark or no one understood it, for there was a surprising lack of reaction. Her voice seemed oddly unreliable; Lindsay cleared her throat.

"I've resigned," she repeated, so loudly this time that heads at the nearby tables swiveled. "I've resigned from the paper. I am no longer a fashion editor. That is, I am, but only for a bit. I shall cover the New York collections next week and then I'm owed some holiday time, and then, soon, I'll be free. I'm giving up fashion. I'm giving up journalism. I'm remaking myself. I'm going to write a book: a biography of Coco Chanel, probably. So now you all have to congratulate me and drink to that."

This announcement *did* produce a reaction. There was a brief, surprised silence, then a babel of questions: How? When? Why? Into this babel, Lindsay continued with her speech.

"I decided months ago really," she went on. "I just had to make myself do it. I've been working in fashion too long. I need a change. . . ."

"Challenges!" Colin Lascelles put in. "Quite right! Fresh fields and pastures new! I've *always* believed in that. . . ."

"Woods. Fresh *woods* and pastures new," Katya corrected. She leaned across and kissed Lindsay. "Well done. You were *wasted* in fashion. I think that's totally brilliant. . . ."

"Brave!" Tom said, rising and also kissing her. "That's

great—do I still get my allowance? Only kidding. Wow! I never thought you'd actually do it. . . ."

"A toast." Lascelles refilled glasses. "To the fair Lindsay— may she succeed in whatever she does next. . . ."

There was another buzzing outburst of questions and exclamations; Lindsay found these made her curiously blind and deaf. Then, as the blindness and deafness began to recede, she began to realize: Rowland McGuire had taken no part in this.

He left the food in front of him unfinished. With deliberate care, he aligned his knife and fork on the plate. Slowly and reluctantly, Lindsay raised her eyes to his face; his expression at once made her want to look away, but she found she could not.

"I see," he said finally, in a quiet voice. "Is this definite? Have you talked to Max?"

"I've given Max my letter of resignation, and talked to him. Yes."

"When did you do that?"

"Last week. One day last week."

"While I was away?"

"Yes, as it happens. That—that has nothing to do with it. I don't work with you anymore, Rowland."

"No, indeed not."

Rowland's displeasure was very evident. His expression was cold; his tone was cold. Upon the convivial table a frost settled. Lascelles glanced at Lindsay, then at Rowland, his brow puckering, and his blue eyes puzzled.

"Well, I say good luck to Lindsay. . . ." he began.

"I've no doubt you would." Rowland's cold green gaze turned in his direction. "Since you know nothing about the situation, that's easy enough."

"Oh, come on, Rowland, what's the matter with you?" Lascelles frowned. "I'm in favor of change. What's Lindsay supposed to do—stick it out for the pension plan and the gold watch? Nobody does that anymore. If she doesn't feel fulfilled working in fashion, she ought to move on. . . ."

"Is that the problem?" Rowland's gaze returned to a hot-faced Lindsay. "You don't feel fulfilled?"

He pronounced the final word with distaste. Lindsay glared at him.

"As a matter of fact, yes. And there's no need to be so supercilious. 'Fulfilled' is as good a word as any other. Colin's right. Lots of people change jobs at my age; they have to, these days. I've been doing this too long. I'm sick of offices and deadlines. I'm sick of all the bitchiness and neuroticism. I'm sick of trying to find something new to say about some damn stupid dress. I'm sick of studios and crazy locations, and planes and hotels. I want to be in one place, and above all, I want to do something else."

Rowland heard her out in silence. He frowned.

"This isn't one of your snap decisions then? You've been considering it for months? You never mentioned it to me."

"You never asked," Lindsay retorted. "And I don't make snap decisions."

"Oh, but you do."

"Well, this isn't one of them. Listen, Rowland, if we were still working on the same paper, yes, I probably would have asked your opinion, but we're not. You edit the Sunday now; you're stuck up in that vast editor's suite, having meetings morning, noon, and night. . . ."

"We work in the same building; we work for the same group. What is this? I see you virtually every day. Three weeks ago, I was round at your flat and I raised this very issue; I got no response. You could have discussed this any time you wanted, Lindsay."

"Well then maybe I *didn't* want to. Maybe I just wanted to make up my own mind, Rowland. I am capable of that. And you may find it hard to imagine, but there are other things I can do besides edit fashion pages."

"I'm aware of that, as you have every reason to know." This remark, quietly made, produced another silence. Katya, who had been watching this exchange with close attention, saw that Rowland's words seemed to distress Lindsay. Her face had been bright with defiance; she began some defiant reply, then something in his tone, perhaps a note of specific reproach, made her reconsider. She turned to Tom, who had also been watching with growing indignation.

"Tom? I haven't done the wrong thing, have I? I *had* to decide."

"Whatever you decide's okay with me." Tom shot Rowland

an angry glance. "Mum's had lots of other job offers," he went on. "People are always trying to poach her."

"Oddly enough, I'm aware of that too."

"There was that TV company, last year. They wanted her to work on a big series—a history of fashion. That American magazine was chasing her. That publisher's been pursuing her for ages. Markov told me. . . ."

"Markov. I see. I might have known it." Rowland's expression hardened. "Is he privy to all this? Is he behind this decision? That's bloody typical."

"Who's Markov?" Colin Lascelles interrupted, swiftly. "Can someone explain? I don't understand any of this. Why is there a problem? Lindsay—"

"Who's Markov? Well now, let me see." Rowland leaned back in his chair, a dangerous glint in his eyes. "Markov is a fashion photographer—a very gifted one; a somewhat subversive one. Markov is, without a doubt, one of the most affected men I've ever met in my life. However, he's clever. I even like him—up to a point. The trouble is, Markov is wildly irresponsible. . . ."

"No, he's not," Lindsay interrupted hotly. "You scarcely know Markov. He's changed a lot since he met Jippy. He's a good, clever man, and I've known him for fifteen years, Rowland. I adore Markov, so you can just stop this—"

"I don't deny any of that," Rowland cut her off. "Will you listen? I said Markov is irresponsible, and if you think for ten seconds, you'll know I'm right. . . . You've always been blind to Markov's faults—"

"Shall we have some more wine?" Colin interrupted, signaling at the waiter. "Rowland, why don't you calm down? I—"

"Just stay out of this, Colin. Listen to me, Lindsay. Markov loves nothing better than stirring up trouble; he's an inveterate *meddler*, and he loves a drama. Is Markov going to worry if a job falls through? If you're out of work? All he's interested in is gestures and *schemes*. . . ."

"Just a minute, Rowland. Could I speak?"

"And you, for some reason I'll never damn well understand, actually *listen* to Markov. He comes to you with some harebrained plot and you buy it. He says 'Jump,' and you jump. That man has an irrational, disproportionate influence over you

Lindsay, and I can hear him talking now. Californiaspeak. 'Fulfillment'? 'Challenges'? Give me a break."

"Dammit, Markov has *nothing* to do with this," Lindsay snapped. "And yes, I will have some more wine, Colin, thank you. Amazing as it may seem to you, Rowland, I made this decision on my own—without your help; without Markov's help. I didn't need your advice then and I don't want it now. Stop being so damn pompous. What gives you the right to run my life?"

The final question silenced Rowland, who had been about to interrupt. Possibly her remarks hurt him, Lindsay thought, at once regretting them. Rowland colored, then turned away. From inside the hot swell of anger within her, she felt misery and shame welling up. Why, why, why did I do this? she thought. For several reasons, as Rowland had implied, she owed him a better explanation than this. Now, at a table with three other people present, and with a pleasant lunch irretrievably ruined, she could see no way of retracting that last unjust statement, or making amends. Then she realized that the reactions of the three other people present were rather different from her imaginings. Tom and Katya, she saw, were suppressing smiles; Colin Lascelles, who had seemed somewhat anxious, was refilling glasses; catching Tom's eye, he winked.

"Cat and dog," Tom said. "Tooth and claw. Argue, argue, argue. Sorry, Colin, they always do this."

"They never agree on anything," Katya put in. "Not a movie, or a play, or a book."

"She tells him he's interfering. . . ."

"And arrogant, Tom. Don't forget that."

"He accuses her of—What does he accuse her of, Katya?"

"I've lost count. Not listening. Not thinking. Talking too much. Being a typical woman—that's certainly come up."

"Wasn't he dominèering? Blind? Insensitive?"

"Definitely." Katya made a delicate pause. "And there, of course, Lindsay was right."

"He had a point too; Mum does *talk*. Never draws breath."

"Oh, Rowland does as well," Colin said, joining in with a smile. "He may take time to warm up, and he may choose his company, but once Rowland *starts* talking, there's no stopping him. Opinions too. When I first met Rowland, he was insufferable. If you *coughed*, he had an opinion. If you *sneezed*, he had an opinion. My sister, who was once very much in love with Rowland, used to say that . . ."

"Enough. That's it. Stop it right there. . . ." Rowland raised his voice. "We get the point."

He hesitated, then smiled, then extended his hand to Lindsay across the table. His green eyes rested thoughtfully, but no longer coldly, on her face.

"I was wrong. I'm sorry, Lindsay. I wish you every possible good in anything you may do. I hope you know that."

"I'm sorry too. I take back what I said."

Lindsay clasped his hand; the handshake that then followed was so warm, so friendly, so fraternal, that Lindsay wanted to weep on the spot. Since she could not weep, she drank another glass of wine, and since that made her feel extraordinarily strengthened, another after that.

She waited until conversation resumed and the atmosphere eased. She waited until Rowland, Katya, and Tom became embroiled in an argument first about books, then Thomas Court's *Willow Song*, its connections to *Dead Heat*, and the significance of the spider sequence.

Katya was speaking with force; Lindsay sometimes suspected that Katya felt challenged by Rowland's Oxford first; always trenchant, she tended to become more so when Rowland was present; indeed Tom had once accused her of showing off. Now, she whipped *Othello* into the argument, then harnessed Freud; she crunched Tomas Court's view of women under her chariot wheels, then quoted some German philosopher Lindsay had never heard of, at length. Rowland listened patiently enough until Jung's aid was also marshaled, at which, seconded by Tom, he launched a counterattack.

The air in the room was altering, Lindsay thought; cigarette smoke, perhaps; anyway, it was now eddying pleasantly, and was assuming a mauvish hue, wafting like mist. Realizing there was a key question she needed to ask, she turned back to the amiable, blue, innocent eyes of Colin Lascelles, and interrupted him.

"Tell me *all* about your sister, Colin," she said.

* * *

Colin did tell her all about his sister, and very interesting it was. This subject, and variations upon it, opened a door, she found. Through that door, Lindsay began to see a younger Rowland McGuire, a different Rowland McGuire. She was busily inspecting these Rowlands, and trying to work out how they related to the Rowland she knew, although, of course, she did not know him enough, when she realized that other, less metaphorical doors must have opened, since they were no longer in the restaurant, but walking past glorious buildings, in a now darkening street. She was arm in arm with Colin Lascelles; he was leading her through a gateway, advancing into a large, misty quadrangle; there were lighted windows, dark-gowned, hurrying figures; a chapel bell was tolling.

"It was here! It was on this exact spot!" Colin, releasing her arm, waved his own like a windmill. "Chateau Margaux 1959! Two and a half bottles! And I was still standing up. Then I started to topple—very slowly, like a great pine; an eight-hundred-foot pine. I'd braved the storm for thousands of years, and then some giant took an ax to my roots. One blow! That's all it took. It took me a century to fall. I could see the paving stones coming up . . . and then Rowland caught me. He saved me! He's been saving me ever since. It's thanks to Rowland that at this exact moment my life makes perfect sense! I have to thank him. Where is he? He was here a second ago. . . ."

Colin whirled about, arms semaphoring. Rowland, who was standing two feet away, watching this performance with Tom and Katya, moved forward, and caught hold of his arm firmly.

"Tom, we may have a problem," he said.

"That was a wonderful speech, Colin," Lindsay said, with warmth. "I can see it. I can imagine it. Was it a cold night?"

"Cold? Bitterly cold. The witching hour! It was three o'clock in the morning. The night was pitch-black. . . ."

"It was June. You take his other arm, Tom," Rowland said.

"A pilgrimage!" Colin shrugged off these arms and took Lindsay's instead. "I have to explain! Oh, God, *God*. Lynne, there's another place I have to show you. It's not far. It's on the way back. It's just round this corner and up the street. . . ."

It was neither around the corner, nor up the street, but they eventually found it. In an ecstasy, Colin paused on a bridge.

"Lisa," he said, clasping Lindsay's hands, "you have wise eyes, d'you know that? You have these beautiful wise, sad, gray eyes. I could look at your eyes all night."

"Thank you, Colin." Lindsay hugged him. "I think they're gray too—in certain lights."

"They're *brown*," said Tom. "Give me strength."

"Or hazel," said Rowland, his manner meditative. "Tom, you know that sofa in your room? Well, I rather think . . ."

"Down here, darling!" Colin plunged toward some steps. He helped Lindsay down them with great gallantry. Lindsay found herself on what might have been a towpath. It was very dark. She could smell river water, and then see the gleam of light on its surface.

"This is the canal! Do you see those barges, Linda? Can you see the barges up ahead?"

Lindsay found she could see them.

"People live on these barges, Lynne. It's just along here. It's this one. No, that one! That's it! The one with poppies painted on it. Well, on this barge here, lived a most beautiful woman. She was a painter, I think. My Lady of Shalott. She had long golden hair. What was her name, Rowland?"

"I forget."

"This was a long time ago, Lisa—you do understand that?"

"I do. Years and years ago, Colin." Lindsay leaned over the water. Rowland pulled her back.

"Exactly. Decades. And this beautiful girl—I was mad about her. Completely mad. Obsessed. This was when I was an undergraduate—before I met you, of course."

"Of course."

"I wrote sonnets! Songs! I dreamed about her every night! I wrote her letters, Lindsay. . . ."

"But you never sent them. . . ."

"No, never. Then I'd weep. Just once or twice."

"Occasionally, Colin. You wept occasionally, when despair hit."

"That's it! Despair! Oh God, *God*. I'd forgotten that. But I despaired all the time, because she didn't love me; she loved someone else. It was *hell*. Unmitigated *hell*, now I look back."

"Oh, Colin." Lindsay put her arms around him. She looked at him very closely. The towpath was beginning to ripple pleasantly. Colin put his arms around her waist. "Colin, that's so sad. I know exactly how that feels. Tell me, did you get this sort of *ache*?"

"In the heart? Yes, I did. But none of that matters now, Lindy, because . . . Oh God. You have the most beautiful eyes I've ever seen in my life. What shall we do? Shall we sit down? Walk? Talk? I want to talk to you all night. There's something I have to tell you. . . ."

"Time to go, Colin." Rowland had been listening to this exchange with the closest attention. Now, as Lindsay and Colin began to sit down on the edge of the barge, he took Colin's arm in a firm grip. He led him toward the steps.

"Up you go, Colin. No, no arguments. Tom, if you pull him, and Katya, you push . . . That's it. Well done. Your room's not far, luckily. You go on ahead with him. . . . Now, Lindsay, these steps are a bit slippery."

"They're not."

"It's deceptive. The light here's not too good. If I just took your arm, perhaps? There. You see? Now, take hold of my hand. . . ."

"You have very nice hands, Rowland. They're warm. I noticed your hands the first time I met you; they're strong. Strong hands."

"It's the climbing, I expect."

"I worry about the climbing." Lindsay came to an abrupt halt on the bridge. "Where's Colin?"

"He's gone on ahead. Don't worry about Colin."

"All right, but I do worry about the climbing. I was worried last night, that's why I called, I think. . . ." She frowned, shook her head, raised her face, and inspected Rowland closely.

"I could see you, Rowland. The rope broke. You were tumbling over into this *chasm*. . . ."

"Yes, well, that's happened to me once or twice."

"Really?"

"No, not really. Maybe if you lean on me a little, Lindsay."

Lindsay leaned on him; it felt pleasant. She gave a small shiver of delight. Rowland put his arm around her waist and they began walking again. Dimly ahead of them, on some other planet, Lindsay could see her son and his girlfriend, and someone else. The someone else was singing; Lindsay liked the song the someone else had chosen; it was a sweet and melodious lament. Neither she nor Rowland spoke; they advanced along a heavenly road; its paving shone; the dark air was necklaced with lights. Rowland sighed. "Lindsay, Lindsay," he said gently. "Whatever's wrong? You never do this."

"My life's changing. . . ." Lindsay emitted a sobbing sound, which startled her. "My life won't lie down, Rowland. It won't obey the rules anymore. I can't . . . I can't . . ."

"What can't you?"

"I used to know where north was. Now I don't. It's moved, Rowland. Sometimes it's in the south, or the east. . . ."

"That happens."

"I hate it. I hate it happening. Rowland, it makes me afraid. Does it happen to you?"

"Sometimes. Yes, it does."

"I might cry, Rowland. I can feel it coming on. Oh, *damn*."

"I don't mind, Lindsay. Truly. Cry all you like."

Lindsay did so. She wept piteously for several streets. Then she found they were standing outside a house that looked familiar; its front door was open. Lindsay leaned against Rowland, who put his arms around her. She watched this door; from it, eventually, emerged her son and someone who proved to be Katya. This confused Lindsay, who had been expecting someone else.

"He's out cold, on the sofa. Dead to the world," said her son.

"Tom, I'm sorry about this—"

"It's cool. No worries, Rowland. Cressida-from-upstairs did it the other week."

"Now listen, Tom. He may feel he wants to fight you. If he does, say you'll fight him in the morning—then he'll go back to sleep. Coffee when he wakes; lots of it. Oh, and Katya, one thing . . ."

"Yes, Rowland?"

"He may propose, at a certain stage; he's been known to do that. . . ."

"So I gather."

"It's a good idea to accept him; that way you avoid the maudlin stage, which generally comes next. I'll take Lindsay's car and drive her back to London. Meanwhile, just to be on the safe side . . . Lindsay, lean on Tom for just a minute, would you? Oh, she's asleep. Hang on. . . ."

There was a pause while Tom propped his mother up and Rowland opened the hood of the Aston. He removed the rotor arm and handed this and the car keys to Tom.

"That's usually the best solution. He knows how to put it back, but he can't manage it until he's completely sober. I'm very grateful to both of you. I'll call you in the morning. . . ."

There was movement and Lindsay began to wake up. Someone soft, who smelled of rose petals, kissed her. This was comforting, although a small voice in Lindsay's mind kept insisting that there was something wrong with that kiss. She was still trying to puzzle out what that might be while her son reproved her, and possibly lectured her, but appeared to forgive her. She had the sensation that this son of hers found something amusing; she was hugged, heard footsteps, then a door shut.

Immediately, as the door closed, two very strong arms encircled her and she found her damp face pressed against wool; the voice in her head now spoke with clarity; a clarion call. Of course, it was not the nature of that kiss that had been wrong, it was the *identity* of the person who bestowed it. She lifted her head and inspected Rowland's features. He did not appear to be angry; he might have been amused. He looked puzzled by something. He had the greenest eyes she had ever seen. She looked at the lamplight on his hair. She looked at green affection, green regret.

"Lindsay, Lindsay," he said, and smoothed back her hair and looked at her face. "You really are terribly drunk, you know. . . ."

"I am," Lindsay agreed. "It feels wonderful, Rowland. Wondrous. Your eyes are very green. Astonishingly green. . . ."

"And yours are hazel; not brown, not gray. Around the iris, they're darker. I've never noticed that." There was a pause. "What are you doing, Lindsay?"

"I'm kissing your sweater," said Lindsay, who was. "I think I might kiss you. Yes. You're so tall. If you could just bend down a little bit, Rowland. . . ."

Rowland did. Lindsay gently kissed his cheek, then his nose, then, as her aim improved, his mouth. Rowland did not appear to resist. They kissed chastely, in the lamplight, and when they drew apart, Lindsay saw that Rowland's expression was now sad. She made no comment on this.

Her handbag was found, and her keys, and her car. One minute Rowland was lifting her into it, the next second he was lifting her into what she recognized as her bed. He removed her shoes and neatly aligned them next to the bed. He turned her on her side and covered her with a duvet. He switched off the bedside lamp and then stood in the stripe of light from the hall, looking down at her, his hair ruffled, his hands in his pockets. Lindsay, opening her eyes, then closing them again, thought he still had that puzzled, thoughtful expression on his face. During the night, at some point in the night, negotiating a dream, then a nightmare, Lindsay woke. She did not know where, when, who, or what she was: she gave a little cry, swung her legs out of bed, and felt her way into the shadows of her living room. At first she thought that it was empty, then she saw it was not. Arms folded, Rowland was seated on the sofa, frowning into space. Lindsay came to a halt in the doorway.

"Would you talk to me, Rowland?" she said.

"Of course." He held out an arm. Lindsay curled up on the sofa next to him and rested her head against his shoulder. Rowland put his arm around her; minutes ticked.

"So, what shall I talk about?" Rowland said after a while.

"Anything. Ordinary things. I just like to hear your voice."

"Well, let's see." She thought he smiled. "I've been useful. I've washed one cup, one saucer, and one plate. I checked your answering machine for you, because the light was driving me mad—flash, flash, flash."

"Oh, I hope someone interesting called."

"Markov did, from Greece. He said he and Jippy were sitting outside a temple; I forget to which god. Max called. Someone called Lulu-something called; I've written it down. . . ."

"Lulu Sabatier? I won't be calling her back."

"Then I'd called—this morning. So I listened to myself, which is always disconcerting; I sounded like someone else." He frowned. "Then, let's see, I read for a while, but I couldn't seem to concentrate. I thought about Scotland: Skye, where I've been climbing. . . ."

"Tell me about where you were climbing. I had a horrible

dream. It will make my dream go away. Make me see your mountains, Rowland."

"Well, you've seen those photographs at my house. I remember you looking at those, the first time you ever came there."

"I remember too." Lindsay closed her eyes. She could remember the occasion only too well, since it was then she had first realized she was in love with Rowland McGuire. It was then this entire debacle had begun; this, of course, could not be said. "There was one particular mountain," she went on. "A mountain with an impossible name . . ."

"Sgurr Nan Gillean. I climbed it again on this visit. Provided the weather holds—and in the Cuillin the weather can change within minutes, which is why they can be dangerous, of course—there's a place you can reach; it's technically quite a difficult climb, a nasty overhang, but once you're around that—if the weather is clear, and it was last week—you're rewarded with an astounding view. You can look out across the Minch, and each one of the Outer Hebrides islands, you can see them, or their outlines; a black necklace of islands on the horizon. They look . . ." He hesitated. "They look too beautiful to be real, like the Hesperides, perhaps. Then, sometimes, the rain comes in, or a mist appears from nowhere, and you lose sight of them. They disappear, and you think you imagined them. . . ." He hesitated again. "Whenever I'm there, I feel . . ."

"Tell me, Rowland."

"I feel as if, finally, I've arrived in the right place, as if questions were unimportant, as if I were beyond questions, maybe. I can't explain, I just like being there, looking at those islands. After those islands, there's nothing, just open sea, thousands upon thousands of miles of sea—sea all the way to America, or to Newfoundland, perhaps. . . ."

He stopped speaking and silence fell. The silence, to Lindsay, felt huge and deep, like a benign ocean. She could see herself and Rowland very clearly, sailing across this Atlantic in some small yacht or skiff; the wind caught its sails; for the first time in her friendship with Rowland she felt she could ask questions—questions could be risked.

"Are you happy, Rowland?" she asked quietly, tensing a little, for he might resent this.

"Now?" He showed no sign of resentment. "I feel happy now, oddly enough."

"No, I didn't mean that. I meant, generally. Day by day. Night by night."

"Not really, no. Not in that sense. But I'm happy—enough."

"May I ask you something else?"

"You may." He smiled. "I'll even answer, I expect."

"Have you ever loved anyone, Rowland?"

"Yes, twice."

"And what came of it?"

"Nothing came of it." He paused. "The first woman I loved is dead; her name was Esther. She was killed in Washington, D.C., a month before our marriage; that happened a long time ago. And the second . . ." He paused again. "Nothing came of it. It ended some time ago."

Lindsay heard the decision to disclose no more in his voice; she had expected the closing of that particular door.

"Nothing ever came of my marriage," she said, in a rushed way, bending her head. "It took me years to see that. You could say Tom came of it, of course, except that I never think of Tom as coming from my marriage. Tom is my blessing, my gift from the gods. But Tom actually came from—you can imagine, Rowland—nothing special; nothing glorious. A night when I was miserable, when my husband was drunk . . ."

"Don't, Lindsay."

"No, you're right. I won't. It doesn't matter anyway, because Tom changed my life. He—as soon as I held Tom in my arms—he wasn't a pretty baby, even I could see that. He had this dark hair then, Rowland. He was born with dark hair. I was so proud of that lovely hair, then later, he rubbed it off, on his pillow, in his cradle, and the next hair that grew was fair, like his father's. . . ."

"Lindsay. Dear Lindsay. Don't cry."

"I don't mean to cry. I don't know why I'm crying. I'm happy really. I love Tom so much. I just wish . . . I just wish . . . I wish he'd grown up with a proper father. Some man—not the man who is his father, because he didn't care, and he should have cared, and I'll never forgive him for not caring for Tom as long as I live. . . ."

"When did he leave? Tell me, Lindsay."

"When Tom was six months old. There was some girl, I think; there usually was. All the time, really. When I was pregnant, before, after. I didn't find that out until later, of course. He—well, he lied a lot."

"Lindsay—"

"It's all right. I can see it in perspective now; I couldn't then. He turned up again, when Tom was about eighteen months old. He'd turn up, beg to come back, then he'd stay a day or two, sometimes a week. After a while, I began to see—he only came if he wanted to borrow money, or if he had nowhere else to sleep, so I threw him out. But even then, I still used to write and send him photographs. I sent him pictures of Tom for years. First as a baby, then as a little boy, on holiday, his first day of school—things like that. I was so bloody *obstinate*. . . ."

"Lindsay, don't get upset. Here—"

"I kept thinking, it didn't matter if he didn't love me, but he had to love Tom. Even if he wasn't a good father, he was the only father Tom had, and Tom needed him. So I kept on *hoping*, in this weak, stupid, futile way—and then one day, I suddenly stopped. I realized—he was such a shit. I didn't like him; I didn't respect him, and Tom was better off without him. After that—"

"You never thought of marrying again?"

"No."

"Why not?"

"No one asked me, actually," Lindsay said, in a small voice. She began to laugh, then cry. "Which is just as well, because I might have said yes, and I can see now that would have been a terrible mistake. I've had quite a lot of unmemorable lovers, Rowland. . . ."

"So have I."

"Dull as ditch water, most of them. *Prudent*. I had a thing about prudent men, for a bit."

"Because of Tom?"

"I expect so. And—there was one who kept his loose change in a purse; he was pretty bad. There was another one who, when we went out to dinner, he always tipped precisely eight and a half percent. It took him hours calculating it. I left him in midsoup. . . ."

"Midsoup?"

"I just got up and walked out. It was minestrone. He was talking about pension plans. I think he might have been about to propose, actually, now I look back. I expect that's why I fled. I don't really like prudent men. I—I'm not very prudent myself—I expect you've noticed that—and I didn't really want a husband anyway; I wanted a father for Tom, which wasn't fair to them, and—I'm sorry about tonight, Rowland. I've been a fool. I'm ashamed. Reeling around on that bridge. I've embarrassed everyone. . . ."

"You haven't embarrassed me."

"Oh, *hell*. Now I'm really starting to cry. I'll make your jacket all wet. Rowland . . ."

"I've got a handkerchief somewhere. Wait, I'll do it. There." He dried her eyes, then kissed her forehead. "Now, look at me, Lindsay. . . . No, look at me properly. Now, do I look embarrassed?"

Lindsay looked at him for a long time. She looked at his dark hair and his shadowed eyes; any harshness in his features was softened by the half light. She lifted her hand and rested it against his face.

Rowland took her hand and clasped it in his own. He gave a sigh, leaned back, and gathered her more comfortably against him. He looked away across the room and made no reply. Lindsay, positioning herself so she could look up at him, saw his expression was now bleak.

She tightened her grip on his hand and rested her head against his shoulder. She watched the quiet rise and fall of his chest; she let the quietness of the room enter her veins. All the words she would have liked to say, and all the comfort she would have wished to give, rose up in her heart like a tide. Her feelings were of the utmost eloquence, but words would not contain them. Perhaps silence could speak, she thought, hoping it was so. She pressed his hand, then raised it to her lips. She kissed his knuckles.

"You're still crying," Rowland said.

"Only a bit. I'll stop soon. I'm glad you're here."

"I'm glad I'm here too."

"I wish things were different for you, Rowland. I wish that things had worked out. That you weren't alone . . ."

"I'm used to it."

"You ought to have children, Rowland. . . ."

"I know that."

". . . I watch you with Tom sometimes, and I think—you'd make such a fine father. . . ."

"Would I? I hope so." He hesitated. "I sometimes wish—"

"What do you wish?"

"Oh, the usual things: that the plot had worked out differently, I expect."

"Tell me, Rowland; talk to me. You're too reserved; it's not good to be as reserved as you are. . . ."

"Maybe not." He shifted her position a little, so she was curled in his arm, and they sat for a while in silence. Lindsay closed her eyes; was it three in the morning, four? The city was almost silent; its stir had subsided; no cars passed; it was quiet in the dusky room, the only sound their breathing, and quiet in the streets.

After a while, Rowland began speaking again. He continued to hold her hand, and he told her innumerable things, in no particular order, but perhaps, she thought, as they played before his eyes, or swam into his head.

He described the small farm his Irish father had owned on the west coast of Ireland, which he had left when he was eight, after his father's sudden death. He described living in London with his English mother, and his school, his scholarship; then, jumping over years, spoke of his mother's unyielding character and her lingering death. He talked of the purchase of his strange and beautiful house in the East End of London, and then—houses being perhaps the association—he described Colin's search for Wildfell Hall and the house near the sea, which he and Colin had eventually found, and which Tomas Court appeared to like.

From this house, he said, a path led down to a remote and little-visited beach, a horseshoe between two headlands. There, only a few days ago, while Colin remained at the house, taking his photographs and making his notes, Rowland had walked. Shells underfoot, shells pulverized by the waves; the cry of gulls as they swooped; a heavy sea, the tide racing in, and engulfing the rocks.

Lindsay, eyes closed, her body warmed by his, listened to the crunch of those shells underfoot; she listened to the scream of the gulls, the heave of the tide, and listening to them, watching Rowland alone on a pale, shrinking strand, she fell asleep.

The next morning, that morning, when it was light, she woke to a changed Rowland, or perhaps to a more familiar Rowland, a man who had reverted, who was considerate, but distant again, kindly and polite. It was only six, but he was preparing to leave. Lindsay watched him numbly. She felt as if someone had injected Novocain into an artery; Novocain was numbing the muscles of her face; Novocain impeded her breathing and interfered with her voice.

"I haven't been fair to you, Rowland," she said, finally, when he was almost at the door, the words jamming, then coming out in a rush. He turned.

"I'm sorry. I wanted to say something at lunch yesterday and then I couldn't. I wanted to say something last night—and I forgot. . . ."

"Lindsay, it doesn't matter. It's irrelevant now, in any case."

"It isn't. It isn't. Three weeks ago you made me a proposal, an offer—a very generous one. You gave me the time to think about it, and . . ."

"Lindsay, you obviously don't want the job. That's all right. I was a little confused, when you announced your resignation, your plans. And disappointed, obviously. But I understand now. . . ."

"No. No. I shouldn't have done it like that. I don't even know why I did. I should have talked to you first. I should have talked to you before I resigned. I should have explained when we were on our own, not sprung all that on you at lunch, with three other people there; I owed you that. Oh, why was I so stupid, *stupid*. . . . I was afraid, I think."

"Afraid? Am I such an ogre?" Rowland gave her a puzzled look. He hesitated, and for one singing moment Lindsay thought he was about to change his mind and stay. He unlatched the door, then turned back.

"I blame myself, not you," he began awkwardly. "You're right, I can be arrogant. I assumed—I thought you might like to work with me again. I thought you might want to move on from fashion. It seemed such a good plan. . . ." He paused. "Do you remember, Lindsay, when I was Max's features editor? You never stopped telling me how to do my job. . . ." He smiled. "I'm sure I never admitted it at the time, but your ideas were good. I haven't forgotten that. I can delegate the heavier stuff and leave you as features editor, with responsibility for everything else. All those damn columns: gardens, property, restaurants, food, cars; they matter to the readers, and they're not good enough. I'd give you a completely free hand. You could continue to oversee the fashion, if you want. If you want to reconsider, the offer's still open—you do understand that? If it's a question of salary . . ."

"No, Rowland, it's not money; truly. What you were offering was more than generous."

"Then what's the problem? Were you worrying about Max? I told you, Lindsay, Max wouldn't be pleased at my stealing you. But he'd accept it. Max is a realist. In fact . . ." He began to smile. "Why don't we *really* annoy him? Persuade Pixie to come with you, to run the fashion side of things, but still reporting to you. We could do that. We could . . ."

"Stop, Rowland. Please don't. I'm so sorry, I hate myself for this. You've shown confidence in me and look how I've repaid you. I sat there at lunch, letting Tom and Colin and Katya criticize you, and I didn't explain the real situation. You could have given me away if you'd wanted to, taken me to task—and you didn't. Oh damn, damn . . ."

She turned her face away to hide her distress. Rowland took her hand and turned her back to him.

"Forget about that," he said. "Lindsay, I don't care what they said or thought. Listen to me, we've always worked well together. I know you could do this job. Won't you at least think about it?"

"Rowland, no. I have thought about it, and I've decided. I've signed the contract for this book. I'm committed. . . ."

"It isn't that. I don't believe you." He was watching her closely. "There's some other problem. You don't want to work with me, is that it?"

Lindsay looked away. To accept this job would mean working with Rowland McGuire in the closest proximity; that would destroy all her peace of mind. The only way in which she was going to cure herself of Rowland was to see him less and to put distance between them. She was now even more certain of this.

"Tell me," Rowland said, when she had not replied. "Look at me, Lindsay. Is it that you don't want to work with me? Is that so bad a prospect? Why? I know I can be infuriating—you tell me often enough. But we understand one another now; we know one another so well—don't you feel that?"

"In certain ways, maybe. But—"

"We make a good team. We spark ideas off one another. Even the fights are useful. . . ." A glint of amusement came into his eyes, then his expression became doubtful again, and his manner somewhat awkward. "I'd rather you said, Lindsay. I— well, I didn't expect you to turn me down. I thought—I can only assume now . . ."

"Rowland, *don't*. You know I like working with you; I always did—and you taught me a great deal. I've told you that often enough. . . ."

"No, you haven't actually."

"Then I'm telling you *now*. This decision has nothing to do with you personally, Rowland. Try to understand. I've spent twenty years, more, in an office. I've spent twenty years going to the collections, twenty years catching planes and chasing around the world. I've had *enough*, of fashion *and* of journalism; I don't want deadlines to dictate the rest of my life. Rowland, I never had a choice before—Tom depended on me, my mother depended on me; we had to have my salary, come what may. But now I *do* have a choice. I can write this book; I *want* to write this book—and if it's a success, maybe I could write others. I'm looking forward to it, Rowland. You wait. . . ." She smiled. "In a few months' time, you won't recognize me. I'll have become an archive junkie, a library addict. I'll be filling up all these notebooks with research. . . ."

It was, she thought, a seamless blend of truth and falsehood, and it was effective.

"An archive junkie?" Rowland also smiled. "I admit I can't quite imagine that." He paused. "You promise me that this is what you truly want?"

"Ah, what do women want?" Lindsay made a face. "I wouldn't go that far, but it's what I want to do."

"I'll miss you, you know. The office won't seem the same

without you. Who's going to cut me down to size if you aren't there?"

"You'll find someone. You know you never listened anyway. . . ."

"You're wrong. I did."

There was a silence. During it, Rowland suddenly seemed to realize that he was still holding her hand; he released it at once. Exhibiting an indecision that was not characteristic of him, he turned to the door, then back again.

"Lindsay, I'll have to go. I have a mountain of work to get through before tomorrow. The trouble with going away is that the workload doubles when you get back. I'd have liked . . . I have a bad week coming up, meetings back to back. . . . When are you leaving for New York?"

"Later this week. I'm staying on after the collections to do some fashion shoots. Then—Max has been generous about notice, and I'm owed that holiday time—I'll come back after Thanksgiving, maybe. I thought of going down to Washington, D.C., for a few days to—"

Lindsay stopped abruptly. She feared that Rowland might query Washington as a destination, in which case she would have to say her friend Gini's name and watch him feign indifference. To her surprise and relief, he did not.

"Washington? I have to go over there sometime too—we're having negotiations with the *Post*. Except, no, it's not likely our visits would coincide. Damn! Perhaps—look, I'll call you later this evening, shall I do that?"

"I'm going out this evening, Rowland," Lindsay replied untruthfully, staring hard at the floor. The reply checked Rowland, whose air of agitation and indecision increased.

"Yes, well, I'll talk to you before you leave for America. We could—you might like dinner one night. . . ."

"I don't think that will be possible. I'm rushing about this week, and . . . I'll see you when I come back, Rowland."

Steeling herself, Lindsay reached up on tiptoe and briefly kissed his cheek.

"Thank you for everything," she said, in a steadier voice. "You sorted me out, yesterday, and last night. You're a very good father confessor, Rowland. I feel much better now. A bit hungover, of course . . ."

"Sleep. Get some sleep. . . ." Rowland replied. "Promise me now. . . ."

"I promise," Lindsay replied meekly, and with this assurance, Rowland finally left.

Lindsay watched the door close. Everything and nothing, she said to herself. She found she was trembling with the effort of deception; the unspoken and the unspeakable rose up in a wash of regret. She returned to her living room and looked around her blindly. She had done what she had promised herself she would do, and now Rowland's absence emptied the room of all content.

She touched the cushion he had leaned against the previous night; she touched the sofa arm where his hand had rested. She tried to remember the strange calm and peace she had felt as he talked to her in those predawn hours; it had been the first, and presumably the last time that he had let her into his life.

Remembering his words, she took out the pale jade teardrop earrings she had removed the previous day and weighed them in her hand. Her friend Gini had given her these earrings, and it was her friend Gini, she knew, to whom Rowland had referred the previous night.

Nothing might have come of it, as he had said, but Rowland had been in love with Gini, and she had possibly returned that love. They had had an affair, briefly, in Paris, three years before, after which Gini had returned to her lover, the war photographer Pascal Lamartine. Reunited, they had married and had a son. None of the participants had ever discussed these events, but she had been their mute witness. Possibly Rowland still retained a lingering regard for Gini; perhaps he did not. She would never have countenanced asking him, and she knew he would have given her no answers if she had.

She looked down at the earrings, a gift from a friend younger than herself, and beautiful in a way Lindsay knew she could never be. Not for the first time in her life, she protested silently at the unfairness of beauty, an accident that could make the best of men blind, then she thrust the earrings in a drawer, out of sight.

The endlessness of the day weighed upon her; but Lindsay had learned resilience and she took comfort in the knowledge that she had executed the first part of her plans. She took greater comfort from the fact that, very soon, she would not be here in this empty apartment, but in a different city, one she had always loved—New York.

Bright lights, a heavy schedule, no time to think; she was sitting contemplating the advantages of that city when she remembered Jippy's curious parting words. "York," he had said, and of course "York" might indicate a city in America, every bit as much as Yorkshire.

At precisely this moment, her telephone rang; it rang twice, in swift succession. The first call, from some mumbling person claiming to work for Lulu Sabatier, she allowed her machine to field. The second, from an apparently sober and chastened Colin Lascelles, she answered herself.

Part Three

BONFIRE NIGHT

Chapter 7

"Remember, remember, the fifth of November—Gunpowder, treason and plot . . ."

Rowland, locking his car doors, turned, was about to walk on, then stopped. The speaker, he saw, was a young Bengali boy, aged about ten. He and another older Bengali boy had stationed themselves outside the Hawksmoor church opposite Rowland's Spitalfields house. Between the boys, propped up against the railings of the churchyard, was a guy, a well-made guy. It was stuffed with newspaper and shredded computer printouts, some of which were escaping from ankles, fat waist, and throat. On its feet was a pair of women's Indian slippers; on its head was a turban; the ensemble was completed by a torn, very English tweed jacket and a tattered Nike track suit. In the dim street lighting, the guy's face mask grinned at him; from some distance away, a rocket fizzed into the dark sky and exploded in a burst of golden stars, high up.

It was years since he had seen a guy, Rowland realized. When he was a boy, when he first came to London to live, these straw men, these hollow men, had been commonplace in the weeks leading up to Bonfire Night; children stationed them outside subway stations, on street corners, outside shops. He paused, looking at the malevolent mask, and with a rush, his childhood came back. He remembered the gorgeousness and gaudiness of the fireworks themselves, the black aromatic powder that leaked from them; he thought of the solemn ceremony every year, his mother and himself, wrapped up in coats, alone in a neglected North London back garden, positioning rockets in milk bottles, lining up magic on a garden wall: Vesuvius, Krakatoa. Light the blue touch-paper, stand well back.

113

He looked at the two boys, who were shivering with cold. This area in the East End of London, always a refugee area, lived in over the centuries by French Huguenot, then Jewish immigrants, was now predominantly Bengali. Rowland wondered if these two boys knew the history of Guy Fawkes and the gunpowder plot, and if so whether it could have any meaning to them: it had little meaning to him. He put his hand into his coat's breast pocket, and the two boys looked at him expectantly.

"The going rate used to be a penny," Rowland said, with a smile. "I imagine it's gone up. . . ."

The boys exchanged glances; they looked pointedly at the upturned hat next to the guy on the pavement. It contained a collection of ten- and twenty-pence coins; prominently displayed, in the center, were a one-pound coin and a fifty-pence piece.

"Inflation, innit?" said the older boy, giving Rowland an impertinent look.

Rowland withdrew his hand from his pocket and took out his wallet. The boys tensed. Rowland dropped a five-pound note into the hat, complimented them on the excellence of the guy, and then, ashamed at his own sentimentality, walked away fast. Whoops of jubilation and derision greeted this generous evidence of his own gullibility; glancing back over his shoulder as he reached his house, Rowland saw that the two boys had decided, perhaps on the strength of his contribution, to pack it in; they were departing, dragging the grinning corpse of the guy up the street.

Rowland let himself into the cold and the silence of his early-eighteenth-century house. It did not possess central heating, and modern heating systems might have damaged the paneling, in any case. Rowland had never minded its familiar winter chill, and its calm, its silence, he had always loved. Taking pity on it, buying and rescuing it fourteen years before, when it had been in a state of ruinous neglect, he had found he wanted to change it as little as possible. The creeping dangers that threatened its structures and its beauties, the damp, the dry rot, the leaking roof and decaying timbers, had been cured. Standing alone in the unfurnished first-floor living room when all this work was finally complete, he had closed the shutters to the tall windows, and for the first time lit a fire. It caught instantly and burned well; its flames burnished the paneled walls and danced upon the bindings of his books.

With the crackling of flames and the creaks of old timbers adjusting to heat, Rowland had had an acute sense of his home's past: he had thought of the French Protestant refugees who had been the first occupants here over 250 years before, several of whom lay buried in the somber city churchyard beyond, and he had felt that, like them, he was not truly the owner of this house, but its tenant or custodian. It would outlast him, as it had outlasted them. In a new millennium, others would stand here, as he did, and perhaps sense, as he did now, past joys and past griefs, some of which he would no doubt have contributed himself.

This thought, that he was part of the house's continuum, destined to become one of its spirits and whispers, had contented him then. Now, he found he was restless, less calmed by these four walls; for reasons he could not grasp, and was reluctant to examine, the silence and familiarity here now agitated him. He would sometimes have the sensation that the house was waiting for something to happen, that it resented being empty by day, and underoccupied by night. It possessed four bedrooms, only one of which was regularly used; the other three, occupied occasionally by friends passing through London, had a melancholy reproachful air; Rowland kept their doors closed.

That evening, his first free evening since returning from Yorkshire, he had brought work home with him, as he usually did. He lit the fire in the living room and waited for the warmth to dispel the house ghosts. These ghosts, of past losses, approximations, and ill timings, of hopes that had once fired Rowland, but no longer did, were reluctant to depart. They lurked in the corners of the room; angry with them and with himself, he switched on all the lamps in an attempt at banishment. The lamplight was ineffective since, as Rowland knew perfectly well, these ghosts had their being in him; it was his blood they fed upon, and they emanated, gray and disconsolate, from himself.

It had perhaps not been such a good idea, he thought wryly to himself, to have bought a refugee house; nor was it wise to indulge the kind of early evening melancholy hundreds of city dwellers no doubt experienced. He was tired; he felt overworked and hungry—that was why, as soon as the front door closed, he now heard the whispers and reproaches of the dispossessed.

Hunger, anyway, was easily assuaged. Rowland went downstairs to his kitchen—a kitchen Lindsay described as charming but primitive. In one of the old battered saucepans—he could remember Lindsay cooking him scrambled eggs in that saucepan, the first time she came here—he heated up some canned soup. He made himself a sandwich, and ate it.

The food revived him. He returned upstairs to find the fire blazing, the room warm, and the ghosts suppressed. He telephoned Lindsay, who was departing for New York early the next day, and found her line was busy. In a desultory way, he began dealing with the backlog of mail, which had been reproaching him all week. A month before, he had sent a brief, formal letter of condolence to Gini, formerly Hunter, now Lamartine, on the death of her father. He had half expected that a reply, no doubt equally formal, might be here, amid this pile of buff envelopes; it was not, and he found he could accept this without disappointment; maybe he had begun to acquire indifference.

He sifted through the bills, and found buried among them a postcard in writing he did not recognize, which proved to be from Tom's girlfriend, Katya. She gave a lively account of Colin Lascelles's recovery on the cerise sofa; she requested the details of a book Rowland had recommended over lunch in Oxford, the title of which she had now forgotten, but which she felt was essential for her literature course. She sent love and best wishes, as did Tom, who was out, she wrote, playing in a university rugby match. The words "rugby match" had been underlined in a scornful way; their inherent absurdity was emphasized by an exclamation mark.

Rowland looked at this missive for a while. Much pursued by females, he had learned over the years to be wary of all communications from women, even those—especially those— that appeared innocent. He frowned. On a postcard, he wrote the name of the book, its author, and publisher. He added, "Best wishes to you both," signed and addressed it, then gathered it up with the rest of the mail to be posted.

He looked at the work he had brought home with him, then, discovering it could wait, poured himself a whiskey. He put more wood on the fire, and in a thoughtful way examined the black-and-white mountain photographs Lindsay had referred to, which he could remember her inspecting the first time she came here.

The photographs, pinned to a bulletin board, were the sparsely furnished room's only personal element, apart from its many books. Beneath them were notes Rowland had made that detailed previous climbs of these particular peaks, routes used, weather conditions, and so on. Little tongues of firelight moved across these notes, and he recalled Lindsay's complaints about the jargon used here, with its terms—arêtes, corries—which she could not understand.

"It's a foreign language, Rowland," she had said. "You'll have to translate."

"On reaching the Three Sisters north face overhang," he read now, "a traverse is needed across the buttress to reach the flake where the wall meets the overhang. The flake is positive; there is a small crack for the right foot, but the left has to smear. Behind the flake, just room for a Number Three Friend, and this can be backed up by a Number Five Rock Placement in the offset crack in the roof. Note, this placement is marginal after rain. Only a dyno can get you to the one substantial hold under the roof, but the swing out on gripping is nasty: thirty-five meters' drop. . . ."

Rowland read on, and as he did so, these words opened out the mountains to him; he saw, simultaneously, their immensity and the minute details of the cracks and crevices that made ascent possible. He considered that route and the sense of triumph he had felt on completing it. He considered, in particular, the use of a "dyno," or dynamic movement, as referred to here. In essence, when effecting a dyno, a climber leaped—and although, to a watcher, that move might appear one of fluidity and acrobatic ease, it was dangerous. There was a moment, the tiniest of moments, when the climber moved through air, up and across the rock face, springing toward the smallest projection or indentation in the rock, over which, or in which, his fingers could obtain enough purchase to support his body weight. The maneuver required nerve and physical strength; it required route knowledge and experience and a very precise degree of judgment. If mistimed, or ill executed, the climber fell—in which case, his safety depended on the skill and care with which he had secured his protection ropes.

Rowland considered this maneuver, and the crux of this route. Coming to a sudden decision, he picked up the telephone and again called Lindsay.

This time, she answered almost immediately. Hearing her familiar voice, Rowland felt less sure of his reason for calling.

"Your line's been busy," he said.

"Yes, I know." Lindsay, as she often did, sounded breathless and jittery. "I—someone from the States was calling me. I'm packing for New York. Why do I pack so badly, Rowland? There's clothes all over the bed and the floor. I can't decide what to take."

"Take that red dress," Rowland said, after a pause. "I like that."

"Really? It's a bit . . . Are you sure? I suppose it would do for parties."

"Will you be going to many parties?"

"I might. Yes, probably. But I've lost the knack for parties, Rowland."

"I suspect I never had it."

There was a silence, during which Rowland watched a red-dressed Lindsay move across some New York party space. In his mind's eye, he saw her do this very clearly—and she was not unaccompanied.

"I had a postcard from Katya," he said, with some difficulty, and with detectable awkwardness. "She wanted the details of some book I mentioned. I gather my friend Colin recovered." He paused. "I gather he did at least call you to apologize. . . ."

"Oh, yes, he did. That next morning, after you left. He rang first thing—he is *nice*, Rowland. He sent me a bouquet of flowers; it was so beautiful. Roses and lilies and things. It was huge; it used up all my vases. I'm in my bedroom, and it looks like a bower. . . ."

Rowland frowned.

"Also those clothes," Lindsay said, still breathlessly, "so it looks like a bower *and* a bomb site. Oh, I've just seen a rocket. They're having a fireworks party next door. There's this enormous bonfire. It's like a war zone here, explosions, firecrackers going off. Can you hear fireworks, Rowland?"

Rowland listened. He realized that all evening, the other side of some barrier in his mind, he had been hearing muffled explosions, the whine as rockets took off.

"Yes, I can. Just. The shutters are closed though and that blocks out the sound."

"I love those shutters. Is the fire lit?"

"Of course. Otherwise I'd freeze. Lindsay—"

"How nice." Lindsay gave a breathless sigh. "Are you working? Have you had a horrible week?"

"Fairly horrible. It's easing up. I should be working and I'm not; I couldn't concentrate for some reason. I—I just rang to wish you a safe journey."

"Thank you. I'll give your regards to Broadway, Rowland."

"I'd like that." He paused. "Give my regards to Colin as well. I haven't set eyes on him since lunch in Oxford."

"Colin?"

"Well, Katya mentioned that he was about to go off to New York. I'm sure he'll look you up there."

"Oh, he said something about that. He's having meetings with the evil genius, I think, and he's going to be staying somewhere odd—I remember, with some American aunt. Some batty ancient aunt."

"That'll be his great-aunt Emily. She is ancient, but not batty; quite the reverse."

"Well, I don't expect I will see him, Rowland. Or the aunt. I'll be rushing about."

"Lindsay—"

"Going into ecstasies about dresses and hats. I'm quoting you now, Rowland. You said that once, years ago, before I taught you to understand fashion."

"Lindsay—"

"I was *so* angry with you when you said that. It's taken me nearly three years to admit that all your criticisms were right. . . . Oh heavens, did you hear that? The most enormous explosion; like Semtex. I'm sorry, I'm talking too much. Why do I do that?"

"Because," Rowland said, in a measured way, "because you're a woman, Lindsay. Because you think that if you talk fast enough and long enough, I won't hear what you're actually saying. And it does make it difficult. It's like decoding something; it's like listening to Morse."

"What nonsense. I always say what I think."

"Do you?" Rowland gave a sigh. "In my opinion, Lindsay, you say what you truly think even less often than I do, and I virtually *never* say what I think."

"You don't need to," Lindsay replied, with spirit. "I can tell what you're thinking, whatever you say. Women can do that; it's our great strength."

"Oh really? Then tell me what I'm thinking now."

"That's not fair. I can't see you."

"You mean you have to see me? So much for female intuition, Lindsay. I'm not impressed."

"Wait a minute. Wait a minute. You sound . . . dry. You're smiling, Rowland, in that dry, infuriating way you do. You're thinking—are you smiling like that?"

"Yes."

"You see! I knew I was right. And I know what you're thinking too. You're thinking Lindsay talks nonsense; she's a complete airhead."

"Wrong. A million miles out."

"You're thinking about work."

"Wrong again."

"Damn, these fireworks must be putting me off. Colin; I think you're thinking about Colin, about that very drunken lunch."

"Wrong yet again. You may be thinking about Colin; I'm not."

"There's no need to sound so irritable, and I definitely know what you're thinking now. You're thinking, why doesn't this damn woman get off the phone? She's a pest."

"Utterly wrong. I can give you my word—I've never thought that in my life, not once."

Rowland spoke with great firmness. There was a silence, then, in answer, a sharp intake of breath; a strange moaning sound came down the line; this was followed by Lindsay, explaining she was moaning in despair. She still had so much packing to do; it was late; she had to be out at the airport at dawn. Rowland interrupted these excuses.

"Where are you staying in New York?" he said.

"The Pierre. I'm staying at the Pierre."

"Maybe I should call you at the Pierre sometime. You could tell me what I was thinking. We could see if your intuition improves. Then—"

"Then?"

"Then you could call me—when you get back. You could call me when you get back from the airport, after you've closed the door, before you've removed your coat. Is that agreed?"

"All right. Agreed."

There was a silence; a long silence. Lindsay made a coughing sound, then cleared her throat.

"Why?"

Rowland considered. He thought of a call made to Yorkshire, which he had missed. He thought of Colin's remarks to him when describing that call. He hesitated. "I'll have missed you, Lindsay," he replied quietly, "and it's always good to hear your voice."

Had she said good-bye? Lindsay, replacing the receiver, was not at all sure. Possibly; she could not recall, because the room was suddenly bright and the whole conversation was whirling in her head. Its words would not lie still, nor assemble themselves in the correct order. The room was fizzing with words, and the undersides of words, and the spaces between words. The words were protean—they might have meant *that*, and they might have meant *this*.

She began to roam about the room making odd, inarticulate sounds. She clasped and unclasped her hands and stared unseeingly at the chaos around her. Dresses and blouses, trousers, skirts and snaking tights; sentences that led in one direction and then doubled back. She prayed hard and silently not to hope, because hoping was the most painful emotion of all and the one she was most determined to cure. She pinched herself and read herself more of the usual silent lectures, because she knew she had been here before, in this stupid demented state, and she had learned, again and again, just how deluded it was.

Affection was not love, and she had to learn to distinguish the two in Rowland's voice. It was pathetic, pathetic, that a man's voice could produce this effect. Had she been twenty, there might have been some excuse, but she was not twenty, and something was badly wrong with her. Somewhere and somehow the past decades had never happened and she had failed to grow up.

No—she could not accept that. If to outgrow love was to grow up, then she would have none of it; she would be content to remain foolish and immature until the date of her death. So no, she would not denounce or renounce the need or the desire, but she would cure herself of imagining a response where it did not exist. She must stop her own emotions from spilling over, so that the words she could not say overflowed into his, and her imagination rewrote Rowland's scripts. On the other hand— and here she felt again an irrepressible delight—Rowland had liked her red dress; he had said, with great firmness, that he liked, no, that it was *good* to hear her voice. He did intend to call her in America; he wanted her to call him, the instant, the very instant, she got back. And this request, Lindsay found, had a soaring resonance; its wings beat about her heart and her head. Such a glorious night, this, she thought, dancing across to the window and gazing out. There was a moon, a full, high, powerful, pregnant moon, and instead of stars, which the lights of London blocked out, there was the lovely artifice of rocket star trails, showering gold on wintry gardens, and exploding over the shine of slate roofs.

She had been talking to Gini in Washington, earlier, when Rowland had been trying to reach her. Now, watching these streaking stars and listening to these thunderclaps, it was clear to her that she must, at once, call her friend back.

No sooner thought than done. She dialed Gini's number and spoke with a sparkling precision; she rearranged all the plans they had made less than an hour earlier, and, having done so, hung up and began to repack. Such a transformation: now, she found, the clothes folded themselves into suitcases and lay obligingly flat, shoes tucked themselves cunningly in corners; instead of bulging and protesting and refusing to shut, as the cases usually did, they closed with ease—one touch of the fingers and the locks snapped shut. One last case remained. Inside it, Lindsay prepared a nest of tissue paper; she danced across to the closet, and on this nest, interleaved with more tissue, she folded her newly beloved red dress.

* * *

In Washington, meanwhile, in her dead father's house, Gini had replaced the telephone receiver, and—looking at her husband and half-sleeping baby son—was shaking her head.

"That was Lindsay again, and she sounded completely *mad*," she said.

"Lindsay? But you'd only just spoken to her."

"I know, and she sounded fine then. Now, I couldn't make out half of what she was saying. It's Bonfire Night in England; I could hear fireworks in the background. She was scrambling up all her sentences and she was out of breath; she sounded as if she'd just run a marathon . . . no, panic-stricken. She sounded panic-stricken, as if she'd just been attacked."

Her husband smiled. He moved across to the windows and looked out at the quiet, charming, brick-paved Georgetown street. He adjusted Lucien's weight in his arms so he was more secure and kissed his brow.

"Oh, you know Lindsay," he said carelessly, "she often sounds as if she's run halfway up the Empire State Building. Lucien's sleepy—I'm going to take him out in a minute. What did she want anyway?"

"She wanted to cancel her Thanksgiving visit here, I think. Half an hour earlier, we had everything planned. Now she says she may have to rush straight back to London. . . ."

"How odd. Did she say why?"

"No, not really. Some garbled excuse." She gave a small frown and glanced at Pascal. "I think there's some man at the back of it."

"Well, I hope there is," Pascal replied. "I like Lindsay; she deserves to be happy."

"A man doesn't necessarily provide happiness, you know," Gini said, a little sharply, turning away. "Lindsay's lived alone for years. She's perfectly happy as she is."

There was a small silence. Pascal looked at his wife thoughtfully; she had moved away to the dining table, which she had been using as a desk. It was piled with folders and files, most of them containing the paperwork pertaining to her father's death. This room, like most of the house, was in the process of being dismantled prior to its sale. There were faded patches of wallpaper where pictures had once hung and one wall was lined with packing cases. He had never liked Gini's father and he had found these necessary weeks in his former home difficult. This, he knew, was even more true for Gini, and he was prepared to make allowances because of that.

"She might not wish to continue living alone," he said, in a mild way. "She might even wish to marry again, and marriage can bring happiness, don't you think?"

His wife colored. "Of course. I didn't mean that. It's just—Lindsay has no judgment whatsoever where men are concerned."

"I wouldn't say that. Who is this unsuitable man she's interested in?"

"Oh, I don't know. Someone she works with, I think. Pascal, I don't have *time* for this. I have to check through this stupid Natasha Lawrence article I've written and fax it off to her and I just *know* she's going to start raising objections. I wish I'd never said I'd do it. I hate showbiz profiles; this is the last one I'll ever do."

Her husband, watching her change the subject in this way, thought he knew the reason. He hesitated, wondering if he could bring himself to mention Rowland McGuire's name, with all its attendant risks. He decided not to do so, although he now felt certain that McGuire was the unnamed man concerned, for he had heard jealousy in his wife's voice—or possessiveness, perhaps.

Could you be possessive about a man you no longer cared for? A man you had not seen in three years? He doubted it; but then his wife did not relinquish her hold on others easily, even after they had ceased to be part of her life. But there were reasons for that—her relationship with her father above all. It had not been easy for her, he thought, as she bent her fair head over her papers, to come here to her father's house and discover the degree to which he had eradicated her from his life. So far, they had not found the least hint of her existence—not one photograph, none of the letters she had written him, none of the newspaper articles she had written and religiously sent to him. The thanklessness and cruelty of this angered Pascal; with the death of her father, he had believed that Gini might at last break free of his influence. A sojourn here in this house had shown him that death made no difference; for many more years, he feared, his wife would be haunted by her father's indifference and neglect.

Moving across to her now, he drew her against him and kissed her pale hair.

"Send the article off, darling," he said, "then come out with Lucien and me. It would do you good to walk, to get some fresh air. You've been working so hard: clearing up this place, writing a thousand letters to lawyers and banks. Come out with us—the sun's shining; it's a beautiful day."

"No, I won't—I'd like to, Pascal, you know I would, but I need to check this through before I send it. There are some letters I have to write. If Lindsay *isn't* coming for Thanksgiving, I suppose we could leave here a little sooner. . . ."

"We could." He hesitated. "And that might be a much better plan anyway, darling. It was never going to be easy, having her here—the place is in chaos. I know you were very set on it, but we can't delay forever. You'll feel better once you're out of this house. We could go to friends for Thanksgiving, then we could start work on our book."

"I suppose so." She moved away from him. "You go, Pascal; I'll come with you tomorrow. But I must get on with this."

"Do you want me to read your piece before I go?"

"No, I hate it. It's adequate at best. I got nothing out of her. You know the only interesting fact in here?" She gestured at the printout of her article. "It took fifty-five takes to shoot that spider sequence in *Dead Heat*—and Natasha Lawrence is terrified of spiders or so she said. I thought that was revealing. That sequence is one of the vilest things I've ever seen on film. Why would that ex-husband of hers put her through that fifty-five times? He's a sadist, I think."

"I doubt that." Pascal smiled. "That sequence is very complex from a technical point of view, Gini. There's those mirrors; there's that three-hundred-and-sixty-degree pan. I've seen it three times; I work with cameras and I still don't know how he did it. . . ." He paused. "You're sure you won't come with us? No? Then we'll see you in about an hour."

He went out. With a sigh, Gini sat down at the table; she moved papers and files in a desultory way, back and forth. She glanced over her shoulder, because when the house was quiet, she could never rid herself of the sensation that at any moment the door would open and her father would come in and ask her what right she had to be here, in his house.

She had no right—she felt that. In front of her now were all the files and papers that confirmed her daughterly role: the letters from lawyers and real-estate agents; the letters from the IRS, from brokers, from banks. To these correspondents, she possessed the authority of daughter, executor, and sole heir, as certified by a brief cold will made some twelve years before and never revised: "I hereby give and bequeath to my only child, Genevieve Hunter." Only her father, she thought, could contrive to leave her everything, yet make her feel disinherited. And she saw him again, as he had been in the last week of his illness, when he realized he was dying, and that the years of alcoholism had finally caught up with him. It had been the day before they put him on a morphine pump and he lapsed into unconsciousness. She had been sitting there, holding his hand, until she had realized that, for a while, he had been struggling to free himself.

"Just for Christ's sake let *go* of me," he had said. "And for the love of God, go somewhere *else*."

She knew, with a dull and painful certainty, that those words, spoken with a bitter amusement very characteristic of him, would remain with her for the rest of her life.

Pascal was right, she thought; she had to escape from this house—and the sooner she did it, the better.

She picked up the *New York Times* interview she had written, together with its cover letter, and fed it into her fax machine; she had asked Natasha Lawrence to reply by the end of the following day and to restrict any queries she might have to facts, but she felt no great optimism that the actress would listen to either request.

She glanced toward the windows and the quiet, empty street beyond, hesitated, and then drew toward her the file of condolence letters. Only half of these had been answered, although she had set aside an hour each morning for the task. Here were all the gentle fictions from her father's past friends, erstwhile editors, and colleagues. They wrote kindly and with ingenuity, avoiding the issue of his drunken, wilderness years; she answered with similar evasions and reticence.

Pushing aside the topmost letters in the file, all of which

Pascal had seen, she drew out the one letter she had *not* shown him, the letter received almost a month before, from Rowland McGuire.

The letter was brief, handwritten, and formal in tone. "I was sorry to hear the news of . . ." Rowland wrote in black ink, on white paper, his handwriting firm and clear. The phrases he used were those of a polite acquaintance, observing the formalities, yet she could not hold the letter in her hand without remembering their brief affair. His letter brought him back—the strokes of his pen made her see his face and hear his voice; worse still, they made her remember a particular expression in his eyes, at a particular time. Closing her eyes now, she let herself watch an act impetuously and urgently begun, then repeated throughout a long night. She allowed herself to remember and, to her shame, she felt a brief pulse of physical longing for him, a faint echoing in her body of past sexual excitement and desire.

This had never happened to her before. With a low exclamation of anger and distress, she rose from her chair and began to pace the room. A car passed in the street beyond; the air in the room suddenly felt thick with a choking despondency. Too many ghosts, she thought, and this house was to blame. She met her childhood self in the dark at the turn of the stairs; the past spilled out of these packing cases; uncertainty was disgorged from these files.

She moved toward the door, then stopped, catching sight of herself in a dusty mirror that had not yet been packed away. There, behind the veiling of dust and mercury scars on the glass, she saw herself: a pale woman, with pale hair and a striving expression. Examining her, she realized that this woman, with her vacillating gaze, had lost the first bloom of youth, was visibly in her thirties, and would soon look middle-aged.

Wife. Mother. She mouthed these words at her own reflection. She thought of her son, whom she loved with the greatest intensity, and of Pascal, a gentler, quieter man now than he had once been. Fatherhood became him—but she was afraid sometimes, although he never spoke of it, that he regretted the decision to give up photographing wars.

It was the right decision, she told her own reflection: his work had contributed to the breakup of his first marriage, and photographing wars as Pascal did was dangerous; it was not a suitable occupation now that he was the father of her child. She looked in the mirror uncertainly, but her face did not reproach her for a decision she knew was influenced by her. "The *right* thing to do," she said, turning away from the mirror. She sat down again at the table, and quickly, before she could change her mind, wrote a brief answer to Rowland McGuire.

Rowland wrote formally: she found she could master this language equally well. A sentence of thanks for his letter; a sentence for her father and the funeral; a brief mention of the planned book; a final sentence for herself, Lucien, and Pascal. She ended the letter "Yours sincerely," as he had done. She was about to fold it into its envelope when the fax machine rang, then whirred. She had been concentrating on her task so deeply that the sound made her jump; she swung around, as if someone unseen had just crept up behind her and touched her arm.

To her surprise, she saw that Natasha Lawrence was already replying. A brief handwritten note from the actress was scrolling out from the machine. She thanked Gini for an interesting interview, complimented her on her understanding of the acting process, and assured her that she had no objections to raise.

This letter made Gini unaccountably uneasy. It was too complimentary; it was oversweet and artificial in tone. The lady doth protest too much, she thought, and wondered why.

Tossing it to one side, she picked up her own letter to Rowland McGuire. On second reading, its tone seemed less unequivocal than she had intended. She would rewrite it tomorrow, she decided, and glancing up, she saw that Pascal and Lucien were returning from their walk. Pascal was laughing and lifting Lucien up; his son, who resembled him so strongly, with the same dark hair and the same gray eyes, was also laughing and chattering away in his touching approximation to language, a tongue composed of recognizable words and invented ones of his own.

She saw them as if in a photograph, a shutter clicking and freezing this moment in time. As they were then, she would always remember them, she thought; in this she was correct. She would also remember her own immediate response, which was to hide Rowland McGuire's letter, and her reply to it, at the bottom of that condolence file.

In New York, at the Carlyle, Tomas Court watched his wife return to the living room with the faxed *New York Times* interview in her hand. He had arrived here only a short while before, and the atmosphere in the room felt edgy and duplicitous, although he could not have said why.

He was sitting in front of the television set and talking on the telephone to Colin Lascelles in London; as he spoke and listened, he flipped the video controls, and on the TV screen a perfect Wildfell Hall fast-forwarded, rewound, paused. He examined a gloomy doorway, dark ranked windows, a crumbling facade; he surveyed moorland, then tracked down to a deserted horseshoe-shaped beach, while in his ear, Lascelles's very English voice continued to explain the security arrangements his assistants were making at various English location hotels. Behind and through his words came the pop, thunder, and fizz of mysterious explosions. Court covered the mouthpiece with his hand.

"You've passed that article?"

He glanced across at his wife. She nodded, then, as he snapped his fingers at her, handed the pages across.

"You can't watch, listen, *and* read, Tomas," she said, in a mild tone.

"You're wrong, I can."

She gave a small shrug, then crossed to her son, who was waiting in the doorway with a stout, well wrapped up Angelica. Natasha adjusted his scarf and zipped up his scarlet ski jacket. Jonathan and Angelica, together with a new, recently hired bodyguard nicknamed Tex, were about to make an expedition to see the zoo animals in Central Park.

Apparently, they did this once a week; *apparently*, the new bodyguard was a great favorite with everyone, especially Jonathan; *apparently*, no one had expected Tomas Court until later, and Jonathan would be disappointed if this expedition were postponed. *Apparently,* in the month since his father had last seen him, Jonathan had become obsessed with animals, birds, bats, reptiles, and insects, books on which now surrounded Court on all sides. Court looked at the *Times* article and the books somewhat sourly. It seemed to him that *apparently* Jonathan had grown used to being mollycoddled by his mother and all the other attendant women who came and went here; Jonathan was *apparently* in danger of being spoiled.

"For God's sake," he said, "leave the boy alone, Natasha. He's going to Central Park, not the North Pole."

The response, as he could have predicted, was a female closing of ranks, a shushing and scurrying, a furtive maternal embrace. Angelica turned her back on Court; Jonathan was hustled out; the door closed.

Colin Lascelles, Court thought, with a certain dour amusement, returning his attention to the telephone, was now sounding more confident than he had in weeks. The particular game Court had played with him, a game often employed before, had proved effective. He had wanted to see if Lascelles buckled under pressure, and had Lascelles done so, Court would have discarded him. Lascelles had *not* buckled, and he had finally found a house that was everything Court desired, the Wildfell Hall of his imagination, that place of exile and retreat that, for nearly two years now, had occupied his thoughts and appeared to him in dreams.

One day, he thought, he would perhaps tell Colin Lascelles why he had hired him—a decision he had reached during their first meeting in that Prague hotel room when Lascelles, vulnerable, voluble, and ill at ease, had told him a story about a woman once encountered on a Qantas flight, a story Court had found touching and absurd.

Lascelles probably imagined, he thought, listening to him, that he had been hired for his professional abilities, which were considerable; and indeed, those abilities had weighed with Court, obviously so. Before even speaking to Lascelles, he had viewed every major movie on which he had worked and talked to numerous directors who knew him. He had acquainted himself with every detail of Lascelles's background: his family, his privileged schooling, and his training.

He had known that Lascelles was the heir to a large estate in England, and had been since the death of his elder brother. He further discovered that at the age of eight, and on the death of his American mother, he had inherited a fortune from her family, the Lancaster clan. That fortune had been held in trust for him, but from the age of twenty-one Lascelles had been a very rich man, one who need never have worked again. He *had* worked, however, and worked hard. That fact interested Court, whose own background was poor.

Court, meeting Colin Lascelles for the first time, had discovered that he resolutely avoided all mention of this background; he let not one single detail slip regarding his parentage, his wealth, his privileged schooling, or his celebrated home, Shute Court, where his family had lived for over four hundred years. Court found that he liked this somewhat innocent and engaging man. He could see that Lascelles was trying to perfect the classless argot of the international movie world, and that he was not altogether succeeding. He noticed—such details always interested him—that Lascelles had the English gift of appearing elegant and shabby at once. He noticed too that the camouflage of the clothes was imperfect: Lascelles might be wearing jeans and a shirt with fraying cuffs, but the discreet watch half hidden by those cuffs was a Patek Philippe, and the shoes were handmade.

"I first saw her at the Qantas check-in," Lascelles had been saying. "I wasn't in very good shape. I had a hangover. It was the anniversary of—well, of my brother's death, actually. I managed to get my seat changed, so I could sit next to her, then I saw she was wearing a wedding ring, so I never said a word. I just sat there and looked at her for twelve thousand miles. . . ." He had paused. "So when you told me your ideas . . . I can understand that *hope*. I think everyone secretly believes that one day they'll meet the—well, the right person. Only no one ever admits it these days. . . ."

And then, right then, Tomas Court had decided to hire him—not, ultimately, for his professional abilities, considerable though these were, but because he saw that this troubled, inarticulate Englishman might understand obsession. The discovery had surprised Court, who believed all Englishmen to be cold-blooded, particularly Englishmen of Lascelles's class.

Court looked across at his wife, whom he had been carefully ignoring. "Checking the fire-escape situation," he heard Lascelles say now. Again, he placed his hand over the mouthpiece. He flicked the faxed pages of the *Times* article, written by some woman journalist called Genevieve Hunter, of whom he had never heard.

"*Why* did you pass this? You scarcely read it, Natasha." His wife, back to the door, looked at him uncertainly.

"It's only short, Tomas. It's fine. I was careful; I had to be. She'd been talking to someone and she mentioned the Conrad building."

"She doesn't mention it here." He gave a gesture of annoyance. "And it wouldn't have mattered if she had, since you're not going to live there."

"You may have decided that, Tomas; I haven't. And I'm not going to have that argument again."

"Fine. Drop the subject."

"I was alarmed when she mentioned the Conrad, Tomas—obviously. People will gossip. Word gets out. And I have to be so careful. . . ." She hesitated. Her voice, which had sharpened a moment before and taken on that tense obstinate note he most disliked, now softened and became conciliatory.

"Anyway, Tomas, you'd have been proud of me. I told her I'd bought a house in the Hollywood hills. I made up all this rigmarole about it on the spur of the moment—and she bought it. She mentions that plan, and I knew she would. Journalists always love it when they think they've prized some new information out of you." She gave a half smile. "So you see, I can lie quite well, Tomas, when I have to."

That reply did not appear to please her husband, whom she could never think of as her ex-husband. He scanned the pages, then tossed them aside.

"Maybe. You lie better when I'm scripting you."

"Do I?"

"Yes, but you're right, the article's fine. She didn't get close; a million miles wide. Look." He flicked the video controls again. "Here's your Wildfell Hall."

His wife, and Court knew he would never be able to think of her as his ex-wife, moved slowly forward a few paces and looked at the screen. She examined the stern, gabled facade, the moorland, then the track, the cliffs, and the horseshoe-shaped beach below.

"Yes," she said, on a slow exhalation of breath. "Yes. Except—the house isn't that close to the sea in the novel."

"We're not filming the novel; we're filming *my* script from the novel. I need the sea; it's better that way."

"Maybe so. Maybe so."

She retreated again a few paces and stood looking at him quietly, her long pale hands clasped at the waist of the gray dress she was wearing.

Quiet as a nun, her husband thought, and with a sense of anger realized that it was a double quotation, from a poem by Milton in the first place, from the taped telephone calls of their persecutor in the second. He thought: the *Collected Works of Milton*; the *Collected Works of Joseph King*. Did the use of such quotations mean that King, who had a flat midwestern accent, a somewhat mordant sense of humor, and an undoubted gift for language, was an educated man?

King could be lyrical, also crude. The police might choose to categorize him as yet another weirdo, as wacko, as some sleazeball or screwball; Court did not agree. King was subtle and certainly intelligent; his phrases stuck in the mind. In one recorded call, he had described, for instance, this gray dress Natasha was wearing. Natasha, who had been protected from some of King's calls, was not aware of that fact, but King had described the dress, its soft cashmere, the way her body shaped the material, very well.

Something small, fiery, and malevolent began to stir deep in the recesses of Court's mind. In his ear, Colin Lascelles had continued to speak all this while. He was explaining that they needed to discuss weather cover, and that he would be arriving in New York the next day, in the morning; he had switched to an earlier plane.

"Come to Tribeca," Court said. "I have a loft in Tribeca. You've got that address? Come there."

Lascelles agreed and reverted to the question of security. Court's requirements, he said, had astonished the various hotel managements. They had emphasized that Yorkshire was not like New York or Los Angeles, and that the crime rate was low. Why, so secure did their guests feel, even their American guests, that they often did not bother to lock their doors. . . .

"You've tied your hair back." Court covered the mouthpiece once more. "I hate it that way. Undo it. . . ."

"Now? Tomas—"

"Undo it. I've been away a month. It's not much to ask." He could see, almost smell, her reluctance. She hesitated, glanced toward the door, then lifted her arms. Her long hair was tied back with a black grosgrain ribbon. Slowly, she untied it and began to wind it around her hand. Blood mounted in her neck, then suffused her face. She lowered her eyes.

"Tomas—Jonathan will be back soon. They'll all be back. . . ."

"This new bodyguard—how old is he?"

"Tex? I don't know—young. Twenty-five, twenty-six. He's been protecting some oil billionaire. The agency said—"

"Good-looking?"

"Tomas, what does that matter? He does his job—"

"Is he good-looking?"

"I guess so. He's tall, blond. A country boy. He has a fiancée, Tomas, back home in some little town near Fort Worth. You'll like him—"

"Maybe."

"Tomas, please—can't you get off the phone? I wanted to talk to you. . . ."

"What about?"

He looked at her steadily; Lascelles's words, punctuated by those explosions, now blurred. He waited, knowing the answer, feeling amid the stirrings of an irrational anger, the stirring of a familiar desire.

"About that newspaper clipping you sent me. That man they found in Glacier Park. About what the police told you, and the detective agency. You said . . . You said they had checks to complete, and—I have to know—is he really dead, Tomas? Was it Joseph King they found?"

"New locks," Colin Lascelles said, into Court's ear, "and an adjoining room for the bodyguard. Now—"

Behind his words came the soft thud of another explosion; some atavistic British festival, Court thought; the burning of a traitor in effigy. He sniffed; the air in the hotel suite, purified, humidified, smelt acrid.

"We'll discuss it tomorrow," Court said. "I have to go now."

He replaced the receiver and looked long and hard at his wife.

The thick, long, dark weight of her hair had now fallen forward; one strand, coiled like a question mark, rested against the roundness of her left breast. Beneath that breast, invisible to all but a lover, his wife had a small mole, a velvety aberration of the skin that he cherished. In his movies, he had always rendered this alluring defect invisible. He hid it religiously with makeup, with lighting, with camera angles, for it was *his* mole, part of his secret knowledge of her. That mole, in some detail, and with relish, King had described. He looked at his wife levelly; King's knowledge, of which his wife remained ignorant, could have only one possible explanation. Yet that explanation was *im*possible, since his wife recognized neither King's voice, nor his writing—or so she had told Court many, many times.

"Do you want him dead?" he said, his tone cold.

"Tomas, please." She gave a helpless gesture of the hands. "How can you ask that? You know I do. I prayed he'd die; and if that's wicked, I don't care."

"Their inquiries are inconclusive." He kept his eyes on her. "They need more time. . . ."

"Why? *Why?*" The color had now ebbed from her face, and her skin was ashen.

"They just do, that's all. It's complicated." He paused, and for a second he could hear King's voice, mocking, knowledgeable. Just a fragment from one of the many, many tapes of his calls; the words used were effective—Court could feel the kick and pulse of them in his groin.

Still looking levelly at his wife, he held out his hand to her. She began on excuses at once: there wasn't time, it was too soon, Jonathan would be returning, she would have to leave for the theater, she needed to talk, just talk. . . .

Court scarcely heard her words behind some crackle and hiss in his mind, a sound that could have come from a defective tape, or from a fire.

"Come here," he said, in the tone that always guaranteed she would obey him. Still she hung back, and he flexed his fingers. He listened to the thud in his blood, the bang of his heart.

"It's been a *month*," he said. "A *month*. Trust me. Come here."

Part Four

FRIDAY THE THIRTEENTH

Chapter 8

"On the beach," Tomas Court said.

"But . . ." said Colin Lascelles.

"But . . ." said Mario Schwartz, Court's first assistant director.

Mario and Colin glanced at each other; both were keeping count and so far Colin was winning. He was averaging twenty "but's" an hour; Mario, limping behind, was averaging fifteen.

"Fucking *hell* . . ." said the neat, gray-haired, bespectacled woman who was sitting next to Court and recording these proceedings in microscopic script. Her name was Thalia Ng; she was one of Court's oldest associates, a woman resembling some mouse of a librarian. One week into his protracted meetings with Tomas Court, Colin was still adjusting to her habitual mode of speech—it clashed with her woolly cardigans.

"On the *beach*," Court repeated, ignoring these interruptions. "When Gilbert Markham sees Helen for the first time, he has to see her on the beach."

"Why?" said Thalia Ng.

"Because I say so," Court replied, with charm.

"Personally," Thalia Ng replied, in cozy tones, "I think Gilbert Markham is a prick, and Helen is one tight-assed bitch. *Personally,* I don't give a flying fuck *where* they meet, but . . ."

The eyes of Mario and Colin locked; Thalia Ng's score was ten and rising.

"They don't *meet*," Tomas Court fixed her with a cool glance. "I said he *sees* her. She's down by the sea; he's up on the cliffs. He *watches* her. She's only just arrived in the neighborhood and he doesn't yet know who she is. In case you haven't noticed, Thalia, there's a lot of voyeurism in this book."

"Sure, and there's a whole lot more in your script. And okay, I can live with that, but you've changed your mind four times. *Four times,* Tomas. First, they're meeting on the moors, and I think, Oh shit, been here before—it's 1939, it's Sam Goldwyn's *Wuthering Heights.* I mean, *please,* it's Merle fucking Oberon and . . ."

"Larry fucking Olivier," Court interjected politely. "Precisely, Thalia."

"Then," Thalia Ng continued. "*Then,* like major rethink, they meet in Gilbert Markham's house, the same way they do in the novel—big *yawn.* Then—I'm on idea number three now, Tomas, I'm keeping track of this horseshit—then, it's night, and Helen's inside Wildfell Hall, and this jerk Markham is creeping around in the garden, trying to get a first look at her, and I'm thinking: *Rear Window? Peeping Tom,* perhaps? Now it's moved *again.* She's on the fucking *beach.* That beach is giving me problems, Tomas. That beach is saying *French Lieutenant's Woman,* a colostomy bag of a movie. So perhaps you'd tell me, before you comprehensively gang-bang the schedules yet again, are you *serious*? Are you *sure* about this?"

Tomas Court gave a small tight smile. Colin could not decide if he was annoyed or delighted by Thalia Ng's comments. The suspicion was growing in Colin's mind that these arguments between Thalia and Court were a little double act they both enjoyed. He suspected they were rehearsed; he suspected that, right from the first, Court had intended this scene to take place on the beach, and that Thalia knew that. Why Court should want to play Prospero in this way, Colin could not decide; all he knew, as the long day wore on, was that Thalia was an unlikely Ariel, and he seemed destined to play Caliban, Prospero's deformed and discontented slave.

This role was familiar to Colin, since he had once actually played it, at age fourteen, at an end-of-term culturefest at his public school. He had given a vigorous and, it was widely agreed, triumphant performance, leaping about grunting like a chimpanzee, with a fish in his mouth in the drunk scene. Even his father, not known for his interest in or respect for theater, had enjoyed the evening. He had motored up from Shute in his ancient silver Rolls-Royce, and sat in the front row, mustache bristling, laughing loudly and slapping his thigh every time he considered Caliban had made a joke.

"By Jove, he's got something, that Shakespeare johnny," he said to Colin afterward. "Bloody fine costumes too. Who was in charge of costumes?"

"Matron," Colin said.

"Who was that playing Prospero?"

"Hicks-Henderson major, sir. I hate him."

"Don't blame you. Can't act for toffee. Complete and utter berk."

Compliments on his own definitive playing of Caliban had followed. Now, Colin drifted off and away to the islands of nostalgia, to a land of lost content where his brother was still alive and all was well. "Be not afeard" he heard his own reedy fourteen-year-old voice pronounce. "Be not afeard; the isle is full of noises, sounds and sweet airs, that give delight and hurt not. . . ." His head began a slow descent toward the table; sleep gathered him gently in its arms, then Mario Schwartz stuck an elbow in his ribs.

Colin jerked upright, trying to radiate alertness.

"But . . ." he said.

Mario noted this addition to his score; no one else took the least notice.

"Those schedules are provisional, Thalia," Court was saying, "so just stop arguing, and fix it—all right?"

Thalia Ng gave a small enigmatic sigh, and wrote a note in microscopic script. Court stretched and flexed his fingers.

"Right. Let's move on. Scene eight," he said. Colin waited until the director was well into the depredations he intended for scene eight. He wondered how long he could decently wait before interjecting another "but," and whether, in any case, he had the energy. When he was certain Prospero was not looking his way, he rested his wrist on the edge of the table, then, very, very discreetly, eased the cuff back against the edge, so that he could look at his watch.

It was now nearly six in the evening. He had been sitting at this long black table, in Court's Tribeca loft, since eight o'clock that morning. The previous meetings with Court had been bad, but this was undoubtedly the worst. It began with the news that, after protracted wranglings, Nic Hicks had finally signed to play Gilbert Markham. Nic Hicks, or Nic Prick as he preferred to call him, was the man Colin most loathed in the world. He recalled his meeting with him in that theater bar; he contemplated the appalling prospect of spending the entire twelve-week shooting schedule in the closest daily proximity with this man: Nic Hicks, whose conceit was boundless, Nic Prick, who had whining down to a fine art.

He was just recovering from this blow, announced by Tomas Court with a small sly smile, he had noticed, when Thalia reported during a coffee break that Nic had been on the phone, would be arriving in New York shortly, and sent word that he and Colin must *get together very soon*. Colin had assumed that, if there were any justice in the world, this had to be the lowest point of the day; he was wrong. He was now frantic for a cigarette, exhausted, frustrated, and confused.

On the table in front of him, next to the usual array of Court's asthma inhalers, were piles of different-colored papers: pink, green, yellow, blue. These were the various schedule revises already made; buried somewhere beneath them, and now altered beyond recognition, was the immaculate location plan he had proudly brought with him from England. Buried somewhere else under this multicolored litter was the original first draft shooting schedule he had helped to compile in those few heady days of optimism when he first arrived in New York.

This pristine, sensible document, its every detail overseen by Tomas Court, was now in the process of being unpicked, slashed, rent, trampled upon, patchworked, and restitched. The alterations made by Court over the previous couple of days had been substantial; today, he had outdone himself. He had juggled locations, so far changing the settings of fifteen major scenes and ten minor ones. Thalia Ng's function, apart from abusing Court by rote, was to keep a record of these alterations, each one of which had a domino effect. Cast, crew, availability, transport, accommodation, costs—Colin watched a mile of dominoes topple down; he had long ago lost track of which scene was now happening where; he was starting to feel sick and dizzy, on the edge of some cliff, watching the seas of despair.

Visconti was worse, he told himself. Visconti, a genius, was a total megalomaniac; yet he had managed to work with Visconti. He had worked with a tetchy, aging, punctilious David Lean, on a film never actually made. He had survived Lean, the quixotic Truffaut, that kung-fu Korean, the lunatic Pole, the deranged Australian, several certifiable Brits, and those two new-wave Germans who needed straitjackets. I can *deal* with this, he told himself grimly; very few movie directors, in his experience, were men of sweet reason, so of course he could deal with it. He would, however, deal with it a whole lot better if he could have a cigarette.

"Excuse me a moment," he said, rising to his feet.

Tomas Court went on talking; Thalia Ng tapped his arm.

"Colin wants the john."

"Oh." Court looked up, his expression preoccupied.

"Didn't Thalia show you earlier? The far end, turn right, first door on the left. Now, that scene you mentioned, Thalia, with Gilbert Markham in the garden at night—I want to keep that, but I'm moving it. . . ."

A low groan escaped Colin's lips. He moved away from the table fast. He was supposed to be meeting lovely Lindsay Drummond at seven-thirty. He was taking her out to dinner; this prospect alone had kept him sane all day.

No problem, he thought, negotiating the long, bare, improvisatory loft area that comprised Court's main living and working space. The space offended Colin's educated eye: it was bleak and looked unloved; no effort had been made to furnish it; it looked as if Court had just moved in, or was about to move out. Colin avoided stacks of cardboard boxes—there were piles of them everywhere. A *cigarette*, then he would feel revived and confident, he promised himself. He would return to the table and *contribute*, which would probably amaze everyone, since he had scarcely opened his mouth all day.

Then he would simply announce he was leaving—just like that. The rest of them could go on until midnight if they felt like it—and they probably did; he would be sitting at a quiet table in a quiet civilized restaurant, eating wonderful food and *advising* Lindsay.

He had now been advising Lindsay, on and off, for the past week, whenever he could contrive a gap in his or her frantic schedules. At every opportunity, he had been prompting

Lindsay on the subject of her prospective biography, her inadequate advance, her economic pressures, and her hope to relieve these by renting her London apartment and finding somewhere cheaper out in the sticks. Whenever Lindsay attempted to change the subject, Colin gently led her back to it; he now knew a great deal about Gabrielle Chanel, and Lindsay's hoped-for hovel with the roses around the door.

The role of adviser to Lindsay was not, perhaps, the one he would have chosen, but he had to start somewhere, and he now felt he was perfecting the role. Quiet, concerned, wise, *prudent*—that was the line to take. Colin was aware he was somewhat miscast in this role—quietness did not come easily to him and prudence felt unnatural—but he was trying hard. Colin's experience of women, considerably more extensive than most women assumed on meeting him, told him that Lindsay needed careful handling. She was quite odd anyway (he liked her for this) and she appeared to be in some odd stressed-out state; it was very important, therefore, to take things slowly and not to rush.

Considering what a bad start they had made in Oxford, Colin felt he had a lot of territory to cover, but so far they were making progress, bowling happily along at a prudent speed: this evening, he had decided, was the moment to step on the gas and accelerate.

He had reached a bare brick wall, a completely bare, brutal, black brick wall at the far end of the loft. Opening a door, Colin found himself in a dark narrow corridor. He turned right, as instructed, and felt about for a light switch. He found one, proceeded a few yards farther on, as an ugly neon strip flickered above his head, then he stopped and gaped.

When, directed by Thalia earlier on, he had found his way to the bathroom here before, all the other doors in the corridor had been shut. Now, a door opposite the bathroom, a door that clearly led into Tomas Court's bedroom, was wide open. *Private, Out of Bounds,* pronounced the voice of Colin's rigorous upbringing, but it was already too late.

He had seen through into the bedroom beyond, which was eerily lit by the bluish neon from the corridor, and by the streetlights shining into the room through its wall of metal-framed windows. He could see that the room contained one very large, monstrous bed, draped with a dark cover the color of dried blood. Next to the bed, on a wheeled table that had a surgical look, was a large old-fashioned recording machine, of the kind that took spools of tape, not cassettes; Colin had not seen such a machine in years. It was flanked by two towering black speakers and by a cliff, a precipice, a cascade, of audiotapes. Mounted behind the bed, blown up very large, so the photograph was the size of some Renaissance altarpiece, was the celebrated black-and-white still of Natasha Lawrence in *Dead Heat*. Colin stared, transfixed. It could not escape his notice that the image had been slashed—a huge jagged knife cut had been made at a diagonal angle, slicing through her body from the left shoulder, with its little crouching spider, to the pale delicate jut of her right hip.

"Oh Christ," Colin muttered under his breath, and took a step back. It then occurred to him that perhaps Mario and Thalia had not seen this, that it might be better if they did *not* see it. Gingerly, he moved forward, intent on closing the door and concealing what he had seen. As soon as he moved into the doorway, a light lit—a small red light, mounted on some invisible piece of machinery high on the opposite wall, above the bed. Colin looked at it nervously; it was possible that the light was part of some security system, was similar to those body-heat detectors that his father, for instance, had recently installed in the great hall at Shute, at vast expense. On the other hand, given Tomas Court's profession, or predilections, it could be a camera; he might now be being recorded on some closed-circuit device.

Colin blushed from hairline to neck. He would look like a snooper; he now *felt* like a snooper. *Act casually,* said some demented voice in his head; he planted a nonchalant expression on his face, whistled a tune, slammed the door, shot across the corridor into the bathroom, opened the window, stuck his head out and smoked, very fast, that much-needed cigarette.

One hour later, to Colin's astonishment, Court seemed suddenly to bore of his alterations. He rose to his feet, announced he was going to see his son, and allowed them all to escape. Colin felt greasy with fatigue and unease; the day's events were now conducting a tribal dance in his head; all he could hear were tom-toms drumming out the signals of danger and distress.

In silence, he, Mario, and Thalia descended in a grim elevator. Outside, Mario paused by a stack of trash cans.

"Sweet Jesu," he said, with feeling, then gave them all a high five and went loping off.

Thalia, who, despite her surname, was an Italian-American who hailed from the Bronx, looked Colin up and down. Colin bore her scrutiny humbly; the usual sirens, ceaseless in this city, wailed and whooped in the distance; the beat of some Rasta sound pulsed from a loft across the street. Colin had never felt more English, more inadequate, more out of his depth.

He was longing to ask Thalia if she knew about the slashed picture, but his antique code of honor prevented him. Was Court some kind of pervert? This idea distressed him terribly. What did it all *imply*? What did it all *mean*? he wanted to shout. He began pacing up and down, making inarticulate noises; when these gave no relief, he banged his forehead hard with his fists.

"Oh, God, God, God," he said.

"You'll get used to it. Hang on in there," Thalia replied, her manner kindly for once. Colin rounded on her, pulling at his hair so it stuck up in auburn tufts.

"December!" he cried. "December! We're supposed to start filming in under a *month*. Postpone, I said. Wait until the spring, I said. But no, he says it has to be after Thanksgiving, and it has to be December. It's a twelve-week schedule. Does he *know* what Yorkshire's like in December? January? Does he *care*? It *rains*. It pisses with rain the entire time. It *snows*. Villages get cut off. . . ."

"Cool it," said Thalia.

"We have a start date! My sanity *depends* on that start date. We're *never* going to start—I see that now. If he moves the whole shoot to California, I won't be surprised. California? What am I saying? Why not Indonesia? Anne Brontë in Ecuador? How about the Zambezi? We could shift the whole fucking thing to the Amazon basin, how about that?"

"Relax. He likes you," Thalia said.

"*Likes* me? *Likes* me? He's destroying me. He's ripped up months of work—"

"He always does that."

"That bloody man is driving me insane. *Nuts.* Twelve hours—nearly twelve hours I've been sitting there, and what's been my contribution? 'But's.' But, but, but, but . . ."

Colin kicked a trash can violently, hurting his foot.

"Listen," said Thalia, when the echoes of his anguish had died away, "if you're going to survive this, just remember one thing. I've worked with him ten years, and I know. . . ."

"What?" Colin cried. "What?"

"He's the best, okay?" Thalia patted his arm. "Supercunt, obviously—but still the best . . ."

"He's playing games with me! I know it! I can feel it!"

"So?" Thalia gave a little smile. "Play some fucking games back. Ciao, Colin." She gave him a matronly wave. "Have a nice evening. See you tomorrow. Oh—he wants us an hour earlier. He's altering the end. Seven A.M., all right?"

In her bedroom at the Pierre, Lindsay was getting ready for her dinner with Colin. She was sitting on her bed in her bra and underpants while her friend and senior assistant, Pixie, applied a peculiar pungent gel to her hair. Pixie had taken a liking to Colin, and was exhibiting great interest in the imminent dinner, which she referred to as a hot date. She had decided that, in honor of the occasion, Lindsay needed a complete makeover. This makeover, involving a bath, then the application of various potions, unguents, scents, restorative creams, and foot sprays, had been going on for a while. Lindsay, who had covered six fashion shows that day, was too tired and dispirited to argue. Pixie, born bossy, was taking full advantage of her uncharacteristically passive state.

"Keep *still*," she said, dragging a comb painfully across Lindsay's scalp. "I'm *transforming* you, sod it, and I can't do it properly if you keep jiggling about."

"Give it a rest, Pixie. Who cares what I look like anyway? I'm trying to read my goddamn phone messages, and it's not easy when I'm being scalped."

"Colin cares. You've read those messages five times already. Look left, I need to check the back."

Lindsay sighed and obeyed. It was true, she now knew these messages by heart. During her absence, Markov and Jippy had called (they were now in Crete; "Off to the Minotaur's lair any minute," the message read). Gini Lamartine had called about Thanksgiving arrangements, as yet undecided; some sad person from Lulu Sabatier's office had called (for the seventh time in seven days); various dull, work-connected people had called, and Lindsay's mother had called to suggest a few thousand purchases Lindsay might like to make for her in Saks.

Rowland McGuire had *not* called. He had not called once in the past week. He was, presumably, not interested in testing her intuition after all, or perhaps he had simply forgotten, been distracted. Lindsay's intuition, ever acute, could put a shape to that distraction. Given Rowland's past conquests, it was likely to measure 34-24-34; it would be a great deal younger than she was, and would in a short while be discarded—such was life.

"I don't even know why I'm *doing* this," she said snappishly.

"You're just nervous. You're having dinner with this very handsome, sexy man. You're about to get lucky. Relax."

"Handsome? Sexy? Who is this?"

"Are you blind?" Pixie giggled. "One glance from those blue eyes and my nipples go hard. . . . He's delicious."

"He's *nice*," Lindsay corrected. "Kind, gentlemanly, rather old-fashioned . . ."

"He won't be old-fashioned in bed. I can always tell. Ah well, you older women get all the luck. . . ."

"I don't even want to go out." Lindsay sighed. "I want to stay in, eat chocolates, and lie in bed. What's in that hair stuff anyway? It smells *weird*."

"Magic." Pixie sniffed. "Yams, actually. And don't worry, the smell wears off after a bit. It's absolutely the latest thing. Ecofriendly, one hundred percent pure natural ingredients, *and* it attacks the free radicals. . . ."

"I have free radicals in my *hair*?"

"At your age, Lindsay, you have free radicals lurking everywhere. Face facts."

Lindsay faced them. She could sense the free radicals crawling around. They had long given up on such minor targets as her complexion, she thought; they were now infesting her head and heart; they were swimming up and down in her blood.

"Turn your head this way. . . ." Pixie examined her. "Oh yes—*excellent*. I'm aiming at a soignée look, très 1930s debutante, with Berlin nightclub undertones. Think Dietrich, then think Nancy Mitford. I want sultry *and* debonair. . . ."

"I've never looked sultry in my life, and I've never felt less debonair. Get a move on, Pixie, I'm fed up with this. My feet feel sticky. . . ."

"They're *meant* to feel sticky. It's the papaya juice in that foot spray. Just wait awhile—you'll feel you're walking on air. . . ."

Pixie made a face at her and continued her ministrations. Pixie was a *believer*. She believed in tofu and aerobics and mantras and collagen injections and miracle creams that cost $200 for a very small jar. She believed in the beauty industry, where science and voodoo interlinked, and she believed in *clothes*. In the gospel according to Pixie, there were very few problems in life that could not be solved by intelligent shopping, and spiritual fulfillment could be bought for the price of a new dress.

Pixie's religion, as Lindsay was aware, had once been her own. If she had never been quite such a born-again evangelist as Pixie was, she too had bowed down before fashion and worshiped at the high altar of couture. Now, finally, finally, she could admit at long last that she had lapsed. Farewell false gods, Lindsay thought, feeling virtuous.

Pixie stepped back, her task completed, and Lindsay turned to the mirror, examining her handiwork. The new hairstyle, more intricate than her usual one, was surprisingly effective. Lindsay's gloom diminished.

"You know I think that papaya stuff is actually working?" she said. "I feel quite refreshed."

"Sure you do. Now we have to find you something to wear."

Pixie moved off to the closets and began rummaging about. Lindsay stretched and examined her ringless hands, the nails of which Pixie had painted a curious but interesting purplish black. How revealing that Pixie should consider Colin Lascelles handsome, she thought; could she be right? She must look at him more carefully tonight.

"Tell me, Pixie," she said, looking at her with affection, "will you ever get married, d'you think?"

Pixie was twenty-one. "No way," she said.

"What about children? You'd like children one day, I expect."

"Maybe. But only if I'm rich enough. Having kids finished my mother. That's not going to happen to me."

"And what about love, Pixie—how d'you feel about that?"

Pixie straightened up with a hiss; she held up her two index fingers in the shape of a cross, as if warding off a vampire.

"Bad magic," she said.

Lindsay was impressed. She did not altogether agree, but she was impressed. Pixie, one of six children, born in Liverpool, and brought up in hardship, had already come a long way. Lindsay, who had given her a start five years before, intended to help her go further. Accordingly, when she resigned, she had advised Max very strongly to promote Pixie to fashion editor. Max, who did not consort with lowly fashion assistants, but who had glimpsed Pixie—she was hard to miss—in the elevators and corridors at the *Correspondent,* had groaned.

"She has green hair," he said.

"Don't be ridiculous, that was *years* ago. Now she looks like Susie Parker, supermodel circa 1958. You must have seen her—tailored suits, a little hat with a veil, high-heel shoes, stockings with seams, gloves, and a Queen Mother handbag. . . ."

"That was *her?*" Max had wavered, then entrenched. "She's a *child,*" he said.

"She's twenty-one. Fashion editors need to be young. Hire her."

"I'll think about it," said Max.

Lindsay had continued her promote-Pixie campaign ever since. Before leaving London, she had conceived a cunning plan that, she had been certain, she could slide past Max. She and Pixie would spend roughly a week covering the actual collections, then roughly ten days in New York on fashion shoots. Over Thanksgiving, Lindsay would take some vacation time and Pixie would return to London. During Lindsay's absence, Pixie could nurse these fashion stories through to press, and Max could see how she progressed.

Lindsay kept these dates and plans somewhat vague, and

was careful to present them to Max late on her last day in London, when he was in the middle of a news crisis.

"Fine, excellent," Max had said, when he finally had time to see her. He smiled a small feline smile. "In other words, Lindsay, I pay your airfares and your hotel bills at the Pierre for around three weeks, during part of which period, you research the American end of your Chanel biography—a biography that has nothing to do with this newspaper. Am I right?"

Lindsay cursed under her breath. "I'm being paid peanuts for this biography," she said. "I won't be able to afford airfares. It would only be the odd hour off, Max."

"No, it wouldn't. You intend to hole up in some archive and let Pixie handle those New York fashion shoots. Then, when I congratulate you on how good they are, you're going to inform me that Pixie did them, thus clinching her appointment." He sighed. "Lindsay, you make a lousy Machiavelli; I can read you like a book. This is out of character; you're the only journalist I know who *doesn't* fiddle her expenses. I've always felt you lacked creativity in that respect."

"I'll bet Rowland doesn't fiddle them either."

"Rowland?" Max shrugged. "Oh, Rowland's probity wears one out. Ah well, I'm really quite fond of you, I'm feeling charming today. Okay. Done."

He scribbled his initials, authorizing these plans with a speed that made Lindsay suspicious at once.

"What about Pixie?" she said. Max's manner became opaque.

"I'm still thinking about it. I'm consulting. I haven't ruled out the idea. Not yet . . ."

Lindsay had informed him tartly that this was wise, since he knew nothing whatsoever about fashion, whereas she knew a great deal and was always right. Max acquiesced to this pronouncement with his customary grace. Lindsay continued to mull this over, to plot and plan, and had finally decided, in New York, the previous day, to inform Pixie. "The job's yours, Pixie," she had said, "if you play your cards right."

Pixie had blushed beneath her layers of perfect 1958 *maquillage*; then the story came out. As Lindsay well knew, Pixie said, she had a brilliant career plan. She intended to be editing English *Vogue* by the time she was thirty, and American

Vogue as soon as was feasible after that. Accordingly, half an hour after Lindsay resigned, Pixie had marched upstairs to the sanctum of Max's offices. There, his trio of stuck-up secretaries had first ignored her, then told her an appointment with Mr. Flanders was not possible. Pixie had not budged. She had sat there for two and a half hours until finally, at eight o'clock in the evening, Max had taken pity on her and agreed to see her for three and a half minutes.

"Very Max," Lindsay said, thoughtfully, working out the time scheme of these events.

This was fine, Pixie continued, since she only needed two minutes anyway. Inside the sanctum, she had informed Max that she had earned promotion, that if she didn't get it she would go to *Vogue*, who had been chasing her for months, and that if she did get it, she would want to make changes.

"Changes?" Lindsay said, in a faint voice.

Pixie had presented Max with a list of these changes, fifteen in number. Max read it, laughed, and offered her a drink. They had then discussed his five children and Pixie's budgerigar. Pixie had decided that, despite his suit and his posh accent, she could do business with Max. The upshot of all this was that, provided Lindsay did not change her mind, the position of fashion editor was within Pixie's grasp.

"Oh, and I raised him five thousand," Pixie added, in a nonchalant voice.

"Five thousand? That bastard. That lying, devious . . ."

"It was *easy*, Lindsay. You could have done it any time. You never push hard enough on the money front. Max is a sweetie, a pussycat . . ."

"Yes, with very sharp claws. Make sure he doesn't claw that five thousand back from your budget, Pixie, because he'll certainly try. . . . You actually discussed *salary*?"

"Sure. On a putative basis, of course."

Lindsay, by then coming out of shock, had begun to laugh. She laughed at Pixie's ambition and Max's poker-game skills, and she laughed at her own vanity most of all. Fond as she was of both Max and Pixie, it had not truly occurred to her that she was dispensable. She had assumed Max would fight to keep her, and that Pixie, with luck, might find her a hard act to follow. Her disillusionment hurt at first. She had been dispensable as a wife, Lindsay thought; now she was dispensable as a mother *and* as an editor. She felt a flood of self-pity at this realization, which she was wise enough to indulge to the full for an hour or two. Then, gradually, her natural optimism reasserted itself. Such lessons were salutary; the little rehearsals life organized for everyone—in the final analysis, after all, death ensured everyone would be dispensable, she told herself.

Now, watching Pixie sashay back and forth between closets and drawers, selecting a costume for a meeting that, alas, was not the hot date Pixie supposed, it occurred to her that Pixie's revelations were doubly useful. Not only had they induced a saintly state of forbearance and wisdom, they had also ensured that there was now no going back. The luxury of changing her mind, a luxury Lindsay was aware she indulged in too often, was ruled out. This was good—now the bridges were burned, the Rubicon was crossed. She at once felt a surge of energy and bounced off the bed.

"That red dress," she said, "that's what I want to wear—the red dress."

Pixie rolled her eyes. "Puh-leaze," she said.

"What's wrong with it? It's great. People like it. Rowland McGuire likes it."

Pixie thrust the red dress to the back of the closet. She pulled out a black suit, a white silk T-shirt, a pair of stockings, black shoes with kitten heels, and some fake pearls that looked like Chanel fake pearls in a kind light.

"Take the bra *off*," she said. "I want *subtle*. Just the occasional hint of nipple, for Colin's sake. Don't argue—*trust*. And never quote Rowland McGuire on clothes to me. I may lust after Rowland, but he knows *nothing* about what makes a woman look good. Rowland should concentrate on women's underwear. . . ." She paused, smiling. "As, of course, one gathers he does . . ."

"Yes, yes, yes," Lindsay said very fast, removing the bra and diving into the T-shirt. She knew Pixie was about to launch herself on the subject of Rowland's physical charms, alleged sexual prowess, and past amatory exploits. This recitative, of which Pixie was fond, and which might or might not be accurate, could continue at Homeric length. Lindsay did not want to hear about Rowland's rumored past amours, and she certainly did not want to hear the details of any present ones. Pixie's reading, in any case, was useless; she came at the subject of Rowland from the wrong philosophic and moral viewpoint. As far as Pixie was concerned, Lindsay thought crossly, it was a truth universally acknowledged that any man in possession of a woman's company must be in want of a fuck.

She closed her ears to Pixie's lewd commentary and emerged from the T-shirt red-faced.

"So tell me truthfully now," Pixie was saying. "Am I right? Did you and Rowland ever . . ."

"What? *What?*" Lindsay said. "Certainly *not.* For heaven's *sake* . . ."

"Pity, because it *is* heaven, by all accounts. I'd have liked to know if it was true. . . ." She gave a dreamy sigh. "Just, like, the best sex *ever.* Eight times a night."

"Don't be so goddamn ridiculous." Lindsay began to yank on the stockings. "*No one* does it eight times a night. Less is more, Pixie. Remember that."

"If you say so, Lindsay," Pixie replied, in the most irritating manner possible. "If you say so . . ." Her eyes narrowed. "Are you telling me the truth? You're sure you never—not even once?"

"No, I damn well didn't. Rowland is a colleague. Can we change the subject and change it now, please?"

"Okay. Okay." Pixie looked thoughtful. "It's just—I've noticed him *looking* at you, once or twice, and I could have sworn that . . ."

Lindsay put on the skirt, the jacket, and the shoes. This took her at least thirty seconds and demonstrated consummate self-control, she felt.

"What could you have sworn?" she said.

"Nothing, nothing. Put it this way, *maybe* he was admiring your work, but I got a rather different impression. . . ."

"Twaddle," Lindsay said, with firmness. "Tosh. Romantic drivel. When was this?"

"Oh, back in the summer sometime . . ." Pixie made an airy gesture. "You were wearing that cream dress."

"Really? I've always liked that dress."

"And another occasion—when you were going straight to the theater with him from work, September sometime?"

"I remember vaguely. September the eighth."

"He helped you on with your coat, and I caught that *look* on his face. . . ." Pixie shrugged. "I was probably imagining it. You were putting him down as usual, telling him how arrogant he is—that's why you didn't notice, I expect."

"Putting him down?" Lindsay began, frowning. "No, Pixie— I don't do that. . . ."

"You never *stop* doing it, Lindsay." Pixie gave her a kind look. "*I* know you don't mean it, and so does he most of the time, but you've got a wicked tongue and you hurt him sometimes. Pity about that—you might have been in there with a chance. . . ."

Lindsay turned to look at her own reflection. She would *silence* that tongue of hers, she thought; she would cut that tongue out if necessary. Never ever again, no matter how provoked, would she give Rowland McGuire a sharp answer. From now on, in her capacity as his friend, of course, she would speak with a becoming, a womanly sweetness; she would anoint Rowland with the balm of her female discourse. . . . I shall be *dulcet*, she resolved, and not just to Rowland, but to all the male sex. Perhaps a certain tartness, even a shrewishness, had been her problem all along, she thought. And how astonishing that Pixie, whose instincts were usually acute for such nuances, should think she might have been in there with a chance.

Resolving to reform, and to start practicing this new mildness of tongue immediately—she could practice on Colin over dinner, she realized; how fortunate—she executed a little pirouette. Pixie examined her, critically, from head to foot. The two women's eyes met in the mirror; both smiled.

"Well, I have to say it—you look great. I've improved you no end. Your skin's radiant, your eyes are shining. . . . Quite a transformation." Pixie gave her a sidelong sly glance. "I can't take all the credit; there must be another reason. . . . Anticipation, perhaps?"

"What?" Lindsay looked at her blankly. "Oh, of Colin, you mean? Well, it will be nice to have a quiet dinner somewhere."

"Quiet, huh?" Pixie smiled. "You like him, maybe? I wouldn't blame you. Thin but Byronic. Nice butt. *Wild* hair.

Great line in Levi's. Well hung. Dresses to the left—that's always a good sign. . . ."

"How observant you are, Pixie. I must remember that."

"And quite an operator too, I'd say. . . ."

"An *operator*?" Lindsay shook her head vehemently. "No, Pixie, you've got hold of the wrong end of the stick. He's sweet. Volatile. A bit naive. Not very sure of himself . . ."

"Oh yeah? Like, he finds out what flight you're on, and switches to it himself. then he chats up that stewardess at Heathrow—I watched him do it, Lindsay—and gets you both bumped up to first class? I've seen him with you, in the bar, gazing at you with those innocent blue eyes, looking like butter wouldn't melt in his mouth. . . . I *read* this man, Lindsay, and I know *exactly* what he's after." She giggled. "And if I were you, I'd give it to him. After dinner tonight."

Lindsay listened to this speech in thoughtful silence. From the vantage point of her new-won maturity and saintliness of character, she gave poor one-track-mind Pixie a pitying look.

"Pixie," she said, "you're getting cynical, you know that? When you're older, you'll understand. Sometimes men and women like to meet and simply *talk*. There is no hidden agenda. . . ."

Pixie gave a snort. Some of Lindsay's new saintliness deserted her.

"Look, Pixie," she continued, the sweetness of tongue also momentarily failing her, "you know where we're going after dinner? We are going uptown to this apartment he's staying in. There, Pixie, I'm going to meet his aunt—his great-aunt to be precise—because, God alone knows why, she's expressed an interest in being introduced. Now I hate to disabuse you, but she's around eighty-five years old, so I scarcely think . . ."

"Wow! You're meeting his *aunt*?" Pixie appeared to be thinking fast. Her face lit. "Well, what d'you know, this must be *serious*. That's good. That's great. I'm really pleased for you, Lindsay. I'm getting the picture now—like, this could be *long-term*, I mean, several months, right? Lucky we did the makeover; this is obviously the big night. I see it all. . . . You charm the old lady, get her *approval*, so to speak, then it's good night to grandma. . . . He brings you back here to the Pierre, like the gentleman he is, then it's soft lights, sweet nothings. . . ." Pixie took her hand in a confiding way. "You'd like me to lend you some grass, maybe? I have a stash downstairs. It can help with a first fuck sometimes, I find; kind of eases all the tensions, revs you up for the *second* fuck, makes sure it goes all right. . . ."

At this, saintliness deserted Lindsay completely. She snatched her hand back.

"Are you totally mad, Pixie? Stone deaf? How many times do I have to say this? It's dinner, it's the great-aunt's, it's back to the Pierre *on my own*. Read my lips, Pixie: *no fucking*. Have you got that?"

Pixie was mortally and morally offended. She gave Lindsay a look of shocked disbelief, made a few pungent remarks about women who hoarded their supposed virtue, then stalked to the door.

"Poor Colin," she said. "That is so mean and miserly, Lindsay. I'm disappointed in you." She opened the door. "You know what I call behavior like that?"

"Don't bother telling me," Lindsay began.

"I call it fucking *immoral*," Pixie yelled, nipping out through the door and slamming it.

Colin's idea of a quiet restaurant surprised Lindsay. It proved to be on East 55th Street; it was called Temps Perdu, had long been famous, and was very grand indeed. Realizing that it was their destination, Lindsay came to a halt on the sidewalk, a few yards shorts of its pinkish entrance canopy. She was about to suggest that this choice was an extravagant one, since Temps Perdu was celebrated for being very expensive, as in Third World debt, when she remembered she was practicing sweetness of tongue.

She rephrased. "Won't this be—well, a little *grand*, Colin?" she said.

Colin looked at her nonplussed. Such a concept did not appear to be familiar to him.

"Oh, I don't think so," he said. "It's terribly nice; you'll like it. The food's wonderful. There's a great wine list, and there's a very jolly headwaiter; his name's Fabian. He'll look after us."

It was on the tip of Lindsay's tongue to say that, in her experience, headwaiters in such New York restaurants were many things: haughty, intimidating, insultingly rude, for instance, but rarely jolly. The old Lindsay would have said this; the new Lindsay made some simpering vacuous disclaimer, and both Lindsays started praying as a flunky in uniform held the doors back.

Please God, the Lindsays said silently, to a deity in which neither quite believed. Please God, let them honor Colin's reservation; please God, don't let them relegate us to a Siberian table so conspicuously ill placed that even Colin will notice; please God, don't let them treat Colin like a worm, and please let them see that he means well and he's really very sweet. . . .

Lindsay was so busy with these prayers and with squinting around trying to work out which table was nearest the rest-room exit, and whether they were being inexorably led to it, that she was seated at a banquette opposite Colin before the details of their reception began to penetrate.

Then she began to realize: the table at which they had been placed was a delightful one, and someone—she was not sure who it was, but someone pleasant with a deep, French-accented voice—had used the phrase "your usual table." This usual table, moreover, was in a quiet, even an intimate corner; it had a snowy linen cloth, candles, charming flowers; beyond it, a wine waiter, supervised by a smiling benignant gray-haired man, was opening a bottle of champagne. It occurred to her that the benignant man must be Fabian—this *aperçu* being assisted by the fact that Colin addressed him as such.

"With my compliments, Mr. Lascelles," benignant Fabian appeared to be saying. "The seventy-six. I remember you liked that." A large leather-bound folder was placed in front of her. Opening it, Lindsay saw that although it listed three types of caviar and five ways of serving lobster, the menu she had been given did not list price.

"Bon appétit," said Fabian, a man Lindsay realized she now liked very much. He withdrew. Colin gave some Gaelic toast, which he said he had once learned in Scotland, and which ensured long life, love, and happiness.

Lindsay took a sip of the champagne; it was nectar; it was a revelation; it was—no contest—the most delicious champagne she had ever drunk in her life. A tiny silence fell; remembering her new womanliness, Lindsay sweetly and sympathetically asked Colin what sort of a day he had had.

"Ghastly. Unspeakable. Agonizing," he replied. "Here, feel. My hands are trembling."

Lindsay took the hand he held out.

"It's fine. Not a tremor," she said, after a while.

"Really?" A glint of amusement appeared in Colin's innocent blue eyes. "I *am* surprised. Try the pulse."

Lindsay tried the pulse. She frowned, concentrating.

"It's fast," she pronounced eventually. "Definitely feverish."

"I thought it might be. Entirely the fault of the evil genius, of course."

In his easy way, Colin then began to discourse on the subject of the evil genius—or Prospero, as he had apparently now decided to call him. He moved on to shred the character of the famous actor Nic Hicks. He did this with some wit, but Lindsay was distracted and listened with only half her attention. Various suspicions were inching their way forward from the back of her mind, and she wanted to examine them in detail. This was not easy; they kept entangling themselves in Colin's sentences and the choice she was trying to make from the menu. Concentrate, she said to herself.

In the first place, there was, possibly, an alteration in Colin's demeanor tonight; she could have sworn that there was a flirtatiousness in his manner when he took her hand, and an accomplished flirtatiousness at that. Perhaps, though, this thought was unworthy and had been planted by Pixie. In the second place, there was the question of Colin's suit. She had never seen him in a suit before, and this three-piece masterly garment, dark gray in color with the narrowest, most discreet of pinstripes, was of a kind Lindsay had believed almost extinct. It could only have come from Savile Row, and it made her understand what Englishmen meant when they spoke of having a suit *built*. The suit; the choice of restaurant; Colin's reception there . . . the suspicions swelled and took on a monstrous shape. It occurred to Lindsay that, judging from this evidence, Colin Lascelles might be rich.

This idea distressed Lindsay, who was wary of the rich in general, and wary of rich men in particular. Sooner or later, a lordliness and a crass insensitivity, which in her experience almost always accompanied wealth, became apparent. Sensing Colin's gaze, she bent her head to the menu. Fish or meat; flirtatious or merely friendly; rich or normal?

"I can't decide," she said.

"Well, the caviar's always reliable," Colin said, in a gentle, helpful way. "If you like caviar, of course. The lobster's generally excellent. Great-Aunt Emily swears by the softshell crabs."

Lindsay saw, in both senses, her entrée.

"I shall begin with the lobster," she said. "Cold, poached. Then the grilled sole, I think. . . . That's a wonderful suit, Colin; is it in honor of Aunt Emily?"

"Most certainly not. It's in your honor. I'm glad you like it; I found it in an Oxfam shop. I'll have the same as you, I think."

He placed these orders with a waiter who had instantly appeared at his elbow. He opened the tome of a wine list, flicked the pages briefly, closed it, and made a tiny movement. The wine waiter materialized.

"They have some very good Montrachet, Lindsay, would you like that?"

Lindsay, to whom alcohol was alcohol, and useful when nervous, felt pretty sure that she had drunk Montrachet on some occasion and liked it very much. She said so.

"I love all sauvignons," she added.

"Oh." Colin looked confused. "Well, this is a white burgundy, but if you'd rather have . . ."

"No, no, no. I love burgundies too. I love everything, in fact."

Colin smiled. "We'll stay with the champagne for the moment," he said. "Then, the Le Montrachet DRC, I think. The 1978. If you'd bring it with the fish." The waiter departed.

Colin gave Lindsay what she felt was a curious look.

"Better be prudent, I think," he remarked, in a meaningful way.

"Yes, yes," said Lindsay, still weighing the provenance of the marvelous suit. "Ever since that lunch in Oxford, I've reformed. I'll never get drunk again in my life."

"Nor I," said Colin, laying some stress on this.

"They seem to know you here, Colin?"

"A bit." He met her gaze unwaveringly. "It's because of Aunt Emily. This place is sort of her local."

Lindsay opened her mouth to say, Local, huh? and shut it again.

"Really?" she said, in an encouraging tone, and, to her surprise, found no more was needed; Colin was off and away at once.

"Well, she lives not far from here, you see. She has an apartment in this amazing building, 1910, Hillyard White was the architect. I wanted you to see it—that's partly why I thought we'd pop in on Emily tonight. It's one of the most extraordinary buildings in Manhattan, and it's absolutely untouched—not a single detail despoiled, for once. Only the Dakota is in the same class, but even the Dakota can't compete. The staircase . . ."

Lindsay had no intention of being deflected by architecture.

"But you obviously come here often yourself, Colin?" she said.

"If I'm in New York, I usually drop in—with Emily. She's been coming here for about three hundred years, you see; in fact I think she used to come here with her father. And she first brought me here when I was eight, so it's become a tradition, and it always cheers her up. She gets lonely—not that she'd ever admit that. Too many of her old friends are dead or housebound, and Emily's still packed with energy, indefatigable, a true daughter of the revolution. . . . I hope you'll like her. I do, very much."

Lindsay was impressed by this speech, for its sincerity was transparent, and she warmed to Colin. Her suspicions backed off a little way, and Lindsay felt glad. The counsel for the defense was trouncing the prosecution, she decided, as the lobster arrived; Colin was far too sweet-natured to be rich.

"So, is she an aunt on your mother's side or your father's?" Lindsay asked, too occupied by the appearance of the lobster to notice that, at this question, Colin exhibited a faint constraint.

"My mother's. My mother was American." He paused. "She—well, she died when I was eight."

"Oh Colin. I'm so sorry—" Lindsay at once looked up and placed her hand on his arm. To her astonishment, she saw that he was blushing. He blushed slowly and agonizingly, from the neck of his impeccable shirt to his hairline; he blushed like the heroine of a nineteenth-century novel, and Lindsay, appalled that she seemed to have inflicted this, took his hand in hers at once.

"Whatever's wrong, Colin?" she began.

"Everything," Colin burst out. "Why did I do this? Why didn't I *think*? I should have known—you don't like it here, do you? It's not your kind of place. I could tell when we came in—but I thought it might grow on you. And now, you're trying to be polite, but it's a *disaster*. Dragging you off to see my aunt—why did I decide to do that? I must have been mad. Insane. We should be going on to a nightclub, something like that. . . ."

"I hate nightclubs," Lindsay said.

". . . And this place! I must need my head examined. We should have gone somewhere new, somewhere fashionable; one of those minimalist places, in Soho, somewhere like that. Hundreds of tables, lemongrass in everything, Californian food . . ."

"Colin—will you listen to me a minute?"

"I *know* those places. I could have rung them up. *Why* didn't I think of that? Why did I start talking about architecture? *Architecture!* Christ! I could see you were bored; you cut me off, and what do I start on—my *aunt*. My aunt and the evil genius, it's a wonder you haven't gone to sleep. . . ."

"Colin." Lindsay pressed his hand, and the tirade bubbled a bit more, then stopped.

"That's better. Now listen to me. I hate those Soho restaurants. I hate those restaurants wherever they are. I loathe lemongrass, I loathe the waiters auditioning when they recite the menu, I loathe the table-hopping and the celebrity-spotting. I like it *here*; I like it very much."

"Really?" Colin looked at her in a doubtful way. "You're not just saying that?"

"No. I promise you I'm not. It's wonderful here—an immense treat. This is the best champagne I've ever tasted in my life. I'm looking forward to meeting your aunt and I'm quite looking forward to eating this lobster, which I'll do once you've calmed down. And while I eat it, you can talk to me about architecture, or your family, or the evil genius, and I won't be bored in the least. Now . . ." She hesitated. "I'll tell you what was worrying me earlier, if you like."

"Go on."

"To tell you the truth, I was mainly worrying about the bill, because it's going to be catastrophic, Colin."

"Well, yes." Colin was showing signs of recovery. "I expect it is."

"Exactly. So you shouldn't have done this. It was very sweet of you, but it wasn't necessary."

"Sweet?" Colin frowned, but the glint of amusement had returned to his eyes.

"All right—kind, thoughtful. But unless you've come into a fortune recently . . ."

"Recently? No, alas." Colin smiled. "But Tomas Court is quite generous, you know, Lindsay. It won't hurt to push the boat out a bit, once or twice."

He answered her with such frankness, with such an engaging smile, that Lindsay felt ashamed of her suspicions. They were low things and they all scurried away at once. Her face cleared and she gave a sigh of relief.

"Well, I'm very glad about the fortune," she said. "I hate riches; they get in the way, don't you think? You know, Scott Fitzgerald, 'The rich are different from you and me'—all that."

"Have some more champagne." Colin paused. "I agree. A very good quotation, that."

"But you're being extravagant," Lindsay continued. "So I want you to promise we can split the bill, then it will only be semicatastrophic, all right?"

Colin hesitated then. He looked at Lindsay for a while, an odd expression in his eyes. He looked faintly bewildered, Lindsay thought, and faintly stunned, as if some unknown assailant had crept up behind him and struck a blow from the back. Then he began to smile. The eyebrows Katya had described as diabolic rose in two quizzical peaks; the blue eyes lit with a deepening warmth and amusement. Katya had been right, Lindsay realized, and so had Pixie: Colin Lascelles was not only good-looking, he was an attractive man. He did not attract her, obviously, but she was beginning to see how he could be extremely attractive to someone else.

"It's a deal," he said. "You can eat your lobster now, but you'd better take your hand back first."

Lindsay, who had forgotten where her hand was, removed it from his. She began to eat the lobster, and very delicious it was. As she did so, she considered Colin's character, which she now felt she understood. He was very English, she thought—that was the key. English, sweet-natured, perhaps not as inexperienced with women as she had previously imagined, touchingly vulnerable and incapable of subterfuge or deceit. She was beginning to see now why Rowland liked him so much, for Colin, like Rowland, could be both dry and ironic. Of course, he seemed younger than Rowland, although they must be almost the same age, and because there were no complications here, she found him easier to talk to than Rowland ever was. She must remember, she resolved, how easily his confidence was dented—almost as easily as her own. Sometimes, in his insecurities, he reminded her of Tom; which was why she felt quite protective toward him, she realized, and, glancing up, anxious to allay any further uncertainties, she gave him a warm, somewhat maternal smile. Colin, noting the quality of that smile, felt a passing frustration. Since he was indeed very English, he did not express it, but concealed it behind his excellent manners—natural to him, but also useful on occasions such as this.

He reminded himself that he had just improvised—and improvised with some brilliance, he felt. A combination of luck and guile had enabled him to steer them around a very tight corner. Now they were back on the open road. Open the throttle, accelerate, he reminded himself, and patted the breast pocket of his masterly jacket to make sure a certain envelope he had brought with him—the fatal envelope—was in place.

It was. He debated the best moment to produce it: before going on to Emily's? Over coffee here, perhaps? Or later, when he escorted Lindsay back to the Pierre? He decided he would play it by ear. In the meantime, he thought, it would be wise, given Lindsay's opinions, to be more careful. Lindsay noticed *details*, ill considered details, giveaway details such as suits.

When Lindsay was looking away, he seized his opportunity, and, hidden by the tablecloth, removed from his wrist the leather-strapped, wafer-thin gold Patek Philippe watch. He could hardly claim to have found *that* at Oxfam. He stuffed it into his pocket, feeling much more confident at once.

"So," said Lindsay, leaning forward and smiling in the most enchanting and feminine way, "tell me more about your aunt's apartment building, Colin."

Colin, who was not intoxicated, instantly felt so.

"Well," he said, "it's called the Conrad and it's a very strange, even sinister place."

Chapter 9

Alone in his loft at Tribeca, earlier that evening, Tomas Court had also been conducting a dialogue about the Conrad, a dialogue none the less forceful for being imagined. The two speakers were himself and his wife, and the dialogue began as soon as Thalia, Mario, and Colin left.

The minute the door closed on them, it burst out in his mind, a cacophony of contradictions, interruptions, and pleas, of ill-phrased assertions and ill-timed *non sequiturs*. Court stood quietly in the shadows of the room, outside the circle of bright light that lit the worktable, and let this chaos into his mind. He was used to this form of possession; when he ceased working, a process that demanded all his energy and willpower, he always felt drained and bloodless, emptied and light-headed; an energy vacuum had been created, and into this vacuum anything, including malevolence, might rush.

Today it was to be the Conrad. So be it, he thought, and waited, not allowing his breathing to quicken or tighten. He knew that, given time, this cacophony and havoc would resolve itself. He fixed his eyes on one feature of the room—it never mattered which feature, and in this case it happened to be the bars of the window, opposite which he stood. The bars, eight feet tall, and at least six across, formed a crucifix shape, which amused him distantly, since he was without religious belief. He looked at this cross, and was aware that outside in the street some absurd commotion was taking place; he could hear that his English location manager was giving vent to his feelings, but as far as Court was concerned he might just as well have been shouting his protests in Urdu. Lascelles's laments were a cry from another country and Court felt an absolute lack of curiosity in anything Lascelles said.

After a while, as Lascelles's voice died away and silence fell in the room, the dialogue with his wife quieted; her interruptions became fewer, then ceased altogether; he was left listening to his own voice. Why? said his voice. Why, why, why? Why live there? Why invite rejection? Why do this?

He felt stronger at once, the moment of mental palsy over and done with, he told himself. The *why* questions were familiar demons; they had been plaguing him for months. It was now safe to move, safe to begin functioning again, although he truly functioned, as he well knew, only when he worked. He picked up one of the cardboard boxes that littered the loft, and carried it across to the circle of light on his black worktable.

He took no second look at the welter of colored papers still strewn across its surface; he had not the least inclination either to reexamine them or tidy them up. Each day, embarking on work, whether here, on location, or in a studio, he would know, before he began, exactly where he aimed, and how much expenditure of spirit, energy, and willpower would be necessary that day to take him there. When he reached that preordained point, he stopped, and had been known to do so in midsentence, or midtake. If necessary, he would drive or drag others on with him to this stopping place; if necessary, he would manipulate, annoy, abuse, frighten, trick, or charm them *en route*, but get there he would.

He opened the lid of the box and moved the tumble of shooting schedules to one side to make space. During the day, these papers held magic, for they were the raw materials of his art, as essential to it, in their way, as celluloid, cameras, actors, and light. Now, since he was at rest, they were inert, and merely his instruments; they were without power until tomorrow at seven in the morning, when he again picked them up.

From the box he took out the material that various researchers had been gathering for him for months. Every scrap of information here concerned the Conrad. There were old architectural journals; batches of photographs new and old; photocopies of the original plans for the building, plans that had been lying in some city hall archive for decades. Court laid them all out on the table and began to examine them minutely; it was not the first time he had done this.

He examined the, to him, grotesque facade of the Conrad, with its baroque excesses and its Gothic turrets. It seemed to him that the architect had given the building a forbidding and secretive look. He disliked the extravagance of its great gaping maw of an entrance; he disliked the *oeil-de-boeuf* windows that ornamented those turrets and punctuated the roofline, and that gave the building a menacing, many-eyed look, as if it were continuously hungry, and continuously vigilant.

His wife was seeking to buy apartment 3, situated on the north corner of the building, overlooking Central Park. She had already viewed this apartment several times; she had refused to allow him to accompany her—proving to be obstinate on this point.

"Tomas," she had said, "you don't want me to live there and you don't believe I'm going to be allowed to live there. No. What's the point?"

Thwarted in this desire, he had turned to this research material instead. Now, he inspected the architectural plans, drawn up by Hillyard White over eighty years before. He traced the walls of apartment 3, examined its orientation, dimensions, and fenestration. He could see the disposition of the rooms; the photographs and descriptions in the various books and journals gave him an idea of how this interior might look. He could half see some rich space with many closets, with rooms that led into further rooms, and with yet more rooms beyond that. The apartment was very large; he now realized for the first time that it was a duplex. Toward the rear, there was a second story, secreted away; this would be the site of the main bedrooms; this was where his wife would sleep. His wife had her final meeting with the board of the Conrad, with the committee who would decide her fate, the following morning; she would be given their decision then. Suppose that decision, against all the odds, was yes? How did you *reach* that second story, that bedroom?

He bent more closely to the plans, which, to a nonexpert, were not easy to decipher. There was the staircase—he saw it now—but how did you reach the staircase?

He only half saw, half glimpsed, he realized. It was like looking into some marvelous lighted room from the street outside, and then, just when all its secrets were about to be revealed, some officious person came along and closed the shutters in his face.

He was suddenly seized with anger; his hands began to shake. With a furious, violent gesture, he swept the papers to the floor. Immediately, the chaos returned, and those two voices began arguing again in his head. "Oh, it torments me, Tomas, it torments me," his wife said. This time, he shouted his wife down and drowned her out, anger giving him an eloquence that, when they actually had this argument, he rarely possessed.

He spelled out to her the insanity of this plan, a misconception from the first. Why was she continuing with the shaming procedures inflicted on her by the Conrad board, who for months now had been vetting her finances and every other aspect of her life? Why had she hired, at huge expense, first a real-estate broker, then one of Manhattan's most expensive law firms to press her suit? All this money and effort would be wasted, he shouted, raining his reasons down on her now-bowed, imagined head. Neither money nor lawyers turned the key of admission at the Conrad, and if the broker—some man called Jules McKechnie—was claiming otherwise, she was being taken for a ride. Could she not *see* that?

The Conrad, he reminded her, was a cooperative; its board could choose whom to refuse and whom to admit. For decades, the Conrad board had weaseled its way around the law, in particular the laws regarding discrimination on grounds of color, race, or sex. It was a *bastion*, and it did not raise its drawbridge to actresses, divorced women with young children, or the *nouveau riche*. Did she not know, had her precious broker and her overpriced lawyers not *checked*: no member of the acting profession, let alone a movie star of her fame, had ever lived in the Conrad, though many had sought admission. And no young children had been brought up in the Conrad for a quarter of a century at least.

The occupants of the Conrad, he continued, were aging, rich, white, Anglo-Saxon Protestants. They believed in the Social Register, since they, and everyone they cared to know, were listed in it; they believed in money, provided it was inherited, and thus disinfected of all taint; and they believed in an Episcopalian God, while failing to practice any of His teachings. They are *evil*, he thundered; that building is *evil*, and I will not allow my son to be brought up in that place.

"*Our* son," his wife's voice quietly corrected him, and he heard again her one attempt to justify her decision. "I want to live there, Tomas. I see it differently from you. I shall feel safe there. This has nothing to do with you. It's *my* choice."

That reply, which had infuriated him when she gave it, and which infuriated him now, explained nothing. It was in his wife's nature to explain herself and her actions as little as possible, and it was this intransigency in her, this refusal ever to allow him to be sure he understood her, that bound him to her—or so he sometimes thought.

In a sudden rage with her and with himself, he slammed out of the apartment, wearing only a jacket and unprepared for the cold of the streets. He had a car available to him, and a discreet, reliable driver whom he could have called upon, but he disliked others knowing his movements as much as he disliked them knowing his thoughts, so he flagged down a cab, knowing he should go back for a coat, but refusing to do so. He had to be careful of cold air, of course, just as he had to be careful of dust, pollen, pollution, smoke, and a thousand other hidden substances in the air; this disability he loathed and resented. His anger deepening, he told the cab driver to take him uptown to the Carlyle, where his son would be waiting for him. Then, changing his mind, and knowing he needed something else, he told him to go to the Minskoff Theater, where his wife would be onstage, and that night's performance of *Estella* would be taking place.

Why? Why? Why? This question pursued him uptown in the cab; it pursued him across the noisy, crowded space of Times Square, where he abandoned the cab, and it pursued him to the theater, where he paused, looking at the lights that spelled out his wife's name on the marquee.

Why live there, and why exclude him in this way, when he was sure she still loved him and wished for a reconciliation as much as he did? Why, when she was eager to work with him, did she still refuse to live with him? Did her continuing fear of Joseph King explain this decision—or was there some other, hidden reason? He glanced over his shoulder, having, as he often did, the sensation that he was being watched. No one appeared to be watching him, so he turned down the small alleyway leading to the stage door and entered the theater, feeling as he had on many occasions that he would find the answers to all his questions here, that they lay very close, within reach.

He was known at the stage door, and no one detained him there, for these visitations of his were frequent. He went first to Natasha's dressing room, where his way was blocked, first by the strange androgynous creature Natasha insisted on having as her dresser, and then by one of the bodyguards—the favorite bodyguard, the Texan.

Court was a tall man himself, but the Texan was even taller. Court looked coldly at his blond, muscled good looks. He looked like an overgrown child, and was possibly more intelligent than he appeared.

"I don't see that you can offer my wife much protection if she's onstage, and you're here by her dressing room," he said.

"I agree. But Ms. Lawrence insists."

"Give my wife a message, would you? Tell her I need to talk to her. I'm going up to the Carlyle now to see my son. I'll wait there until she gets back after the show."

An expression of doubt passed across the man's face. "I'm afraid she's going out after the show, sir. She's having dinner with her real-estate broker, Jules McKechnie."

"Then tell her I'll call her tomorrow."

"I surely will." He paused. Tomas Court felt his blue eyes, eyes that appeared as innocent as a summer's sky, rest on his face. "Is there anything else I can do for you, Mr. Court?"

"No, there is not."

Court turned away. He went into the backstage maze at the Minskoff, along corridors, through fire doors, up flight after flight of stone stairs. He paused on one of the upper landings, a warning constriction beginning to tighten around his chest. Then he went on, up more stairs, until, right at the top of the building, he came to the place where he had to be next.

He opened a series of doors and stepped into the lighting box, high at the back of the auditorium, above its topmost tier seats. This dark, boxed-in coffin of a room, glass-fronted, soundproof, jutted forward over the heads of the audience and gave him an eagle's-eye view of the stage. The two technicians there, used to these unannounced visits of his, looked up, nodded, then returned their attention to the winking lights of their computer consoles. One silently passed him a pair of headphones, and Court stood there, holding them, watching the console, watching their hands moving back and forth among the switches and slides and myriad tiny green and red cue lights. He had a confused sense of being piloted, of being in flight; they were taking off, banking, gaining height. He felt that at any minute, all the answers to his questions would be there in his mind, and he would understand his wife.

He took a step toward the glass wall, felt a second's vertiginous fear of falling as he saw the deep, dark declivity of the auditorium open out beneath; then moved again, and saw across the gulf of the audience, infinitely distant, silent and gesticulating, the figure of Estella, the figure of his wife.

He watched her lips move, her mouth open and close, and her throat pulse. He watched her tenderly as, beautiful in her young girl's first-act white dress, she moved center stage. He savored her silence, then, with a slow reluctance, he put on the headphones. The music hit him in a wave; soaring up through the currents of the song came the sound of Estella's voice.

They had reached the fourth scene of the first act; he was hearing the duet between that cruel child, Estella, and poor, humiliated, confused, besotted Pip. Court had no liking for musicals, most of which he despised, and scant admiration for the composer of this one. He had advised Natasha against taking this part, and had had forebodings of failure for her when she did. None of those factors was relevant now.

This particular song, one of the great hits of the show, was not even a song he liked. He could see that technically it was difficult, and that melodically it was intricate—it interwove major and minor keys in a haunting way—but he had always found its bittersweetness not to his taste. Even so, it left him defenseless. To his anger and incomprehension, the power of his wife's song bypassed his mind and sent a shock to his heart, just as—no matter how he resisted—it always did.

Again he felt that warning constriction in his chest; he heard himself make some strange wounded sound; he removed the headphones and fumbled his way out of the darkness of the box. He descended the stone staircases without seeing them, still hearing the voice of his wife, both on the speaker system and in his head. Halfway down the stairs, he took a wrong turn and found himself lost in that labyrinth of backstage passageways. He turned, leaned against a wall, retraced his steps, descended again, and arrived, at last, at the stage door. He ignored the man on duty there, who, on seeing him, rose with an exclamation of concern. Pushing his way through the doors, he fought to control his breathing and fought to control the anxiety that always made these paroxysms worse. Finding himself in that dimly lit alleyway, he blessed its darkness; he moved away from the door, away from prying eyes, and slumped back against a wall, now gasping for breath.

It was a bad asthma attack and the pain was acute. He listened to the sirens of this city, to the incessant growl of automobiles pumping out their poisons, as he fumbled for the inhaler he always carried. He tilted his head back and depressed the plunger once, then again, sucking hard. At the third attempt the beta-adrenoceptor stimulants at last took effect. They soothed his breathing, if not his mind, and the fist that had been squeezing his lungs slackened its grip.

He waited, breathing quietly and shallowly. Two women entered through the stage door; one man came out. No one took the least notice of him and perhaps no one saw him; Court, who hated for others to witness these attacks, was grateful for this.

He watched the man, the unremarkable man, walk down the alleyway, turn into the street beyond, and disappear. It came to him, in the clear but distanced way that ideas often did after an attack such as this, that the man could be Joseph King, who—as he had informed his wife—could be alive or dead. That man could be King, and so could any other man he encountered today, tomorrow, any day of the week.

King could be driving his taxicab, or taking his order in a restaurant; King could be the man he sat next to in a screening room, or met briefly at some movie festival. King might have worked for him, or with Natasha in the past—this last suspicion, that King was connected with the movie industry in some way, having deepened recently, for King's knowledge of movies, he had come to see, was as deep and as intimate as his knowledge of Tomas Court's wife.

King was no one, and could be almost anyone; indeed, when Court slept badly and had nightmares, as he often did, it was in Court's own mirror that he often manifested himself. And King, who had administered his poison so well, pouring the substance into his ear drop by drop, was not a man who was easily killed off. Court thought of him as immortal and invisible; even if he were dead—and Court never felt he was—he lived on in the minds of those he persecuted. In this capacity lay his peculiar evil and his peculiar strength.

Tall, short, dark, fair, old, young? After five years he still could answer none of these questions. He leaned back against the wall, waiting for his heart rate to slow and his breathing to relax. When they had done so, he moved away from the protection of the wall and began to walk slowly up the alley. He stationed himself at the curb in the street beyond, averting his eyes from the flash of his wife's name on the marquee. He watched the flow of traffic, waiting for the one cab with its light lit that would take him out of this cold foul city air and uptown to his son. Cab after cab, all occupied, and he could sense that although the pain was subduing, his disquiet was not.

Natasha had claimed, closing her bedroom door to him some months before their separation and divorce, that it was he himself who gave King power by believing, or half believing, by dwelling on all the lies King wrote or said. She further claimed that his obsession with King had not only poisoned their marriage and permeated his work, but was slowly but surely eating away at his health. "That man will be the death of you," she had once said.

Court did not view his concern with King as an obsession, and if it were, that was excusable—presumably he was allowed to be obsessed with a man who knew his wife's and son's movements so precisely, and constantly issued threats. But he did acknowledge some truth in her remarks: he admitted that, for several years now, it had been King's actions or communications that brought on the worst of his asthma attacks.

The cure, then, ought to be to forget King, to put out of his mind all those whispering suggestions King wrote, or said—a process that should become easier if King had been silenced and was actually dead. Yet Tomas Court was not sure he wanted to be cured; there was a part of him, and a vibrant part, that clung to King, even as he watched him destroy his marriage and endanger his health. He now missed King's communications; sometimes, at night, when he lay on his bed, listening to replays of King's past calls, he found himself frustrated at the five months of silence. What he wanted was a new message, another revelation, an update.

He needed that dark side, he thought, as a cab finally pulled in at the curb. He needed to listen to the unspeakable. He wondered, in a distanced way, as the cab eased forward into gridlocked traffic, whether he ought to explain that to his wife. Not necessary, he decided; such ambivalences lay at the very heart of his marriage, as he had been reminded when assaulted by the power of his wife's singing, tonight.

"So this is the Conrad," Colin Lascelles said to Lindsay, coming to a halt beneath a huge encrusted entrance portico. "Now do you see what I mean? It is powerful, don't you think?"

"I certainly do see what you mean. Dear God, Colin . . ." Lindsay looked up at the portico, which towered over them both. The architect of the Conrad, as Colin had just been telling her over dinner, had been a strange man; the twin Conrad brothers, both financiers, who had commissioned him to design the building, had been equally strange and—if Colin's account was accurate—the building had a strange checkered past. It boasted several ghosts, the most fearsome and vengeful of which was said to be Anne Conrad, unmarried sister to the twins, who in 1915, or thereabouts, had leaped to her death from one of the windows of the apartment she shared with her brothers. Stepping back to examine the Conrad's facade, Lindsay wondered which window this was.

Anne Conrad's manifestations were infrequent but ill

omened, Colin had said. Further details had not been forthcoming; Lindsay had intended to prompt Colin, but now that she saw this building, she changed her mind. She was too suggestible: if Colin described these hauntings, she might imagine herself into an encounter with the dead woman, who had been young, beautiful—and deranged, or so people said, Colin had added, by way of an afterthought.

She must have passed the building dozens of times, Lindsay thought, yet she had never paused to look at it. Now that she did, and at night too, she realized just how magnificent and grim it was. This was how she had always imagined the House of Usher might look. She glanced across, over her shoulder, to the great tract of darkness at the heart of Manhattan that was Central Park, then looked back more closely at the Conrad's huge entrance mouth.

A cluster of liver-colored Corinthian columns flanked its approach steps, giving it the air of a somber classical temple. These columns supported a vast dark carved pediment; even Lindsay's untrained eye could see, however, that the proportions here were infelicitous, for the pediment was oversize, so that the pillars seemed oppressed by its weight. They looked squat, and their appearance was not enhanced by the surface treatment of their massive stone plinths. "Vermiculation," according to Colin, was the correct term for this doubtful form of decoration; to Lindsay's eyes, the plinths looked as if their stone had been eaten away by millions of blind, hungry worms—or maggots, perhaps.

She gave an involuntary shiver. She began to see that Hillyard White's heart had not been in the rigors of classicism in any case. There might be a suggestion of a Greekish temple, but the whole facade was a monstrous and heterogeneous sprouting of embellishments. This detail had been plundered from the French, this from the Venetians, this from the Egyptians, that from the Spanish; a smorgasbord of past centuries and architectural styles had been gobbled up and spewed forth.

"Dear God, what's *that*?" she said, realizing that even the pillars were not unadorned, and that from some clustering stone vines mounting the wall behind them, a dark face was peering out.

"A gargoyle." Leaning across, Colin patted its ugly head

with affection. "I wouldn't look too closely, Lindsay—some of the detailing is quite nasty."

"What's that in his *mouth*? Oh—" Lindsay frowned; from one angle the gargoyle was biting the head off a snake; from another angle it was possibly not a snake, and the gargoyle was otherwise employed.

"In we go," Colin said, somewhat hurriedly, taking her arm.

He drew her into a foyer (*Citizen Kane,* Lindsay thought) and greeted first a doorman, then a porter. It took Lindsay a moment even to see the porter, who was dwarfed by the altar that served as his desk. They approached a wall of linenfold paneling, and Lindsay realized that although she knew how she had entered this cathedral—the entrance maw was somewhere at the other end of this nave, several miles back—she could see no other way out of it.

"Full of tricks, this building," said Colin, delighted. "I did warn you. *Not* easy to find your way around unless you know it. Even Hillyard White's plans are deceptive—which is one of the reasons why it's so secure, of course."

He glanced around at the porter, then smiled at Lindsay.

"Don't worry," he said. "It gets worse, or better, depending on your point of view. Are you of a nervous disposition?"

"Very."

"Hold my hand." He nodded at the porter. "We'll go up by the main stairs, Giancarlo."

There was a low buzzing sound, and the linenfold in front of them opened up. They walked through into an inner hall, the paneling closing behind them with a hiss.

"There is an elevator," Colin said, "but I thought you wouldn't mind walking up. Emily's only on the second floor, and I didn't want you to miss this."

"No, *indeed*," Lindsay said.

She walked forward a few paces, across a cold paved floor. She looked at the wide bloodred-carpeted oak staircase rising in front of her, which was lit at intervals by statues of blackamoors holding lamps aloft. It rose before her, then twisted back, and was cantilevered, story by story, so she found she was looking at the undersides of the stairs as they mounted up and up to a huge domed space that settled over the stairwell like a lid. She was in the gut of the building, she realized, and all the apartments must lead off this vast central digestive tract. The dome was at least ten stories above her head, each floor was galleried, and an army could have marched up the stairs ten abreast, yet the effect was claustrophobic. The space was hushed, warm, and curiously expectant, as if the stairs, blackamoors, and shadowy galleries were waiting to see what these two new arrivals might do next.

"What do you think? Monstrous, isn't it?" Colin was looking around him with affection and pride. "*Sublimely* monstrous. I never get over it."

The fat coils of the radiator next to Lindsay emitted a digestive gurgle, then a faint, satisfied hiss. She shivered again.

"Hitchcock would have killed for that staircase," she said.

"Wouldn't he just?" Colin sighed. "Embarrassing, those blackamoors. There was a move to get rid of them, a few years back. Emily nipped that in the bud *very* quickly."

"She likes them? Colin—she can't possibly like them."

"I'm afraid she does. She's not exactly politically correct." He hesitated. "The thing is, she was right, from a purist point of view; they *are* original. And Emily's lived in this building all her life. In fact, she was born here. In fact . . ."

Lindsay, who was growing less keen on this visit to Aunt Emily by the second, sensed that Colin too might be having second thoughts. His manner, confident a moment before, was now becoming doubtful. She was beginning to recognize the symptoms of Colin's insecurities, she thought.

"I'm just wondering," she began, "isn't it a bit *late*, this visit, Colin? We stayed longer in the restaurant than we meant to do, and . . . She's eighty-five years old, after all. . . ."

"Oh, *that's* not the problem. Emily's a night bird; she keeps very strange hours. She nods off during the day, though she denies that, of course, and sometimes it's hard to know when she *is* asleep. She'll be in her chair, I'll tiptoe about, and then suddenly she'll speak and make me jump like hell. . . . So this is early evening for Emily. Around midnight, she gets very lively indeed."

Lindsay was now sure she recognized the symptoms of nerves, which included loquaciousness.

"But there *is* a problem," she said. "Come on, Colin, what is it?"

"Well, she's a bit deaf."

"And?"

Colin considered. "She can be a bit *odd*," he said finally.

Lindsay wondered whether he might mean senile. Dotty? Eccentric? Slightly demented? Ninety-five percent crazed? Since Colin was given both to overstatement *and* understatement, his remarks could be difficult to interpret. He was now looking both anxious again and downcast. Lindsay took his arm. "Well, I'm very glad you're with me," she said. "With you here, I feel safe."

Immediately upon saying this, it struck her that she truly meant it; Colin's presence, for reasons she could not exactly define, was reassuring. Her compliment, or perhaps the fact that she took his arm, seemed to allay his anxieties; his confidence returned at once.

"Not *very* odd," he amplified, leading her toward the staircase, "just odd occasionally. A bit of a tease, you might say. You may find it helps if you remember that. . . ."

Lindsay braced herself for this teasing great-aunt. The stairs were not really *Psycho* material, she decided—more *Gone with the Wind*, more Tara. Hello, Scarlett and Rhett, she thought, as they began to climb them, dreamily imagining herself as a feisty O'Hara, and Rowland McGuire as an improvement on Clark Gable. Hello, Polanski, and hello *Repulsion*, she thought, as they turned into a long, galleried corridor, where hands thrust from walls holding lamps. Colin rang the doorbell to Emily's apartment and Lindsay waited for Dracula's servant to answer it. Instead, Mrs. Danvers opened the door, and led them into a very large and daunting drawing room with a du Maurier whisk of her skirts.

An old, a very old, very wrinkled, and very imperious woman held out her hand; introductions were made. Lindsay looked at Aunt Emily narrowly. Well, hello Miss Havisham, she thought.

"I want a word with you. You're late," Angelica said, as Tomas Court entered the quiet living room of his wife's Carlyle suite. Court moved past her without greeting her or looking at her, but his manner was often curt, even rude, and Angelica was used to this.

"I've been talking to the bodyguard. . . ." he said.

"Which bodyguard?"

"The one here." Court's manner was irritable. "John. Jack—whatever his name is."

"Jack." Angelica gave him a dismissive glance. "That's why you're over an hour late? You've been talking to the bodyguard for an *hour*? Jonathan's been waiting up for you. . . ."

"I was delayed. I got held up."

"He won't go to sleep until he's seen you." She paused; Court had not looked at her once and had now turned his back. She sighed. "Maria stayed on to sit with him. He's showing her his new animal books. He wanted to show them to you. There's one on big cats."

"Maria?" Court said.

Angelica sighed again. "You've met her. You met her the other week. The one who comes to give Natasha her massage before the show sometimes. The aromatherapist. Dark hair, glasses. Jonathan likes her; she's a nice girl."

"Well get rid of her. There's enough women in and out of this apartment as it is."

Angelica, used to this complaint, did not reply. She left the room, and in the distance, Court heard the sound of women's voices. The aromatherapist, the voice coach, the two secretaries, the yoga expert who taught Natasha relaxation techniques, the personal trainer, also female; Natasha's days seemed to him spent amid a retinue of female helpers and supporters, and he loathed the way in which they treated her with a reverent concern, tending the hive, tending their queen, cosseting and protecting, grooming, feeding, and honing. He found it unhealthy; Natasha had always had a tendency to surround herself with priestesses, and since their divorce, the tendency had worsened; he had often told her this.

"Hi. Good evening," said a woman's voice. Court glanced around to see Angelica and this Maria, who was being helped into her coat. Like most of Natasha's priestesses, she was ugly, Court noted; overweight, cheaply dressed, with greasy hair tied back in an untidy bun, and hideous thick-lensed spectacles. He was making her nervous, he saw, as she glanced at Angelica in a faltering way, and then gave him a shy smile that was not, he supposed, unsweet.

"Your son's still wide awake," she said. "We've had a lovely time. He's a really bright little kid. He's waiting to show you his whale book, Mr. Court. . . ." She glanced again at Angelica. "I thought—better avoid the fairy stories tonight. You know, if he's still having those nightmares . . . so we just looked at the animal books. He's so cute. Hey, it's late. . . . I'd better be off."

Tomas Court gave her a curt nod; he listened to the sounds of female conversation and laughter as Angelica showed her out.

"Nightmares?" he said, when Angelica returned, closing the door behind her. "What nightmares? Natasha never mentioned that."

"He wakes up sometimes." She avoided his gaze. "It's been going on for a while now."

"How long?"

"Well, it started around the time of the divorce, then it got better for a bit. Now it's started up again."

"He never gets nightmares when he comes out to Montana. He was fine last summer. It's this place. Cooped up here; his mother out night after night."

"She has to work. The run's nearly over anyway. She'll be leaving the show any day now, then . . ."

"Well, it can't be soon enough. I don't know why she did it in the first place." He gave an irritable sigh. "I'll have to talk to her about this. If Jonathan has nightmares, I should be informed. Why wasn't I?"

"You didn't ask, I guess."

Angelica's tone was insolent, but then she never bothered to disguise her dislike of him. It was, indeed, more than dislike; Angelica's hostility to him had always been unwavering and forceful; it was returned in good measure. The best that could be said of their relationship was that they eyed one another with the respect of combatants fighting their own weight.

In their contests, unceasing since his marriage, Tomas Court had had one supreme advantage: he was male, and he was the husband, with all the husband's rights. This advantage, as they were both aware, had diminished since the divorce.

"Are you okay?" Angelica said now, looking him up and down. She always delighted, as Court well knew, in the least evidence of his physical disability. "You're white. You don't look so good. You had an attack?"

"I'm fine." He turned away. "The pollution's bad. The traffic was bad. I'm tired. I've been working since five-thirty this morning. You can make me some coffee. Bring it through to Jonathan's room. . . ."

"You want it black?"

"Yes, I do. I'm going to wait for Natasha—"

"I wouldn't do that. She'll be late. She told you, she's having dinner with that fancy broker of hers after the show, then she has an early start in the morning. The trainer comes at seven. She's having breakfast with Jules McKechnie, then . . ."

"Dinner *and* breakfast? Why's that necessary?"

Angelica gave a small gloating smile and a shrug.

"It's the committee meeting at the Conrad tomorrow, and they have to get the details right. It's important to Natasha— and she's nervous. She doesn't want anything going wrong, and it's Friday the thirteenth tomorrow—not too auspicious, right?"

Tomas Court profoundly hoped it would *not* be auspicious. He might have liked to say this; he might have liked to question Angelica further; he would certainly have liked to know whether Natasha was dining with Jules McKechnie alone, or with others. Just the mention of McKechnie's name set off those Joseph King whisperings in his head; King, his very own Iago, was always prompt on occasions such as this. Such questions, evidence of weakness, would have delighted Angelica. He looked at her bulk, at the flat hard planes of her face, at her small and malicious black eyes, and an exhaustion close to anguish flooded through him. Sometimes, especially after an asthma attack, he no longer had the energy to fight.

"There's something you wanted to say to me?" he asked quietly.

"Sure. I want to know some things. About Joseph King. About what happened in Glacier." She paused. "I know what you told Natasha. . . ."

"I'm sure you do."

"And I want the truth." She hesitated, the hostility in her face softening a little. "I'm here with Jonathan. I'm the one who's right by his side, day and night. I need to know these things."

"I wouldn't argue with that. I had intended—"

"I won't tell Natasha. But I need to know."

Across the space of the room, their eyes met. Court turned to the door.

"Fine," he said, "I'll explain when I've seen Jonathan. Bring the coffee through here instead, Angelica. I won't be long."

"Don't be. It's way past his bedtime; he should be asleep."

"I want to show you the bat book now, Daddy," Jonathan said, "and this one on whales. They *talk* to each other, bats and whales, they have this special language, look. . . ."

Court looked at his small son with sadness and with love; he made an effort, fighting fatigue.

"What, the bats talk to the whales? I didn't know that."

"No." Jonathan laughed. "Don't be silly, Daddy. They talk to each *other*. Bats talk to bats; whales talk to whales. It's *excellent* how they do it. Look—"

Court bent to the books. His son had a touching didacticism, a longing to educate, and a passion for facts. He looked at the diagrams his son was indicating; these diagrams explained bat radar to him, and the frequencies of bat squeaks; similar diagrams, accompanied by a barrage of information, explained the communication systems of whales. His son chattered on and Court sat quietly, holding his hand from time to time, or stroking his hair, and waiting for this room, and his son's presence, to bring him the peace they usually did.

In the recesses of his mind, images stirred; he saw dark leathery shapes flit through a jungle night; he watched lianas coil like pythons, and he saw, rearing up from this terrifying fertility, the hot mouth of some orchidlike flower. "Oh, it torments me; Tomas, it torments me," his wife's voice said. The words had been said many years before, when his wife had been six months pregnant with Jonathan, and had discovered that her husband's infidelities were continuing. Court could not now remember the details of that particular infidelity; he rarely could. It might have been with a man, or with a woman, and it would have been brief, for Court never had prolonged liaisons, and with the exception of his wife, who came into a completely different category, he never had the same sexual partner twice.

These sexual encounters he could walk away from without rancor or regret; they were a brief sharp need, which he could satisfy as quickly and easily as he could hunger or thirst. His wife knew—he had told her often enough—that they in no way impinged on his love for her; that love, the determining force of his life, and the inspiration for much of his work, was unchanging; it would neither alter nor diminish with time. It was one of the many mysteries of his marriage, he thought, turning a page of his son's book, that Natasha both believed in and doubted this love. Perhaps also, like him, she preferred the lightning flash of uncertainties to the long, calm summer of faithful married love. He was not sure on that question. During the course of his marriage, he had given Natasha periods of fidelity and periods of infidelity: he had come to believe that the periods of infidelity, with all their attendant pain, insecurity, and indeed torment, were the ones when their marriage was most alive to her—though he was less certain of that preference since his divorce.

"Look, Daddy," Jonathan said, picking up the whale book again and turning to its photographs. He began to speak of ice floes, of the Arctic, of the unimaginable depths to which, with one flick of their vast tails, these wondrous creatures could dive, and, as he spoke, Court became a little more tranquil; into his mind eddied the memory of his wife as she had been on the day he first met her. She had already been famous; he had been unknown; he had sent her a script, and through the offices of a shared friend, she had agreed to meet him. She had come to the small, humid, cramped office he had been renting in downtown Los Angeles. He had known what was going to happen, and he knew she had also, from the moment she quietly entered the room. Her beauty had astonished him; he had been unprepared for it, even though he had seen her many times on-screen. Her hair was loose on her shoulders, her face was without makeup, and she had been wearing—he could still see its every detail— a simple, cotton, madonna-blue dress.

"Daddy. *Daddy*." Jonathan tugged at his sleeve. "You're not *concentrating*. I'm telling you about the *whales*. They sing to one another—it's like singing. And they can hear one another through the water, from miles away sometimes. . . ." He smiled. "And you're miles away too, Daddy."

"I'm sorry, Jon. I just drifted away a bit. I'm tired I guess. I was thinking about the first time I met Mommy, and how beautiful she was. . . . Now." He looked at his watch. "You should be lying down, young man. You should have been asleep hours ago. Down you go. Let me tuck you in."

He hugged his son tight against him, some emotion he could not define welling up: a rich mixture of love, pain, loss, and fear for his son—none of which could be expressed. His son, small for his age, clung to him; he felt so thin, his father thought, and so light and frail. Tears came to his eyes, and he laid his son down in the bed and tucked him in, averting his face.

"Now tell me," he said, sitting down on the edge of the bed and taking his son's hand in his, "what's all this about nightmares? Is something worrying you, darling?"

"A bit." Jonathan lowered his eyes and began to pleat the edge of his duvet. "It's Thanksgiving soon. Mommy says we'll be living in the Conrad by then. . . ."

"It's possible, darling. It's not fixed."

"Will you be coming for Thanksgiving, Daddy? I hoped you might."

"If you want me there, I'll be there. I'll arrange it with Mommy. You know you don't need to worry about that." He paused. "And just think, very soon after that, we'll all be in England together—for three whole months. I'm looking forward to that."

"I am too." His son's face brightened, then clouded again. "It's just . . ."

"Tell me, Jon."

"I don't really like that Conrad building, Daddy. Mommy says I'll get used to it, but it's spooky. I'll have a big room there, Mommy showed me, with all those closets for my toys, and Mommy knows this artist man, and while we're away in England, she says she'll get him to paint these animals for me, on the walls. Any animals I like."

"Well, that sounds good." Court looked closely at his son. He had a small, somewhat melancholy face, expressive, with its fears and its joys easily read. He pressed his son's hand and added, as if it were an afterthought, "Which artist man is that?"

"He works at the theater; he painted some of the sets for *Estella*. He made that horrible spooky room Miss Havisham has. . . ." He hesitated. "I hated that Miss Havisham. Nasty spooky old witch."

"Well, you know there's no reason to be frightened of her," Court said gently. "That's just an actress playing her—and Miss Havisham doesn't exist; she's just someone made up, for a story."

"I didn't like the artist man much either. . . ." his son continued, in a low voice. "I met him one day when Mommy was rehearsing. He looked at me in this funny way. He shook hands, and he had this horrible damp hand. . . . He looked at Mommy too; he stared. She didn't notice, but I did."

Court felt a quickening of alarm then, but controlled it. He would find out the man's name, he thought wearily, and get him checked out, just as he always did. But Jonathan's reaction probably meant little; it was not the first time he had expressed feelings of this sort. They were a by-product of the restrictions that encompassed him, of the bodyguards, of the constant, unremitting suspicion of every male who came to this apartment, every male who lingered, or approached on the street. King had imprisoned his son, Court thought, as effectively as he had imprisoned Natasha and himself, and Jonathan's fear of strange men, exacerbated by Natasha and Angelica, was a legacy he deeply regretted.

"Jonathan, people do stare at Mommy," he replied now, in as reassuring a manner as he could. "It's because she's famous and because she's beautiful; it doesn't mean anything. Now I want you to promise me—no worrying about this. I'll have a word with Mommy. If you don't like this man, maybe she won't use him. Besides, remember that these Conrad plans may not work out; the people at the Conrad may decide to let someone else have the apartment."

"It's very big, Daddy." His son clasped his hand more tightly. "There's all these rooms. I thought, maybe you might come back and live there too. I wish you would."

The plea in his eyes and in his voice cut Tomas to the heart.

He leaned forward to kiss him, and it was a few minutes before he felt able to trust his voice.

"We'll have to see, my darling. These things—well, they're complicated, you know that. Mommy likes this city more than I do, and it's not very good for my asthma. I imagine we'll sort it all out in the end. Meanwhile, just remember how much I love you and Mommy. Now, lie back and I'll read to you for a bit. . . . Which book? This one?"

Jonathan nodded. The book, one with which Tomas Court was not familiar, was *The Secret Garden*, by Frances Hodgson Burnett. His son found the chapter he wanted and the section he wanted. The story took place in Yorkshire, he said, which was where they would all be going shortly; Court agreed that this was so. It took place in a large house, Jonathan went on; there was a little orphan girl called Mary, who was plain and sour, but got nicer as the book went on; and there was a little boy, called Colin. Colin was ill, his son explained, pointing to the paragraph where his father was to begin reading, and this section here was Jonathan's favorite. Court could see why that might be so, as soon as he began reading. Like Jonathan, the boy in this story was isolated and troubled; the chosen chapter concerned Mary's reaction when she awoke to the sound of Colin's cries in a strange house at night. The girl went in search of him, Court noted, and—he found the tone sentimental— they began a mutual process of healing.

"I need the *facts*," Angelica said, pouring coffee. "Tell me the things you left out when you spoke to Natasha." She gave him one of her black-eyed, scornful glances. "I know your techniques. You never tell a story straight; you fast-forward past the awkward facts; you backtrack; you throw in these diversions— well, that won't work with *me*. I've seen you do it too many times. You do it all the time in your movies."

"Yes, well you're not too likely to understand my movies." Taking his coffee and moving away from her, Court gave her a dismissive glance. "Stick to your women's magazines if you want a simple story."

"Romance, crime; that's what I like." She gave him an unapologetic stare. "I like true love. I like a mystery solved. I like happy endings."

"You surprise me. And life isn't like that unfortunately, so, no romance, no ending yet—happy or otherwise. I fear this mystery may not be solved, but I'll give you the facts, such as they are, including the ones I didn't tell Natasha, and you can play detective."

Angelica gave him a look of sour amusement. She sat down heavily and spread her hands on her thighs, turning her slab of a face toward him.

"So why *didn't* you tell Natasha the whole story?"

"Because I want to protect her. I don't want her to worry any more than she needs. . . ."

"And?"

"And, all right, the more worried about King she is, the more convinced she is that he could still be alive, the likelier she is to make this move to the Conrad. I don't want her going there."

"I don't like it there either," Angelica said, surprising him. "No point in saying so. The more you argue with her, the more she digs her toes in. I figured—keep my mouth *shut*. They probably won't let her take that apartment anyway."

"Jonathan's afraid of it. Does Natasha know that?"

"She knows and she doesn't know. I guess she thinks he'll come around to it." She paused. "And it is secure; it's a real secure building. Famous for it. Keep anybody out, that building would. I guess that's why she chose it."

Court gave her a pale glance. The taunt under her words was obvious enough, and she made little attempt to disguise it.

"Well, it won't keep *me* out," he replied quietly, "not as long as my son's there, and Natasha would do well to remember that." He turned away. "Now, do you want these facts, or don't you?"

"Sure I do." She paused. "What Natasha told me, I couldn't really understand. Why all these tests and checks? It seems pretty clear to me—I mean, they found the *body*. . . ."

She continued speaking for a while, and Court listened, interested to see just how accurately his explanation to his wife had been reported back. As he had expected, few details had been left out—but then Natasha had always confided in Angelica minutely. He had never had any privacy in this marriage, he thought with a flare of anger. Natasha ran to Angelica the way a good Catholic ran to the confessional; he was certain that Angelica knew Natasha's version of every one of his infidelities.

It had always seemed to him that Angelica would find them undisturbing, and just what she would expect from a member of the male sex. Angelica did not *judge*, he sometimes felt, she just watched, and very little either surprised or shocked her. He wondered now, watching her as she spoke without emotion of violent death and the details of that body in Glacier, whether Angelica knew of, and understood, the final paradox: that it was the advent of Joseph King that had cured him of the need for adulteries.

Had Angelica's keen hard mind made that connection? He thought it probably had. He thought Angelica would have seen the link between a letter or call from King and his own haste, immediately afterward, to get his wife back upstairs to their bedroom. He felt sometimes that Angelica had been able to see through those walls and locked doors, and that she had known, as precisely as he did, what then provoked the ensuing excitement, desperation, and physical abandon.

"He's *sick*," Angelica was saying now, gazing off into space, her slab of a face hard with concentration. "He's sick and obsessed, and the way I figure it is, he went out to Montana because he knew Jonathan was there, then he finally cracked. He went out to Glacier and found a real quiet private place, and he *jumped*. Good riddance. It took him a while to die—I hope it did. I figure . . ."

Had Angelica made that connection? Court wondered, looking at her, then moving away as she continued speaking. Sometimes he felt she had not only seen the link, but pointed it out to Natasha. At other times, he felt that his wife had understood that link and had done so alone and unaided. It would not have been difficult; besides, it had seemed to him that Natasha shared his needs initially. He had been able to see a certain dark excitement in her eyes, which, on occasion, she had disguised with weeping.

"Oh, I can't bear this," she would say, letting one of King's letters fall from her hands. "Take me upstairs, Tomas. I want to be with you."

Being with him was a euphemism. The instant the door had

closed and they were alone, he had seen her face light up; she might not admit it, but he had known that she responded as strongly as he did to promptings others might have judged perverse or transgressive.

"So he finally went over the edge," Angelica was now saying, still frowning off into space. "But what I don't understand is, how come he was always so well informed? How come he knew where you'd been? Where Natasha had been? I mean, that wasn't guesswork. He must have been following. He must have been *watching*. . . ."

Court turned his back to Angelica. He leaned up against a table; he could hear his wife's voice very clearly. "He must have been *watching*, Tomas." She closed the bedroom door, and, beginning to tremble, turned to face him. "How else could he have known that? He must have watched you with that boy. In a *parking lot*? Tomas, how could you do that? It makes me *ache*. I can't bear—you *let* him? What did he do? Is it different when a man does that to you? Did he do it more than once? How long did it take him? Tell me. . . ."

Her husband had told her. Her response, agitated and disguised, was immediate; he had been able to feel the electricity in her hands when, bolder than the boy had been, she began to touch him.

"But what I can't figure out," Angelica was saying, "I can't figure out why it *stopped*. I mean, why would he give up so suddenly? Like this has been going on five *years*, and then he ups and kills himself? How come?"

Court passed his hands across his face. He stared at a pale wall hung with watercolors. For three of those five years this newly charged relationship with his wife had continued; then he had made a very foolish mistake—he had admitted, under close questioning from his wife, that for the last two and a half of those years he had had no other sexual partners; he had neither wanted nor needed them; he had desired only her, and had been faithful. She had wept in his arms with apparent joy; her bedroom door had been closed to him thereafter.

Separation had ensued; divorce had swiftly followed. In the period since the divorce—and it was nearly two years—he had remained celibate, if not in the strictest sense, at least in the sense of having no other sexual partners. He was beginning to see that this too was an error; when it was admitted to his wife, here in this room, a week ago now, her lovely eyes had darkened with an expression of sympathy and disappointment. He had reacted as he always did: angry yet filled with longing for her, he returned to Tribeca and lay there alone in the darkness, listening to those tapes, finding some release as he communed with ghosts and took his wife by proxy.

"You still keeping all those King tapes?"

Angelica voiced the direct question suddenly, as if even while speaking she had been able to follow his thoughts with unerring accuracy. "You still listen to them the way you used to do?"

Coloring, Court kept his back to her.

"No," he replied, "the police have most of them. I never listen to them now. I'm over that."

"He had you hooked." There was a malicious triumph in her voice; in this weakness of his she also exulted.

"Night after night you used to listen and reread the letters. I told you then, it wasn't healthy."

"I can remember what you said."

"It was all lies anyway. Filthy lies." She spoke with sudden venom. "All those lies about Natasha. She isn't like that—never has been."

She paused, as if waiting for confirmation of this statement. When she received none, she gave a sigh.

"Accurate about *you*, though. Chapter and verse. Where you'd been, who you'd been with . . ."

"Accurate in some ways." He turned and gave her a pale steady look. "And those tapes told Natasha nothing that I hadn't already told her. You might remember that, Angelica."

"You're honest with her, I give you that." She paused, eyeing him. "She won't take you back, you know."

"Then I shall have to find a way of taking *her* back," he replied evenly. "Believe me, I will. And when I do, I won't be consulting or informing you, Angelica."

That angered her; he saw the blood creep up into her neck and suffuse her face. Her expression became set.

"She's free of you now."

"I wouldn't count on that."

"She's free of King as well. She can start a new life. He's dead; he has to be *dead*. Not one call, not one letter, in nearly five months. They found that body. They found the ID with it." Her voice had risen. "I have to *know*, is it *finished*? Is he dead, or isn't he?"

Court gave her a long still look. He wondered if she was aware of the duality of her own question; he thought not. She wanted to believe King was dead because, for some primitive reason, some reason buried deep in her mind, she believed that if King was dead, Natasha's marriage would similarly be dead. It was himself, he thought, as well as King that she wanted to eradicate from Natasha's future.

"The indications are that he *is* dead," he replied, "as you've been saying, and as I told Natasha." He paused. "But I don't believe he is. I believe he's very much alive. . . ."

"Biding his time?" Angelica leaned forward.

"Precisely."

"But they found the body. . . ."

"They found *a* body," Court corrected.

Giving her what Colin Lascelles would have described as one of his Prospero looks, he crossed the room. With a sigh, seating himself opposite her and speaking quietly, he began to tell her the story.

"I didn't tell Natasha this," he began, "but I know the place in Glacier where they found the body—and I know it well. I went there, Angelica. I went there last July first, with Jonathan, while he was staying with me in Montana. We went with a bodyguard, because I'd promised Natasha I would do that, and we took a back-country trail. It takes you through the mountains and on down to Kintla Lake. . . ."

"You camped." Angelica nodded. "I know, Jonathan loved it there; he told me."

"We were away three days. It's a very beautiful part of Glacier and it's remote—hardly anyone uses that trail. Even in high season you can walk all day and not see a single person. We had . . ." He hesitated, looking away and seeing the place in his mind's eye as he spoke. "They were three of the best days of my life. We walked, we fished, we had cookouts—it took me back to my childhood. We slept out under the stars; we didn't even need the tents. We had three days and nights of perfect weather and absolute peace, and I was glad of that—for Jonathan.

"He'd spent months cooped up here in this city," he continued. "I wanted to show him that there's another America; a place where he could breathe pure air, where he didn't have to worry about telephone calls, or what the mail might bring. A place where he didn't have to keep looking over his shoulder."

He paused. "At the end of those three days, we went back to the ranch, and then, months later, when the body was found, I discovered we hadn't been alone in Glacier. We'd been watched and followed—and someone went to considerable lengths to ensure I knew that. Do you know where they found the man's body, Angelica? What was left of his body?"

"By some water, in scrub. Right under this great wall of rock—that's what you told Natasha."

"Yes—and that was accurate, up to a point. What I *didn't* tell her was where that rock wall was located. The trail we took goes over it, Angelica. They found that body by the lake shore, not two hundred yards from one of our overnight camping sites. The body had been smashed up by the fall and left there to rot; and I'm certain that wasn't accidental. It was a place where I'd been happy, where Jonathan had been happy—and anyone watching him there could have seen how happy he was. So they took that place and they polluted it. They've certainly ensured I'll never go back there."

"Ah, Jesus." Angelica made one of her superstitious little signs. "He'd followed you there, then."

"I'm afraid there's no doubt about that, as you'll see in a minute. Wait awhile. Look at the chronology. In October, the rangers patrol the park before the snows come, and it's closed for the winter. That's when the body was found; by which time, it had been lying there, they think, for around four months, in the heat of summer. There are bears in Glacier, Angelica. You can imagine; there'd been decomposition, animal interference, some bones were missing. The only way they're going to make an identification is through dental chart records. It could take months, longer, before they find a match—if they ever do. At the moment, they're going through the records for missing persons state by state—it's slow, and it may well lead nowhere.

Meantime, shortly after the body was found, I was contacted. You know why? Because someone had gone to considerable lengths to suggest an identification for that body. Someone wanted to suggest, to the police, to me, to Natasha, that the body was Joseph King's. Now, you know how careful King is, and how ingenious. How do you think he did that?"

"There was a backpack," Angelica said, with some eagerness. "They found a backpack near the remains, and in the backpack . . ."

"In the backpack, Angelica, or in what was left of the backpack, was something that wouldn't decay, or rot away—something that would be preserved, and could communicate a message however long it had to lie there. There was a plastic box. A very ordinary plastic box; the kind you might use to pack sandwiches in. Only this one, of course, had rather more unusual contents."

There was a silence. Court looked around the room, knowing he would continue, yet reluctant to do so. To speak of Joseph King, he always found, was to empower him. He could almost sense his presence now, and so, he knew, could Angelica. He saw her face tighten, and he knew she was remembering, as he did, various little packages Joseph King had sent in the past—packages with suggestive and unpleasant contents.

"Tell me," she said. She rested her large, square, ugly hands on her thighs. "Tell me. Was there a photograph?"

"Yes. I'll come to the photograph in a moment. First of all, inside the box, there was a hunting knife; the kind you can buy in a thousand stores across America—a thin-bladed knife, the sort you use to debone animals. Then there were some shotgun cartridges, though no gun was ever found. And, just to make sure I knew that I'd been watched in Glacier, there was a T-shirt of Jonathan's. He'd been wearing it the day we camped there by Kintia Lake; it was missing the next morning, and we'd thought no more about it. He'd taken it on and off ten times that day—we'd been swimming, and we assumed it had simply been mislaid; it wasn't. Someone had been down to our campsite, while we were sleeping—and he wanted me to know that. He could have killed Jonathan then; that's how close he was."

"That bastard." Angelica flushed with anger. "That bastard. I want to kill him. . . ."

"Wait, Angelica, that's not all that was in the box. There was also a wilderness permit—they issue those in Glacier if you're going to walk the longer, more dangerous trails, or if you're going to camp out. That permit was in the name of Joseph King; issued for the same three days we were there. The home address was some street in Chicago that doesn't exist, and never did exist." He paused, his voice becoming less steady. "And finally, Angelica, there was a photograph. Not one of the publicity pictures of Natasha that he's used before, but a family photograph, of Natasha and Jonathan—a photograph *I* took, when Jonathan was still a baby, in the garden of that house we had years ago in California."

"A photograph *you* took?" Angelica stared at him. "But that's not possible. . . ."

"A photograph I took over five years ago now." Court gave a weary gesture. "Jonathan was about eighteen months old. Natasha and I had just finished work on *The Soloist*—you remember?"

"I remember." She looked at him in confusion. "But I don't see—how could he get hold of it? That's got to be *before* we got any letters or calls from King. . . ."

"Exactly. The police have checked; I've checked; the agency has checked. I know exactly when I took that photograph; it was two months before the first of the calls and letters from King— so we have to redate the start of his obsession. Except, for all I know, he's got pictures I took even earlier, and he's just waiting to produce them. . . ."

"But how did he *get* it? He stole it somehow?"

"No, easier than that. That photograph was the last on a reel of family pictures I took. Jonathan was walking by then, beginning to talk—Natasha loved that house. . . ." He broke off, then after a pause, continued. "Anyway, I had it developed at the same laboratory in L.A. that I always used. They sent back the prints and the negatives, and I still have them—but, of course, for anyone working in that lab, it was easy enough to run off extra prints, and no one would be any the wiser. . . ."

He gave a sigh and rose to his feet. "So, they've now launched a new set of checks: who worked at that lab then?

Where they are now? There were over thirty employees who could have had access to that film. It's over five years ago. Most of them have since left the firm, moved out of state, married, changed their names, dropped out of sight. . . . It's going to take *months*, yet again, to trace them and question them. And it will probably lead nowhere. It will probably be another dead end." He stopped abruptly. "You know what he'd done to the picture?"

"Cut it up? Like the others?"

"Yes. He'd cut it up." He gave an angry gesture. "Cut it up into these neat squares, each one about a quarter of an inch. It was very precise. Natasha's face was on one little square; Jonathan's was on another. And they both had crosses on them, gouged across their faces. When I saw that . . ."

He turned away, feeling his breathing start to tighten. He could feel King's presence in the room acutely now. He felt the old helpless instinct to open doors, search closets, look for a man who was not there—and stay by his son's bedside in case he came through a locked door or a barred window.

"Don't get upset," Angelica said, to his surprise. In this respect, of course, they were at one, he thought, turning back to look at her, and seeing on her face an expression not of hostility, but sympathy.

"Don't," she said again. "It *could* be him; it could be. I don't see that this proves otherwise. He's crazy. I always said he'd kill himself one day—so maybe he did. He jumped, but he had to leave one final message. . . ."

"You could read it that way, and Natasha does." With a sigh, Court returned to his chair and sat down. "But you see, I haven't explained about the permit."

"The permit? I don't see. . . ."

"Think, Angelica. They issue those permits for a *reason*. If someone doesn't come back and check in, the rangers raise the alarm and send out a search party. They have to do that: someone could be hurt, or lying injured somewhere. . . . But that didn't happen in this case. You want to know why there were no alarms, no search parties when the permit *wasn't* handed back in? The answers are all there in the record books at the rangers' station. On Independence Day, the day the permit expired, the day Jonathan and I left Glacier, a man calling himself Joseph King rang the rangers' station. He apologized for not returning the permit, said it had slipped his mind, but he was perfectly safe and had left the park. Now, why do you think he did that, Angelica?"

Angelica hesitated. "So you'd know he was alive? Dead men don't make phone calls?"

"Partly, perhaps. But it's more than that—don't you see? He didn't *want* search parties. He didn't want the body found too soon. The sooner it was found, the easier it would be to identify, so it suited him just fine that it lay there for over three months. That's what I think, anyway."

"But if he placed that call. . . ." Angelica frowned. "That must mean he's alive after all. . . ."

"No, it doesn't. It means someone *calling* himself Joseph King placed the call. It might have been King himself; it could have been some friend. *Think,* Angelica." Court rose again, with an impatient gesture. "He *wanted* there to be doubts and uncertainties, don't you see? How many ways can you script this? I can think of at least five ways, straight off, and they're all equally plausible."

There was a silence. Watching her, he saw the realization slowly dawn. She rose to her feet and looked at him uncertainly.

"Then if it isn't his body, whose is it?"

"I don't know; no one knows. It could be his—it could equally well be someone else's. Some walker; some hitchhiker he picked up, some vagrant, even."

"But that would mean he *had* killed someone—not just talked about it, not just threatened, but actually done it. Oh, Jesus, I see now. . . ."

"It's possible, Angelica. I think that. For what it's worth, the police also think that way, and so does the agency."

"That bastard. That son of a bitch bastard." The blood rushed into Angelica's face. "So we just have to go on waiting— that's his idea? Waiting, the way we always did? That's what we have to live with? Jumping every time the phone rings, having taps on the line, checking the mail, checking the locks. . . ." She drew in her breath, pressing her hand against her chest. "*That's* what we have to do—go on living with the bodyguards, looking over our shoulders every minute of every livelong day, waiting for that bastard to *resurrect*?"

"It would amuse him to play Lazarus." Court turned away to disguise his unease. "So, yes, I'm afraid that's exactly what we have to do. We go on being careful; we go on being vigilant— for as long as it takes."

He moved away, feeling suddenly exhausted. He looked around this pale dull room where his wife had chosen to live for the past year; his longing for her presence intensified. He began to wish that he had never had this conversation, necessary though it was. He began to wish that he were alone, and that of all the words Angelica could have used, she had not used the word "resurrect." That word made him deeply uneasy.

Angelica made a strange and ugly sound—a harsh, rasping intake of breath. Turning to look at her, he saw that she was trembling; the force of her animosity came off her like heat.

"I'm going to fix him, and this time I'm going to fix him *good*. There's something I have to do—it won't take long. I'll be back."

She hastened from the room. Court looked at his watch. It was past eleven. Should he leave now, or stay? His wife would have only just left the theater. She would be on her way to have dinner with Jules McKechnie, possibly alone, possibly with others; it might be hours before she came back.

He began to move about the room in an irresolute way, trying to find in it some trace of the woman he knew and loved. Its neutrality and its tastefulness appalled him. The room was white on cream on beige—a thousand permutations of color-lessness. Natasha had hung some of her own paintings, he saw—and his wife's taste in paintings was not his.

Since the divorce, she had begun to collect eighteenth- and nineteenth-century watercolors; the vaguer and washier they were, the more she liked them. Court stared at what might have been a seascape—a wash of indigo, a wash of yellow-white, some inky hieroglyphs that might have been trees, or birds, or ships.

On the opposite wall, she had hung some of her own artist mother's oils—paintings he had always refused to give house room. Natasha's mother, now dead, had been a flower child of the sixties, and like many children of that particular decade, never grew up. Her amateurish paintings, large and violently colored, were all depictions of monstrous flowers, close up. Their stamens, sepals, and pistils had a moistly sexual insistence; Natasha said they were powerful and reminded her of the work of Georgia O'Keeffe. To Court, who loathed O'Keeffe's work too, but could see its strengths, this proved how curiously blind his wife could be. She could see so much sometimes, yet she could also be, or affect to be, myopic. "I will get her back. I will take her back," he said to the throaty flower in front of him, and he began to see ways in which that might be done, if he was careful, if he scripted them correctly.

It was unbearable to remain in this room any longer, he found; its quiescence and opacity oppressed him. He could still hear his own voice, explaining uncertainties to Angelica, and the air here was filled with uncertainty, ambivalence, and doubt. Also, he could now smell burning, a peculiarly unpleasant burning smell too, like hair singed. He could hear, faintly, the sound of rustling and crackling.

He could not bear the jealous hours of waiting, he decided. He would prefer not to know how late it was when his wife returned; he would prefer not to stay here and speculate as to her activities. He went out into the corridor and paused by the entrance to the small bedsitting room that was Angelica's. Here, the smell of burning was stronger; he could glimpse, through the open door, the cluster of crucifixes and saints' pictures and religious knickknackery with which Angelica adorned every space in which she lived.

"I cursed him," she said, appearing in the doorway from nowhere, and startling Court. "I cursed him—and this time I cursed him real good. I got through. I could feel it; I could feel *him*, like some fish wriggling on a hook. . . ."

"Yes, well you've cursed him plenty of times before," Court said coldly, "and without conspicuous success."

He looked at Angelica's flushed face; a vein stood out on her temple; her heavy body was giving off heat like an electric plate. He tried, as he had often done before, to tell himself that Angelica was an ugly, overweight, vindictive virgin of fifty-five, whose sole redeeming feature was her love for his son. She was *without powers*, he told himself, and he was the last person in the world to be impressed by the mumbo jumbo of her semi-Catholic, semipagan prayers, curses, and jinxes.

He told himself this, but as before, it did not convince. She muttered a few more words, lapsing as she always did, from English to her native Sicilian, to a dialect filled with liquid threat, with razor-sharp sibilants, with saints' names and obscenities intermixed.

She was trembling; the light in the hallway was poor. Court, acknowledging his fear, backed away from her.

"I *fixed* him," she said, turning her bright black eyes on Court. "He's starting to die right now—but slow, from the inside out. I'm going to let him suffer awhile, and then I'm going to finish him off. I fixed him. He tried to hide, but he couldn't hide from me this time. I summoned him up."

The last phrase had a hissing sound to it. Court turned, and without speaking further, quickly left. He felt followed the instant the door closed, and he blamed Angelica and her dramatics for this. The sensation remained with him when he left the Carlyle; he could not shake it off. He decided to walk to the Conrad building, as he sometimes did at night, and it pursued him there. He stood outside the Conrad, on the north corner, looking up at the dark windows of the apartment his wife wanted—and he knew he was watched.

He swung around, staring toward the shadows and shrubbery of the park; nothing moved; no one spoke. He looked up at a thin and sickly moon, riding high above that many-eyed roofline, and then, sometime after midnight, hailed a cab and directed it back south.

The sensation of being pursued remained. He could blame it on fatigue, on lack of food, on superstition, on the conversation with Angelica, which still rippled through his mind—but he could still sense some watcher, some follower in his street; he could sense eyes as he stepped into the elevator.

Instinct, recognition, the influence of some sixth sense—whatever the explanation for that sensation of unease, he saw how timely its warnings had been as soon as the elevator doors opened.

He felt his body come alive with adrenaline shock; the door to his loft stood open, its locks smashed. He could see that in the room beyond, vandalism had been at work. The lights were on; the floor was a sea of paper, and the perpetrator of this, whose identity he did not doubt for one second, was still present. He could hear that low, pedantic, murmuring, midwestern voice, and it was murmuring an old message. "Under the left breast," he heard. "Under the left breast."

He hesitated, flexing his hands, summoning his strength; then, with the eagerness of one greeting an old friend, a familiar not seen in a long while, he moved forward and pushed the door back.

Chapter 10

━━━◆◆◆━━━

"Breeding," Colin's great-aunt Emily said, with an air of getting straight to the point. She leaned forward and tapped Lindsay on the knee. Lindsay, who had been daydreaming, jumped.

"She's bred once—will she breed *again*?" Emily asked, in a sharply interrogative manner, glancing toward Colin. For one confusing moment, Lindsay thought this particular question might refer to her.

"Fecundity," Emily continued, turning back to Lindsay, and giving her a glare. "She is unquestionably *fertile*. In my opinion, *that* is what's giving them the heebie-jeebies—bunch of old women. But, darn it, do they have a point? I want to know what you think, Lindsay. Advise me, my dear."

Lindsay did not know what she thought. To give advice was a little difficult, as she did not have the least idea what Emily was talking about. She tried hard to think of some noncommittal reply. For at least the last ten minutes, she realized, Aunt Emily had been rattling away to Colin, and Lindsay had allowed her own attention to wander.

She had been looking at this room, which was large and packed with a glorious accumulation of *stuff*. Some of this stuff was superb and some was kitsch. She had been wondering why Emily chose to put a vase of green ostrich feathers on a Hepplewhite desk; whether the magnificent portrait above the fireplace was a Sargent; whether the two strikingly beautiful women depicted in it could be related to Emily, who was strikingly plain; and whether the grand piano in the corner was supporting fifty-five ancestral photographs in silver frames, or fifty-six.

She had also been wondering why Emily had reminded her of Miss Havisham, since she could now see that, beyond a tendency to pursue a private agenda in conversation, Emily did not resemble her in the least. This was no mad Dickensian bride, but a tall, lean woman, with a shock of white hair, bright, iris-blue eyes, and a good line in tweeds. She was wearing three pairs of spectacles on leather thongs about her neck, yet so far had used none of them; she was seated at one end of a gigantic sofa—Colin, looking nervous, was seated at the other end—and somewhere among the plenitude of its exquisite tapestry cushions there was at least one, possibly two, pug dogs. The lighting was subdued, which made the number of pugs difficult to confirm; they, or it, snuffled and snored constantly. Lindsay and Colin were drinking prudent mineral water; Aunt Emily was knocking back a serious bourbon on the rocks.

Inattention, as Rowland McGuire had often remarked, was Lindsay's besetting sin. She was always too busy examining the leaves of each tree in the forest to notice where the forest road led. With a woman like Emily, whose conversation was given to abrupt swerves, this tendency was disastrous. Emily was still waiting for a reply to her question, and Lindsay's brain was in midskid. Breeding? Fertility? Lindsay eyed the pug, or pugs; it came to her that Emily was discussing the breeding of dogs, or, more specifically, bitches.

"Pedigree very dubious *indeed*," Emily now said, rattling off again, to Lindsay's relief. "Who *sired* her? No answer to *that* question, my dear. And then there's the matter of her fame. She is excessively *famous*." Emily cocked a sharp eye at Lindsay. "What's our reaction to that, my dear? Is famous bad or good?"

Dogs could be famous, Lindsay thought—if they won at shows. Yes, she was almost sure she was on track. Emily was on the subject of dog breeding, of pedigree, about which Lindsay, who liked only strays and mongrels, knew nothing and cared less. Still, old ladies had to be humored. She gave Emily what she hoped was a smile of bright intelligence.

"Tricky," she said.

"And then there's the *money* question." Emily's face became grave, as did Lindsay's two seconds later. "Too much money, my dear—and very *recently* acquired, or *earned*, which makes it rather worse." She paused, eyeing Lindsay. "*Loot*. The acquisition of loot. Always a delicate subject. Better not investigated sometimes. As I said to Henry Foxe, 'Henry, where d'you think *this* came from, darn it?' "

She thrust out a skinny hand and waggled a finger. On this arthritic digit was a very large diamond, Lindsay saw; it was one of the biggest rocks she had ever seen in her life.

"And d'you know what Henry said? *'Tiffany's.'* " Emily gave a delighted snort of laughter. "I always admired Henry's sense of humor; very droll. In fact, Lindsay, my dear, there was a time—Lord, back in 1932 this would have been, when Henry Foxe and I . . ."

"More bourbon, Em?" Colin rose quickly to his feet.

"You are one sweet man," said Emily. "Don't you agree, my dear? Colin, just wave the bottle over the top."

Colin poured an inch of bourbon into the glass. Emily declined ice and suggested he wave the bottle a bit more. Colin added another inch of bourbon, opened his mouth to speak, shut it again, and sat down with a defeated look. Lindsay eyed Emily; she gave no signs of being in the least intoxicated. *Mad*, Lindsay decided. Totally mad; barking; off the wall, permanently out to lunch.

There was method to this madness, she suspected, however. Emily had some objective in view, she felt, even if, for reasons of her own, she was approaching it by a peculiar and indirect route.

"So, to summarize," Emily continued, "she's bred once— which reminds me, my dear. You have a son, I think Colin said?"

"Yes. Tom. He's reading modern history at Oxford now."

"Ah, Oxford. Brideshead. Delightful. I can't believe it, my dear—you look so young."

"I married young," Lindsay said, with some firmness.

"And divorced young too I hear. Quite right. If they're no good, ship them out. . . . Of course, I never risked marriage myself, not that I regret it now. . . . So, let me see, your son must be eighteen, nineteen?"

Lindsay sighed. She debated whether to claim Tom as a

child prodigy who had gone up to Oxford aged fifteen, remembered Colin had met him, and decided against.

"Twenty any minute now," she said.

"Colin was charming at that age." Emily gave her a measuring look. "Wild, innocent, muddled. Ah, youth." She paused, eyeing Lindsay. "Of course, he's still charming now. As I expect you find, my dear?"

"Very," said Lindsay.

The drift of Emily's questions was now clear, she decided, hiding a smile. She looked at Colin, who appeared both agonized and mortified. She looked at Emily, who clearly suspected Lindsay of designs on her great-nephew. She considered saying plainly that if Colin had been wild, innocent, and muddled at twenty, his character did not appear to have changed greatly in the succeeding two decades. She considered saying, even more plainly, that she was not trying to hook Colin, so his vigilant great-aunt could relax her guard.

She rejected these possibilities: the second was ill mannered; the first was hurtful—and she had no wish to hurt Colin, whose demeanor now indicated profound and desperate dejection. He shot Emily a pleading look.

"You're rambling about a bit, Em," he said. "I expect you feel tired. Maybe we should—"

"Nonsense, I'm just waking up. Hitting form. Besides, I haven't finished, and I want Lindsay's views on this. Where was I? Ah yes, I was summarizing—the case for the prosecution, point by damning point! Breeding, pedigree, money . . . and *fans*, of course. The fans will almost certainly present problems, my dear, don't you think?"

Fans? Lindsay, now hopelessly lost, looked up at the ceiling.

"And finally, my dear . . ." Emily had been ticking off these points on her fingers. "Finally, we come to the single most important question of all. S-E-X, my dear—and also *love*, of course."

Love? Lindsay began to see that dogs could not possibly be the subject of discussion here. Colin, who had blushed painfully when the words "sex" and "love" were used, was now staring hard at the air, in the manner of a man who believed that, if he concentrated hard enough, he could teleport himself elsewhere.

"I'm afraid I don't quite follow," Lindsay began.

"My, dear, there is the *ex-husband*!" Emily said, as if this made everything clear. "A most *peculiar* man—or so our spies report. Like you, my dear, if you'll forgive my saying so, she has *not* loved wisely, and she has *not* chosen well. Will she choose more wisely the second time around? Can we trust her to find a suitable mate, someone who will fit in? Alas, not necessarily. She will imagine she is in love, as women do, and her judgment will be impaired. . . ."

"What absolute rubbish, Em," Colin interrupted, five seconds before Lindsay. Showing signs of recovery, he gave his aunt a combative look. "You're in no position to judge her first marriage, and she's far likelier to make the right choice the second time around. . . ."

"I agree," said Lindsay. "Having one's fingers burned improves the judgment no end."

"Do you think so? What a charming pair of optimists you are." Emily gave them a sprightly look. "I remain dubious. The next husband—do we know the nature of the beast? No. What about lovers? There are likely to be lovers. More problems there. I foresee disturbances! I can sense them in the air."

She gave a quick glance over her shoulder, then peered around the room as if disturbances might lurk here, among the crowded furniture, behind the thick folds of the curtains—or beyond the room perhaps, Lindsay thought; beyond it, in those shadowy galleries, in that womb of a staircase hall. A clock ticked softly; Emily appeared to be listening; from the plenitude of cushions came a low pugnacious growl. Lindsay, suddenly remembering the ghost of Anne Conrad, felt something cold slither along her spine.

"Did you hear something, Colin?" Emily, paling a little, cocked her head on one side.

"No, nothing. It was probably just Frobisher in the corridor."

Colin rose, moved to the door, opened it, and looked out. A cold draft issued into the room and wrapped itself around Lindsay's ankles. She shivered. Colin closed the door.

"Nothing," he said. "Frobisher's in her bedroom watching television—I can just hear it. You probably caught the sound of that, Em."

"Maybe. My hearing is acute at times." She hesitated. "This

building is full of noises, and not always sweet ones. Occasionally, it expresses its opinions and its desires. It used to frighten me when I was a child. . . . Did you hear anything, Lindsay?"

"No, not exactly. But something—when your little dog growled. And my hands—my hands feel terribly cold."

"You didn't see anything, I hope?" The question was sharp.

"No, no. Nothing at all."

"Stop this, Em." Colin moved across to Lindsay and took her hand. "Stop it. You're making Lindsay's blood run cold."

"*I* am? I did nothing at all."

"Lindsay, this is my fault. I shouldn't have told you those ghost stories at dinner. . . ."

"Perhaps. I'm susceptible to stories. I'm fine now—it's passed whatever it was. Where were we?"

Colin released her hand. Lindsay could sense his unease. As he crossed back to the sofa, a long silent look was exchanged between aunt and nephew; as a result of that look, and for the first time that evening, Emily was quelled. She retreated back into her nest of cushions and Colin, to Lindsay's great relief, took charge.

"I doubt if you've followed half of this," he said. "Emily can have a rather circuitous approach. In fact, it's straightforward, Lindsay. The Conrad is a cooperative—there's really no equivalent in England. Its board decides whether or not someone can acquire an apartment here. At the moment, one of the apartments, number three, which is directly beneath this one, is available. It used to belong to one of Emily's oldest friends, and she died earlier this year. The woman who now wants to buy it— and we won't name her, I think, but she's an actress and she's very well known—has been pressing for a decision, because she wants to move in as soon as possible; in fact, she wants to celebrate Thanksgiving here."

"We've been given a deadline," Emily piped up. "We are not used to ultimatums. We don't like them at all."

"*I'd* have given you an ultimatum, Em," Colin said, with impatience. "This has been dragging on for months. Bankers, stockbrokers, the IRS, references—it wouldn't surprise me if you had her medical records. It's absurd." He turned back to

Lindsay. "Tomorrow, the decision has to be made, one way or the other. Emily is on the committee. . . ."

"Along with four dithering males!" Emily cried.

"And the Henry Foxe she mentioned chairs it. But don't listen to Emily when she says 'dithering'; two of those men are carved in granite, and as for Biff Holyoake—well, can you describe him as a man?"

"I *adore* Biff!" Emily protested. "Biff is a sweetheart. Biff is Peter Pan on his fourth divorce. . . ."

"Precisely. Say no more."

"Biff's very pro her anyway. When the subject of orgies came up, Biff was charmed. He said, in that case she'd certainly get *his* vote. Dear Biff! Two martinis for breakfast these days, I hear."

"*Orgies?*" Colin and Lindsay said in unison. Colin sighed. "I don't need to ask who raised that possibility, do I? It was you, wasn't it, Em?"

"I might have mentioned it, in passing." Emily, showing signs of resurgence, gave a gleeful smile. "One has to consider the worst. Remember her profession! I foresee parties, alcohol, substance abuse . . . people coming and going day and night. . . . I know what goes on, you see! Frobisher fetches me the gutter press, and I pay it the very *closest* attention. I fear the worst! What about *cocaine*? Angel dust. Snow. Nose candy— I know all the terms! I think nose candy is in the cards, myself."

"Em, please." Colin sighed. "In the first place, she doesn't live like that—as I've told you a thousand times. In the second, what about Biff? Biff Holyoake, to everyone's certain knowledge, has a four-hundred-dollar-a-day coke habit, and he's had it since 1952."

"Biff's mother was at Chapin with me. Biff's grandfather was your great-grandfather's best friend. They founded . . ." She stopped short, glancing from Colin, who was frowning, to Lindsay, who was amused.

"They founded a firm *friendship*," she continued, her manner somewhat flustered. "A loyal friendship. They were lifelong friends, like you and poor dear Rowland McGuire. So, so—where was I? Ah yes, Biff. Biff may be a lost soul, but he is one of *us*. He is a fine good man, and I will not have a word said against him. . . ."

"Christ," said Colin indistinctly.

"What was that, Colin?"

"Nothing."

Colin, who had sunk his head in his hands at some point during the peroration on Biff Holyoake's ancestry, now raised it. He gave Lindsay a look of blank misery.

"You see?" he said. "You see what I'm up against here?"

Lindsay considered. She indeed saw what Colin was up against in an obvious sense, since Emily's views were a swamp of prejudice, and arguing with her was like mud wrestling. But she suspected Colin's words had a deeper meaning. She was still trying to work out what that might be, when Emily stirred, preened, emerged from her nest of cushions, and fixed her with a very intent look.

"So, my dear," she said, "now you know *everything*, and I want your considered opinion: Should we admit her to the Conrad, yes or no? I feel you can help me here. I'm not young anymore—but you, you also have a child, you're also divorced. You're a modern young woman, and Colin thinks you have *excellent* judgment. . . ."

"He does? Thank you, Colin."

"Of course. He admires it immensely. It was Lindsay's judgment you were admiring, wasn't it, Colin? Just the other day?"

"Yes," said Colin, somewhat fixedly.

"So there you are then. You must tell me how to vote tomorrow, Lindsay. I rely on you entirely, my dear."

"Well, I think it's very simple," Lindsay began. "It seems to me that you're proposing to blackball this woman for the most appalling reasons. How can you reject someone for being a woman? Or divorced? For having earned a lot of money? For having a *child*?"

"Orgies, rumors, fans," said Emily. "Don't forget those."

"Have your sources—I think you called them your spies—produced any evidence of anything remotely resembling orgies?"

"Well, no," Emily replied, with deep regret. "There remains a lack of evidence, although the inquiries have left no stone unturned."

"I know those stones," Lindsay said, with some asperity, "and I know what comes out from under them when you lift them up. Surely . . ."

"I remain suspicious of the *fans* myself." Emily bridled. "And of journalists who, in my experience, are unprincipled people capable of insinuating themselves anywhere. Even here."

"I am a journalist."

"So you are, my dear, but of a very different kind. I was referring to seedy little men in raincoats. Scandalmongers. I'm sure you know the breed."

There was a silence. Lindsay began to see that Emily was very far from mad—and she played a mean game of conversational tennis. The harder Lindsay hit the balls, the harder they were returned. She was losing all sympathy with Colin's Aunt Emily, Lindsay decided.

In particular, she disliked the way in which Emily insistently coupled her with this unknown woman seeking admission to the Conrad. Where were the similarities between them, beyond the fact that they both had children and were both divorced? Why all that stress on fertility, on breeding? The sensation was growing on her that, for some incomprehensible reason, it was she herself who was now on trial.

"Have you met her?" she asked now. "You must have met her presumably? Did you like her?"

"I have met her once. I thought her a consummate actress. As to whether I liked her, I couldn't say."

"But you found nothing to dislike? Or distrust?"

"Not on that occasion, no."

"Then you must admit her," Lindsay said. "You must see, you can't let prejudice and rumors influence you here."

"Interesting," said Emily.

"I *knew* you'd say that." Colin revived. He gave Lindsay a warm smile. "There you are, Em. Maybe you'll listen to Lindsay, since you won't listen to me."

Lindsay at once felt encouraged; she warmed to her theme. "The only thing is," she continued, "it's no good wasting your vote. So, if the other four are opposed to her, you'd have to find a way of bringing them round to your view. You only need two additional votes. . . . I wonder, are the granite men against?"

"So I believe."

"Then could you influence Biff, perhaps? I'm sure you could, by the sound of him. . . ."

"Of course she could!" Colin rose, with an air of excitement. "Biff always listens to Emily; he does whatever she tells him to do. She can twist him around her little finger. He's putty in her hands. . . ."

"Colin, you are mixing your metaphors," Emily said. "Calm down."

Lindsay gave Emily an appraising look. She could see it would be more productive to appeal to Emily's power lust— well developed, she felt—than to her sense of fair play.

"I don't suppose you could influence Henry Foxe," she began, in a doubting tone. "No, almost certainly not. That's a shame. . . ."

Emily drew herself up, resentful of this slight to her powers. "Not impossible," she said, eyeing Lindsay in a thoughtful manner. "A woman of ingenuity might find a way."

"Really?" Lindsay gave her an innocent look. "He's not decisively against then?"

"My dear," Emily drawled, "Henry Foxe is on the fence— which is where he's been for most of his life. One of the problems in 1932, and if you'll forgive my being frank, not the only one, my dear . . ."

Emily gave a slow, ribald, reptilian wink. Lindsay, startled, decided to take this as a sign of encouragement.

"Well, I'm sure you could get him off the fence," she said. "I'm sure you could persuade him."

"Possibly." To Lindsay's delight, she saw that the light of battle had begun to dawn in Emily's eyes. "Henry Foxe is the kind of man who likes having his mind made up for him. . . . You know the type, my dear?"

"Yes, unfortunately."

"For the first thirty years of Henry's life," Emily continued, still eyeing Lindsay in a thoughtful way, "Henry's mother made up his mind for him, then his wife took over, for the next four decades. His wife, a tedious woman *not* one of my dearest friends, is now *dead*. . . . However, like many men—and I'm sure you'll be equally familiar with this phenomenon, my dear—Henry Foxe requires the illusion that he has made up his own mind without assistance, especially from a mere female. So any persuasion has to be undertaken with *stealth*. . . ."

"Difficult." Lindsay frowned. "I do know the type—only too well. I work with at least ten of them. I wonder, does he have any sense of gallantry? A spark of chivalry? That could help. . . ."

"Yes, yes, yes," cried Colin, animated again. "That's brilliant, Lindsay. The white knight rides to the rescue of the beleaguered damsel."

"Chivalry, my eye," said Emily, somewhat grumpily. "Henry Foxe's instincts are not yours, Colin. He is not chivalric; he is *cautious*—as I discovered in 1932."

"Reasoned argument?" Lindsay ventured.

"You jest, my dear."

"Then I give up." Lindsay gave a sigh and a smile. "There's only one thing to do: you'll have to use your womanly wiles."

This remark, not intended with any great seriousness, produced in Emily a sudden and dramatic change. Her expression became cold.

"Really? Isn't that somewhat underhand? I have never approved of such manipulations myself—one of the feminine characteristics I *least* admire."

"Em." Colin rose, his expression suddenly anxious. "Don't be absurd. Lindsay didn't mean . . ."

"Besides . . ." Emily, ignoring him, pressed on. "Besides— do I want to change Henry's views? I'm not at all sure that I do. Henry will almost certainly come down against her, in the end, and I feel he is right."

She gave a small fretful gesture and rearranged her pug. Her feathers were ruffled, Lindsay realized, and there was now disapproval in those cold, blue, raptor eyes.

"Forgive me, my dear," she continued, "but I feel you are being more than a little hasty here. You seem to assume I agree with you. I don't recall saying that. This is a serious issue, after all. I have lived in the Conrad all my life. I plan on *dying* in this building. . . ."

"But I thought—you asked for my view. . . ."

"My dear, you have been trying to railroad me—you, and this nephew of mine here."

"Persuade, Em, not railroad. Look, it is getting very late, and I really think . . ."

"Festina lente," Emily pronounced, magnificently, turning that blue-ice gaze back upon Lindsay. "That is and always has been the motto of this building. Do you know what it means? Colin will translate, since he had a classical education. . . ."

"It means 'hasten slowly,' " Colin said, his tone now openly mutinous, "and everyone knows that. Emily, it's time for us to go."

"Hasten slowly. Precisely." Emily, still ignoring him, swept on. "A very wise dictum, as you will appreciate, Lindsay, should you ever reach my age. Change should always be gradual—especially so in a place such as this. The Conrad is an institution, one of the last of its kind in Manhattan. It has its traditions and its standards. You can buy or maneuver your way into most places these days, but neither money nor manipulation will gain you admittance *here*. We do not lower the drawbridge without the most careful consideration, and we are not taken in by sweet talk and feminine wiles."

She fixed her eyes on Lindsay even more intently as she made this final remark, and Lindsay found she was becoming angry.

"Consider," Emily continued, gesturing at the room, crammed with all its costly spoils. "This is a safe building. There may be crime on the streets of this city, but it never infiltrates here. People lead quiet lives in this building; they honor its traditions, because that is and has always been our way." Emily fixed her gaze upon Lindsay. "You see, my dear, we are like a little state here . . . or you could say, perhaps, that we are like a *family*. We have to be very careful not to admit the wrong element. By admitting into our circle the wrong type of person, we could sow the seeds of our own destruction. I have seen it happen so many times. We have to be sure that anyone we admit to our little family not only understands our ethic, but shares it. For anyone seeking admittance, there really is only one question: Are you one of us? Do you *belong*?"

Lindsay, unlike Colin, had listened to this speech quietly and without signs of impatience. It had left her very angry indeed. She had heard this argument, or variations upon it, many times; it shored up a variety of causes, and she was in sympathy with none of them. She was now in no doubt as to why Emily had raised this whole issue; Emily evidently still suspected her of designs on Colin, and she was being told, in no uncertain terms, that if she wished to be acceptable to his great-aunt, she had better toe the line.

She looked at Emily carefully and saw that a game had been being played with her throughout the evening. Emily had treated her to an odd ragbag of personae: there had been the Miss Havisham hauteur, the dotty aunt diversion, the dragon lady, and the sibyl. Now Emily had morphed—and morphing was what it resembled—yet again. She understood that Emily had been playing a game of several sets with her; now, having tested her, and maneuvered her, and finagled her into some unwise net play, she seemed convinced that these final hard baseline drives had won her the game. Lindsay was not sure which aspect of all this angered her most: Emily's assumptions as to her own marital intentions, or her calm conviction that, having stated her case thus, Lindsay would promptly back down.

Lindsay rose. "We obviously think very differently," she said, with great politeness. "I'm sorry, but you asked for my opinion, and it hasn't changed. Now it's very late, and I've stayed far too long. . . ."

"Oh dear, oh dear," said Emily, with a sidelong glance at Colin. "I suspect you think I'm a dreadful old reactionary, my dear."

This was a well-timed lob; Lindsay decided to go for the overhead smash in return.

"Mistaken," she said, "unjust, and probably unwise."

"Unwise, my dear?"

"Of course. All institutions have to adapt; even the Conrad. If they don't, they ossify. They become—fossilized."

She paused. Emily had not taken either "ossify" or "fossilized" too kindly—and indeed, they sounded backhanded, Lindsay realized, given Emily's age. She at once regretted the terms; however strong her own feelings, she had no wish to upset a woman of eighty-five.

"Can we not agree to differ?" She held out her hand with a smile. "I'm very glad to have seen the Conrad, and it was good of you to invite me."

Good manners failed to conciliate. Emily stretched out her ossified and arthritic fingers, so the magnificent diamond flashed against the light.

"Do you know, Colin," she remarked, her manner peevish, as she briefly took Lindsay's hand, "I feel rather tired. All this idealism must be exhausting me. Ring for Frobisher, will you? I think I must retire, and you must show this charming young woman back to her hotel. . . . No, no, my dear, I insist. New York can be a very unsafe place at night. You need a man at your side."

She took Lindsay's arm and began to guide her toward the door.

"*So* nice to have met you, my dear. I do hope we meet again." She peered at Lindsay, as if trying to remember who she was. "And now, I must have a brief word with Colin. . . ."

Emily was morphing again, she could sense it. They were now inching toward duchess, and there were symptoms of Lady Bracknell too.

Game, set, and match, Lindsay conceded, as with thanks and courtesies she escaped. Frobisher closed the door firmly, and for a while there was silence in the drawing room beyond.

During the silence, Colin walked around in a complete circle. He returned to the chair in which Lindsay had been sitting and sank down in it, clasping his head in his hands. Emily, who had been rocking with silent laughter from the moment Lindsay left, now laughed aloud. She sat down on the sofa, still laughing; she kissed her pug on its crinkled snout, settled it on her lap, and took a congratulatory swallow of bourbon.

"My Lord, I haven't enjoyed myself so much in ages," she remarked. "The last time I had that much fun was at Maud Foxe's funeral. And you enjoyed it too, you wicked boy—so don't pretend otherwise and don't glower."

"*Enjoyed* it?" Colin groaned. "I was in torment. *Torment.* Why couldn't you stick to the script?"

"Because it was too darned boring, and a whole lot less effective than my approach. That was *inspired* to ask her about the Lawrence woman. I gave a virtuoso performance. I deserve an Academy Award."

"It was several *miles* over the top. It was way up in the *stratosphere.* Why did I let you talk me into this? I should have known you couldn't be trusted. You know what she's going to think now? She's going to think insanity runs in my family. It didn't occur to you that might be a little counterproductive? Oh God, God, *God*." He rose and began to pace up and down. "I was in *agony*. Poor Lindsay—how could you be so unfair?"

"Poor Lindsay coped very well. Her footwork could have been a little faster, but she has *grit*. I approve."

"I *told* you that. Courage, a kind heart, and the most beautiful eyes in the world. Oh *God*. Give me the verdict. Have I a hope, Em?"

"*Fossilized!*" Emily laughed again. "I did so enjoy that. She was outraged, you know—quite pink in the face. And I'd put my argument so *well*."

"You were intolerable. You put her in an intolerable position. Why, why, why couldn't you stick to the lines I wrote?"

"Because I'd have learned *nothing*. Instead of which, and entirely thanks to me, I've learned everything I need to know."

"Oh sure, and she's learned to hate you. Bloody great. That's really going to help me. Well done, Em."

"Nonsense. She'll come around; she has a generous nature, and next time I'll be on my best behavior, I promise. . . ." She paused. "Thanksgiving?"

"Maybe." Their eyes met. "But I'm not sure yet. I'm having to be very, very careful. I'm not going to mess this up, and none of it's easy. I want . . ."

He hesitated. "I just want to take her in my arms all the time."

"So I observed."

"Oh God, *God*. You can't have. You don't think she noticed? When I took her hand?"

"Oddly enough, no. But then she doesn't know you as well as I do. . . . Could you stop walking up and down, Colin? It's making me quite dizzy."

"I'll have to go; she'll be waiting. Come on, Em, I want to know what you *think*."

"We have a couple of minutes. Frobisher will keep her well out of earshot. Why can't I tell you when you get back from the Pierre? Always assuming, of course, that you *do* get back from the Pierre . . ."

"Because I have to know *now*. Em, please—"

"Have you given her the envelope yet?"

."No, I haven't. But I'm about to. . . ." He stopped pacing and his whole demeanor changed. "Come on, Em," he said, more quietly, "put me out of my misery. I've made so many bloody mistakes, and this time it really matters. Am I right— yes or no?"

Emily found herself moved by his pallor and by the expression in his eyes. She knew the answer he wanted, for it was written in every line of his handsome face. Her expression became serious, and she looked at him in silence for a while.

"You're sure?" she asked at length.

"Totally."

"You've considered the question of her age?"

"Oh, for God's *sake*, don't start on fertility *again*. It was inexcusable when you did that. . . ."

"Colin, your family have lived at Shute for over four hundred years."

"I don't bloody *care*."

"There is the entail to consider, Colin."

"Fuck the entail."

Emily sighed. She saw the flash in his eyes as this statement was made and it affected her, since she had a weakness for passion and iconoclasm; she was also devoted to Colin and wished to see him happy, though in her experience, romance and contentment rarely went hand in hand.

"Colin, someone has to say this to you, so I will. She has a son approaching twenty; she may look much younger, but she must be forty at least. You are aware of the biological clock, as I believe it is called these days? Colin, do I have to spell this out to you?"

"No, I've already done those calculations."

"And it doesn't alter your view?"

"It couldn't." The blood washed up into his face. "I love her, Em."

Emily sighed. She found her nephew hard to resist when he looked as he did now, and she felt, looking at him fondly, that many women, perhaps even Lindsay, might have shared this view. Colin was indeed chivalric; he rode to the lists careless of the fact that he was vulnerable, and deeply so.

"Well, well—I begin to see that," she said quietly. "Colin, don't say any more, it will make me sentimental, and to be sentimental, at this juncture, will be of no assistance at all." She sighed again. "I'm not going to give you advice. Young men in your condition rarely listen to advice, however wise. And I have to admit, I liked her. The age is a very definite drawback— though, of course, even at forty, or forty-one, there is hope. . . . But in many ways, she is just what you need, and I am not blind to that. She is honest—not an ounce of calculation, I thought. Also quite smart, amusing . . . Your father would adore her, and I think she would adore him. I can even see her at Shute. . . ."

"So can I."

"You're going to have to confess. A palace is a rather different kettle of fish to a hovel, Colin dear."

"Shute isn't a palace; it's my *home*. And I'm going to explain all that to her. . . ." Colin, recovering somewhat, gave her a glance that was half anxious, half amused. "I have it all planned out, Em. I told you, I'm not going to risk losing her. This is a *campaign*."

"So I see." She laughed. "I also see my verdict doesn't make two cents' worth of difference. If I'd said the opposite would that have changed your mind?"

"No."

"So resolute! Well, well, you'd better go."

"Do I have a chance, Em?"

Emily smiled, then sighed. "As to that, I never make predictions. She likes you, which can be a good start. I wonder— have you any rivals, though?"

"Oh *God*, I don't know. I don't *think* so. I can't believe there aren't, but she claims there's no one. . . ."

"Does she indeed?" Emily gave Colin a small glance. "Well, you've always been good at getting your way when it mattered, Colin. You've been smart so far, I think."

"I intend to go on being smart."

"But I'm not too sure about the platonic approach; I wouldn't overdo it. Interesting what she said about indecisive men . . . I've always felt that the great secret of seduction is knowing *when* to make your move. Now, kiss me good night, you wicked boy, and don't keep her waiting any longer. Full speed ahead—"

"*Festina lente,*" Colin corrected, the glint of amusement returning to his eyes. "*Festina* very *lente* for at least the next two weeks. So I'll be back in half an hour."

In the taxi—and Colin proved as expert at summoning cabs as he was at summoning waiters—Colin established a most gentlemanly three inches of seat between them. Lindsay admired this.

"I'm sorry I was so long," Colin said. "I just had to calm Emily down a bit. She really is worried about the decision tomorrow."

"She's obviously going to vote against—"

"I'm afraid so."

"Ah well. I hope I didn't upset her. I'm feeling guilty now. I hope I wasn't too sanctimonious. She's not young, and it's predictable she'd feel as she does."

"Don't worry about it, I've given her a far harder time. She doesn't mind, and she loves a good argument. In any case, she liked you. She's just been singing your praises."

"I find that hard to believe."

"No, no, you're wrong. She thought you were very pretty. She thought you had extraordinary eyes, truly beautiful, *candid* eyes."

"Heavens," said Lindsay, secretly gratified.

"And then, she admired your dress sense. . . ." Colin gave her a sidelong glance, suppressing a smile. "She particularly liked that white T-shirt thing you're wearing. . . ." Lindsay, remembering Pixie's comments on that T-shirt, blushed in the darkness of the cab.

"She said she liked your voice. She said it had a most attractive catch in it. Your sense of humor, she mentioned that. . . ."

"Stop. Stop. I'll get swollen-headed."

"Oh, and when you stood up to her, held your ground—she *adored* that."

"Are you sure, Colin? I didn't get that impression at all."

"I warned you she was odd—you mustn't be misled by her manner. Once you know her better, you'll begin to see—" He broke off. "That is, if you meet her again. I hope you'll come

to like her. She's a very good judge of character—of everything, in fact. I never make an important decision without consulting her."

"And do you take her advice?" Lindsay asked, struck by
his tone.

"Not always, but I listen to her views." He took Lindsay's
hand in his. "So, all in all, she was very glad to have met you."
He raised her hand to his lips, kissed it, then released it. "Very
glad," he repeated.

Lindsay, thrown by the kiss on the hand, stared at him.
Colin, who had been gazing out at the passing streets in an
abstracted way, glanced back with a smile.

"And so, in conclusion, she hopes you weren't too bored by
a crotchety octogenarian, and that you'll visit her again before
you leave New York. . . . Ah, the Pierre. Here we are. I'll just
see you safely in. I'll tell the cab to wait, if I may."

Lindsay preceded him into the Pierre. She felt flurried and
dazed as a result of that kiss on the hand. The cab actually was
waiting, she noted, as Colin completed his negotiations with its
driver; that meant that Pixie's predictions were very wide of
the mark.

Realizing this, Lindsay felt a certain disappointment. She
did not want Colin Lascelles to make any advances to her—of
course not—and she would certainly have rejected them had
he done so; but after three years of being invisible to Rowland
McGuire, it might have been pleasant, she thought, if just one
man had found her desirable in a mild way, now and then.

This evidence of her own triviality and vanity alarmed her;
she advanced on the front desk, reprimanding herself. She collected her key, picked up her messages, glanced through them,
came to a halt, and made a small moaning sound as Colin Lascelles, appearing agitated, reached her side.

"You're worrying about the cab," Lindsay said, noticing
that he looked edgy, even pale. "You mustn't keep it waiting.
Thank you, Colin, for a marvelous evening and a delicious
dinner—but don't imagine I've forgiven you yet for paying
that bill. You broke your word."

"I said, 'It's a deal.' I didn't give you my word."

"Even so, it was cunning and underhand. I shall take you to
a burger bar in revenge."

"I shall keep you to that. Meanwhile, I meant to give you this earlier."

He produced an envelope from the breast pocket of his masterly suit.

"For me, Colin? Whatever is it?"

"Nothing, nothing. Just some photographs that might interest you. I've added a note. Let me know what you think. I'll call you tomorrow. Oh, damn and blast than man. . . ."

The driver of Colin's cab had just punched his horn hard, on cue, and exactly as this weird Brit had just tipped him ten dollars to do. As the sound died away, Colin's blue eyes rested upon Lindsay intently. Drawing her toward him, he kissed her cheek in the most decorous manner possible, thanked her, then turned and disappeared.

Lindsay retreated to her room, which still smelled of magic unguents, of yams and papaya juice. She leaned against the closed door for several minutes, until her heart rate slowed down. A short while later, she permitted herself to read the only one of her messages of any significance. It informed her that Mr. McGuire had called at eleven P.M., and would call again the following morning, at nine, New York time.

Lindsay kissed this message several times and rescheduled her next morning's activities in her mind. She reminded herself that, when this call came through, she would rigorously observe her new womanliness and sweetness of tongue. She paced about the room in a fervor; then, discovering that only two minutes and not a lifetime had passed, she examined Colin's mysterious envelope and opened it.

Inside was a brief note, in large writing she found difficult to decipher. Eventually she made out the words: "This place belongs to someone my father knows," she read. "It needs a loving tenant, I gather. Rent low. Maintenance negligible. Available now. Terms negotiable, but long let preferred. Could this be of interest? Colin."

The style of this note surprised Lindsay, who would not have expected terseness from Colin. Having read it carefully twice, she turned to the enclosed photographs. She stared at them in disbelief, then gave a gasp of delight. They showed an old, beautiful house, of medium size, that might once have housed a farming family. It had a steep lichened roof and walls of honeyed stone. Next to it was an ancient stone barn, in front of which chickens pecked in a perfect courtyard. It had a perfect cottage garden, with hollyhocks and lavender. There was a perfect stream, flowing through a perfect orchard, and the boughs of the trees there were weighted down with ripening apples. Beyond the garden and the orchard, lay the green serenity of English fields, bathed in the gold of an English summer afternoon. "Shute Farm," Colin had written on the back of one of the pictures. "Twenty miles from Oxford."

Lindsay could not believe her eyes. It was uncanny how closely this resembled the house of her dreams, as described several times to Colin. When she saw that, although it was not by any means a hovel, it did have a rose, a crimson rose, trained around its door, she surrendered her heart to it.

She went to bed thoughtful and lay in the dark, suddenly fearful that she might dream of those ghosts at the Conrad. But her sleep was benign: she dreamed she was living in the magical house, writing an inspired biography, enjoying frequent visits from those two good friends, Colin Lascelles and Rowland McGuire. One afternoon, under those boughs of ripening apples in that orchard, Colin proposed to her again. This time, he was sober, and this time the proposal was witnessed by a silent Rowland McGuire. Lindsay was plucking an apple, and just about to give Colin her answer, when the dream took a new turn.

At the Conrad, Colin Lascelles did not even attempt sleep; in a fervor from that kiss on the cheek, in an agony of suspense as to Lindsay's reaction to the photographs, he felt it unlikely he would ever sleep again. He left Emily, together with Frobisher, watching a late movie on television—it was one of their favorites, *Terminator 2*. He retired to his own rooms at the far end of Emily's very large and labyrinthine apartment.

There, he paced up and down, tried to work, failed to work, discovered an urgent need to express himself, and picked up paper and pen. He wrote a long and impassioned letter to Lindsay Drummond, baring his heart. He covered six pages in his large sprawl, reread them, found them ill-phrased and inadequate, and decided instead to write to Rowland McGuire. He penned five pages to Rowland, explaining how grateful he felt to him for bringing the miracle of Lindsay his way, then decided in midsentence that this confession might be premature.

Rowland was discreet, it was true; indeed, he was one of the most discreet men Colin had ever known, remaining as reserved and silent on the subject of his own affairs as he was on those of his friends. He was, however, an old friend and colleague of Lindsay's; it was not impossible they would be in communication during her stay in New York, and not entirely impossible that Rowland might let something slip in conversation. Better to wait and apprise Rowland of his hopes, fears, and joys later, he decided, remembering that he had already, a few days before, sent Rowland a postcard that was somewhat overemotional in tone. He reread what he had written and found both letters weighty with adverbs. They had tried to cure Colin of adverbs at his public school; now a rash of them had broken out. There were "deeply" and "tenderly" and "unbelievably" and "eternally" just in the space of two lines.

He ripped both letters into confetti, consigned them to his metal wastebasket, then, knowing both Emily and Frobisher were capable of snooping, set fire to them. He burned his hand, scorched a fine Persian rug, and filled the room with choking smoke. Waving his arms and swearing, he leaped across to the window and flung it wide open. It had begun raining; the air was chilly and a fine mist hung above the trees of Central Park. He stared out at the same moon Tomas Court had found thin and sickly, and it seemed to him enchanting, creating a silvery city, a Manhattan of monochrome. Only the constant restless surge of the city and the ceaseless panic of its sirens disturbed him. When they intruded too much into his reverie, he closed the windows again and leaned against the glass, surrendering to the homesickness for Shute that was never far from him, and which now welled up in his heart.

He thought of the peace of its parkland, the grace and charm of Shute Court's south facade. Beautiful in all weathers and all lights, the great house had a particular magic by moonlight. Perhaps, he thought, he could contrive it so that Lindsay saw Shute at night and by moonlight, when he showed it to her for the first time.

A week after she moved into the estate farmhouse, perhaps? Two weeks? He wanted her to have time to fall in love with the beauties of the place, but he knew that once she was actually there, his deceptions could not be protracted too long, and the risk of accidental discovery was strong. He would have liked to take her there now, he thought; he wished that, at this very moment, they were walking hand in hand through the copse and out into the enchantment of the deer park.

Within seconds, he was seeing, then scripting, this first encounter; then he was scripting Lindsay's first meeting with his father—a little difficult this, for although Colin loved his father dearly, he knew his eccentricities were marked. Then he was introducing Lindsay to his two beloved lurcher dogs, Daphnis and Chloe; now they were in the great hall, now in the kitchen, and suddenly, he discovered, in his bedroom, in the peace and privacy of which room, Lindsay began to say and do the most marvelous things.

Colin lay down on his bed and closed his eyes; his imagination now beginning to gallop, he gave it a lover's free rein. He worshiped the roundness of Lindsay's breasts and the smoothness of her thighs; he discovered she possessed a loving agility; locked in each other's arms, they were just moving from a long adagio of kisses and caresses toward a crescendo of desire, when the telephone rang.

Colin looked at his bedside clock, discovered it was three in the morning, and was immediately certain that only one person in the world could be telephoning now. He grabbed the telephone, waited for that wonderful voice with a catch in it, and discovered he was listening to the very different voice of Thalia Ng.

His mind grappled with this disappointment and its detumescent effect. Gradually it began to register that Thalia, for once, was not swearing, and that she sounded both shaken and alarmed.

"I need your help," she was saying. "Get a cab, Colin, and come down to Tribeca—"

"Tribeca? Now?"

"Yes, Tomas's loft. And make it fast."

Colin's cab dropped him on the corner of Court's street. As he turned into it, he heard voices and running feet, then the slam of a vehicle's doors. He saw that a long white unidentified van, too small to be a hospital ambulance, but possibly a private one, was pulling away from Court's building. It moved off fast, without sounding its sirens, but with the red light on its roof flashing fear out of the shadows of the street and striking panic into Colin's heart. He ran the last few yards, entered the building, and, ignoring the elevator, ran fast up the stairs. The door to the loft was wide open and he could just see Thalia Ng, standing on the far side of that long black worktable where they had both spent most of the preceding day.

Colin moved forward into the doorway, questions on his lips, then stopped dead as he saw the extent of the damage in the room beyond. He stared around him, in shock and bewilderment. "Oh dear God," he said, in a low voice. "Christ—what's happened here?"

Thalia was supporting herself, he realized, by leaning against the table. Her face was drained of all color and she was trembling.

"He called me," she began, in a low unsteady voice. "He called me an hour ago. I came straight over. I called his doctor from home, before I left, because I could tell—from his voice, the way he was breathing . . ." She fumbled for a chair, then sat down. "Shut the door, Colin. I need a drink—find me something. Brandy, Scotch—whatever. I don't care."

"He doesn't drink. . . ." Colin closed the door and looked around him helplessly. He took a step forward, heard glass crunch under his feet, and realized that there was blood on the floor.

"I know, but he keeps some for other people. In that cabinet over there."

Colin made his way to the cabinet with care. His passage was blocked by upended, smashed chairs, by a blizzard of paper, ripped photographs, and coils of film stock. One of the cabinet doors had been wrenched off its hinges and most of its contents lay smashed and spilled on the floor. At the back of it, he found an unopened bottle of bourbon and one wineglass. He brought these back to the table, righted a chair, and sat down next to Thalia.

"Here," he said. "Drink it slowly."

Thalia took a swallow, half choked, then swallowed a little more. Colin looked at her untidy frizz of gray hair and at her clothes, which had obviously been bundled on in a hurry. He realized that she was much older than he had first thought, nearer sixty than fifty, and that she had been crying. Gently, he took her hand.

"Take your time. Thalia, can I get you something else? Tea? Sweet tea? You've had a shock—"

"Tea? Are you kidding?" Some color had returned to Thalia's face. "You have a cigarette? I know you smoke sometimes—"

Colin hesitated, his eye caught by one of Court's asthma inhalers, lying amid shreds of paper on the floor.

"It's okay. Tomas would forgive us, under the circumstances. Besides, he isn't here. . . ."

Colin lit cigarettes for both of them. Thalia inhaled, then, to Colin's consternation, began crying again.

"I thought he was dead," she began. "I thought he was dead. I walked in and he was lying on the floor right there, and I thought I was too late. Oh shit." She pulled off her glasses, and rubbed at her eyes ineffectually. Colin produced a handkerchief and handed it across. Thalia looked at this immaculate square of white linen, laughed, then began to cry again.

"I might have known you'd carry one of those. You're just so goddamn English, you know that?"

"Sorry," said Colin, "I do try. I just seem to revert now and then."

Thalia laughed again and dried her eyes. She took another swallow of bourbon and another deep inhalation of her cigarette.

"You're okay," she said at length, in a shaky voice. "Tomas thinks so. I think so—and that's why you're here. Tomas doesn't have any friends. I couldn't call Mario, because he talks. In fact, I couldn't think of anyone who *wouldn't* talk, and then I thought of you."

"I won't say anything." He looked around at the chaos of the room. "Thalia, what in God's name happened? Is Tomas all right?"

"No." She blew her nose. "Shit, my hands won't stop shaking." She swallowed a little more bourbon. "No, he's not all right. He hasn't been all right for quite some time. The asthma's worse and—there are other problems: stress, overwork, lack of sleep, anxiety." She looked away. "So—something happened here tonight, and I don't know what it was. There'd been a break-in, I guess. Tomas—someone had hit him. His hands were bleeding and there was this gash on his face, but the doctor said that wasn't serious. . . ."

"But he'd collapsed?"

"Yes. He was semiconscious; he couldn't speak. It was a bad asthma attack—one of the worst I've seen." She broke off and stubbed out the cigarette, grinding it in an angry way in a broken saucer that lay among the ripped papers on the table. "But he's going to be okay—the doctor says so. He will be okay. Rest, medication—they'll pull him around. Meantime, I need your help. You're going to help me clean this up." She gestured around the room. "And you're going to help me fix up a convincing cover story, because we need one, fast."

"A cover story?" Colin looked at her in confusion. "Why, Thalia? Shouldn't we call the police? Natasha Lawrence—have you called her, Thalia? She has to know—"

"She'll know in my good time, if at all. I don't want her involved now, and Tomas wouldn't either. As for the cops—no way. Give me another cigarette and I'll explain."

Colin lit another cigarette for her; she drew on it, then sighed. "You know how hard it's been for Tomas to get health insurance on this movie?" she began. "Very hard. He had to have three different medicals. The doctors didn't like the condition he was in, and they liked it a whole lot less when they found out he was facing a tight twelve-week shooting schedule in the north of England, in winter. The insurers finally signed a week ago, but they put in a back-out clause: any worsening of his condition before the start date and they withdraw cover. You know what that means? No movie is what it means. This movie has a seventy million dollar budget—you've seen the figures. Unless Tomas is insured, the studio stands to lose most of that if he cracks up during filming; they won't risk that. No insurance, and they'll pull the plug on the entire project. . . . So, no one finds out what happened tonight, you understand?"

"Of course I understand. But Thalia, this can't work. You can't keep this sort of thing under wraps. What about the doctor tonight? The ambulance men?"

"His doctor will keep his mouth shut. He's paid to do that, and paid well. They've taken Tomas to a private clinic so fucking discreet you'd think the CIA was running it. He's been there before. He goes in under an assumed name and he comes out under an assumed name, and if anyone there recognizes him, they get a fit of amnesia, you understand? The doctor says two or three days should do it. Then he flies back to Montana and he *stays* in Montana. I'm going to make him do that until we're ready to film. And as far as the studio is concerned, or anyone else connected with this movie is concerned—including Mario motormouth—Tomas is in Montana now. Change of plan: he flew out there tonight—you got that?"

"Will that work?"

Thalia shrugged. "It's worked before."

There was a silence. Colin began to understand. He began to see why there might have been those months of uncertainty as to Tomas Court's exact whereabouts. He began to see why, when he was scouting locations, it had sometimes proved so difficult to locate his director. He began to understand, now, the numerous occasions when, unable to reach Tomas Court himself, he had had to wait for Court to contact him.

"Thalia, how ill is he?" he asked.

"I don't know." Her face contracted. "I just know he's better when he's actually working. He's better when he isn't breathing in all the filth in this fucking city, and he's better when he's away from that ex-wife of his, as well."

"Why?"

"Because he loves her too much. It's like a sickness with him." Her face took on a closed expression. She rose. "Anyway— that isn't my business, and it certainly isn't yours. I'll call her later today and tell her Tomas had to go back out to Montana. I'll say some suit is flying out from the coast to see him there—"

"Thalia, you can't do that. He's ill; he's in hospital—what if something happened to him?"

"It won't, and I can't think of a quicker way to bring on another attack than have her weeping by his bedside. I'm telling you, he won't want her to know. He never does—"

"Why not, for God's sake?" Colin burst out. "Why all this secrecy? They were *married*; they have a child—"

"He doesn't like her to see him sick." Thalia made a grimace. "He doesn't like her to see him weak. And you know what? He's right. That woman can smell weakness in a man the way a shark scents blood in the ocean."

"That's ridiculous. That can't be true."

"It is true. I know her. Take it from me."

Her tone was very certain. Colin looked at her, then sank his head in his hands. He could feel unease welling up inside him; his mind felt dazed and confused. Lack of sleep was beginning to tell on him, but he knew the problem lay deeper than that. He did not have the right kind of intelligence, or perhaps character, to understand the complexities here. Love was love, he said to himself, and he could not understand why it should be twisted into some power game. How could love be a sickness? Love seemed to him both direct and simple: he loved his father; he had loved his brother; he loved friends such as Rowland; he tried to imagine his relationship with Lindsay in terms of deceit or malaise or a power struggle and found it unimaginable. Just to prevent himself from making a declaration, from flinging himself at her feet as it were, required all his self-control. Love ought to be freely and openly given, he thought, looking around him at the chaos of this room. He could not wait to tell Lindsay the truth. Why did people feel the need to distort love with lies and evasions and pretenses? Then it occurred to him that those who did so perhaps enjoyed greater success than he himself had. His own record, of pursuit by women who proved to be interested only in his money, or of rejections from women who preferred colder men to Colin, was no advertisement for the virtues of baring the soul.

He rose to his feet and tried to focus his mind on the realities of this room. It looked as if a fight had taken place in it, as if Tomas Court had surprised an intruder, yet the damage here, it seemed to him, was greater than any fight could explain. A fight might account for the broken chairs, smashed china and glass, but surely not for this blizzard of torn papers covering the floor, and not for a leather sofa, oozing rubberized stuffing, a sofa that someone seemed to have tried to disembowel.

He passed his hands across his face and turned back to Thalia.

"I still don't understand. What can have happened? When Tomas called you, did he explain?"

"No. He could barely speak. He just asked me to come over.

When I got here, the door was wide open and Tomas was on the floor, like I said. There was no one else here—"

"But who would do this? Has anything been stolen?"

"There was nothing to steal."

"Is it just this room?"

"No." She hesitated. "He'd been in the bedroom too. I—I closed the door. You'll have to deal with that. I'm not going in there."

Her tone was flat. Colin bent and picked up at random some of the papers torn and scattered at his feet. He leaned toward the light on the table and began to examine them. The first was a copy of the *New York Times* Arts section, dated a few days earlier; it was folded back at an interview with Natasha Lawrence he had already seen, an anodyne piece written by someone called Genevieve Hunter, whom Lindsay had mentioned she knew. The photograph of Natasha Lawrence had been smeared with some whitish substance. The quote referring to her future home in the Hollywood hills had been circled in green ink; the words LIAR BITCHCUNT had been written next to it in capitals.

He began to feel sick. He dropped the newspaper and examined the other fragments of paper one by one. Some he recognized as the various revised shooting schedules that had been littering the table the previous day. There were several others that concerned the Conrad building, some torn from books, others, to judge from their paper and wording, from architectural journals. Finally, there were scraps of what appeared to be letters, handwritten, again in capitals, and again in green ink. He peered at the words, which seemed to concern Natasha Lawrence and bodyguards; then he came across the first reference to animals. He crimsoned and let the scraps of paper fall.

Thalia, who had been watching him in silence, gave a gesture toward the sea of fragments covering the floor. Colin saw there were more communications in green ink, hundreds of them, perhaps more, all of them ripped and shredded and trampled upon.

"You've heard about Joseph King?" Thalia said, her face expressionless.

"Yes. Mario told me."

"You heard he might have died, last July—killed himself maybe?"

"No, I didn't know that."

"That was what people hoped. Those are his letters. Five years' worth of letters—"

"But he can't be dead." Colin picked up the newspaper, then held it out to her. "Green ink, the same writing. This paper is dated four days ago."

"I know. I saw it before you arrived. In fact . . ." Thalia paused. "It's partly why I called you. I got afraid. I think he's been here tonight. I think Tomas caught him in the act of going through these letters. I think he's been listening to the tapes of his phone calls as well. . . ."

"Those tapes in the bedroom? Those are *his*?" Colin stared at her. "I saw them yesterday—the door was open. Thalia, why would Tomas keep them? I don't understand."

"He likes listening to them. Don't ask me why. I wouldn't dare ask him and I prefer not to know. But those tapes were playing when I arrived and they're probably still playing now. I wasn't going to go into that room and I won't now." She gave herself a little shake. "So you're going to have to do it. You're going to switch the fucking thing off, then we're taking all the tapes and we're going to box them up along with the rest of this filth. Then I'm taking it all away and I'm getting it burned, which is something I should have done a long time ago. . . ."

"Thalia, we can't do that; we don't have the right. This is Tomas's property, in the first place—and in the second, it's evidence. We have to call the police."

"This stuff is killing Tomas." She turned away. "I've watched it poison him and I'm not watching it anymore. And we *don't* call the police. We do that and this whole story's splashed across the tabloids tomorrow. There'll be reporters and photographers crawling all over this. They'll have tracked Tomas down to that clinic by tonight. Some asshole cop will be slipping those tapes to some contact of his, and before you know it, this shit will be all over the front pages, and the *National Enquirer* will be taking their marriage apart. . . ."

"Thalia—I said call the police, not Reuters."

"Same thing in this city."

"Thalia, no newspaper would print this stuff." Colin gestured toward the sea of papers. "They *couldn't* print it—and they wouldn't. Why would they? King isn't sane, that's obvious. Who would print this kind of sick allegation?"

"You've been reading the wrong newspapers." Thalia gave him a derisive look. "And don't make the mistake of thinking King's just some crazy fantasist; he isn't. He likes to mix a little fact in with his fictions. You think this would have obsessed Tomas the way it has if it was all sick lies from start to finish? No way. King's *better* than that, and a whole lot smarter. It's because Tomas knew King was telling the truth about *his* activities, that he thought he just might be telling the truth about Natasha as well."

Colin felt that sick unease begin to rise in his stomach again. He picked up a scrap of one of the letters, then quickly let it fall.

"He couldn't have believed this—*surely* he couldn't have believed this. . . ." he began.

Thalia gave him a tired look. "I think he believed some of it, some of the time. Maybe he even *wanted* to believe it. I'm not arguing with you about this; I'm getting rid of this stuff, the tapes *and* the letters, so you've got a straight choice: either you help me or you go."

She sat down at the table as she said this, as if suddenly exhausted, and ran her hands through her frizz of gray hair. Colin hesitated. His instinct was still to call the police, to believe that they could bring order, justice, and due punishment to whatever crime, or crimes, had been committed here. He looked at the blood splashed on the floor and the sea of incriminatory paper.

"Let me check the bedroom," he said. "I'll switch that tape off, then I'll decide."

He crossed to the far end of the loft, opened the door in that bare, brutal brick wall, and moved into the corridor, feeling for the light switch. The ugly neon flickered into life; he could hear a low, level, midwestern voice, speaking with a pedantic insistence, as soon as he opened the door.

He paused in the bedroom doorway, feeling suddenly afraid, watching the small red warning light come on above the bed. The room was tidy and apparently untouched. That brownish bedcover was uncrumpled; the pillows bore the faint impress of a head, but might have been that way before.

Although the havoc of the outer room was not repeated here, he could sense disturbance in the air. It emanated from the tape recorder and the quiet murmuring voice, and it made him feel he was breathing in contagion; he could sense it as soon as he entered, some toxicity breeding here.

He moved across to the surgical table and the large, outdated machine. He began to fumble in the half light with the machine's unfamiliar switches and dials. "Hot, hot and moist," said a voice, very loudly, right in his ear; he started back, realizing that by mistake he had turned up the volume control.

He backed away to the door, trying to close his mind to this spillage of words. He found the light switch and depressed it, but no light came on. He returned to the machine and bent over it, his hands now unsteady, trying to make sense of its battery of controls. He began pressing switches at random, but the twin spools continued to rotate and the voice continued speaking. "Naked in bed," Colin heard. He turned another dial and the voice sank to a whisper, a whisper he found more insidious and more discomfiting. "Absolute lust, shall I tell you what she did next?" whispered the voice, and to his horror Colin found he wanted to know.

He slammed his palm against a whole row of switches, then, when that produced no effect, began a frantic search for the plug. The machine's cables snaked away from the surgical table and disappeared under the bed. The outlet seemed to be at the head of the bed, under the *Dead Heat* altarpiece. He began to push and pull at the bed in order to reach behind it, but the bed, monstrously large, monstrously heavy, mounted on a box-like plinth, refused to move.

Abandoning this, he straightened, stared at the machine, and found himself mesmerized. *"Such dexterity . . . were satisfied . . . the supervisor grossly . . . swallow them up."* Colin watched the tape wind from the right spool to the left. The room seemed to be growing hotter and hotter; he could feel himself being lured down some whispering corridor of words, around this corner and into room after hidden room.

He knew that the words were affecting him; his body began to stir in response to the description of acts he abhorred. He felt a giddiness, a compulsion to continue listening, then the voice made a small mistake: "She loved it," it pronounced with a sigh, and Colin's senses returned, for love was not the emotion being described here.

A sudden cleansing anger surged through his body. Reaching across, he grasped hold of the tape and wrenched it out of the machine. It coiled about his wrist and voided itself with a high-pitched squeaky scream. He pulled harder, and yards of the stuff spilled out like entrails; he caught hold of the machine, which proved immensely heavy, picked it up bodily, and flung it down. Its casing cracked open, sparks flew, there was a blue, scorching, flashing tongue of light, a smell of burning, then a fizzling sound.

Colin returned to the main room of the loft. Thalia, who was kneeling on the floor, stuffing handfuls of papers in boxes, looked up at him.

"You'll help me?" she asked.

"I've already started. I'll find a trash can," Colin replied.

They worked side by side, in virtual silence, for several hours. Shortly before six, Thalia telephoned Mario to cancel that morning's meeting and to inform him that Tomas Court had returned to Montana; Mario received this information without surprise.

Half an hour later, when the first thin light began to tint the sky, their task was completed. The bags and boxes of toxic waste, as Colin now thought of them, were stacked at the door awaiting disposal. Thalia was about to call the clinic, to check on Tomas Court's progress; Colin, exhausted and troubled, was standing at the tall loft windows, watching a slow Manhattan dawn. A thin cat, he saw, was emerging from an alleyway; he watched it nose the trash cans. He was trying to think of Lindsay, and finding he could not do so here, when the telephone rang.

"Tomas never picks up. He always lets the answering machine screen the calls." Thalia looked at him uncertainly. "But it could be the clinic. . . ."

Colin crossed to her side, feeling a sudden unease. They both waited as the telephone rang three times. The answering machine kicked in. "Leave any message after the tone," said a tinny mechanical voice; silence ensued. Thalia gave a nervous gesture; Colin leaned close to the answering machine. He thought he could hear breathing, then a strange rhythmic sighing sound, like the sea. When the now familiar midwestern voice finally spoke, it startled him.

"Testing, testing, testing," said the voice. "Just checking your machine, checking your machine . . ."

Chapter 11

"Not a nice place, that labyrinth," Markov was saying to Lindsay, at 9:23 the same morning. "All those sacrifices, Lindy. A definite reek of blood and bone. Even I could sense it, and Jippy didn't like it at all. . . ."

Not for the first time in her life, Lindsay cursed Markov's addiction to the telephone. Since 8:55, the entire world had decided to call her. First it had been Pixie; then, at nine on the dot, Gini Lamartine, wanting to cancel Thanksgiving in Washington ("I'll call you back," Lindsay had cried); next, Max had called and received very short shrift. There were then two minutes of agonizing silence, before the next caller proved to be that mumbling person from Lulu Sabatier's office, wanting to speak to Ms. Drummond urgently.

"She's *dead*," Lindsay cried. "She died suddenly. Go *away*."

At 9:15, it had been Markov. Lindsay had already had four minutes on the subject of the lunch he and Jippy had just finished—retsina and moussaka; delicious, but Jippy had no appetite at all—and four minutes on the palace of Knossos; she did not intend to have any more.

"Markov," she interrupted, "will you get off this line? I'm not *interested* in minotaurs. I told you, I'm waiting for a very important call."

"You're insensitive, you know that, Lindy?" Markov yawned. "Thanks to the miracles of modern technology, darling, this is your friend calling you from the other side of the world. How's Gotham City? Whose call?"

"I'm hanging up, Markov. I'm hanging up in twenty seconds. . . ."

"Tell me, Lindy, just to set my heart at rest, sweetling—this

236

call wouldn't be from a certain Rowland McGuire, would it? You remember him? The answer to every maiden's prayer? Otherwise known as Mr. Blind, Mr. Unobtainable, and Mr. Conspicuously Bad News?"

"No, it damn well isn't. It's—it's work, that's all. Go *away*, Markov. Ten seconds and counting . . ."

"Jippy wants a word."

Jippy might have wanted a word, but as usual he had difficulty in pronouncing it. Desperate now, Lindsay stared at the hands of her bedside clock; she could hang up on Markov without compunction, but not Jippy—that would be too cruel. She listened to Jippy fight sounds; she saw his gentle, steady, brown-eyed gaze, that expression of doglike fidelity; she remembered the last time she had spoken to him and felt the brush of unease. It took Jippy one and a half minutes to utter a sound.

"H-h-hell," he said finally. Lindsay waited for the last "o" of the greeting; it never came.

"Sorry about that." After a pause, Markov came back on the line. "I told you, Jippy's upset. He's picking up some *baad* vibrations here. . . ."

"Where?" Lindsay asked, jolted by Jippy's truncated greeting and feeling a small shiver. "Where? In Knossos? In Crete, you mean?"

"Kind of." There was a pause; some whispering. "Anyway, he sends love. He says, take care."

"Listen Markov, I send you both my love too, but I'm hanging up, I have to—"

"No problem. We'll see you soon anyway. Back for Thanksgiving in the Big Apple, that's the plan. I might go for a swim now. The wine-dark sea beckons. . . . Give my *fondest* love to Rowland, darling. Oh, and here's *un petit message* for him. Tell him, he who hesitated has lost. Tell him, serves him *right*, because if he'd listened to me *years* ago, he wouldn't be up shit creek without a compass now. And tell him Jippy says—"

"What? What?"

"Jippy says, Frailty thy name is woman." Markov laughed. "Bye, *mia cara*," he added, and with his usual annoying timing, hung up.

Lindsay glared at the telephone. The trouble with gay men, she told herself, was that they did not understand women at all. They might like to think they did, but they were invariably wrong.

Minutes ticked. Mr. Blind, Mr. Unobtainable did not call. She would give him another five minutes, Lindsay decided, at 9:40, and then she would leave.

It had taken Colin and Thalia a long time to load all the bags and boxes of toxic waste into her station wagon. Thalia announced that when she had disposed of them, she would be going out to the clinic to see Tomas Court; she would call Colin at the Conrad later that day.

"You know that ex-wife of his is trying to buy an apartment there?" she said, standing arms akimbo, out of breath, next to the open door of her car.

Colin felt as if he were drowning, possibly in unhappiness, or confusion, or slime; he focused on her question with difficulty.

"I know. It seemed better not to mention it—"

"Wise," said Thalia. "With Tomas, the art is knowing when to speak and when to keep your mouth shut. He respects silence." She frowned. "Have you met Natasha?"

"No."

"Well, when you do, you'll see. She perfected the art of silence a long time ago."

Her tone was pejorative. "Perfected?" Colin said.

"Sure. In her case, silence can be a weapon, you know." She made no further comment. Colin watched her car disappear. He stood in the deserted street, looking at darkened buildings; a steady rain had begun to fall. It was still early, not seven yet; the day seemed reluctant to begin and the city was unusually silent. Distant, and filtered by buildings, he could just hear the growl of traffic, as if some somnolent leviathan sensed dawn and stirred.

He felt light-headed and disoriented from lack of sleep. He knew there was a cross street less than two blocks away where he could pick up a cab, yet felt he had no idea which way to turn. He was tired, yet hyperalert; he felt dirty and anxious to wash off all trace of King's communications from his hands;

he felt afraid, and had ever since he heard that low, oddly mocking voice come through on the answering machine.

"Testing, testing, *testing*." He glanced over his shoulder, swung around, suddenly sensing someone behind him, as close as a shadow. There was no one there; the street was empty. From some domain beyond the stacks of trash cans, a cat yowled.

He had to walk, he discovered, when he had already covered two blocks. He had to walk, move his body, breathe air; he had no wish to wait for a cab, or to be in a cab, or to have to speak to anyone, even to give directions. He had to walk and force the night's events out of his mind. He paused, looking back at the towers of the financial district to his south, where the light was beginning to crest the money citadels with gold. Then he set off north, swinging his arms, breathing in carbon monoxide as if it were the freshest mountain air. He skirted Little Italy, plunged on north through the charms of the West Village, and found himself in the garment district, where the trucks were already drawn up, disgorging rails of clothes. It was winter and it was cold, yet he was pushing past diaphanous summer dresses. He brushed against something gauzy, thought of Lindsay, whose professional territory this was, and felt a longing to be with her so fierce and so sudden it was like being punched in the heart.

This was where his footsteps had been leading him, he realized. Lindsay could heal him; she could rid him of this sensation—which he still had, long after leaving the chaos of Court's loft—that he was treading on broken glass.

But he could not see Lindsay as he was now. He felt dirty, coated with grime, besmirched; he could not rid himself of the sensation that Joseph King's words had gotten under his fingernails and were adhering to his hair. Two men, he felt, had stood in Tomas Court's bedroom a few hours before, and two men had confronted that tape recorder. One, the Colin he recognized and thought he knew, had wanted to silence that voice; the other, some *doppelgänger*, some other Colin whom he loathed and feared, liked the voice and its story. It was familiar to him, as if he and not King had determined it; he knew every twist of its plot, longed to hear its climaxes, and saw, with a dark and resonant pleasure, how it must inevitably end. Which man had failed to find the switch-off mechanism? Colin thought now, quickening his pace—and was he entirely sure which of these two selves was drawing him north to Lindsay now?

He crossed Forty-second Street, that Manhattan divide, and pressed on, the rain falling more heavily now. He was on Fifth, and approaching a gilded area of the city, although he scarcely saw the lighted windows and was blind to their promise of luxury. He did not see the furs, the exquisite shoes, or the jewels; he did not see the temptations arrayed for Thanksgiving, or sense the allure of commerce's pre-Christmas display. Blind to Saks, to Tiffany's, and to Bergdorf's, he fixed his eyes on the bare trees of Central Park up ahead, crossed by the Plaza, caught the smell of the poor blinkered horses who waited there to ferry tourists, even in winter, even in rain, and finally glimpsed, up ahead of him, the dark, squat bulk of the Conrad, the bellying of its rounded turrets and the expectancy of its many dormer eyes.

How many blocks had he walked? Fifty? Sixty? More? He had lost count. He stumbled into Emily's apartment, drenched to the skin. There Frobisher, who had known him all his life, fussed over him and exclaimed, but he brushed aside these ministrations; all he could think about was a bath, a shower, the cleansing effect of water, and the urgency of seeing Lindsay. Pushing past Frobisher, he was waylaid by Emily, who seemed to be in a great state of excitement about something. She bombarded him with sentences; she was getting ready for the crucial board meeting; she couldn't find her pearls; she had discovered she was *wearing* her pearls; she had already spoken to Biff and Henry Foxe on the telephone, and *something was going on.* . . .

"Going on? Going on?" Colin did not know what his aunt was talking about; nor, at that moment, did he care.

"What time is it? What time is it?" he said over his shoulder, hurrying on down the corridor.

"Wheels within wheels," he heard her call after him. "*Wheels*; and I can darned well hear them turning. Frobisher, Frobisher, which purse shall I take? The lizard, or the crocodile?"

Colin slammed his door on her agitations. He went to look at his watch, a twenty-first birthday present from his father, and found he was not wearing it. He began a frantic search, on his chest of drawers, bedside table, on the floor. Then he remembered, felt in the pocket of his coat, felt in the pocket of his suit and discovered it. He peered at its dial in disbelief. Past nine? How could it be past nine? What had happened to the hours?

He plunged across to the telephone and dialed the Pierre.

"I have to see you," he said. "Lindsay—I have to see you this morning, *now*. Can you wait for me? I'll—I have to—I'll be there in an hour. . . ."

He thought she said yes, she would wait. He put down the phone, turned on the shower, and started pulling off his clothes. Then he realized he was uncertain what she had said. Was it yes? Was it no? Had a time been mentioned? He dived back to the phone. He punched in the numbers. It rang through to Lindsay's room, his watch told him, at precisely 9:45. Lindsay answered on the first ring.

"Yes, yes, yes, yes, yes," she said. "I told you. I'll be here."

She replaced the receiver at once. Colin felt a soaring of the spirits. He pulled off his clothes, kicked the masterly dirty suit into a corner, kicked the shirt and the silk foulard tie and the handmade shoes and the socks and the boxer shorts after it. He turned the water on full blast. He glimpsed his own nakedness in the mirrors and stepped into the hail of the shower.

Rowland McGuire's call finally came through at 9:52. By then, those demons she fought so unsuccessfully had tormented Lindsay into a great state of nerves. Despite the fact that, of all the female characteristics with which she was richly endowed, a propensity to sit by a telephone and hope was the one she most loathed and despised, she had found herself trapped in that room at the Pierre. She was well acquainted with every inch of its carpet as she paced round and round. It was disconcerting, at exactly 9:45—the time she had convinced herself Rowland would call—to pick up the receiver and hear a man tell her he had to see her, when the voice telling her this was the wrong voice, and the man, much as she liked him, was the wrong man.

At 9:46, having hung up on Colin, she had got herself as far as the door. By 9:47 she was back again at the bed, staring at the telephone with joy in her heart. She had just realized that if Rowland's call the night before came through at eleven New York time, it must have been placed in London at four in the morning. For a brief instant, this fact filled her with hope. She imagined Rowland, in the dead of night, afflicted with torments similar to her own. Then she saw the obvious explanation: Rowland, who did not suffer torments, had called at four A.M. because he happened to have returned home then—and her swift and deadly imagination had no difficulty in seeing just why he might have returned so late, and why he had been detained.

A brief sojourn in heaven; a swift and predictable descent to hell. Will I never be free of this bondage? Lindsay thought, feeling the familiar shackles lock into place. She turned back to the door, resolving on liberty; the telephone rang, and she found all desire for liberty had gone.

She let it ring three times, out of pride, and in an attempt to calm herself. Sweet, womanly, *dulcet,* she reminded herself. She snatched up the receiver, heard Rowland's voice, and experienced, as she always did, the same fatal joy. It was short-lived. Within sentences, she saw that this conversation was stilted and unusually awkward; this panicked her; she sensed an alteration in Rowland's manner, and this panicked her more.

He was not addressing her with his usual friendly warmth; if anything, his manner was cautious and guarded, even cold. He sounded as if he were feeling his way into this conversation with care, trusting neither himself nor her. He sounded, in short, like a stranger, and not like the man she had known for three years.

Where was that usual fraternal ease, that relaxed willingness to discuss what each of them had been doing and where each had been? It was gone, utterly gone—the rules of their dialogue had changed. What could have happened in the space of just a week to effect such a change? Lindsay's mind froze over. She felt like an actor whose script had just been torn from his hand; she was left with scraps and tatters of memorized speeches and an urgent need to improvise her way back into the scene.

It might have been easier to do that, had Rowland been

giving her clear and simple cues, but she found he was not doing that. She was stranded midstage, unable to hear the prompter, desperate to communicate with a fellow actor who sounded as stranded and uneasy as she. She stared at the wall. What was *wrong*? Had Rowland changed or had she?

Concentrate, concentrate, she said to herself. How did this halting dialogue begin? Rowland had prefaced his remarks by explaining, somewhat irritably, that he had been trying to get through since 8:55. Sounding agitated—and Rowland never sounded agitated—he had added that he had a meeting shortly and so could not talk for long.

"I'd hoped," he had said, "to reach you last night. It would have been almost exactly a week since I last spoke to you— and we wouldn't have been worrying about time. . . ."

Time! As soon as he used the word, Lindsay started babbling inanities. She realized that Colin Lascelles would be arriving here soon. She could hear some inexorable clock ticking; she could see its pendulum swing. It was important, it was vital, to strike the right tone, to say the right thing.

Then—what had happened then? Rowland had cut her inanities short. Had he done so in an irritable way? No. He had interrupted in a dry, even patient way, so for a second Lindsay glimpsed the man she knew.

"I received that burst of Morse," he said, hesitating. "At least, I think I did. Lindsay—"

Then he had stopped short. Whatever he had been about to say, he seemed to find it impossible to pronounce. He was as silent as Jippy, and Lindsay panicked again. Some idiot, she thought, some *dolt* has cut us off.

"Rowland, are you there?" she said, now very agitated.

"Yes, I'm here."

"Oh, thank goodness. I thought . . ."

"Can you hear me all right? You sound odd, Lindsay. You sound different. I—"

"Yes, yes. I can hear you perfectly. . . ."

"You're sure?"

Why ever was he insisting on this point? Lindsay thought. It was wasting time; it was using up precious seconds.

"Yes, I hear you as clear as a bell, as if you were in the same room and standing next to me. It's just . . ."

"What?"

"Nothing. You have that meeting. I—I'm worrying about time. . . ."

"Then I'll come to the point. Wasn't I supposed to be testing that famous intuition of yours?"

Rowland did not sound as if the prospect of doing so gave him amusement. He sounded oddly *formal*, Lindsay thought; and try as she would, she could not concentrate fully on what he was saying. She was beginning to worry that Colin, if unable to get through on the telephone from the desk, might come upstairs.

Rowland had continued speaking, she now realized, for some time. He had been speaking throughout this flurried reappraisal of the beginning of their conversation, and he was still speaking now. He had said, after the mention of intuition, something about a visit to Oxford, something about some don, and something about Tom. But now her need to say the right thing, the vital thing, was growing stronger and stronger. She could feel this message rising up from her heart, and the urgency of these words made them take on physical shape; they loomed larger and larger in her mind; they were large, the size of a hoarding, as tall as the Hollywood sign.

". . . Tom's opinion," she heard.

"I have missed you, Rowland," said her tongue. Lindsay clamped her hand over her mouth. She realized that this blurted remark had gone unanswered. She was listening to silence, a silence that went on too long.

"Lindsay—"

He said her name with a sudden lift to his voice, and Lindsay, intent on retrieval, intent on glossing over that admission, an admission that had phrased itself in the wrong way, so that it sounded defensive, began babbling again.

When she said *missed*, she continued, revving up into overdrive, what Rowland must remember was how dispiriting the collections could be, and how good it always was to have a friend to unwind with at the end of a hard day. Preferably someone with little interest in fashion, such as Rowland himself . . . or, for instance, his friend Colin Lascelles.

Her eye fell on those photographs of Shute Farm, and she rushed on. Luckily for her, she continued, Colin had been a

great help in this respect. They'd taken to meeting here in the
bar after work. . . . Oh, and last night, he'd taken her out for the
most delicious dinner. Then he had shown her the Conrad, that
extraordinary building, and introduced her to his aunt. . . .

This speech, a long one, was not interrupted once by Rowland; it was received in absolute silence, until the moment
when she mentioned Colin's aunt. Then he did interrupt, and
his next question was not warmly asked.

"Colin introduced you to Emily?"

"Yes, yes, yes," Lindsay said, accelerating again, and
finding that Rowland's *froideur*, his inexplicable *froideur*, was
making her more nervous. "Yes, yes," she said; then Colin
had brought her back to the Pierre and had produced these
photographs.

This topic took Lindsay off on a very long explanation,
involving her own future plans, her economic strategies, and
finally the uncanny perfection of this house near Oxford called
Shute Farm.

"Could I just get something clear?" Rowland said, his tone
now arctic, interrupting this encomium as Lindsay began to
rhapsodize about roses around doors. "You're planning on
moving out of London, is that correct?"

"Yes, yes. Didn't I mention that was my plan?"

"No." There was a pause. "You did not."

This time his tone was so forbidding, Lindsay did not dare to
speak, let alone babble.

"Shute Farm. Twenty miles from Oxford. Well, well."

"It's the location that makes it so perfect, Rowland,"
Lindsay said, confused and a little hurt that Rowland seemed
displeased at her good fortune. "It will mean I can see Tom
from time to time—but it's not right on his doorstep, so he
won't feel cramped. And then, it's so pretty, Rowland. It's in
the middle of fields, no neighbors. . . ."

"Are you sure about that?"

"There's no other cottages in the picture, Rowland, just
fields. So there'll be nothing and no one to distract me. . . ."

"Possibly." He sounded unconvinced. "It's certainly in a
very beautiful part of the country."

"Oh, you mean you know it, Rowland? From when you
were at Oxford?"

"Yes, I used to drive out that way often. I know it well. And who did you say this place belongs to? Someone Colin's father knows? I see. And it's available? The rent is low?"

"I think so. Colin's coming over to explain all the details today. He'll be here any minute, in fact—"

"Ah. Well, don't let me detain you."

"No, no. He's coming up here—I know he'd love a word with you."

"Somehow I doubt that. And I don't have time."

"It really is the most beautiful house, Rowland. It's everything I dreamed about," Lindsay said, still puzzled by his critical tone. "If it does work out, will you come and see it? I'd like that. You could come over one day for a meal with Colin. . . ."

"With Colin? That should prove diverting, to say the least."

"Rowland, is something wrong? I don't understand. You sound so—I expect I'm making you late for your meeting."

"Lateness is certainly on my mind."

"I don't want you to miss it, Rowland—"

"I have a feeling I've already missed it."

"Rowland, you could sound a bit more encouraging, you know." Lindsay hesitated, disappointment welling inside her. "I thought you'd be pleased. It was so kind of Colin to help. He's obviously gone to a lot of trouble. . . ."

"Oh, I agree."

"He is your friend, Rowland. I was—well, I was a bit worried about the money side of things, and . . ."

"With good cause."

"I'm sorry?" Lindsay felt a sudden distress. "Rowland, don't be disparaging. I know I haven't planned all of this as well as I might have done—and that book contract isn't marvelous, but I am trying to do my best. . . ."

"No, the contract isn't marvelous, and any fool could have told you not to sign it. I suppose that one of these days you'll learn to stand up for yourself on the money front. I certainly hope so, because that publisher has taken you for a ride."

"Rowland—"

"You do realize, do you, that there's no way you can live on that kind of advance? It's going to take you two years, probably three, to write this damn book, and that advance won't pay your electricity bills. . . ."

"Yes it will. Wait a moment, Rowland"—Lindsay, feeling her temper begin to rise, struggled to control it. *Dulcet* she reminded herself. "I don't think you can have been listening," she continued. "I *told* you—it will be a bit tight, but I can manage. I can rent my apartment in London for quite a lot, and somewhere in the country is bound to be cheaper. Colin says . . ."

"Oh, for God's sake. When are you going to grow up, Lindsay? What kind of daydream are you living in? All right, economics was never your strong point, but why don't you *check*? What you can afford wouldn't rent you a boathouse in the Orkney Islands, let alone a desirable farmhouse in Oxfordshire. Why are you so naive?"

"I'm not naive—and you're *wrong*. I *told* you, I consulted Colin and Colin says that . . ."

"Jesus Christ, will you stop parroting Colin's name?" Rowland's voice rose. "No doubt you think Colin is giving you disinterested advice. You thought that shark of a publisher was doing just that. You're *impossible*, Lindsay. Where's your judgment here? You've known Colin for ten minutes. I've known him for twenty years and . . ."

"Then you ought to be loyal to him," Lindsay snapped. "You shouldn't suggest he's a shark. . . ."

"I didn't *say* that. Dear God, do you *never* listen? I'm just suggesting you look at this farmhouse proposal carefully and don't rush into it without thinking, because as we all know, thinking before you act isn't exactly your strong point."

"Goddammit, Rowland, you can be insufferable, you know that?" Lindsay said sharply. "Stop being so patronizing. I'm not fifteen. Can you stop talking down to me for five seconds? I'm not a child you know."

"Well, you can certainly behave like one," Rowland cut in, "in which respect, you and Colin make an excellent pair. As was evident when we all had lunch at Oxford, I now realize. I can't think how it escaped my notice at the time."

"You pompous creep!" Lindsay shouted, losing her temper completely. "What's the matter with you? Oxford? I might have known you'd bring that up sooner or later. The one time in all the years you've known me when I happened to get a little bit drunk. . . ."

"A little bit? You couldn't damn well stand *up*. You were falling over. You had to be propped up by me. It was one of the most . . ." Rowland stopped abruptly. He hesitated.

"Yes? Yes?" Lindsay shouted, abandoning dulcet to the winds. "Go on, list my crimes! I don't give a damn if I *was* drunk. That's the effect you have on me. I could drink an entire bottle of Scotch right now."

"You kissed my sweater," Rowland said, in an altered tone.

"So what?" Lindsay yelled. "I don't care if I did. I'll kiss a hundred men's sweaters, anytime I feel like it. I don't have to ask your permission before I breathe. You're the most pompous, mean-spirited, narrow-minded, uptight man I've ever known."

"Would you like to answer my question?" Rowland said, in a voice that sounded dangerously calm. "Pleasant though it is to be insulted by you on the transatlantic phone, I do have that meeting to attend. So answer the question, if you would, and then I can cease annoying you."

"What damn question?" Lindsay shouted, now beside herself with rage. "You haven't asked me anything—and I'm not insulting you."

"I asked you a question at the very beginning of this conversation," Rowland said, his voice becoming colder by the second. "If you've already forgotten it, it can't have been worth asking. Never mind . . ."

He paused, and for one second Lindsay thought he was about to hang up. Clearly he had second thoughts, because with effort, he continued.

"I told you," he said, "that I have to go to Oxford soon, and while I'm there, I thought I should look in and see Tom. There's something—well, there's something I need to discuss with him."

"Something you need to discuss with Tom?" Lindsay frowned. "Well, of course, I know he'd be delighted to see you. Katya would too."

"I'd rather Katya wasn't there actually. I wanted to talk to Tom alone."

There was a silence; Rowland had spoken with emphasis. Lindsay felt a flicker of unease.

"You don't want Katya to be there?" She hesitated, feeling suddenly afraid. "I don't understand. Rowland, does this concern Katya in some way?"

"You could put it like that. I want to make Tom understand that—"

"Tom loves Katya." Lindsay spoke in a flat voice, panic rising. "He adores her. They've been together more than two years. She's the fixed point of his life, Rowland."

"Precisely. I know that. Which is why—"

"Oh God. She wrote to you, didn't she? You told me and I thought no more about it." Lindsay's voice became unsteady. "I can't believe this. Rowland—wait. . . ."

In a second, a score of past incidents flashed before her eyes. She saw all those occasions when Katya glanced at Rowland as she made some provocative remark; all the occasions when Katya had tried to monopolize Rowland in argument; all the occasions when she had watched Katya mask attraction with antagonism, and had done nothing, assuming that Katya's fascination with Rowland was harmless, that it would vanish eventually of its own accord.

"So what's happened?" she heard herself say. "Has she written to you again? Have you seen her? Rowland—you haven't encouraged her, surely? She's nineteen years old. She's young enough to be your daughter—"

"I'm aware of Katya's age." Rowland's voice had become curt. "Lindsay, will you listen to me? For the whole of this past week I've—dammit, this is impossible on the telephone. . . ." Lindsay could hear the emotion in his voice then, and the urgency; it spoke volumes and it made her afraid.

"Oh, I can't believe this, I *can't*," she burst out. "Rowland, how can you even *consider* such a thing? How far has this gone? You realize what this will do to Tom, do you? He admires you so much—he looks up to you. Rowland, if you've been anywhere near Katya, if you've flirted with her, I'll never forgive you. For God's sake, aren't there enough obliging women in London? She's Tom's *girlfriend*. Don't you *dare* go running to my son with that kind of problem. . . ."

"Have you finished?"

"No, I damn well haven't. What are you proposing to say to him, Rowland?"

"I'm not proposing to say anything now. I'll forget the entire fucking idea. Jesus Christ, I don't believe this. . . . I'm going to hang up—"

"No, you won't. You'll explain and explain now. What's happened? It's something serious, I can tell from your voice. . . ."

"*Nothing's* happened. You expect me to answer that kind of accusation? You think I'm that kind of man? What in God's name has got into you?"

"Yes, I damn well do expect you to answer. I can hear it— you're hiding something. You said you had to talk to Tom alone. You said it concerned Katya. . . ."

"Dammit, I didn't say that. Do you *never* listen? Fine. Just for the record, Lindsay, and to set your mind at rest, I'll spell it out to you. No, I wouldn't set out to seduce or encourage a nineteen-year-old girl who happens to live with a young man I like and admire. No, I wouldn't encourage her in any way if I had the slightest suspicion that she was interested in me. And, finally, *finally,* Lindsay, if such a situation arose, the very last thing I'd do is run with the problem to a volatile boy half my age." He paused. "I'd have thought you might have known that. The fact that you clearly don't hurts me more than I can say." He paused again. "In fact, it makes me so fucking angry, I don't even know why I'm continuing this conversation, so—"

"Wait. Don't hang up. Rowland, listen—" Lindsay hesitated, feeling a rising tide of shame and distress. "I'm sorry. I'm sorry if I jumped to the wrong conclusions, but you sounded—I still don't understand. Why did you want to see Tom?"

"I told you. I won't be making that visit now. It's not really your concern—but Tom's reading history, and it was history I wanted his opinion on; ancient history at that. As to how you think I sounded—no doubt it's the strain of having a conversation with you. For what it's worth, Lindsay, you're one of the stupidest women I've ever known. You leap to conclusions; you don't listen half the time; you're so wrapped up in your own plans, and your own activities, that you never notice what other people are thinking or saying, let alone feeling. . . ."

"Wait—Rowland. That's not true—"

"I'd like to know, before I ring off, just what possible justification you think you have for what you've just said to me. In all the time you've known me, have I ever behaved in that way?"

"No. Maybe not . . ." Lindsay hesitated. "But if we're going to be honest, you have a certain reputation, Rowland, you know."

"Do I? I see." He gave a sigh. "And you believe the gossip you hear. Well, that's good to know. So much for *your* loyalty, Lindsay."

"That's not fair either," Lindsay said, fighting tears. "I've always—Rowland, please, I've said I'm sorry. I was upset and I was confused. You'd been so harsh about all my plans. You sounded so strange. . . ."

"I may have sounded harsh, but what I said was accurate."

"You talk *down* to me, Rowland. You do it all the time. I don't understand why you do that."

Lindsay paused, fighting to steady her voice. She had begun to cry.

"You tell me I'm stupid and disloyal and incompetent, and I get to the stage where I can't think clearly anymore."

"You *never* think clearly, and your failures in that respect have nothing to do with me."

"You see? You're doing it again. Why? I've tried to apologize. You've done it right from the start of this conversation. Everything I do is wrong. Why? My plans aren't that bad. Colin says—"

"I don't damn well want to *hear* what Colin has to say," Rowland shouted, losing his temper as suddenly as she had. "Learn to stand on your own two feet for once in your life."

"What?" Lindsay had begun to tremble with misery and anger. "How can you say that? What do you think I was doing when I spent twenty years bringing up my son on my own? What do you think I'm trying to do *now*, Rowland? Don't you shout at me. Anyone would think you were my father the way you talk to me. Do this, don't do that. . . ."

"Your father? Thanks. I can imagine only one worse fate than being your father. I'm going. I've had more than enough of this conversation. I have better things to do with my time."

"I agree. Just fuck off, Rowland. I'm sick of your preaching. Don't talk to me about not listening to other people, or not noticing what they're feeling. You do it the whole bloody time."

"Oh, go to hell," Rowland said, and slammed down the phone.

Twenty minutes after that, Lindsay was lying on her bed and Colin was lying beside her. Colin, whose perceptions of that morning's events were jagged at best, was not sure how he came to be there, but now he *was* there, he knew it was the right, the only place. A trajectory begun in Tribeca four hours earlier had now completed its course; the laws of dynamics had determined that he had to be here, with Lindsay in his arms, and nowhere else.

He had walked to the Pierre from the Conrad, as not one cab in New York seemed to be free; he had been soaked to the skin for the second time that day, but since Lindsay did not seem to mind that his clothes were wet, neither did he.

"Don't cry, Lindsay. Dear Lindsay, you mustn't cry. Come here," Colin said, as he had already said several times before. He drew Lindsay closer into his arms, so she could weep against his wet shoulder. Every so often, he produced another of the beautiful linen handkerchiefs that Thalia had mocked and dried Lindsay's eyes. Lindsay, who had poured out the whole story of her telephone call to him, would thank him, attempt to calm herself, and then weep some more.

"I am so bloody miserable," she said now, in an indistinct voice, into damp Brooks Brothers cotton. "I'm sorry about this, Colin. I'd quite like to die, but I may recover if I weep for the next week."

"You can cry on my shoulder for the next *month*," Colin said, feeling rapturously happy. "For the next *year*."

"He said such wounding things. . . ." Lindsay continued, wiping her eyes. "And the worst part of it is—they were all *true*, every one of them."

"I know." Colin sighed. "There's always a vile accuracy about a dressing-down from Rowland. I've had a few. Was he cold? Something happens to his voice, have you noticed? It's not just *what* he says, it's the *way* he says it. It makes one want to shrivel up and die."

"I was horrible back." Lindsay made a moaning sound. "I made all those awful accusations. I told him he had a reputation."

"So he does. It's rather longer than your average arm."

"I told him he was patronizing."

"Quite right. He can be patronizing."

"I told him he was pompous."

"Oh dear."

"I told him to fuck off, Colin. . . ."

"Nothing wrong with that. I frequently do."

"He was so scathing about that contract I'd signed. Colin, he made me feel such a fool."

"Well, it wasn't a *great* contract," Colin said gently, "but you'll manage, I'm sure."

"I told him all about that lovely house you'd found and how excited I was. I thought he'd be pleased, but he wasn't. He just got colder and colder, and more and more sarcastic. . . ."

Colin gave another sigh. He could imagine Rowland's reaction, since Rowland knew Shute Farm well, and Rowland did not take kindly to duplicity. He knew that, given Rowland's character, there would be consequences for himself. He could predict them precisely and he knew precisely how he intended to deal with them. On another occasion, the thought of facing Rowland's ire might have alarmed him; not now. Now that he was here in Lindsay's arms, he felt he could have dealt with the devil himself.

He began to stroke Lindsay's hair and then her back—something he had been longing to do since she first burst into tears and he took her in his arms. Lindsay's hair, soft but resilient, smelled of rosemary. In her ear, she was wearing a small gold earring, with a jade teardrop. Colin found he wanted to kiss her hair, and her ear, which was small and delicate.

Lindsay tensed as he began to stroke her; then, soothed by the stroking, she relaxed. "Shall I tell you the worst thing he said?" She turned her head to look at Colin, her eyes brimming with tears. "It hurt me so much. He said I was childish. He said I acted like a child—and I thought that wasn't fair. I wasn't childish when I was bringing up Tom—and I thought Rowland would have known that."

More tears spilled down her cheeks and Colin resisted the impulse to kiss them away. "But he's right," she went on. "It hurts to admit it, but he's *right*. I don't understand why it is—I'm not childish when I work. I can run a department, do my work, and do it well. I feel confident then—but outside of that . . . I just mess everything up. I try and reorganize my life, and Rowland's right, I've done it in the stupidest way. I swear I'll never act on impulse again, and then I do. I lose my temper, just like *that*; I sign bad contracts; I run away from things; I can't make the simplest decisions sometimes—"

"Give me an example. Tell me a decision you need to make."

"Well, Thanksgiving, for instance; that ought to be easy enough. I was going to Washington, but that looks unlikely now. I could stay in New York. I did think of going back to England. I change my mind five times a day. . . . "

"That's easily settled. Stay in New York and spend Thanksgiving with me. I'd like that."

"Do you mean that?" She turned to look at him. "I think you do. All right, that would be nice. Thank you, Colin."

"Anything else I can sort out for you?"

"Oh, just my life. Just my life. Just my life." Lindsay looked up from his shoulder and gave him a wan smile.

"Listen . . ." Colin dried the last tears, kissed her forehead, and positioned her so that she was more comfortably cradled in his arms. "You don't want to take what Rowland says too much to heart. He's always had a fiendish temper; he won't have meant all he said. He can be gentle and understanding as well, you know—"

"I know that. And he did mean it, I could tell."

"If it's any consolation, I'm an equally hopeless case—much worse, in fact. Rowland reminds me of that from time to time, and if I'm in a bad mood, I remind him of the mistakes *he's* made; there are plenty of them. We do all make them, Lindsay—you're not alone."

He paused. "Shall I tell you how I started messing up my life? It was when my brother died. I had an elder brother, Edward, whom I loved very much. Edward was—well, he was everything I wasn't, everything I'd have liked to be. He was brilliant at school—he took a first at Oxford—he was effortlessly clever, very funny, and very kind. I adored him—everyone did. And my father—my father worshiped him." He hesitated, then gave a sigh. "My father's a good man—he was always gentle and encouraging to me as I limped along behind Edward, but I always knew it was Edward he loved the most." He looked down at Lindsay. "When you love someone, when you care more about that person than anyone else on earth, it can't be hidden, don't you think? It shows in the eyes."

"Maybe." Lindsay, who had stopped crying, took his hand in hers. "Go on, Colin."

"Well, Edward was killed in a car crash, just before I went up to Oxford. I can't really talk about this, even now, but what it did to my father was terrible; he aged overnight. It broke him inside. You'd never know that, if you met him, because he's very proud, for one thing, and very much old school in his views. Men should never show emotion, you know."

"I do."

"I was never like that—which was one of the problems—but after Edward died, I made myself this vow: I'd become Edward; I'd give my father back the son he'd lost. . . . I knew it would be hard, but I told myself that if I worked at it every day, if I threw myself into my studies at Oxford, I might get some of the way. . . . And you know what happened?" He gave her a sad smile. "All those fine resolutions—they lasted about five weeks. Then, when I saw it wasn't working, I went to the opposite extreme: I stopped doing any work at all, I never went to lectures, I hung around with a stupid crowd of people I didn't even like, and I drank. I drank all the time. I was drunk by ten o'clock in the morning and I made sure I stayed drunk all day." He shrugged. "They'd have thrown me out, in due course. They're tolerant at Oxford, amazingly so. They knew the circumstances and perhaps they made allowances, I don't know. But I was going out of my way to get sent down and they'd have obliged me in the end. Then I met Rowland—"

"And it was Rowland who helped you?"

"Yes." Colin made a face. "In a very grim sort of way. No sympathy; no indulgences, but he made me see—it was *my* choice: sink or swim. I tried very hard to shift the responsibility onto his shoulders, of course. . . ." He gave Lindsay a half-amused glance. "And I still do from time to time. But he wasn't having that, so, gradually, I learned. I came to admire him. He could make me laugh—he could be dry, even then. He was a hard taskmaster, but I wanted his approval so I reformed, in the end." He glanced toward Lindsay.

"I know what you're thinking: Rowland's my replacement brother—it's obvious, I know. And Rowland's never pointed that out to me, which is his supreme compliment, I always feel. He never rubs in the fact that I can't get through life without a brother figure, without a prop of some kind."

"Colin, *everyone* needs props sometimes." Feeling a rush of affection for him, Lindsay sat up and drew Colin to face her. "Even Rowland does sometimes, I expect, and I don't believe that Rowland thinks you use him as a crutch. Besides, who's propping me up now, and doing it very well? You underestimate yourself, Colin, and you put yourself down, you know."

She looked directly into his eyes as she said this; her expression was so gentle, and so filled with conviction, that Colin was almost overcome. The desire to kiss her intensified.

"Perhaps we're both guilty of that," he said, drawing her down beside him again. "I feel very much as you do. I'm reasonably good at my job, but outside of that, I feel muddled and ineffectual most of the time. I overreact, or I fail to react, or I react much too late, or too soon. . . ." He took her hand in his. "I always feel as if—oh, I don't know—as if I'm running for the last bus, and just as I draw close enough to jump on board, it pulls away—and all the passengers laugh." He paused. "Even if I caught it, it would probably turn out to be the wrong bus, going in the wrong direction. Everyone else always seems to know which bus to catch, and when it runs. Half the time, I can't even read the fucking timetable." He smiled.

Lindsay was moved by the way he spoke. She turned toward him, inside the circle of his arms.

"*Why* do you think that?" she said. "I'm sure it isn't true. You could catch any bus you wanted, Colin, anytime. You're funny and clever and kind. . . ."

"So are you." Colin's voice became unsteady. "You're all those things and more. You have beautiful eyes and beautiful hair, and a beautiful voice. If it's any consolation, which it probably isn't, I watched you with Tom in Oxford. I couldn't help watching you, because I couldn't take my eyes off you. I didn't think you were childish, not remotely so. I could see you were sad about something. I think now—well, I think that in some ways you are child*like*, which is a very different thing, and a good thing. I also think you're very womanly. I can't look at you without . . . You are—Lindsay, you make me . . ."

"Oh God," said Lindsay, seeing what was about to happen next.

"Please keep still," Colin said, with sudden firmness. "I'm going to kiss you. Don't argue. Don't move an inch. Stay still."

To her own surprise, Lindsay obeyed him. He looked at her for a long while, tilting her face to his and stroking her hair. Then, with great gentleness, he rested his lips against hers. Lindsay closed her eyes tight. The kiss, so gentle to begin with, became prolonged. It could not escape her notice that, for a man who claimed always to miss metaphorical buses, he kissed alarmingly well.

When this first kiss finally ended and Lindsay had steadied her voice, she told him so. Colin smiled again and kissed her again, and Lindsay discovered she liked the taste of his mouth; she liked what he did with his mouth, and she also liked what he began to do with his hands. It was gentle, adept, and very determined.

"You have the most beautiful breasts," he said, undoing her blouse—something Lindsay discovered she was prepared to let him do without protest or demur.

"You are lovely," he said, kissing each nipple in turn. "And I have wanted to do this ever since I first walked into that room in Oxford and saw you. I may have had the mother of all hangovers, and my brain may not have been functioning too well, but the rest of my senses were."

"Then?" Lindsay said, knowing she was flattered by this revelation, but excusing this as a weakness of her sex.

"Then and since," he replied. "In the restaurant last night. At Emily's. When I had to leave you here last night. I find it very hard indeed to look at you and not think about making love to you. No doubt that's very bad. Oh, you're wearing stockings. I hoped you might be. Do you know what stockings do to a man?"

"I can *feel* what they're doing to a man," Lindsay said, catching that glint of amusement in his eyes. She found herself beginning to smile, then stopping, hesitating, then touching him.

His response was immediate: a sharp intake of breath, an involuntary leaping of his flesh against her hand. He clasped her against him, and it was perhaps then that she decided. The yes came into her mind when she saw his physical need, saw his desire and her own power to assuage it, and realized that she could give pleasure as well as receive it. It had been too long, she thought, since she had last experienced a simplicity of that kind.

"Oh God, what am I doing?" she said, with a smile, reaching for his shirt buttons.

"It looks to me as if you're removing my shirt," Colin said. "I'd like it very much if you removed the rest of my clothes as well."

"Are you sure this is a good idea?" she continued, undoing his belt and the zipper of his jeans. Colin guided her hand, at which point Lindsay, who had been in little doubt anyway, realized just how good an idea this was.

"Colin?" she said, a while later.

"Mmmm?"

"I think I'd better warn you—I'm out of practice at this."

"I'm not."

"So I see."

There was a long silence, while Colin demonstrated the truth of his last statement. Lindsay discovered that she was losing her residual control.

"Colin," she began again, in a somewhat shaken, husky voice, as he lifted his head from between her thighs, having given her revelatory pleasure. "Yes?" he replied, in a distracted way, kissing her stomach, then her breasts, and moving so that Lindsay could close her hand around his cock.

"Colin—we could stop this now."

"No, dear Lindsay, we could not."

"Wait a minute. I have to ask you something. Do you like me, Colin?"

"Yes. This bit of you especially. This bit I love."

"Listen, I like you too. . . ."

"There?"

"Especially there. But—listen. I don't want to stop liking you, or you me, and sometimes sex has that effect."

"If you imagine," Colin said, with great firmness, "that I'm going to discuss that now, you must be mad. Now be quiet. Open your legs. Is that nice?"

"It's amazing. I—"

"Oh, bloody *hell*. I don't have any condoms."

"I'm on the Pill." Lindsay kissed him. "I don't have any sexually communicable diseases. . . ."

"Neither do I."

"In that case—"

"I agree."

"Colin, as long as you understand—it's so long since I've done this that I'm practically a virgin. I'm practically a nun. . . ."

"I find that an encouragement," he said, with a lift of one diabolic eyebrow. "Especially the nun."

"As long as you're sure. I—"

Colin saw there was only one thing for it. He silenced her with a kiss; shortly afterward, and as he had suspected might be the case, she began to demonstrate a response and a proficiency unlikely to be found in a nun; and although not silent, she stopped talking as well.

Sometime later, Colin disentangled himself from her arms with the greatest reluctance. He went into the bathroom, closed the door, and stared rapturously at the air. He turned on all the taps to drown the sound of his voice, and told the taps and the walls and the bath how much he loved Lindsay.

When he had done this several times, and felt he had gotten it out of his system, so there was no danger of his saying it to Lindsay herself—*festina lente,* after all—he returned to the bedroom. As soon as he saw Lindsay lying back against the pillows, her skin rosy and her hair damp from their exertions, he felt that since he had scrambled his schedule anyway, and just performed an act he had intended not to risk attempting for at least two weeks, he might as well admit the truth.

He was about to do so, indeed it was hard for him to look at

her and *not* do so, when he remembered those occasions in his
past when such lack of caution had served him badly.

He began to walk about the room, and slowly a terrible
uncertainty, a terrible postcoital misery settled about him.
What if Lindsay never came to reciprocate his feelings? What
if she was regretting their lovemaking right now? He began to
see that it was possible, even probable, that Lindsay would
never let him make love to her again. He groaned aloud.

"I need a cigarette," he said. "I need two. *Four.*"

"That's all right." Lindsay smiled and stretched. "You can
give me one as well."

"You don't smoke."

"I need one now. I'm feeling overcome."

Colin found "overcome" encouraging. He lit two cigarettes
and returned to the bed. Lindsay curled up like a cat in the
crook of his arm. She puffed, coughed, and gave up. Colin
stared hard at the wall opposite. Do not mention love, said a
stern admonitory voice in his mind; don't use that word under
any circumstances; no sneaking it in; play it cool.

"That wasn't very good," Colin burst out. "In fact, it was
disastrous. It was an unmitigated disaster, from beginning to
end."

"Was it?" Lindsay smiled and curled closer. "I thought it
was wonderful. I enjoyed it. The beginning, and the middle,
and the end."

"You didn't come," Colin said, in the tones of one approaching the scaffold, "and I came too soon. Oh God, *God.*"

"I very nearly did," Lindsay said, in a comfortable way. "I
was only about two millimeters off. And I didn't think you
came too soon; I think you came at exactly the right moment.
One can't always synchronize, and it felt so good when you
did."

"It makes it worse if you're kind."

"I'm not being kind, I'm telling you the truth. And it *was* the
first time."

"That's true." Colin's demeanor brightened. He found he did
not need the cigarette; in fact, he decided, he would never need
one again. He abandoned it and took Lindsay in his arms. Her
eyes dazzled him. Don't even *think* about saying it, said that
voice in his mind.

"I expect it's me." Lindsay sighed. "I expect I was a disappointment."

"You're mad."

"I have stretch marks on my stomach; I expect they put you off. Tom's nearly twenty and I *still* have stretch marks."

"Where?"

"There, and there, and there."

Lindsay indicated some faint silvery lines. Colin began to kiss them. "You're beautiful," he said. "I love your stretch marks. I love every single one of them. . . ." Be very, very careful, said the voice in his mind.

"I expect my rhythms weren't very good," Lindsay went on in a doleful voice. "I told you I was out of practice. You went into this amazing sort of tango sequence and I was still doing the waltz."

"Oh, God, *God.* I wasn't giving you the right signals. . . ."

"Oh God. I wasn't picking them up. . . ."

There was a small silence. Colin stopped kissing the stretch marks and looked up. Lindsay smiled; he smiled. His diabolic eyebrows rose in two quizzical peaks. Lindsay kissed them. She kissed his marvelous hair. That now familiar warmth and amusement returned to Colin's eyes.

"You're teasing me," he said. "You're sending me up."

"I most certainly am."

"I love you when you do that," Colin said. At which point the admonitory presence in his mind washed its hands of him and gave up in disgust.

Dalliance ensued. During the dalliance, Colin suggested that in view of Lindsay's comments on making love for the first time with a new partner, a second experiment might be wise. Lindsay agreed. After this, they slept in each other's arms very peacefully for a while; on waking, they discovered that Colin did not have to work that day, and Lindsay, who had been going to begin her Chanel research, could put it off with no problems at all.

They lay side by side, talking quietly and companionably. Lindsay, feeling at peace, realized that she was happier than she had been in a long, long while, and Colin experienced an absence of anxiety so unusual he decided it must be bliss. He told her of the long, strange, and painful night he had spent,

and she listened with a care and concern that belied the criticisms of Rowland McGuire. "I'm proud of you. You slew the
dragon," she said, when Colin recounted his battle with that
tape recorder, and Colin, who had not thought of it like that,
felt comforted and hoped this was true.

"So I didn't sleep at all last night," he explained. "I had no
sleep and then I walked about a thousand blocks in the rain. All
I could think about was seeing you. I had to see you, and now
I see why."

He bent across and kissed her hair, then her mouth, which
opened with an already sweet familiarity under his.

"Considering you hadn't slept and I'd been so miserable,"
Lindsay said, "it's astonishing the progress we've made, don't
you think?"

"I do. One millimeter, that time?"

"Less. Half a millimeter at most. Very close indeed."

"I thought so. We're beginning to know each other. I think,
next time . . ."

"Mmm. So do I." She stretched. "What shall we do now? It's
afternoon. Colin, you must be longing to sleep properly. . . ."

"I'm not. I feel astonishingly awake. We could order up
some food from room service. Some champagne."

"Oh, let's. And have it in bed?"

"Of course."

"We could watch some stupid movie on television. . . ."

"We could. I love watching television in the day; it always
feels debauched. So we could watch a movie, or talk, or I could
just lie here and look at your eyes. . . ."

"You could tell me all about this lovely house you've
found. . . ."

"I'll do better than that. I'll take you there, after Thanksgiving. We could go back to England on the same flight. I'll
have a little gap before filming starts. I could drive you down
there. We could stay at an inn and sit by a fire, and I could make
love to you all night. . . ."

Lindsay sat up. "Colin, did you know this was going to
happen?"

"No, not today. I hoped—well, in due course. You know."

"I didn't see it coming at all. Not until just before you kissed

me." She gave a small frown. "At least, I don't think I did."
She hesitated. "Colin, what I said to you before . . ."

"Not the best timing."

"I know, I talk too much, and always at the wrong moment.
I was nervous. . . ." She paused. "Colin, it can be a very bad
idea to go to bed with someone you like. I learned that years
ago. A friend becomes a lover; you lose the lover; you lose the
friend. I wouldn't want that to happen to us."

"It won't happen to us."

"Can we promise each other that? We agree now: no regrets
ever, or complications? Just something that happened to make
us both very, very happy at the time?"

She held out her hand to him. Colin bent over her palm, so
she could not see his expression and kissed it.

"Sure," he said. "It's a deal."

Colin finally left the Pierre at around ten-thirty that night. The
third experiment had fulfilled their predictions, and as they
both agreed, the fourth was a conclusive triumph. Colin walked
along anonymous hotel corridors, missed the elevators, circled
the Pierre several times, and eventually found himself in the
lobby. He walked through it, cloaked in joy. He bumped into a
tall thin young woman with very short blond hair, unsea-
sonably dressed in a crop top, pedal pushers, and ballerina
slippers. Some time after she had greeted him, he realized that
this was Lindsay's assistant, Pixie, who when last seen two
days previously had had shoulder-length black hair.

He examined her, smiling. "Got it," he said finally. "Jean
Seberg, in *Breathless*?"

"Spot on." Pixie looked at him closely and raised one eyebrow. "You look happy," she said.

"Pixie, I am happy. I am extraordinarily happy. Isn't it the
most wonderful world?"

Pixie looked at his disheveled hair, disheveled clothes, and
radiant expression. Aware that she had become invisible to
him, she raised the other eyebrow, smiled, and kindly showed
him to the exit door. Colin left the hotel and soon afterward discovered he was back at the Conrad, though he had no recollection of any period of transit between the two. Emily, seeing at

once that he was in no condition to understand the English language, kept her news to the minimum, despite the fact that she had been longing to impart it for most of the day.

"She's *in*," she said. "Natasha Lawrence is *in*. She has been admitted to the Conrad, God help us all. I voted against, and those four darned male simpletons voted for. This we will discuss further tomorrow, Colin. Meanwhile, Thalia with an unpronounceable surname called. You are to fly out tomorrow afternoon to Montana, and continue your work with that peculiar director man there. Perhaps more importantly, and certainly more urgently, your friend Rowland McGuire has called." She paused. "He first called at ten-thirty this morning, and spoke to Frobisher in a somewhat heated way. He has called on the hour, every hour since, and if I am not mistaken, that will be him calling now. So take this call in your room, Colin, which you will find at the end of the corridor. And collect your wits, because I've already spoken to him, and he does not sound in the most tractable of moods."

Colin did as he was bid. He found his own room. He found the telephone.

"Hello, Rowland," he said. "What a wonderful world."

"Perhaps you'd be good enough to explain just what the fuck you think you're doing?" Rowland said, in tones of great politeness. "I'm now at home. It's four o'clock in the morning. In front of me is a postcard from you which I received four days ago. It reads as follows: 'New York glorious. Lindsay adorable. O brave new world. Love, Colin.' The style didn't surprise me. I wasn't altogether surprised by the content, but now I'm confused. If Lindsay is so adorable, would you like to explain why you've been lying to her? You can thank me for not giving you away this morning, while you're about it. Shute Farm? Owned by someone your father knows? Available at a miraculously low rent?"

"All true," said Colin, gazing out of the windows at the moon.

"Are you drunk?"

"Not on alcohol, no."

"All true? Then your interpretation of truth must be very different from mine. Maybe you'd like to explain why you failed to tell Lindsay the *exact* truth: to wit—that house is owned by your father and entailed to you, as it will be entailed to your sons, or—failing that—your cousin's sons. To all intents and purposes, Colin, you own it—along with Shute itself, God alone knows how many other tenant farms, cottages, and houses, plus an obscene amount of Oxfordshire. I find it surprising that you neglected to mention these belongings of yours. Were you similarly reticent about the forty thousand acres in Scotland, and the umpteen million you inherited from the Lancaster clan? Colin, it was perfectly obvious that Lindsay knows none of this, and you, for some reason I cannot comprehend, are deceiving her and maneuvering her into becoming your tenant at a knock-down rent. You're doing this, what's more, at a time in her life when she's especially vulnerable to assistance of that kind. Now I know your schemes, Colin, and I've seen them blow up in everyone's face a thousand times. So I'm warning you, if you end up harming Lindsay, or hurting her in any way. . . ."

"I love her," Colin said, in a beatific voice, still staring at the moon. "I love her. I adore her. She's the most wonderful woman ever born."

This checked Rowland for rather less long than Colin had hoped.

"Then this is worse than I thought," he said, in a brusque way. "You do *not* love her, Colin. You fall in love the way other people catch colds."

"No, I don't," said Colin, in a robust way. "I *used* to, I admit that, but I haven't done that for at least eight years. I love her. I love her with all my heart. I worship the very ground on which she walks."

"Colin, you've known her less than two weeks."

"That has nothing to do with it," Colin replied, his wits returning, and a note of unmistakable conviction entering his voice. "You can love someone just like *that*." He snapped his fingers. "You meet them, you know you're going to love them, and the love starts to grow. And if you don't know that, Rowland, you're a great deal stupider than I thought."

Rowland hesitated. "Very well," he said. "I concede that can happen. It doesn't last."

"This *is* going to last. I've just left her now. I've been with her all day—and I'm so happy I can hardly speak. She's loyal and good and candid and funny and warm. . . ."

"Colin, I wouldn't argue with any of that. I know her too well; she's also scatty, impetuous, and naive. She has a terrible temper, a nasty tongue, and a marked inability to *think*. She is, without a doubt, one of the most impossible goddamned irritating women I've ever known. . . ."

"You see? You're fond of her too!" Colin proclaimed, on a note of triumph. "I can hear it in your voice. She's a *paragon*. And you know the best thing of all, Rowland? She likes *me*. She can see my faults and she *still* likes me. She doesn't know about the money or Shute—she likes me for *myself*. For the first time in my life I have no doubts about that—in fact, if she knew about the money, I'm afraid she might like me less. So I want her to know me, *really* know me, before she finds out. I want her to see Shute for the first time, and not know it's mine, so she can just love it for itself, and then I want her to marry me. I'm going to marry her, Rowland, and if you come between her and me, I'll fucking well kill you, because she is the best thing that's ever happened to me. Apart from you, she's the one good thing, the one incontestably good thing that has happened to me since Edward died."

There was a long silence then. In London, knowing Colin would never mention his brother unless he passionately meant what he said, Rowland bowed his head in his hands. In New York, Colin thought of Lindsay in his arms and felt blessed.

"I'm going to marry her, Rowland, and I'm going to marry her within six months," he continued, in a quieter voice. "I'm going to ask her the very second I think she might accept, and I damn near asked her an hour ago—so you can draw your own conclusions from that."

"In that case," Rowland said, after a pained hesitation, "I shall say nothing to Lindsay about Shute. I hope you know you can rely on that. But I also hope you know what you're doing, because Lindsay would be very easy indeed to hurt—"

"As you should know," replied Colin, in a flash, "considering how you hurt her today. You reduced her to tears—"

"I did what?"

"You made her cry, and you're not going to do it again. She was in an utterly miserable state—and I'm not surprised. You destroy every bit of confidence she has. She's trying to make a new start in life, and what do you do? You roll in like a fucking Centurion tank, and you tell her she's naive and childish, and only a fool would have signed that book contract. Not everyone has your fucking unshakable self-confidence, Rowland. Why don't you *think*?"

"I made her cry?" Rowland sounded both bewildered and shocked. "That's the last thing on God's earth I'd have wanted to do. I thought—we argue, Lindsay and I. We're always having some fight. I lose my temper, she loses hers, and then the next day—"

"Well, don't lose your temper with her!" Colin cried. "I love her. I won't have you talking to her like that. I saw you do it in Oxford, and I wanted to punch you then. Lindsay's right—anyone would think you were her father, the way you talk to her. . . ."

Rowland, who had begun to speak, was brought up short.

"Her father. I see. Were there any details of my private conversation with Lindsay that weren't reported back?"

"No, since you ask. She told me the whole miserable story from beginning to end. She tried to hide it, when I first arrived, but I *knew* there was something wrong, and then she just broke down. She started crying and she couldn't stop. I put my arms around her, and—" He broke off. "And, anyway, I calmed her down, eventually. I explained you didn't *really* despise her. I told her how you're always bawling me out. We agreed in the end that you were right rather too often, but you weren't such a bad sort and we both quite liked you. None of which means that you shouldn't be ashamed of yourself."

"I'm certainly ashamed to have made her cry. Perhaps you'd be good enough to tell her that," Rowland said curtly. "Meanwhile, if there's anything worse than the thought of the two of you discussing my defects in that particular cozy, nauseating way, I don't know what it is, so—"

"Oh, we forgot about you after a bit," Colin said, in a cheerful, consoling tone. "We never mentioned you again, funnily enough. . . ."

"I'm hanging up, Colin."

"Wait, wait, wait. Rowland—just one question."

"What?"

"Will you be my best man, Rowland?"

Rowland considered this question for what seemed to Colin an unnecessarily long time.

"No," he said eventually, his tone altering. "No. I'm very fond of you, Colin, but I don't think I will. Good night."

Part Five

TWO LETTERS AND FOUR FAXES

Chapter 12

Throughout the following week, the telephone lines between Lindsay at the Pierre, and Colin, staying at Tomas Court's ranch in Montana, were kept very busy. It was a week of *correspondences*, and in more than one sense, Lindsay was later to decide. During it, fax lines, the international mail, and in one case a courier service, were kept busy as well.

The first missive, its formality of tone perhaps explained by the fact that it was the last of six drafts he had written, came in the form of a letter from Rowland McGuire.

My dear Lindsay,

It is early on Saturday morning, and I have been trying to find the right words in which to write to you since I spoke to Colin on the telephone, two hours ago. The conversation with him left me profoundly shaken—I cannot tell you how much it distressed me to learn that I had caused you unhappiness, indeed had made you cry. My immediate instinct was to call you, but when we speak on the telephone, I always feel we are missing one another in some way; this leads to misunderstandings. So I am writing now because I want to apologize to you, and beyond that, make certain things unmistakably clear.

I have had several hours—and they've not been pleasant hours—in which to contemplate my own stupidity, arrogance, and lack of insight. For those failings, and my inability to curb my temper, I seek your pardon—how stilted that sounds! Lindsay, I'm so sorry and so sad to have caused you pain.

The conversation with Colin has made me realize that I

271

have to be very careful how I express myself. I am not finding it easy to write this, and I want to be sure I avoid ambiguities, so will you forgive me for any awkwardnesses here? Everything I say, however clumsily expressed, is written from the heart.

I don't want to make excuses for myself, but I do want you to know that almost everything I said to you yesterday stemmed from my anxiety on your behalf. Lindsay, I look on you as a close and dear friend, for whom I feel an unwavering concern. I want you to find happiness and, yes, fulfilment in everything you do. That is why I question and argue as I do. I now realize just how badly I put my arguments yesterday. You were right to resent the way I spoke, but I would like you to understand that I don't mean to interfere, or snipe from the sidelines. I just can't bear to think that, as a result of all these recent changes and uprootings, you might experience difficulties, hardship, or unhappiness of any kind.

Colin has made me see how inept I am at conveying that concern to you. I'm grateful to him for that. Talking to him was a chastening experience; he made me see—well, many things for which I feel the deepest regret.

He also made me see that I've made one great error, an error I want to correct. I see I've always been quick to criticize, and that I have never told you how much I like, respect, value, and admire you. So I say it now—without reservations. I hope you will believe that.

We have worked so closely together, and seen one another so often, that I realize I have assumed, in my usual arrogant way, that you knew this. I've assumed you would understand the unspoken, and I see now just how mistaken that was. Colin said you felt I despised you—Lindsay, nothing could be further from the truth. I feel for you the very warmest admiration and regard; I rely on your friendship to a far greater degree than you perhaps realize; but then, I trust you completely—and I'm not good at trusting; I trust very few people indeed. I feel the deepest affection for you, Lindsay, even when I am insulting you, even when I have lost my temper, and especially when you are being, as you often are, one of the most provoking, most impossible women I've ever known.

You have great generosity of heart, Lindsay, and despite what I said yesterday, when I was angry for a hundred other reasons that need not worry you, I realize that your intuition and instincts are much sharper than mine. Yes, you jump to conclusions, but they are often the correct ones, whereas I am often too slow to acknowledge a truth, and try to argue it away. Something very obvious can be staring me in the face, and yet I refuse to see it until it is too late and an opportunity has gone. I don't know why I do that: obstinacy, perhaps, or I could blame caution. I think I sometimes fail to act for fear of mistaking the circumstances, or for fear of causing harm.

Well, I won't dwell on these very male defects, and I know I can rely on you to mock them. The point is, I accused you yesterday of acting first and thinking afterwards. I now see that's not always a vice, and can be a virtue. It is a virtue you possess—to act on the impulses of the heart—and I wish it were more often my own.

There are many other things I would have liked to say to you, but now is not the moment; besides, this letter is already too long. So, will you forgive what I said yesterday? There will be no more lectures; I give you my word.

I wish you happiness, joy, and success with your book, with your new life, and perhaps with your new home. In respect of property, Colin is a very good guide and advisor— far better than I could ever be. You can be confident that any proposals he makes are made with your best interests at heart. Colin can be as exasperating as you can be—and as I know I can be—but he is a good and utterly trustworthy man.

If you do go to live at Shute Farm, I hope it will fulfil all the dreams you spoke of—I'm sure that it will. Meanwhile, I'm not certain when you are returning to London—perhaps after Thanksgiving? Perhaps when you return we could all three of us meet? I'd like to see you and try to begin making amends.

I can't stop thinking about your tears. I wish to God this had never happened. I realize that now I've said only a few of the things I wanted to say, and no doubt said them ill.

Lindsay, I trust to your generosity of heart to read between the lines and see the degree of regret I feel.

Damn! More time has gone by. I'm not writing as coherently as I'd hoped, and I've now discovered it's almost impossible to courier a letter to New York over a weekend. I've finally found a firm that swears it can do this, so my letter can go off today and will, I hope, reach you tomorrow, Sunday morning.

I shall think of you reading it. I'll listen for the curses you'll no doubt, and justly, heap on my head. I'll be able to hear them, I promise you, very clearly across this distance of three thousand miles.

Please don't reply to this letter. It doesn't need a reply, and it's better to let it stand. Can you read my writing? I'm not feeling as calm as I should, and I expect my punctuation leaves something to be desired.

My love—best and warmest good wishes to you—I hope I can still sign myself as your friend.

Rowland McGuire

This letter, which Lindsay received without curses and with tears, arrived at the Pierre on Sunday afternoon. On the tenth reading, she still found herself puzzled by that reference of Rowland's to his punctuation. Rowland's punctuation was meticulous down to the last semicolon; in which respect, she thought, it was in singular contrast to her own letter to him, which had crossed with this one, and which she had posted express the previous day.

Dear Rowland,

I am in one of my *states*. I can't sleep, and I've been pacing up and down the room in the stupidest way. It's the middle of the night, and I can still hear myself shouting down the phone at you like some demented fishwife. Oh dear!

Listen—I'm just going to scribble this very fast and then rush out and catch the first post. Rowland, I'm so sorry I said all those horrible things to you. I want you to know—everything you accused me of was true. I see now that I've been a total fool about that bloody book contract. I think I knew that publisher was a complete shit really, but I sort of buried the idea and hoped I was wrong. You're right about the money too—what's the matter with me? I always *intend* to get tough on the money front and then I never do. I think it's that I secretly despise money, so talking about it, let alone angling for more, always seems so *low*. So I'm always v. dignified, get screwed, and end up living on vegetables for the next ten years.

But you don't have to worry, *truly*. I have some money saved, and I think Shute Farm may work out—in which case, I shall be able to afford bread and jam, if not blinis and caviar. I'll be so tucked away too, that I'll have no distractions—no movies, or theatres, or friends, so I expect I'll write the book in record time out of sheer boredom and nothing else to do . . .

Hell. I'm putting off the serious thing. Rowland—when I think of what I said about Oxford and Tom and Katya, I want to *die*. What's wrong with my brain? Whenever I talk to you, especially on the phone, I get into this stupid flurried state—it's like listening to fifteen radio stations simultaneously. Then I tune in on one of them and it's always the wrong one.

Rowland, I'm so ashamed I said those things. No wonder you were so hurt and furious. I just go into a blind panic if I think anything could harm Tom, but if I'd paused for two and a half seconds, I'd have known you would never act foolishly, because you always think everything through too carefully, and there's no way you'd commit a dishonourable act. It's strange, isn't it, that no-one seems to use the word 'honour' any more? I think honour is important; I also think you're the most honourable man I've ever known. Yes, I know you can lie to get your way—I've seen you do it at work a thousand times. And you lie so well: flagrantly and coolly. I wish I could do that. I'm a lousy liar—well, sometimes I am. Maybe not all the time. But I know you would never lie about anything important. I think of you as a man of truth, an honourable man of truth, so there! That's why I want you to know that yesterday I said the very opposite of what I meant, as usual. I didn't mean any of those horrible insults I hurled at you. The truth is, I'm always grateful to you for your concern, your kindness, and your strength. And your wit, too, Rowland. It was good of you, yesterday, when listing my drunken sins in Oxford, to be discreet about that shaming episode when I kissed your sweater. This was gallant of you. Thank you for that.

Anyway. *Mea culpa.* Will you forgive me, Rowland? I shall be coming back to London after Thanksgiving. I've decided to stay on here until then; I have some Chanel research to do—I'm looking forward to becoming an archive addict. Quiet, dedicated and *nun-like*—and Colin is going to be here, so it seemed quite a good idea.

Colin came here yesterday, after you telephoned; he was understanding, gentle, and kind. You have nice friends, Rowland. He told me all about his brother and how you helped him at Oxford. He is very loyal and devoted to you, and so am I.

He's going to take me to see Shute Farm when we get back to England. I'm praying it will work out. I'm praying I'll cope if it does—I've never lived in the country. If you've forgiven me, I hope you'll come and see me there—you could teach me some useful rustic things: how to chop logs, how to light a fire.

Shall I buy some chickens? Or ducks? There's a stream. Oh, Rowland, I feel excited and afraid all at once. Since yesterday, so much has happened—and one day I'd like to tell you about it, but not now.

Are you in your lovely sitting-room as you read this? Are you frowning or smiling? I wonder, are those shutters I admire so much open or closed?

You've been a good friend to me, Rowland. The very best, kindest, and most loyal of friends. I wish I'd said that yesterday, but since I didn't, I'll say it now.

God, what horrible handwriting I have! Can you make out any of this? I hope you can at least see the important bits and read the important words.

I send you my thanks for all your wise advice and your insufferable but accurate insight into my defects of character. I send you my apologies. I send all love and best wishes. Damn! My pen's run out. No ink available at the Pierre at 5 A.M. I'll have to use a Biro. The smudges every-

where are from the Biro. You are a dear friend, Rowland, and I kiss your green Christmas sweater in a very sober way. When you next see me, you'll find I'm a reformed character.
    Lindsay

Something went wrong with the U.S. express mail system, or possibly there were problems at the U.K. end. Lindsay's letter did not arrive in London until four days had passed; then, since Lindsay did indeed have horrible and illegible handwriting, especially when writing numbers, so that all her sevens looked like ones, the letter was delivered to Rowland's neighbor at number 11 in his terrace, and not to his house at number 17. The neighbor was away; he finally dropped the letter through Rowland's door late at night on the Tuesday before Thanksgiving.

Rowland found it on the mat early the following morning, as he was leaving for work. He read it only once on that occasion, but he read it with great care. He returned inside, called his secretary and various colleagues, canceled all his appointments for the next three days, gave his deputy editor instructions, and then left for Oxford before nine.

Meanwhile, Colin Lascelles was finding the telephone an inadequate instrument to express himself.

Saturday. Montana.

Dearest Lindsay,
    Have just spoken to you. Am going to bed. The sky here is amazing—I've never seen so many incredibly brilliant stars. I miss you terribly. I think I said that on the phone, but I'll say it again. I could throttle Tomas for dragging me out here, but I do feel sorry for him; he looks desperately ill. I'm going to fax this to the Pierre, so I can't say what I want to say. Imagine asterisks and all they imply. Can you understand Latin? I need to know immediately. You can fax me at the above number and I wish you would because I feel totally sick at heart and soul. I send you love and *trois mille bises*.
    Colin

Tuesday. Montana.

Darling Lindsay,

Talking to you on the telephone is the only thing that's keeping me sane. When we talk, I feel as if I'm with you, holding you in my arms (and if you're the desk clerk at the Pierre reading this fax, FUCK OFF. This is private, you understand?). I've never known it to be so easy to talk to someone as it is to you. Do you feel that, darling? You've made such a difference to me in such a short time. I feel I can do *anything*: climb a mountain; fly.

I got up very early this morning—I couldn't sleep anyway for missing you. I borrowed one of Tomas's horses and went for a ride. The landscape is spectacular. I could see the peaks of Glacier National Park in the distance. Watched the sun rise and thought of you.

Tomas now much better and visibly stronger. There's umpteen production people here during the day, but they piss off in the evenings to some hotel, thank God, so apart from the odd bodyguard and staff, it's then just Tomas and Thalia and me.

He and I had a long talk yesterday, after Thalia had gone to bed. I forgot to tell you about this. He's a very interesting man—proud. I feel for him. I think he's in agony about—better use initials—NL. And about her move to Emily's building. I heard from Emily this evening, and apparently, NL must have had everything organized, and ready to roll, because the decorators are in there already. According to the Emily bush telegraph, always reliable, the whole thing will be finished by the end of this week. Yet she *can't* have known they'd admit her and the odds were against—most mysterious! NL apparently very thick with Biff already, which was predictable. H. Foxe singing her praises as well, which annoys Emily no end. NL *not* popular with Giancarlo and the other porters though, I hear. Trouble of various kinds, I gather—constant hassle from some anonymous caller—in view of what I told you, worrying, eh?

Listen, darling, we must talk tomorrow about Thanksgiving and all our other plans. I always mean to on the phone, but my mind goes into a whirl the second I hear your voice, and besides, we have other things to talk about then.

Is your friend Genevieve still coming up from Washington with her husband for Thanksgiving? When shall we fly back to England? I can't wait to show you Shute Farm. Isn't it great about the rent? I gather they want a tenant who *loves* the place—money isn't the issue. Money should never be the issue, I say, don't you agree?

Darling Lindsay, I'm very glad you can't read Latin. I'm afraid I had it rather dinned into me at school. Vivamus, dear Lindsay, atque amemus—soles occidere et redire possunt, nobis, cum semel occidit brevis lux, nox est perpetua una dormienda . . . Incidentally, you know that little thing you do that I mentioned (desk clerk at the Pierre, get LOST) the thing you do when I—you remember? Well, I'm thinking about it now. Effect immediate—and wasted alas; most frustrating. I send love, darling Lindsay. Take care of yourself. I hope the research goes well. Gabrielle Chanel sounds odd. Why didn't she marry the Duke of Westminster? I think of you in the archive place, darling. If I were with you there, we could do some very interesting research . . . Will call usual time tomorrow. You can read my writing, I hope? Darling, I kiss all your asterisks.

    Colin

Wednesday. The Pierre.

Dearest Colin,

The desk clerks here are giving me very peculiar looks. I wonder why? It's a great boost to my confidence—I'm perfecting a sultry slink for their benefit. This cheers me up when I get back from work. All day today in the archive at MOMA. Wearying. Escaped finally, and came back feeling a bit low for some reason—having to concentrate, I expect. Then Emily kindly called and asked me round for a drink. We had great fun—I think I'm now getting used to her. I certainly like her a lot. I heard all the latest news about Biff, H. Foxe et al. (Ah, I find I do know some Latin after all.) I'll regale you with it when you call.

Emily told me the whole story of Anne Conrad and the

two brothers. Heavens! It terrified me. No wonder she still haunts the place. The elevator was out of order when I left (overloaded by NL's decorators, and the first time it's broken down since 1948, Emily said), so I had to walk down that staircase *alone*.

I wished you'd been here when I returned. I miss you too, but there are so many things we need to talk about. Hurry up and come back to New York, I'm lonely and V jvfu lbh jrer xvffvat zl oernfgf evtug abj. You are a wonderful ybire, and I am very, very sbaq of you—but don't make me run too soon, dear Colin: I'm always slow off the starting blocks.

I'm faxing this, so you can work out the above. Also this: V jvfu lbh jrer vafvqr zr, in fact, V jvfu guvf constantly. More research tomorrow. Not sure I'm cut out for this— archive libraries awfully *quiet*—no-one allowed to *speak*. Good night, Colin. I can just see the moon. Can you see it too? I send all best wishes and love, kisses too.

Lindsay

Friday. Montana.

My darling Lindsay,

Your letter came today. Darling, it made me so happy. I've read it a thousand times. It's folded up with that wicked fax you sent me—naughty girl! I carry both of them next to my heart. Your code nearly drove me frantic—but, yes, I've cracked it. Wish-fulfilment and memories of prep-school helped me. Very useful! I've been thinking about lbhe oernfgf all day, and how it feels when I pbzr vafvqr you. Do you know what it does to me when you gbhpu zl pbpx? I was thinking about it today, in the middle of a production meeting—concentration badly impaired. Also had the most rabezbhf rerpgvba. Most embarrassing.

Darling, promise me: I don't want you to worry about *anything*. We can go as slow or as fast as you want—at the moment, I can't think beyond the day when I next see you. I just want to take you in my arms. I will never rush you, dar- ling, please believe me. If I should ever sound hasty, it's because I'm so impatient to be with you. Darling, you are in my thoughts, day and night. Everything I see and do and think is only for you. I watch the sun rise and the moon shine and, unless I can tell you about them, they have no meaning at all. Oh, Lindsay, I wish you were *here*. Darling, your absence makes my heart *ache*.

I've been trying to convince myself that this sudden parting could be of use—a baptism of fire, perhaps. When we return to England, I'll have to be in Yorkshire most of the time, and I'm praying that this separation now will help us to bear that one. What do you think? We'll still be able to talk to each other, the way we do now. I'll have a mobile. You can always leave messages—coded or otherwise!—on my machines. Then, if you're at Shute—and I hope you will be, darling—I'll be able to come down to see you on odd days and the occasional weekends. It's about four hours door to door—I've been working out times and best routes! And you might like to come up to Yorkshire, perhaps, to see at first hand the sheer soul-destroying tedium of actual filming, in what will probably be snow or pouring rain, I expect.

Then you could have the dubious pleasure of meeting the famous Nic Prick—you remember? The one who played Prospero to my definitive Caliban at school? He was called Hicks-Henderson then, and he was a world-class jerk aged fourteen. He remains one. He flew in here yesterday from LA—or the Coast, as he likes to call it. I was counting his name-dropping rate: it was three a minute when he arrived; he got it up to six a minute by the time he left for New York. I realize that Tomas is very devious and very smart: the Gilbert Markham character Nic's playing is a smug, vain, sanctimonious, prurient prat—type-casting. After he'd called me 'Col' fifteen times, I remarked on this. Sarcasm wasted: he was delighted—but then *he* thinks Markham is the hero. I think Tomas was *very* amused at that. Have you started reading *Tenant*, darling? I want to know if you agree with Rowland—maybe there were things I missed.

Must concentrate. Darling—two things. First, you remember what I told you yesterday about events in Glacier Park? Well, the police arrived in force not long after we spoke, and apparently that identification *is* now confirmed: an Australian tourist—gay, I think. He'd only arrived in the

States a few weeks before and had been hitching. No family over here, his family back home not close and not sure of his travel plans, didn't know he was heading for Montana etc., etc. That's why it's all dragged on so long. When he hadn't written or called for four months, some cousins finally raised the alarm. They did the ID from dental chart records, I think. Poor, poor man.

This means, of course, that JK is alive—but I always *knew* he was, you remember? Apart from those events at the loft, I could *sense* him there. I can sense his presence here too—the result, well, you can imagine: phones never stop ringing, everyone edgy, security people crawling all over the place, and Tomas utterly silent on the entire issue, though you can see he's in the most terrible state, terrified for his son. He was on the phone to NL for three *hours* today and came back grim-faced—worked us all until nearly midnight, which is when I began writing this.

I can't wait to get out of this place and come back to you. Which brings me to my second point. Darling, about Thanksgiving. I'm so glad! It will give Emily a great deal of pleasure, and it's only dinner, after all. She'll be inviting some other people, I expect—she always makes rather a big thing of Thanksgiving. Don't know who. Don't care. I shall only have eyes for you.

Darling, I've been thinking, I'm so desperate to see you. Tomas leaves early Wednesday morning to join NL for Thanksgiving—I'm going to fly back with him in one of the studio's jets; it's the quickest way I can get back to New York. I'll be there by midday on Wednesday, so here's a suggestion: Darling, why don't I book us a marvellous room at the Plaza for Wednesday and Thursday night? That would mean you'd save on the expense of a room at the Pierre—economy, darling, think of that! And we could meet at the Plaza, like wicked, illicit lovers, wouldn't that be fun? You could show me your sultry slink, then we could go up to our room and stay there shamelessly for a day and a half—until we have to leave Thursday evening for Emily's Thanksgiving beanfeast. Would you like that?

I know you want to see Gini and her husband, and Markov and Jippy—as they're all tied up for dinner, why don't you get them to meet us in the Oak Room at the Plaza for Thanksgiving drinks? Sevenish? Then you and I could go on to Emily's—I'm bribing her to let me sit next to you. I intend to do unspeakable things to you, hidden by the tablecloth—I want to see if you can keep a straight face. . . .

I'd love to meet your friends—especially Markov. Did you realize that I spent our first-meeting lunch in Oxford worrying about him? From the moment Tom and Rowland first mentioned his name, I was in a state of jealous torment: I thought he might be your lover—that's why I started drinking like a fish. Total panic. Very glad *indeed* that he's gay.

Oh Lindsay, Lindsay, what have you done to me? I'm usually a man of great equilibrium, as you know. Always calm, always confident, and yet now—Are you smiling, darling? You have the most beautiful smile in the world; it lights up a room. Of course, you also have the most beautiful, the most desirable oernfgf in the world. I kiss them. Oh God, I wish I were vafvqr lbh now, darling.

I'm sending this by fax—shouldn't really, but the post is so *slow*. Darling, I'll be with you Wednesday. Let me know *re* above Plaza plot etc. when we speak. I'm sorry this letter is so long, but it's been a vile day, and I was feeling miserable without you. I've just read your letter again—Oh, Lindsay. Trust me, darling. It made me so happy, what you said about the *simplicity* of our shpxvat—I feel that too. I kiss all your beloved asterisk bits. I send you my love. Only 101 hours until I next see you. Stars very bright tonight. Almost a full moon. Yours, darling,

   Colin

Part Six

THANKSGIVING

Chapter 13

In Oxford that Wednesday, the day before Thanksgiving, Katya was enduring the last fifteen minutes of a tutorial. It was being conducted by her senior tutor, Dr. Miriam Stark, a woman whose cool intelligence Katya feared; it concerned the use of narrators in two novels by the Brontës. It had begun with Katya reading aloud to Dr. Stark the essay she had written on this subject, comparing Emily Brontë's *Wuthering Heights* with her sister Anne's *The Tenant of Wildfell Hall*; it had continued with Dr. Stark's analysis of that essay; the questions had been unrelenting and the criticisms barbed.

Katya, who had begun writing having done too little preparation, and who had continued writing with her mind on quite a different subject, was aware this essay was a poor effort. For several weeks now, Katya had been suffering a certain mental and emotional turmoil; reading her essay aloud, she had realized that turmoil and confusion were evident in every line. In an obstinate way, she continued reading, praying Dr. Stark might not notice the skimpiness of her arguments, praying she might be impressed by the two obscure critical references Katya had tacked on at the last moment, and—failing that—might be distracted by Katya's aggressive and iconoclastic tone.

Dr. Stark had not been distracted by such frills; she was concentrating on fabric, on basic tailoring, and for the past twenty minutes had been scissoring Katya's offering apart.

Katya glared at Dr. Stark, an American who had graduated *summa cum laude* from Barnard, but whose M.A. and Ph.D. had been awarded by Oxford. She was in her late thirties, was beautiful, highly distinguished, and *thin*, which seemed unfair.

Dr. Stark, famously unmarried, had a cloistered air about her; she possessed an aura, Katya always felt, of steely, determined, female dedication. She was a fellow of Oxford's last remaining women's college, a college to which Katya had applied in a burst of feminism she now regretted, and she was the kind of woman who could spend half an hour dissecting the implications of one word.

"Katya, I can see your mind was not on this essay when you wrote it, and is not on it now. . . ." Dr. Stark paused, having caught Katya staring moodily through the window at the quadrangle and pouring rain outside.

"Yes, well possibly," Katya mumbled, taking refuge in mutiny. "I don't really like either novel." She eyed Dr. Stark. "All that hysterical spinsterish passion. I don't really go for the Brontës at all."

"Evidently," Dr. Stark replied, her voice a block of ice.

Katya was stung. "I thought . . ." she began.

"You *thought* very little, Katya."

Dr. Stark handed back the pages of the essay, now covered in Stark hieroglyphs. She gave Katya a long, cool, and assessing stare.

"One of the purposes of your degree course, Katya, is to teach you to *read*. To teach you the subtleties of the reading process. They will not be acquired by skimming and skipping, or approaching a text with a mind awash with foolish prejudice." She paused. "Such skills, I sometimes fear, are endangered—might even be on the way to becoming extinct. Except, of course, in places such as this . . ."

She glanced toward the quadrangle; Katya glanced at her watch.

"Such skills," Dr. Stark continued, "useful in the study of literature, can occasionally be of use in life." She paused. "Katya, something is wrong. You have ability, and on the evidence of this essay, you are squandering it. You are, when you wish to be, intelligent. You were most certainly not in an intelligent frame of mind when writing this, nor are you in a receptive frame of mind now. Katya, you are clearly distracted by some other matter—would you like to tell me what that is?"

"No," said Katya.

"*Deal* with it," Dr. Stark replied, gathering up her skirts and rising to her feet. "You are at liberty to waste your own time, but not mine. Six thousand words on the complexities and significance of the heavily disguised time scheme in *Wuthering Heights* by next Tuesday. Should you feel disposed to rewrite this particular essay, it would be of benefit."

Sod it, thought Katya, rising hastily, as Dr. Stark whisked past her and moved to her desk. She thought of her own novel, begun on a sudden impulse earlier that week, at three o'clock in the morning, when Tom was fast asleep. It was told, in the first person, by a woman twenty years older than Katya: she had been pleased by its world-weary tone, its éclat, and its bite. It now occurred to her, as Dr. Stark began to gather up armfuls of papers and books, that perhaps first-person female narration was a mistake. Why not have two narrators? Four? Omniscient third person? No, far too dated. A subtle *combination* of first and third? Stream of consciousness? Diaries? Some metafictional folderols, perhaps? It came to Katya that her narrator, who was of course not a heroine, but merely a *voice*, would function far more effectively with testicles. She was perfecting this sex change in her head, and wondering whether it might toughen up that interesting section on page four, when she realized that Dr. Stark, saying something about picking up lamb chops from Sainsbury's, was accompanying her out of the door.

They crossed the quad together and turned out into the street. There, Katya, striding along in a bad temper, combat cap pulled low on her brow, head lowered against the rain, collided with someone in a black suit and a black overcoat.

"Good heavens," said Dr. Stark, coming to an abrupt halt. "Rowland? It is Rowland, isn't it? I can't believe it. It must be fifteen years."

It was indeed, and undeniably, Rowland McGuire. His hair was very wet; his coat was soaked; his expression was grim, dazed, and dark. Katya, lip curling, thought he had a Rochester look.

"Miriam," he said, as Dr. Stark blushed a slow, deep crimson. "I—this is a surprise. I've been looking for Katya—"

"And now you have found her. Fortunate."

"This city is *impossible*. You can't *park* in it. You can't *drive* in it. Katya, I'm looking for Tom. I need to see Tom.

Urgently . . . Yes, almost fifteen years, Miriam." He paused, frowning. "After the 'Commem Ball.' Yorkshire, I think."

"How accurate you are, Rowland. But then you always were." Dr. Stark smiled in a somewhat dangerous way. "I agree about the traffic in this city. One always ends up going around in circles, don't you find? And now I must leave you. I'm late for a lecture, as it is. . . ."

She disappeared. Katya had decided twenty seconds before that she did believe in destiny after all; she glared hard at the walls of her college.

"She's not going to a lecture. She's going to Sainsbury's to buy lamb chops," she said, in an angry voice. "Why did she blush? She never blushes."

"I haven't the least idea," replied Rowland, in a tone that precluded further questions. He began walking away in the direction Dr. Stark had taken, then halted abruptly and turned back.

"Tom," he said, in what Katya felt was an odd, wild, and highly agitated manner. "I have to see Tom."

"Well, you can't. Not today." Katya was dressed in jeans and a workman's jacket; she turned up its collar against the rain and scowled. "Tom's in Scotland—Edinburgh. He flew up this morning for some stupid debating thing."

"*Scotland?* Today? *Christ.*"

Katya gave him a venomous look. "And he doesn't get back until tomorrow night," she continued, setting off up the street. "So you're out of luck. You should have phoned."

"*Phoned?* I've been phoning since nine o'clock this morning. I've phoned his house; I've phoned his college, your college. . . . I damn near drove off the motorway calling on the mobile. . . . *Scotland?* It's term time, for God's sake."

"Even so," Katya said, walking faster, "he doesn't have lectures. He rejigged his tutorials. Things have *changed*, Rowland, since your day. This place isn't the prison it used to be. *Shit.*" She came to a sudden halt. "That bloody woman."

"What woman?"

"Dr. Stark. She just took an essay of mine apart."

"That's her job." Rowland had caught up with her; he frowned along the street. "I didn't realize she was your tutor. It wasn't a good essay then?"

"No, it was a fucking awful one." Katya glowered. "My mind wasn't on it. My mind was on *other things*."

She looked at Rowland closely as she made this remark; he seemed to pay it little attention.

"The Brontës," Katya said, in furious tones. "*Wuthering Heights. The Tenant of Wildfell* fucking *Hall*. Passion. Much that bloody Stark woman knows on that subject. Love—yawn bloody yawn."

"She must know something on the subject. Miriam Stark wrote an excellent book on the Brontës." Rowland continued to frown along the street. "She was researching it when I knew her. I went to the Brontë parsonage in Haworth with her once. . . ." He broke off and turned back to Katya. "Never mind that now. Is there somewhere I can reach Tom? Do you have a number for him? Damn, no. That's no good. I need to see him. . . ." Rowland looked up and down the street in a distracted way, as if expecting Tom to materialize at any second.

Katya gave him a withering look and strode off again.

"I can give him a message if you like," she said, over her shoulder, "or you can leave him a note. I'm going over to his room now. It's up to you."

"A note. Yes, a note. That's an excellent idea. . . ." Rowland accelerated his pace, overtook her, and set off up the street, Katya finding it difficult to keep up with him.

"Is that your car?" she said, in an accusing tone, as they finally reached Tom's house, having walked a considerable distance, in heavy rain, without a single word's being spoken. Katya glared at the car in question, which was drawn up outside the front gate and parked in an impetuous way, one wheel on the pavement.

"Yes. Yes, it is—"

"Interesting," said Katya, kicking the wheel. "I always wondered what you drove. . . ." She followed Rowland through the gate and caught up with him at the front door.

"And strange as it may seem," she continued, in a poisonous tone, "it's no good pushing and shoving at the door like that. You need a key. Luckily, I have one."

"Here," she said, as they entered Tom's room, a room that seemed to have a peculiar effect on Rowland McGuire. He was staring at the cerise sofa, then at the bookshelves; Katya held out a notebook and a pen to him. The pen was a ballpoint, an unremarkable one; looking at it, Rowland appeared transfixed.

"Christ," he said again, directing his remark to the bookshelves. He looked at the notebook. "What shall I say?"

"That's up to you, Rowland," said Katya, in an acid voice. She gave him a measuring look and slowly unbuttoned and removed the jacket. She pulled off her combat cap and shook loose her long, damp, russet hair.

"Tom—I need to talk to you," Rowland wrote. He paused, frowning, then added, "as soon as possible." He frowned again, then added, "I'll call you next week."

"What day is it?" He looked up at Katya. "What day is it today?"

"It's Wednesday." Katya gave him an unpitying stare.

"Oh, yes, of course. Thanksgiving tomorrow. *Hell*," said Rowland. He added the date to the note, frowned again, and added "Kind regards, Rowland" and made for the door.

Katya panicked. "I can make you a cup of coffee if you like," she said, in an ungracious tone.

"No time," Rowland replied. "Thank you, but no time—I have to get back to London. I have a plane to catch. . . ."

Katya listened to his footsteps descending the staircase. It was at this window, just a few weeks before that she had watched him arrive in Colin Lascelles's astonishing Aston Martin. It was then, she thought, that she had first sensed the tremors; it was beside these very bookshelves, as Rowland McGuire examined that Anne Brontë novel, that everything right in her life had begun to go wrong.

She strode up and down the room, clasping to her chest one of Tom's discarded sweaters. She found she was angry, confused, and close to tears. Tossing the sweater down, she crossed to her worktable and picked up the chapters of her novel, printed out early that morning, after Tom had left.

She had not wanted him to see what she had written, and now, rereading it, she saw why. She began to see the nakedness and duplicities of her own fictions. Snatching up the pages, she tore them into halves, then quarters, then eighths. Overwhelmed with guilt and misery, she threw this confetti on the floor. "Fuck, fuck, fuck," she said aloud, filled with rage against Rowland McGuire and herself, and furious at discovering that her novel was not about alienation, as she had supposed, but about love—a feeble topic, a woman's topic, after all.

She picked up one of the Brontë novels that had been the subject of her essay, and scowled at it. She flicked the pages, and then, her eye caught by a particular sentence, began reading. She carried the book across to the cerise sofa and curled up with it there.

What had she missed? What, exactly, had she missed? She began reading, mindful of Dr. Stark's corrective scorn; to her surprise, the craving she now felt for Rowland McGuire diminished somewhat as she began to concentrate. Perhaps the exercising of her intellect would effect a cure, she thought, hoping that might be the case, for the craving was unlike any she had experienced before, and its nagging, obsessional vitality was something she had come to fear.

To her relief, this prose kept Rowland at bay for a while; despite the passion she had sneered at in her tutorial—or, possibly, because of it—she was still reading two hours later, completely absorbed. Three hours later, stirred by what she had read, she felt a need to confess. Picking up pen and paper, she began writing to Tom.

"It's going to snow—there's a storm threatening," Colin remarked as the limousine that had picked them up at Kennedy turned out of the airport precincts. Beside him, Tomas Court, who had not spoken to him once on the flight from Montana, gave a sigh.

"It'll hold off. It's hours away yet," he replied. He gave Colin a shrewd glance. "What time are you meeting your friend?"

"Around one o'clock. One-thirty. At the Plaza."

Colin craned his neck to look at the clouds bunched over the western horizon; they were edged with a jaundiced light. With difficulty, he prevented himself from consulting his watch, which he had been checking at five-minute intervals throughout their flight.

"Relax." Court gave a half smile. "I won't make you late for your appointment. I guess you're pretty anxious to be on time. . . ."

"Does it show that badly?" Colin asked.

"I recognize the symptoms," Court replied, his manner kind enough, but faintly bored. "What's her name?"

"Lindsay," Colin said, his heart lifting as it always did when he pronounced, heard, thought of, or saw this name.

"We'll drop you at the Conrad," Court continued. "You find those pictures and notes, bring them down to Tribeca. . . . It won't take us long to go through them. Half an hour at most, then you'll be a free man."

His tone, Colin felt, was slightly mocking. He considered arguing, then rejected the idea. The photographs concerned, in which Tomas Court had previously evinced little interest, showed the moorland landscape around their chosen Wildfell Hall. They were now lying in their file in Colin's room at the Conrad; overnight, Tomas Court had decided that he had to reexamine them urgently. Colin, not pleased by this decision, which indeed threatened to delay him, was wary of protest. He now felt a growing respect, even affection, for Court, but he retained a keen sense of the man's perversity. If he demurred now, Court was more than capable of keeping him working throughout the afternoon.

Let him try, Colin thought; he had every intention, should that situation arise, of proving to Prospero that he had a will of his own. Meanwhile, it was simpler to humor his whim, produce the required pictures, which would almost certainly turn out to be irrelevant, agree with everything Court said, and then make his escape from Tribeca to the joys that lay in wait for him uptown.

Court, meanwhile, had relapsed into a moody silence. Colin patted the breast pocket of his jacket, where Lindsay's letter and fax to him lay folded against his heart. Not for the first time that morning, he blessed the fact that he and the uncommunicative Court were traveling alone. Thalia Ng had left that morning to spend Thanksgiving with her widowed mother in Florida; Mario Schwartz had left to join his family in what he called Hicksville, Idaho; the rest of the production team had dispersed to various places, leaving Colin to travel with the person least likely to interrupt his reveries. With relief, touching that precious letter, Colin began to rehearse its phrases in his mind.

There had been a "but" in Lindsay's fax, a "but" that drew

Colin's eyes every time he reread it; there were fewer "but's" in the letter, however, and this gave Colin heart.

He was almost certain that he could hear a new note in these sentences, as if Lindsay, writing to him from her hotel room, had begun to hear the same music that haunted him; Colin's mind dwelt on that music and its melodies. His hopes rose as they approached Manhattan; this city contained Lindsay and very shortly she would be on her way to meet him at the Plaza. Find the photographs, he told himself, deliver them to Court's loft, make his escape. He dived out of the limousine in great haste as it pulled up in front of the Conrad, and entered that building blindly, praying that he would be eloquent, not tongue-tied, when he took Lindsay in his arms.

In the limousine, Tomas Court continued his journey south to Tribeca; he watched the streets of Manhattan as they drove, and felt a familiar despondency settle upon him. He felt a brief, passing longing for the pure air, and the spaciousness, the great spaciousness, of Montana; then, remembering the interviews he had had with the police there, and the subsequent sleepless nights, he passed his hand across his face and closed his eyes.

On reaching Tribeca he dismissed his driver, shouldering his bag himself, and stepped into the grim confines of the elevator. As its doors closed, he tensed; he had heard a sound, a small unidentified sound, perhaps the scrape of a shoe against concrete, and it had come from a landing above. The air in the elevator was faintly perfumed: the residue of a woman's scent clung to the air, and when he reached his floor and stepped out, he saw that a woman was there before him. She was in the act of tapping at his door; hearing the elevator, she started, then swung around.

She gave a low exclamation, then blushed, then took a step backward; Court saw that she was carrying a small package—a package with his name on it written in large capitals—and that she was clutching this package to her breast, somewhat defensively. Court gave her a wary look, hesitated, then moved forward. He did not recognize her, but he recognized her type instantly: an out-of-work actress, he thought, with irritation—either that or, possibly, some fan.

He came to a halt beside her and looked her up and down. He saw that she had a pretty if unmemorable face; her eyes, of an unusual yellowish hazel, were large and set too close together; they were fringed with short lashes to which thick black mascara had been clumsily applied. These eyes—their expression awed, excited, and half fearful—were now fixed on his own.

"Yes?" he said, his manner cold. "You're delivering something? That package is for me?"

"It is." She made no attempt to hand it over. "I didn't expect—I mean, I hoped I might meet you, obviously, but I thought I'd probably have to leave it with someone. A maid, maybe . . ."

"I don't have a maid."

"I wanted—if you could just spare me ten minutes of your time . . ."

"I don't have ten minutes to spare. I don't have *five* minutes to spare." He looked at her narrowly. "You're not a messenger, are you? You're not from some courier company? Maybe you'd like to explain just how you got this address?"

"I got it from a friend." She passed her tongue across her lips, then, frowning slightly, lowered her eyes. "He worked on your last movie with you—and he took a whole lot of persuading." She paused, indicating the package. "It's just a videotape. I wanted—" She hesitated, then glanced up at him again. "Can't I come in? If you won't give me five minutes, how about four? Three? Two and a half?"

Court looked at her more closely. He looked at her dark hair, which she wore loose on her shoulders, at her clothes, which were cheap but pressed and clean, and at her figure, the curves of which drew his eye. What she was offering was not a videotape, he suspected; beneath the coat she wore, which she had left open, was a dark blouse of some imitation silk material. The top button of this blouse, intentionally or unintentionally, was unfastened; he could just see the cleft between her breasts. He noted that she had small, well-manicured, pretty hands.

"Two minutes," he said and opened the door.

"You're an actress, aren't you?" he said, once the door was closed. He looked around the unnaturally tidy space of his loft: Thalia and Colin had made a thorough job of their cleansing operation, he saw. Without those piles of cardboard boxes, the room looked unfamiliar and faintly alien. He turned back to the woman with a sense of boredom, wondering how she would script her overtures, whether she would echo the words of her numerous predecessors, or whether she might surprise him by being original. He did not expect originality from women in this situation, nor was he going to receive it, he thought, as with an odd, defiant, half-obstinate glance in his direction, she set her package down delicately on his worktable, and then began to unbutton her blouse.

"Sure, I've been an actress." She gave another small frown. "In a few crummy movies, blink and you miss me—that kind of thing. I've done a few TV shows. That's what's on the tape— kind of a composite: my best scenes, my best roles. The kind where I actually got to speak some dialogue . . ." She paused, an expression of faint mockery passing across her face. "I've done other things besides acting, obviously. I mean, I've held down a whole lot of demanding positions. I've been a model, I worked in a gas station one time. Let's see . . . what else? Waited on tables, of course. But that was way back, when I was a student at UCLA. . . ."

Court looked at her steadily; he could hear a certain anger in her voice, and for an instant saw it flash in her yellowish eyes. Liking the anger, he changed his mind.

"Look," he said, less coldly, "do your blouse up. You've been misinformed, I think. I don't audition this way."

"Don't you? That's not what I heard. I asked around. I take an interest in you—I have for years." She hesitated, eyeing him, clasping her blouse across her breasts. "I really admire your movies—I wanted to tell you that. I've watched them a thousand times. I think you're a really great director. . . ."

Court turned away with a gesture of irritation. Her voice, with its faint hint of Southern California, was beginning to grate on him. He liked neither her voice, nor her sentiments, and the momentary sympathy he had felt for her ebbed away.

"Some people like my movies; some people loathe them, and either way, I'm indifferent," he said. "Also, I'm allergic to compliments—particularly fulsome ones. Do your blouse up. I'm expecting a colleague here any minute."

Her response surprised him: he was used to obedience when

he used that kind of tone. The girl seemed scarcely to have heard him and she ignored the contempt in his voice. She continued to look at him as he spoke, that small perplexed frown still creasing her brow. Then, with a sigh and another yellowish glance in his direction, she began to move slowly around the room, her manner unhurried, as if she were there alone and waiting for someone to return.

She crossed to the tall windows, then back to the worktable; in a desultory way, she removed her coat, then brushed her hand across a pile of scripts, picked up a book, examined it, then set it down. She moved with a grace that interested Court; her silence and her apparent absorption in her activities began to affect him. He wondered whether she had realized that he was likelier to respond to silence, and its ambiguities, far more than words.

As she moved around the room, he began to track her with his eyes as he might have done with a camera; he found the chemistry of the room was altering, thickening, and becoming charged. She had his attention now; he was interested in what she might do next: Spoil the effect by speaking? Move toward the door and leave? She did move toward the door, and at this Court felt a sharp and immediate pulse of excitement; for the first time in many years he was remembering how much such encounters could fuel him, and how reliably, if briefly, they drove all thoughts of his wife from his mind.

He took a step toward the woman and regarded her levelly. He watched the light slide across the planes of her face; he watched a new concentration enter her eyes.

"When did you say your colleague was joining you?" she asked. "Any minute now?"

Her eyes rested on his for a moment; then, with a glance of perfect understanding, she unfastened the door, and left it ajar.

She moved a little to the side of it and leaned back against the wall. Court took a step toward her, then another. He came to a halt just in front of her; he could now smell the scent of her body; he could sense the warmth of her skin, and see the rise and fall of her breasts as she breathed. The desire to touch her deepened and Court's body stirred. From the landing beyond, through the crack of the opened door, came the sound of the elevator. It whirred into life; the clankings and shiftings of machinery came from its shaft. Going up, or down? Court was unsure. He was almost certain that it would be twenty minutes at least before Colin Lascelles arrived, but since the woman had begun to move about his room time had slowed, so he might have been wrong.

The possibility of discovery excited him further, and the woman seemed to share that taste, or at least to accept it. An expression of quiet and concentrated complicity had now entered her eyes. Reaching forward, she took his hand and guided it inside her opened blouse. Her breasts had the unnatural jut that betrayed silicone implants; beneath them, he could just feel the thin ridge of the enhancement operation's scar. This unnatural plasticity, he found, also excited him; the woman gave a small sharp intake of breath that might have indicated pleasure. Court moved his hand up so that it rested against the base of her neck; he exerted a faint pressure downward. This signal, or suggestion, she responded to at once; she smiled, revealing pretty, perfect teeth, then, with a quick caress from her small pretty hand, and a glance that might have been one of triumph, she obeyed him without speaking, and knelt down in front of him on the floor.

"No, no, no," said Colin, darting past his great-aunt Emily, who was intent on waylaying him. "Emily, I can't talk now, I'll be late. I have to go. . . ."

He snatched up the pile of photographs and notes for Tomas Court and, dodging furniture, made for the hall.

"Supposing there's a crisis?" Emily said, pursuing him. "I ought to be able to reach you—in emergencies only, I understand. . . ."

"Crisis? What crisis? Why should there be a crisis?" Colin cried, in desperate tones. "Emily, I'll be *late*. Let me go. . . ."

"Anything could happen!" Emily replied, somewhat dramatically. "Supposing I died? Supposing I fell down the stairs? What about a heart attack? I expect a heart attack at any time, and if I had one, I might need to *contact* you. . . ."

"Christ," said Colin, rolling his eyes.

"I won't tell a soul. I swear I won't call—unless I am actually dying, obviously. . . ." Emily paused. Her voice took on a wheedling tone Colin instantly recognized, since he himself used it when necessary, and knew it rarely failed.

"The Pierre? The Plaza? The Carlyle?"

"Give me a *break*," cried Colin, opening the door.

"The Regency? Not the Waldorf, surely?"

"None of them! I'm not telling you and you won't guess in a thousand years. . . ." Colin plunged out onto the landing.

"It's the Plaza, isn't it? A view of the park! I might have known it! Ah, Colin, what a romantic you are!"

"It is *not* the Plaza," Colin cried, blushing furiously. "I've *gone*. I'm out of here. . . ."

"Ah, love. Too charming," said Emily smugly, closing the door.

Ah, love, thought Colin, racing out of the Conrad and leaping into a cab. "Drive very fast *indeed*," he said to the driver, pressing dollar bills through the screen and spilling out directions to Tribeca. The driver spat out of the window and accelerated. Colin looked out upon a transfigured city, a blessed city; he could hear the conversation he would shortly be having with Lindsay very clearly as they drove. He listened attentively to this tender and delightful dialogue for an eternity of intersections; each red light was an affront to the universe. Gallop apace, he thought, looking at his watch for the twentieth time. He was still on schedule, he realized; he could make it back to the Plaza by one-fifteen at the latest, provided Tomas Court did not delay him. No sooner had he thought this, however, than the driver swung left on what he claimed was a shortcut; they at once came to a halt. Colin stared ahead with tragic eyes at a huge delivery truck blocking the street. The driver hit his horn fifteen seconds before Colin told him to do so, but the protest was useless—they were now blocked both behind and in front, the delivery truck clearly intended to be there for the next century, and all the traffic was snarled.

In his loft at Tribeca, Tomas Court adjusted his clothing and stepped back from the girl. It was not his practice, in such situations, to waste time once the required act was over. The brief allure the woman had possessed for him had now gone, and he was without further interest in her. His one concern now was to extricate himself as quickly as possible from this formulaic event, and, looking down at her, he was just considering which of his old formulaic devices would ensure her swift departure, when something caught his eye.

The woman was still kneeling, head bent, face hidden; during the course of her ministrations she had removed her blouse, which now lay beside her on the floor. As she bent forward to pick it up, Court's eyes rested on her bared back; he had been looking down at the discernible line of her spine as he assessed the best way to get rid of her; as she moved, the strands of dark hair that fell across her shoulders parted, and Court glimpsed—he was not sure what he glimpsed, but he heard himself make a small, disbelieving sound.

The woman's face jerked up toward him; she made another quick movement, but Court was too swift for her. Before she could rise, he stepped forward and forced her back down. With a low exclamation of anger and surprise, he parted the thick strands of dark hair, exposing her left shoulder. And no, he had not imagined it: there, in almost precisely the right place, high on the left scapula, was a tattoo—a tattoo of a small, crouching, and delicate black spider.

He jerked away from her and pushed her aside. He stepped back, his face pale. Slowly, the girl straightened up. She wiped her hand across her mouth, met his gaze, and frowned.

"I told you I admired your movies," she said.

"That's a foolish way to express admiration. Write a letter next time. I'll make sure one of the secretaries answers it."

"Write a letter?" Color swept up into her face. "That's what you advise? Mr. Court, I'll remember that."

She reached for her blouse, put it back on, and began to button it. Court watched her in silence. When she had put her coat on also, and began to move toward the door, his anxieties eased somewhat. He began to tell himself that he had been lucky, that the risk had been greater than he had realized, but that the risk was over now. In the doorway, however, she paused.

"You don't remember, do you?" she said, resting her yellowish gaze on his, and voicing the question in a quiet tone.

"Remember what?" Court replied, moving farther away.

"The last time we did this." She looked slowly around the room; Court frowned.

"You're mistaken," he began. "I think it would be better if you went now. I told you—"

"Oh, *I'm* not mistaken, you are." She hesitated, a shy, almost coy note coming into her voice. "It's okay, I don't blame you. Why would you remember? I was blond at the time. Quite a lot younger. It was very brief—nothing special, I guess, as far as you were concerned. Why would it be? I was the third that week, after all."

"I don't know what you're talking about; we've never met. I don't even know your name. . . ."

"It's Jackie." She gave him a sidelong glance. "No? Well, never mind. I understand how it is. I understood then. I mean, you were under a whole lot of pressure, I could see that. The great director! Only the movie wasn't going too well; you were having technical problems—problems with Natasha too, I think. . . ."

The use of his wife's name startled Court and angered him.

"Whatever problems I was having," he said coldly, "I wouldn't have discussed them with you, I'm very sure about that. So—"

"No, you didn't." She gave a low laugh. "The way I recall it, you didn't say too much of anything. You fucked me that time. . . ." She paused, the tiny frown reappearing on her face. "Think about it and you may even remember. On location, outside L.A.? *The Soloist,* and it kind of bombed at the box office. We went to your wife's trailer. . . . You know I always liked that movie? One of your best. It really made me laugh, all those asshole critics eating their words, reappraising it after *Dead Heat* came out. Boy, are they *dumb.* I could have told them—"

"Look," Court interrupted, hearing a new droning and fanatical note enter her voice, "you're mistaken. I'm sorry, but let's leave it at that, shall we? For your information, not that it's any of your business, I was happily married when I made that movie—"

"Oh, yes? You've never been happily married." Her voice rose. "If you were so happily married, how come you did what you did? You fucked me from behind. I was bent double over your wife's makeup table. I had a picture of your kid right in front of my face; he was only a baby then. It took you less than five minutes, start to finish. Women tend to remember things like that."

There was a silence. Court had been listening with the closest attention. He could remember that location well; he could remember the trailer she spoke of, and he could remember very vividly the difficulties he had encountered when making that movie: the groping after solutions, the script rewrites, the elation that accompanied creation, and the despair.

Of the event she described, he had no recollection at all—but that did not mean she was lying; it simply meant that she had been useful, and having been useful, had been erased.

"Are you threatening me?" he said quietly, after a long pause. "Is that why you're here today? What do you want? Some form of revenge? An apology? If you're waiting for an apology, you'll wait a long time."

"An apology?" She gave him a blank look. "No, I came here . . . I guess I came to see if you'd changed. You might have been different now. I thought . . ." She hesitated. "You're older now; you're divorced. People say you're pretty ill—I guess I thought you might be—kinder, you know."

"And do you find me altered?" Court asked, watching her closely.

"Oh no." She glanced away. "You're exactly the same. I never quite got you out of my head, you see—so I guess I wanted to be sure. . . ."

"Maybe we should meet again," he said, with care. "You might revise your views. Do you have an address? A phone number? You live here in New York? I'm going to be in the city for a few more days. . . ."

A small derisive smile flickered across her features. "I have to go now," she said. "Maybe we'll run into each other—you never know."

And with that, before he could prevent her, she was out of the door. She left it ajar; Court, knowing there were better methods of pursuit, did not attempt to follow her. He could still hear her footsteps on the stairs as he reached for the telephone and began dialing. Then another idea came to him. He replaced the receiver and picked up the videotape she had brought with her. His hands a little unsteady and his breathing tightening, he inserted it in his machine.

He had expected some message, some revelation, some clue. The tape was blank; discovering this, he reached again for the phone.

"Now," Colin heard, through the door, as he reached Tomas Court's landing. "I'm not interested—just find the records; they must be on file. I want to know her name and who hired her. . . . I told you, *The Soloist*—that's five and a half years ago. You check the payroll records. What? No, I don't know. Try Wardrobe, Continuity, Makeup. . . . You think I don't realize that? God dammit, I know it's Thanksgiving tomorrow. I don't give a fuck if it's Thanksgiving, Christmas, and your son's bar mitzvah all rolled into one. You get me that information and you get it now. . . ."

Colin hesitated, tapped on the door, then pushed it open. Court swung around, as if startled; then, seeing it was Colin, waved him toward a chair and continued speaking. Colin ignored the chair; he looked at his watch, placed the file of photographs on Court's black worktable, and edged back toward the door.

"How long to run those checks?" Court was now saying. "Yes, but she could be using several names. What? Everything—credit cards, license, registration, sure, sure. Then cross-check with that L.A. photography lab—you still have their employee records? Fine. Then try UCLA—she could have studied there. Try student records for their literature courses—never mind why, just do it. And any courses that they ran on movies. What? I don't know; it's difficult to say: twenty-five, maybe twenty-seven, no older than that. Go back over the past decade and that should do it. . . ." He hesitated, glancing toward Colin. "And she mentioned a boyfriend. . . . What? Just in passing, never mind how it came up, but you do see? Yes. Yes, precisely. I *know* a man has to be involved, goddammit; you don't need to spell out the obvious. . . . What? I don't *know*. She just said he was some kind of an artist—I hadn't realized it could be important then. No, I was only half listening, I had my mind on other things. . . . What? No, an *artist*, that's all she said, and she was probably lying. . . ."

He paused; Colin, impatient to leave, edged toward the door

again. He considered interrupting, then, seeing Court's expression, thought better of it. When Court's gaze moved in his direction, he embarked on some complicated semaphore. He pointed at his watch, then pointed at the door; he mouthed the words "cab waiting," and when this had no effect—Court indeed seemed blind to him—he gave a small dance of agitation and mouthed the words "late—have to go."

Court gave no sign of receiving this message either; he had begun speaking again. Stealthily, Colin edged into the doorway. He was about to turn and flee when, after a pause Court said, "Ah, God, yes," and replaced the phone

The way in which he spoke halted Colin. There was a note of extremity in his voice that Colin had never heard before, and that awoke an instant anxiety. He began to realize that this was not an ordinary conversation, and that Court was in the grip of some strong emotion. Forgetting his cab and his haste for a moment, Colin saw that Court's face was blanched of color, and that he was now breathing with difficulty. As Colin turned back to him, he leaned against the table as if to steady himself, and stood there in silence, head bowed.

"Tomas, are you all right?" Colin began, moving toward him. "What's happened? Here, sit down. . . ."

He reached for a chair, but Court, straightening up and steadying his breathing, waved it aside.

"Nothing's wrong." His pale gaze rested on Colin's for an instant. "Some problem's come up—casting, nothing for you to worry about; not your concern. Those are the pictures I wanted? Thank you."

"Tomas, you don't look well. . . ." Colin hesitated, fighting his conscience. He thought of his late-night conversation with Court at the ranch, a few days before. He thought of the candor and bleakness with which Court had spoken of his love for his wife and his continuing hopes for a reconciliation. Colin had sensed it was the first time he had ever discussed this with anyone. He had pitied him then, and looking at Court's drawn face, he pitied him now.

"Let me call someone, Tomas," he said. "You shouldn't be alone. Maybe I should call that doctor of yours, just to check you're all right. . . ." He hesitated again, then submitted to his conscience. "I can stay," he continued, "if it would help. I can stay for a while. . . ."

"I think not." A flash of dour amusement came into Court's eyes. "I appreciate the generosity of the offer, but you mustn't keep this Lindsay of yours waiting. I promised you you'd be on time—I don't want to break my word."

"I can call her," Colin began, trying hard to hide misery. "Really, Tomas, she'll understand. You look ill—you're terribly pale."

"It's nothing. It's passed. Off you go. . . ." He gave a dry smile. "And I hope you've remembered a present. It is Thanksgiving, after all."

Colin felt a rush of gratitude and liking. He thought of the elegant pale-blue Tiffany's box safely stowed in his bags.

"I have. I bought it in New York that morning, before I left for the ranch. Just in case I couldn't find anything in Montana . . ."

"Very wise. What one finds in Montana doesn't take too portable a form." Court paused, then added, somewhat awkwardly, "I hope you liked the ranch."

"I did," Colin replied.

"It's isolated, of course. My son loves it. Ah well." He gave a sigh, held out his hand, and clasped Colin's.

"Enjoy your Thanksgiving. I'll be speaking to you on Monday, in England, as arranged. And you can relax—it won't be before."

Colin hesitated still, alarmed by something in his manner, by a note of resignation or fatigue he had not heard in Court's voice before. With another dry smile, Court turned away from him and took out the photographs he had requested. He waved Colin away and Colin, moving toward the door, watched him bend over these images of a bleak northern landscape. He thought of Thalia's assertion that Tomas Court was without friends. He could believe that. Court seemed to him to be a man inexperienced at intimacy, slow to trust, and awkward at indicating regard. His attempts to convey liking, both at the ranch and now, touched Colin. He wished Court good-bye, unease and affection tugging at his heart.

Then he remembered Lindsay; his spirits rising at once, he sprinted down the stairs and out to his cab. He told the driver to get him uptown to the Plaza by the best route, and to break every record when doing so. The driver, amused by this demented Englishman, duly did so. Half an hour later, all thoughts of Tomas Court forgotten, Colin was walking into the lobby at the Plaza, his heart beating hard.

He was five minutes late. Meeting Lindsay, who was waiting for him, and who sprang to her feet as soon as he entered, he saw that she was even more nervous than he was. He took her hand, which felt small and cold, in his own. He watched color come and go in her face; her eyes rested on his, their expression dazed and a little afraid. Colin, who had planned an amusing speech, found he was struck dumb; he could say nothing at all.

He registered them both in under the name Lascelles, told the desk clerk to hold all calls until further notice, overtipped the porter who showed them to their room, and, the second the man departed, hung the Do Not Disturb sign on the door.

He locked it. Lindsay had retreated, he saw; she had backed away, past a table decked with flowers, and was standing in front of the tall windows that overlooked Central Park. Joy welled up in Colin's heart. She was wearing a new dress, and a coat he had not seen before; they were black, like most of her clothes. She was smaller than Colin remembered, and slighter in build; with a sudden sense of her frailty, he saw that her small white hands were tightly clasped at the waist of her funereal coat. He saw the anxiety flare in her eyes, and he sensed a new defenselessness in her. At this he felt a great tenderness for her, and his own anxieties melted away.

"I'm so afraid," she said, as Colin began to walk toward her.

"Don't be," Colin replied.

"I did plan what I'd say and do. Now—you look different. I'm afraid I'll say the wrong thing, or do the wrong thing. . . ."

"You don't have to say anything," Colin answered. "Darling, you don't have to say anything at all."

He took her hand gently in his own and kissed it. Lindsay made a small, nervous, disconsolate sound. Colin drew her back across the room to the bed, which was large. Lindsay sat down on it and looked up at him. Colin saw that her hands were trembling.

"I spent all morning shopping," she said, panic in her voice.

"I bought an illicit coat and an illicit dress. I'm wearing them both—and now I don't feel illicit at all."

"Neither do I," said Colin quietly. All desire for pretense fell away from him; a new, and unmistakable expression came into his eyes. Lindsay, reading that expression, gave him a half-fearful look, then uttered an odd, breathless sigh.

Colin thought of all the things he had intended to say, and realized just how wrong and how inadequate they were. Her face, lifted to his, was alight with contradictions and doubt; seeing that, he felt a second's fear. He could see questions in her eyes, and he could sense some tidal pull in the room, exerting its force on him. For a moment he felt at sea, in uncharted waters, with no experience of how to navigate here.

"I love your illicit clothes," he began, somewhat nervously. "I love you in them, and I know I'm going to love you out of them. . . ."

He paused; Lindsay saw him battle with his pride and struggle against some final constraint. Then his face cleared.

"The truth is—I love *you*," he said quietly. "I expect you've realized that. I tried to hide it when I wrote, and it couldn't be done. I meant to hide it now too—and I can't do that either. I love you so much it actually hurts. That's never happened to me before."

Lindsay, moved by a sadness in his expression, by the directness and simplicity of his words, felt a rush of pure affection for him flood her heart. She gave a small flurried gesture of the hands; she raised her eyes to his, then looked quickly away. "Oh God," she began, her voice catching. "You mustn't—I can't—I don't know who I am anymore, Colin. . . ."

Colin was hurt by that reply, but he hid it; it seemed to him that words were better avoided now. In a way that brooked no argument, he drew her to her feet and took her in his arms. He began to kiss her, and that kiss silenced them both. Feeling blind with sudden happiness, and certain he could see a similar blindness in her eyes, he caught her against him. He felt a mad conviction that they had no need for words, and that the language of his body was one she must understand.

He began to make love to her, in ways which he had had 101 hours to dream of and plan. By the time this eloquence was finally over, it was dark in the city outside, and a full moon was riding above the bare trees in Central Park. Lindsay, her body pleasured, and her mind in disarray, gave a small cry of loss as he withdrew from her. She felt both broken and whole. In a frantic way, she began to press kisses against his throat and his chest, and to murmur endearments; taking his hand, with mingled sadness and happiness, she began to kiss his face, and his eyes, and his hair.

Colin's heart lifted; he felt a certainty of purpose, a contentment, and a calm deeper than he had ever known. He kissed Lindsay with great tenderness, then, having learned when it was wiser to remain silent, lay with her clasped against him, making no comment and asking no questions, when she began to weep quietly in his arms.

"Rowland, you are handsomer than ever," said Emily Lancaster, regarding him with affection and pouring him a very large bourbon indeed. Rowland, who was standing at the window of her drawing room, did not respond. "Close the curtains, would you?" Emily continued. "I don't like to see the moon through glass; it's unlucky. . . ."

"That's only when it's a new moon," Rowland replied. He watched the trees move in the darkness of the park, then obeyed her instruction. Emily, who had been watching him thoughtfully, moved across to the sofa. "Now come sit down," she said. "You must be exhausted—that long flight. Lord only knows what time it is by your body clock. Are you sure you won't let Frobisher get you something to eat? No? Rowland, my dear, I'm sure you must be suffering jet lag—even a man of your determination can't face that down."

Rowland made a polite disclaimer. He seated himself beside her on the sofa; Emily budging her pug with a smile. She inspected him closely, putting on one of her pairs of spectacles to do so; she gave a small frown.

"Yes, you've definitely improved with age," she pronounced. "You have a dangerous look about you these days. An air of *perturbation*. I've always found perturbation attractive in a man. If I were forty years younger, Rowland, I'd fall madly in love with you, and we could have a *very* incautious affair."

Rowland looked at Emily with affection; in the five years

since he had last seen her, she had aged considerably. She could no longer hold herself as straight as she once had, but her spirit, he sensed, was as indomitable as ever. He thought of the first time he had met her, when she came over to Oxford for Colin's graduation. At sixty-five, she had been magnificent; and at eighty-five, wrapped in a shawl of heathery-colored tweed, she was still magnificent. Rowland could see, though, the distortions time had made to her hands and spine; suspecting she might be in pain, he pitied her for the ravages of the last twenty years.

Liking her, and also knowing how astute she was, he tried to shake off his own exhaustion and despondency, to rally himself and respond.

"If you were forty years younger, Emily," he said, "you'd be playing havoc with my heart. And I wouldn't risk an affair: I'd propose."

Emily smiled at this. "Smartest move you could make," she said. "I'm one of the few women I know who could cope with you. I'd sort you out in no time. I'd be more than a match for you. What you need, Rowland, is a woman who's ten jumps ahead of you the entire time."

"Do I?" Rowland said, giving her a glinting, green-eyed glance that made even Emily's eighty-five-year-old heart beat appreciably faster. "Do I indeed?"

"My dear, it is very good *indeed* to see you." Emily laughed. "I'd forgotten how well you flirted. Wicked man! This is a pleasure—an unexpected one too. . . ."

"Yes, I had to leave London rather suddenly. It was a last-minute thing."

"What did you say brought you to New York, my dear?"

"Work," said Rowland, who had not previously explained his presence. "My paper's negotiating various link-ups with the *Times* here. We've suddenly run into a few problems."

"How exciting. Oh dear."

"So I came over to—finalize things."

"Of course. But won't everyone be away, my dear? It is Thanksgiving tomorrow after all."

"That shouldn't present any difficulties."

Emily raised her eyebrows, but taking pity on him, pressed him no more. She began to chat away about inconsequential things, while waiting for Rowland to reveal his true reason for being here in this apartment. Much as she liked him, and flattered though she was by his gallantry, Emily was not under the illusion that he was here to see her.

Rowland listened to her with half his mind. He was finding it almost impossible to sit still and be patient; it required all his self-discipline, and that discipline was usually considerable, to avoid questioning Emily at once. All he needed was a location or a telephone number, then he could be speaking with Lindsay within the hour. What he would then say, he had no idea, but he felt a frantic conviction that once he heard her voice, or preferably saw her, he would be blessed with eloquence; the right words, or actions, must inevitably come.

This address and telephone number, he had been chasing ever since he had finally arrived at the Pierre some four hours before. He had first tried calling Lindsay from Heathrow airport, only to find her number engaged; he had tried calling from Kennedy as soon as he landed, and had been cut off three times.

"What do you mean she's checked out?" He had stared at the two young men behind the desk at the Pierre. "Checked out when? Checked out *where*?"

"Ms. Drummond checked out this morning," said the younger of the two, glancing at his confrère. The confrère smirked.

"That's right," he confirmed. "She collected her *faxes*, then checked out. Around ten."

The mention of faxes produced visible and incomprehensible mirth. Rowland stared blankly at the two men. He felt as if he were still traveling: he was on the highway to Oxford, on a fool's errand to see Tom; he was on the highway back, breaking the speed limit to catch his plane. He was in the limbo of the aircraft itself, and he felt in limbo now. The two men had denied all knowledge of Lindsay's present whereabouts. Grimly, Rowland had booked himself into the small cell that was the only room available there over Thanksgiving, and had started telephoning. Twenty calls later, he still had no information and no leads. As a last resort, he obtained Markov's Manhattan number from a giggling Pixie, in London, and dialed it. He did not expect a kind reception, nor did he get one.

"Looking for Lindsay?" Markov trilled, in his most infuriating tone. "Too thrilling, my dear. I always *wondered* when you'd get round to it."

"Where is she?" Rowland said, swallowing his pride. "I need to talk to her and I need to talk to her *now*."

"Can't help, I'm afraid."

"Please," said Rowland.

"Not a word I ever expected to hear on *your* lips," cried Markov, detectable triumph in his tones. "How are the mighty fallen, my dear."

"Fuck it, Markov—where is she?"

"Sweetheart, I *genuinely* don't know. Tucked up in a love nest somewhere, I suspect. With the new inamorato. I can't *wait* to meet him. He sounds too charming for words."

"Markov—have you ever been desperate?"

"Of *course*, darling. Most of the time."

"Well, I'm desperate. No doubt that delights you. Help me out, here."

Markov made a considering noise. "I'm seeing a little cabin in the woods," he said, in a maddening way. "Could it be out of state? Yes, I think so. A *cozy* little cabin, somewhere très discreet. An *intimate* little cabin, with log fires . . ."

"Christ, Markov—"

"Oh, all right." Markov gave way to the temptation to cause trouble, a temptation he could never bear to resist for very long. "I'm seeing the Oak Room at the Plaza, tomorrow evening at seven; they get back then. Thanksgiving drinks, darling. Jippy and I get to vet the inamorato. I gather . . ." Markov lowered his voice. "I gather he has auburn hair, hyacinthine curls, diabolic eyebrows, an Apollonian body, and a way with women. . . ."

"What fool gave you that description?" Rowland said, in a violent tone.

"Can't *think*, darling. Someone who knows him pretty well, I guess. Have to go now. Bye."

Replacing the phone, Rowland realized that even he, with a journalist's persistence, could not call every hotel with cabins in America; besides, there was an easier way. He dialed Emily's number, as a result, here he was—jet-lagged, exhausted, afflicted with a sense of whirling futile momentum, going no-where exceedingly fast.

"I'm sorry to miss Colin," he said, interrupting Emily and unable to bear prevarication añy longer. "I hear he's staying out of state somewhere with Lindsay."

"Ah," said Emily, bending to fondle her pug. "Yes indeed."

"Have they been away long?"

"Well, now, I'm not really sure. Colin's being a little secretive. . . ."

"He wasn't secretive when I telephoned before," Rowland said, hearing the bitterness in his own voice and realizing that he was losing his capacity to dissemble. Lindsay, he thought, would not judge his untruths to be cool or flagrant now. He turned to look at Emily. "I gather marriage is in the cards."

"He is very much in love," Emily replied, in a quiet, firm tone.

"And are his feelings returned?"

"That I cannot answer. Lindsay would not confide in me. Though I would say . . ." She paused and turned her blue gaze steadily upon Rowland. "I would say they were admirably suited to one another, wouldn't you?"

Rowland's reaction confirmed everything Emily had sus-pected, and told her all she needed to know. She saw his hand-some face darken and an arrogant expression mask his dismay. He gave her a cold, green-eyed glance, and took a swallow of bourbon.

"I always find questions like that impossible to answer. They're foolish. Only two people can judge—and that's the two people concerned."

"Well, I think they're made for each other," Emily said, a little sharply; then, seeing the unhappiness in his eyes, she modified her tone. "Consider," she went on, "they are both vul-nerable; they are both innocents—and I do not mean that in a pejorative way. They both have an open, sunny, optimistic dis-position, though Colin, of course, likes to dramatize his fears. They have a very similar sense of humor—which is very important indeed. . . ."

She hesitated; Rowland, his face set, said nothing. Emily looked around her room, wondering whether to show him mercy or continue. She thought of her conversation here with

Colin on the night she had first met Lindsay; love for her nephew, and protectiveness toward him, rose up in her heart. Continue, she decided, and began speaking again, ignoring the stony expression in Rowland's eyes.

"And then," she went on, "there are the long-term considerations. Lindsay is not in her first youth. She has one miserable marriage behind her. For twenty years, she has had to bring up a child alone. She has a resilience, and a determination I admire—and they would be of great benefit to Colin. . . ."

"They would be of benefit to anyone who married her."

"Indeed." Emily gave him a sharp glance. "But Colin has admirable qualities too, let us not forget that. With Colin, she could rely on unswerving loyalty and devotion. . . ."

"I'm sure she would repay that in kind."

"No doubt. My point is that with Colin she could be secure. He would be faithful, loving, and considerate. He would make the very best of husbands. . . ." She paused, then added, in a delicate way, "Not all men are husband material, wouldn't you say?"

"I'd say appearances can be deceptive in that respect," Rowland answered, somewhat roughly.

Emily made no reply, but continued to look at him, her expression kindly but perplexed; she gave a sigh.

"Well, well, I am very old now," she said, in a quiet way. "I look at these things differently from you, no doubt. I love Colin; his future happiness and well-being are very close to my heart." She paused. "I'm sure you will understand that, since you and Colin are such close friends, and have been for so many years."

Rowland heard the undisguised note of warning in her voice; his eyes met hers.

"I also wish Colin well," he began, in a stiff way. "I like Colin and I respect him. I hope you know that—"

"Indeed I do. I also know what it is to experience a clash of loyalties. That is always painful, and especially so for an honorable man."

Rowland colored. "I don't follow you," he said, looking away.

"Oh, I think you do," Emily said. She paused, her gaze

resting thoughtfully on his face; then she made one of those lightning shifts of attack that Rowland remembered of old.

"You have thought of marrying, I imagine, Rowland?"

"I have thought of it. Yes."

"And no doubt you would like children?"

"Yes, I would hope—" He stopped, suddenly seeing the unerring accuracy of her aim. He turned back to look at her. "I would like to have a family, children—yes. I have no family of my own. So I had hoped to have children one day."

Emily gave a small inclination of her head. Rowland saw pity come into her eyes.

"Colin also wants this," she said quietly. "In many ways, and despite the life he's led, Colin is and always has been, a very domestic man. He loves his home and is never happier than when he *is* at home. With the right wife, and God willing, with children, there is no doubt in my mind that he would be completely fulfilled. Of course, in Colin's case, there are additional reasons—I suppose one would have to call them dynastic reasons—why he should want children. He may deny it, but I know how deeply it matters to him, and to his father, that he should be able to pass Shute on to his son and heir."

"I know that. I know exactly how much that matters to him." Hope had come into Rowland's eyes. "So I would have thought that—"

"So would I." Emily cut him off with a small lift of her hand. Seeing her expression change, Rowland felt a second's foreboding; he could see that she was tiring, but she clearly intended to say something more, and knew it would be unwelcome. She looked at him with gravity and compassion, then sighed.

"You are an intelligent man, Rowland. No, sit down; there's something I want to tell you before you go. This question of children, of heirs. You should know—I discussed that very issue with Colin, here in this room, on the night he introduced me to Lindsay. I reminded him of Shute and the length of time his family has lived there. I reminded him of the entail. . . ." She paused. "I didn't use the word 'sacrifice' with him then, but I will use it with you now." She paused.

"To contemplate marriage to a woman who might, unhappily, be unable to bear a child, is perhaps the greatest sacrifice

Colin could make. Yet he intends to marry her, and he made the decision without the smallest hesitation—I think you should know that, Rowland. Other men, in similar situations, might have acted differently. . . ." She allowed her gaze to rest quietly on Rowland's face. "I would not blame them for that. But I will say that, in these circumstances, Colin's love for Lindsay should not be underestimated. He showed courage—and I have never admired him more than I did then."

The statement was gently made, but it cut Rowland. He rose and turned away. "I've never doubted Colin's moral courage," he said.

"But you do doubt him in other ways? You think he is unsteady, perhaps? Impetuous? No doubt you would feel concern on Lindsay's behalf, if that was your view."

"I do feel concern," Rowland began, turning. "I feel—"

"My dear, I can see exactly what you feel. I am not blind and I am not deaf." Emily gave a deep sigh. "Rowland, what you feel is obvious in your speech, in your expressions, in every gesture you make. You have my sympathy, but I would counsel you to think very carefully and very honestly before you take any action you might subsequently regret. Colin looks upon you as a brother. I would not want you to delude yourself that he is not in earnest here, however tempting that might be. He is *utterly* in earnest. And if I may give my opinion, I think that from Lindsay's point of view and his own, he has made a hard, but a very wise choice."

"I love her," Rowland said, in a low voice. "Emily, for God's sake—" He turned away, and Emily, who had never seen his composure even threatened, in all the years she had known him, watched it break.

Saying nothing, she waited for him to regain his control. She leaned back against the cushions, feeling suddenly that all her energy was gone. The strength of Rowland's reaction disturbed her; now her eighty-five-year-old mind felt fearful, and every one of her eighty-five-year-old bones seemed to ache.

She had suspected this conversation might be necessary as soon as Rowland telephoned and announced his arrival in New York; she had known, beyond doubt, that it was necessary when he entered, and she saw the expression on his face. She had begun this conversation feeling very sure of her ground, but now an old woman's incertitude gripped her. Confronted by the evidence of pain—and a man's pain, which she found harder to witness than a woman's—her mind felt flurried, muddled, and flooded with doubts.

"Rowland," she began. "Rowland, I'm so very sorry. Listen to me—"

"No, *I'm* sorry." Rowland, his back to her, fought to steady his voice. "You were right earlier. I'm desperately tired. I should take myself off. . . ."

"I wish you wouldn't. At least stay and finish your drink." She gave him an anxious look, then, as he slowly turned, held out her hand to him. "If you go now, I'll feel I've offended you."

"You certainly haven't done that."

He hesitated, then, with a gentleness that surprised her, took her hand, with its bent and misshapen fingers, and held it in his own. Emily saw that he could still scarcely speak for emotion; she drew him down beside her, and looking at his drawn face, felt another flurry of remorse and doubts. Those who could not see beyond Rowland's appearance, she thought, were very foolish. Rowland McGuire was a considerable man, to whom Colin, and Colin's family, owed a debt. Who was she to judge whether he was, in her own glib phrase, husband material?

Marriage was a serious subject; love was a serious subject; the bearing of children was a more serious subject still: these issues determined the course of entire lives—what right did she have to meddle here? She was partisan, and had in any case been too long retired from the fray; she had forgotten the agonies of love, and had no doubt underestimated them, for she was preoccupied too often now with the more pressing concern of mortality and imminent death.

"Ah, Rowland, Rowland," she said, laying her hand on his arm. "I never married. I never had children. I'm old. I hadn't understood how strongly you felt. I shouldn't have spoken as I did."

"No. I'm glad that you did." He looked across the room. "I can see now—I suppose I always could—Colin can offer her so much. Not just material things; I don't only mean that. Colin is generous at heart. And you're right, they are alike, in many respects. When they first met, I could see then. . . . It's just that—well, I had thought—I had sensed—"

He broke off, and Emily, pitying him again, and knowing his pride, turned her gaze away from his. With skill and with tact, she diverted the conversation away from this subject to more neutral ones. Rowland, as anxious as she was to regain neutral ground before he left, followed this lead. Prompted by Emily, he began to talk of other things; Emily half listened to him, and half listened to something else.

At first, she was aware only of some shift and disturbance in the room—having lived so long in the Conrad, this was something to which she had long been accustomed. Attuned to the spirits of the building, both malign and benevolent, she could always sense when they became restless and stirred.

This they did, these days, more and more often. Emily attributed their more frequent activation to her own age, to the proximity of her own death, and to the fact that she no longer dismissed them as the products of her own fancy or superstition, as she had done in her youth.

The spirits here were always encouraged, she believed, by perturbation in human beings. Perhaps Rowland had unwittingly summoned them up tonight; perhaps she herself had. She glanced at his now guarded, tense face, then looked down at the rug beneath her feet. It was an Aubusson, still beautiful, and patterned with faded roses; the dusky pink of these flowers, in this subdued light, darkened to the color of blood. Tonight, these flowers, like the shadows in the room, teemed with abundant life. Emily's little dog could also sense this; she felt him stir beside her, and his hackles rise up. She concentrated on the other conversation she could now hear, which she realized had been continuing for a while, beyond and above the sound of Rowland's quiet voice. She tried to hear what was being said, in that other anterior exchange—and something was being said; she could half hear it, emanating from this carpet's warp and weft.

She began to distinguish first a man's, then a woman's voice; their words were muffled, but the reproach and pain in their voices were not. Gradually, as she listened, stroking her little dog and wondering if this message might be indirectly meant for herself, she heard that the woman's voice had come to dominate; Emily listened as an aria of accusation mounted, then faltered. There was a silence, then a long cry of uncertain gender, a cry that might have signified desolation, or delight, or distress.

"What was that?" Rowland said sharply.

Looking up, Emily realized how deeply she had been distracted. Rowland had brought their conversation to a close without her being aware of it; he had risen, and must have been moving toward the door, when he spoke. She looked at him uncertainly, confused and surprised that he should have heard this sound, one with which she had become familiar, and which she believed to be the cry of a woman long dead. It would scarcely do to inform Rowland, a rational man, that the voice was Anne Conrad's. He would assume that age had finally taken its toll on Emily, that she was losing her wits.

She gave herself a little shake and opted for the pragmatic answer, realizing as she did so that it could well be correct. After all, according to Frobisher, who had it from the porter, Giancarlo, Tomas Court was at present in the building; he was in the apartment below this one, visiting his former wife.

"Oh, just a marital argument," she said in a dry way, recovering herself and holding out her hand to him.

"I wish you well, Rowland. I wish you wisdom, my dear." She paused. "When will you be returning to England?"

"I haven't decided yet."

"I see." She released his hand. Somewhere in the building a door slammed. Emily shivered.

"It's darned cold tonight," she said. "You'll have to take the stairs, Rowland, the elevator's playing up again."

"I've already discovered that."

"I dislike those stairs myself." She huddled her shawl more tightly around her. "Well, well, you're a good man, Rowland. I'm glad you came—"

Rowland hesitated. "Are you all right, Emily?"

"Fine. I'm just fine. A little tired maybe." She picked up her tiny dog, and kissed his crinkled sagacious brow. Still Rowland hesitated, suddenly concerned for her; he looked about the shadowy room and felt unease furl its wings about him.

Emily waved him away, her diamond ring catching the light. "Good-bye, my dear," she called after him, as he stepped out into the hall. Rowland passed out onto the galleried landing, with its brandishing arms and inadequate light. He descended the stairs, looking neither to left or right, and left the building. Snow had been falling, he discovered, stepping out onto a thin crust of white. There was an unnatural hush about the city, and more snow would fall during the night.

Chapter 14

"What time is it in England now, Colin?"

With a sigh, Lindsay disengaged herself from his arms; she extricated herself from the tumbled sheets and, sitting up naked and cross-legged, reached for the bedside telephone and began dialing.

"Five hours ahead of us," Colin replied, yawning, stretching, then sitting up and kissing the back of her neck. "I've no idea what time it is here, though," he added, beginning to kiss each disc of her spine. "It could be yesterday, or next week."

"It's six-fifteen. Six-fifteen! How can that be? What happened to the afternoon?"

"Darling, what happened to the morning?"

"They merged," Lindsay said, giving him a mischievous glance. She replaced the receiver, then redialed. "And now we have to reform. The others will be arriving soon. We have to shower and get dressed and go downstairs and be respectable. Gini's always horribly punctual. . . . Damn! Tom's not answering. . . ."

"Tell me about Gini." Colin said, beginning to kiss the back of her ear. "Will I like her?"

"Probably. She's beautiful, so most men tend to like her—on sight." She replaced the receiver. "Bother. I can't get Tom, and I wanted to speak to him. He flew back from Edinburgh this evening. I wanted to know he was safe. Now I'll worry about his flight."

"No, you won't." Colin put his arms around her waist. "Darling, he has this number. It's past eleven in Oxford. If there were any problem, he or Katya would have called."

"That's true." Lindsay's face brightened. "I'll try him in the morning, before we leave for the airport." Her face became thoughtful. "Colin, tomorrow we'll be in England. . . ."

"I don't care where we are," Colin said, "as long as I'm with you."

"You comfort me." In an impulsive way, she took his hand in hers. "You comfort me, Colin. I feel happy. I woke up this morning next to you—and I felt content. The day felt full of promise and prospects. I'd forgotten a day could feel like that."

Dazzled by the expression in her eyes, and too joyful to speak, Colin drew her into his arms. Lindsay rested her head against his shoulder; he began to kiss her hair; her use of the word "comfort," which had surprised him, stirred some memory. For a moment he could not place it, then it came to him. "Comfort me with apples," he murmured, beginning to stroke her breasts. "My beloved is mine. . . . I forget the rest. Something about lilies . . ." His body stirred, and Lindsay gave a sigh of pleasure; her mouth opened under his.

"Darling, we mustn't, we mustn't—it's so late. . . ."

"Let them wait."

"Colin—no. We shouldn't. I—Oh God, that's not fair. We can't, not *again.* I can't go down like this. I have to have a shower. I smell of sex. Darling, stop—they'll know what we've been doing. . . ."

"They'll know anyway." Colin smiled. "It shows in your eyes, and mine. I know that."

"In my *eyes*? It can't. Oh, *yes* . . ."

"It does. It's flagrant. I can see every possible declension of sex in your eyes. Past, present, future—passive and active form. Has fucked, will be fucked—it's beautiful, and it's the most erotic thing I've ever seen in my life. . . ."

"Well, perhaps if we're very quick," Lindsay said.

"Are you still anxious, Jippy?" Markov asked, catching a glimpse of Jippy's pale face over his shoulder, in his hallway mirror. They were preparing to leave for the Plaza, and Markov was in the process of selecting a hat.

"Don't be, darling." He turned. Jippy was wearing a neat suit that made him look like a minor accountant; Markov, moved by this, took his hands fondly in his. He hesitated. "It will all be all right—won't it?"

Jippy did not reply. He could not explain, even to Markov, how it felt to see the aura of future events. For days, ever since they had returned from Crete, he had been afflicted by the buzzings and whisperings and seethings that signified unrest. That morning, he had woken from disturbed sleep to a sense of paralyzing fear. He had watched some dark shape lumber across the room, and he had smelled evil. Evil had a precise smell, a distillation of iron, burning, and salt. It was not a noxious odor, and Jippy suspected others might find it bracing, like sea air, but it left him feeling sick and lethargic, aching at his own impotence, knowing he could glimpse troubles, but that his powers were limited. The troubles, he could foresee, but could not prevent.

As yet, and as usual, the shape of those troubles was still vague; their proximity was now giving him an acute headache, for which he had already taken several doses of codeine, without effect. Standing next to Markov now, he was seeing fizzes and flashes of blinding light; he wished they would go away; he blinked.

Markov, having decided on a black fedora, turned to look at him again. When they were alone together, and only when they were alone, Markov abandoned his affectations of speech.

"I love you, Jippy," he said.

"I l-love you back," Jippy replied in a stout way; his stammer improved when they were alone also; Markov's term for this shared phenomenon was the "certainty effect."

"Does your head still hurt, darling?"

Jippy nodded; Markov put his arms around him. "I'll make the pain go away," he said, kissing Jippy's neat dark hair, then stroking it. "There—is that better?"

Jippy nodded; the pain, indeed, diminished when Markov held him.

"Well, *I* won't do anything to make things worse, I promise you that." Markov looked at Jippy in a penitent way. "I won't say a word out of place—for once. Not even to Rowland, if he turns up. Is he going to turn up, Jippy?"

Jippy did not know the answer to that question, and the minute Markov released him, the sharp stabbing pain had returned to his head.

Markov opened the front door of his small, smart East Side town house.

He grimaced at the sidewalk, and then at the sky.

"Can you believe it? It's snowing again," he said.

Farther south, Rowland stood at the window of his cell at the Pierre, and looked out at the dark sky. He had showered, shaved, exchanged one dark suit for a different one, and was still irresolute. Stay or go? Risk or retreat? It was approaching seven, and he remained undecided. The scales were almost exactly balanced. On the one side was the loyalty he felt toward Colin, given added weight by the reason and dispassion of Emily's arguments; on the other were his own hopes and desires—and instincts, of course.

A decisive man, Rowland hated indecision; he despised it in others and he despised it even more in himself. He took out Lindsay's letter to him, hoping it might resolve the issue. When first read, in London, it had seemed capable of only one interpretation; now, interpretations swarmed. With a dull misery, he saw that it could mean the very opposite of what he had thought it meant. It could even be read, he realized for the first time, as a farewell letter, in which Lindsay looked at something for the last time, and then sadly but decisively turned her back.

To go or not to go. He stared out at the streets, at the groups of people making their way to Thanksgiving gatherings. *Why* had he not acted before? Why, when he was rarely tentative, had he been tentative in this? He lifted Lindsay's letter to the light again, groping at the sense of her sentences. "Colin came here yesterday, after you telephoned. . . . Are those shutters I admire so much open or closed? . . . The smudges everywhere are from the Biro. . . . You'll find I'm a reformed character."

He refolded the letter, a confused and incoherent plea rising up in his heart; he rested his forehead against the glass and watched the snow fall. He began to feel that time had stopped and that the hands of his watch were fixed; he lifted it to his ear and listened to the seconds tick.

"Do we have to go?" Pascal said to his wife, putting on a tie in honor of the Plaza—and he hated to wear ties. "It's snowing.

It's thirty blocks from here. Couldn't we just call Lindsay and say we can't make it?"

"I don't know where she is." Gini was sitting at the dressing table of the guest bedroom, in their friends' apartment on the upper West Side. She was concentrating, pinning back her pale hair in a pleat. She had hoped to look beautiful tonight, and felt, in a dispassionate way, that she did. She examined the serene oval of her face and the luster of her skin; no lines were visible; her father's house was sold; she was free and beginning her new life. She picked up a string of pearls and held them against her dress. "We can't let her down," she said, abandoning the necklace. "We needn't stay long."

"We *can't* stay long. We have to be back here for dinner. This is a crazy arrangement—what if Lucien wakes up?"

"Darling, he won't. And if he does, the others will look after him. He'll be thoroughly spoiled. Don't you want to meet Lindsay's new man? I do. I'm intrigued."

"Women usually are by that kind of thing. It bores me to distraction. I wish them well—beyond that, I couldn't care less."

"Well, I could. I'm interested. It's all so sudden. And I'd begun to suspect she was interested in someone else." She paused, looking at her own reflection. "Someone very unsuitable—he wouldn't have suited her *at all*. So I'm glad she's seen sense."

Pascal did not reply. He moved across to the window, drew back the curtains, and looked out. This apartment, on the fourth floor of a brownstone on Riverside Drive, overlooked the Hudson. River and sky now blurred together; the air was thick with snow. Turning away, his manner edgy and irritable, he began to pace.

His wife watched him do so in the mirror. Carefully, she screwed two pearl earrings into place. She knew what was wrong with her husband, and it had very little to do with the meeting with Lindsay: Pascal was beginning to feel caged by domesticity. Once they began work on their book, this feeling would lessen, but it would not disappear altogether, and she was beginning to realize that.

"You're missing your wars, Pascal," she said, hearing her own voice strike exactly the wrong note.

"My wars?" He gave her a sharp look. "The wars aren't of my making; I merely photograph them."

"You're missing them, nonetheless. Pascal—"

"I miss doing what I do best, possibly." His tone was cold. "Gini, we really should go. Surely you're ready by now?"

Gini experienced a tiny moment of fear. She looked at her own face in the mirror; she felt she was stepping through the glass and watching history repeat. This was the pattern of his first broken marriage; his first wife, Helen, being informed by Gini that Pascal had decided to end his coverage of wars, had smiled a small tight smile.

"Gini, dear," she said. "What a victory for you! I hate to say it, but I give it six months before he reverts."

It was more than six months; it was nearly two years.

"Pacal—you promised me. . . ." she said.

"I know, I know, I know." He gave her a long, still, penetrating look. "You extracted that promise from me after Lucien's birth. You always have good timing."

"What's that supposed to mean?"

"Nothing, my darling. Just that, with marriage to you, I've realized how tenacious you are. You usually end up getting what you want, don't you, Gini?" He have her a regretful, measuring look, then gave a shrug. Dropping a kiss on her brow, he moved to the door.

"We really must leave. Who else did you say was going to be there?"

"Just Lindsay and this Colin man. And Markov and Jippy."

"Thank God for that. I like Jippy."

"Do you still love me, Pascal?" She rose.

"Still? That sounds defeatist. Of course I do. You know that." He took her hand as she reached his side and looked at her closely. "And now you've finally made me into what you wanted, do you still love me? No regrets?"

"Of course I do." She hesitated. "And everyone has regrets occasionally, Pascal. They mean nothing at all."

"Don't they? Tell me, do your regrets take a specific shape?"

"No. Certainly not."

"Good." Her husband's cool gray eyes rested on her face. His wife did not intentionally deceive others, he thought, but he was learning how good she was at deceiving herself. "Then we have nothing to worry about. An ideal couple. Destined for each other from the first." He spoke in a light tone, feeling suddenly tired. "We must leave, Gini. Come on—we'll be late."

"Good evening," Emily said, in crisp tones, to the tall man standing outside the elevator. Behind her, a maid closed the door to Henry Foxe's elegant apartment, on the tenth and top floor of the Conrad building. The sounds of merriment from the cocktail party beyond were cut off. Emily eyed the man and felt a spurt of gossipy interest. This was her first proper sighting of Tomas Court, the ex-husband. He too had been present at the Foxe Thanksgiving party, but since he had not spoken once, and had lingered at its edges throughout, that sighting did not count.

"Going down?" he said.

Emily looked at the ceiling.

"Well, I surely can't go *up*," she said tartly.

"No, I guess not." Tomas Court smiled.

Emily tucked her crocodile purse under her arm and adjusted her fur, a fur that several lynxes had died to make. It gave her a wild, bristling appearance, and it had been the height of fashion in 1958. She gave Tomas Court one of her unabashed sweeping glances, and to her surprise, found herself impressed. She could see fatigue on his face, but she liked his eyes, his graying, close-cropped hair, the quietness of his demeanor, and his air of constraint.

Very different kettle of fish to the *wife*, Emily said to herself. The wife, ravishing in some pink creation, was still lingering at Henry Foxe's party. Though she had said little, and her manner was modest enough, she liked to be the center of attention—or so Emily, unsympathetic to beautiful women, had thought. She had had Henry Foxe running around in circles, proffering canapés and drinks, and poor Biff, swaying on his feet from an excess of dry martinis, had spent the evening staring at her in a besotted manner; every sentence he managed to utter began with her name: Natasha thinks this, Natasha said that. . . .

Emily had decided that Natasha Lawrence was beginning to find this worship tedious; having been useful to her, poor Biff was about to be discarded, Emily had sensed. She suspected Tomas Court had sensed this also; he too had watched Natasha Lawrence give a tiny sigh and a tiny frown; like Emily, he had

seen the two people who had flanked the actress all evening
react. Her real-estate broker, Jules McKechnie, whom Emily
disliked, had drawled: "Biff, darling, don't you think you're
getting the teeniest bit tight?" The actress's bodyguard, a handsome, hulking boy with a Texan accent, had moved forward,
and shortly after that, Biff was detached—and dispatched,
Emily assumed, since he had left the party and she had not laid
eyes on him since.

"This elevator isn't working," Tomas Court said. "I'm afraid
we'll have to walk down, Miss Lancaster. It is Miss Lancaster,
isn't it?"

"Yes." She looked him up and down. "You may give me
your arm, if you would. This elevator is becoming very *trying*.
My nephew Colin is working for you—are you aware of that?"

Tomas Court smiled quietly, as Emily fixed upon him her
most duchessy look; he took her arm and began to assist her
down the stairs. The shadows in the galleries whispered at
Emily as they passed; she glanced at Tomas Court.

"This staircase is haunted," she said, in firm tones, pausing
on one of the lower landings. "Have you noticed that?"

This was one of Emily's tests; Tomas Court passed it.

"Of course. As soon as I saw it, I knew that." He paused,
frowning. "I know what it is to be haunted," he added, in an
offhand way, "so I would notice, I guess."

"It has gotten *worse*," Emily continued, with asperity, "since
your wife arrived. I have my suspicions about the elevator also.
There is a definite *malevolence* in its breaking down when it
does. I, of course, was the sole person on the board committee
to vote against admitting your wife."

"So I heard."

"*Most* strange, the manner in which she obtained the other
four votes."

"Not so strange. My wife seduces people—as you've seen
tonight." His manner remained imperturbable, his tone flat.
"She made a number of donations to various causes, I understand; they happened to be the pet causes of two of your committee members, and they were large donations, but then my
wife is now very rich. Jules McKechnie advised her as to
which causes, I think. . . ."

"Juliet McKechnie?" Emily gave a rude snort. "I can't abide

that darned woman. Never could. She's smart, however. One of *the* McKechnies—which she trades on, of course."

"Ah, I see." He glanced over his shoulder. "I hadn't realized until tonight—I was confused by the name. I'd assumed my wife's broker was a man. . . ."

"Then you weren't far wrong," said Emily, in a dry voice.

"As to the two other committee members," he continued, giving no sign of hearing her last remark, "Mr. Foxe was gently wooed, but then he is widowed, and no doubt lonely, and Natasha would have seen how easily frightened he is. . . ." He paused. "Does Mr. Foxe have a daughter, by any chance?"

"He did. His only child. She died."

"I see. I imagine my wife would have known that. She is always well informed. . . ." His eyes moved along the shadows of the galleries. "As for Biff Holyoake, well, that would have been easy for a woman of her beauty, don't you think?" He paused, looking at Emily in a careful way. "You should under-stand—I approve. My wife fights fire with fire; she always has."

"And you?" Emily looked at him closely. "I get the feeling you're not too enamored of this building?"

"I dislike it intensely." He turned his pale and steady gaze upon her. "That dislike doesn't extend to every individual occupant, of course."

Emily found herself flustered; she looked at Tomas Court with amusement, then with deepening respect.

"This is my apartment right here." She paused. "The Thanks-giving dinner is cooking as we speak, and very good it will be. My nephew will be arriving shortly; if you have no other plans, you'd be very welcome to join us. . . ."

He refused with a small shake of the head. "It's very kind of you, but I'm having Thanksgiving dinner with my wife and son . . . a family reunion. My son's looking forward to it. I must go and join him now. . . . Give Colin my regards."

He turned to the stairs. In a state of great excitement, anx-ious to impart the news of this encounter to Frobisher, Emily hastened in. She made straight for the kitchen, from which mouthwatering smells emanated. There she found Frobisher, looking somewhat *distrait*, basting a gold monster of a turkey. Frobisher, friend, confidante, and factotum, was an excellent

cook, who took her art seriously. Emily sensed that now was
not the best moment to interrupt.

She deposited her purse on the Alice B. Toklas cookbook,
Frobisher's culinary Bible, and eyed a plate of corn muffins.
When Frobisher's attention was distracted, she broke off a
corner of corn muffin and nibbled it surreptitiously. Frobisher
heaved the monster turkey back into the oven and clanged the
door shut. She wiped her hands on her apron. Emily saw that
her handsome face was flushed, and her gray hair in disarray;
this boded ill. She opened her mouth to explain she had just
met the great director, the peculiar ex-husband, and a most
intriguing man he was, then was silenced as Frobisher gave her
a beady look.

"That darned telephone has never quit ringing since you
left," Frobisher said, enunciating the words with a clarity that
presaged trouble. "No way can I answer the telephone and
cook."

"No, of course you can't, Froby," Emily said in a small
humble voice.

"Problems!" Frobisher said darkly. "*Developments*—and
Colin's not going to like them, I can tell you that."

"Oh dear," said Emily, hiding her hand behind her back.

"Ructions," Frobisher said, more darkly still. "I've been
railroaded; ructions—that's what I predict. . . ." She looked at
Emily fiercely. "And there'll be more ructions if you keep
eating my corn muffins. Put that back."

"My lord, did you *see* Emily Lancaster's coat?" Juliet Mc-
Kechnie said, in a low voice, taking Natasha Lawrence's arm,
as they reached the second-floor landing of the Conrad.

"Ssssh." Natasha laughed. "Keep your voice down. We
shouldn't be doing this, Jules."

"It made her look like a grizzly bear, didn't you think?"
Juliet also laughed. "Magnificent, though, in her way. And she
can't stand me—which is a pity. She's an old tartar, but I've
always had a soft spot for her. . . ."

"Why can't she stand you?" Natasha said, taking out a key
and opening a small, unmarked door around the corner from

the entrance to Emily's apartment. She laid her finger on her lips. "And keep your voice *down*."

"My grandmother snaffled Henry Foxe from under her nose." Juliet smiled. "This would have been around 1452. She's been prejudiced against all female McKechnies ever since. . . ."

The two women stepped into a small hallway, and descended a short flight of stairs. Finding themselves in a long arched corridor, hung with watercolors, they stopped and looked at each other. Juliet glanced at a door to her left, which led down to the lower floor of Natasha's apartment; it was closed.

"Tomas hasn't . . ."

"No, no." With a sigh, Natasha shook her head. "He wanted to come up here, of course. He wanted to see everything—a grand tour. He tried to insist yesterday, but I held out."

"You see? I told you you could."

"It's all finished now." Faint color rose in Natasha's cheeks. "I hung the last of the pictures yesterday morning. Jonathan helped me, and Angelica. Do you want to look?"

"Have we time?"

"If we're quick. He's downstairs in the living room with Jonathan. Angelica's keeping guard. She's not going out until I arrive. She won't let him prowl. . . ."

Taking Juliet's hand, she drew her along the corridor. Juliet was shown Jonathan's room, the television room, and sitting room next to it, the bathrooms, and finally Natasha's bedroom. In this room, the two women came to a halt. Juliet found she was moved by the charm and simplicity of the rooms, and by the obvious care that had gone into them. She was moved, too, by the shy, hesitant way in which Natasha showed them to her, her obvious delight in them tempered by nervousness, as if she feared that at any moment Juliet would begin to criticize or accuse her of some unforeseen lapse of taste.

Juliet looked around the bedroom, a cool, quiet room dominated by a four-poster bed. She took Natasha's hand.

"That bed looks superb," she said. "I knew it would."

"I'd never have dared buy it without you." Natasha lowered her eyes. "I'd have argued myself out of it."

"You have to learn to trust yourself. And you *are* learning.

But you haven't been out of prison very long yet. It takes time. . . ."

"Juliet, don't. Don't. That isn't fair to him—"

"If you say so." Juliet gave a little shrug. "But it's beautiful, Natasha. All of it's beautiful." She hesitated. "And you're beautiful too, darling. I've never seen you look lovelier than you look tonight." Turning, she rested her hands either side of Natasha's face, then tilted it up, to hers. She stroked the heavy dark hair back from the pale forehead; she examined the delicate brows, the wide-set eyes raised anxiously to her own. Drawing Natasha into her arms, she kissed her on the lips.

The kiss, prolonged, sweet to both, became impassioned.

Natasha, with a low cry, was the first to draw back. "Darling, we mustn't, we mustn't," she said. "I mustn't be too late—and he'll know. One look at me, and he'll know—"

"He's going to have to know, sooner or later." Juliet drew her closer again. Bending forward, she kissed Natasha's throat, parted her dress a little more, and kissed each of her breasts. Then, with a dry smile and a mocking glance, she fastened the dress again and held Natasha at arm's length.

"There? You see? The picture of modesty. Brush your hair, tie it back, and he'll never know. He doesn't really see you anyway, Natasha. He sees his idea of you. . . . And his idea of you doesn't include me, I'm sure of that. I was standing next to you at that party, wanting you, thinking about the other night—and he never noticed a thing." She smiled. "Too busy keeping a jealous eye on your sweet handsome bodyguard, I think."

"Maybe." Natasha gave a small frown. "Don't underestimate him, though, Juliet. Tomas *sees*—but he always sees from such strange viewpoints." She hesitated. "Juliet, he's such a fine director—"

"He's a great director. I wouldn't deny that. I don't object to him when he's behind a camera. I do object to him when he's directing your life."

"I know, I know. But—ah, Juliet, I did love him once. I loved him so much. . . ."

Color winged its way into her pale face as she said this; she turned away with a sigh. Juliet watched her as she began to move about the room, with her customary grace, but with a certain agitation. She moved toward the bed, then the window, where she looked out at the falling snow. Juliet waited.

"I *will* tell him, Juliet," she said, in an impulsive way, turning back. "I've been trying to tell him for months. I've tried to prepare him, make him see I can't have him here. I can't have him back. But he won't listen to me. I say it and I say it, and he drowns me out." She gave Juliet a sad look. "That's what it's like. Tomas is listening to a different symphony, a different orchestra. . . ."

"One he's conducting, of course."

"I guess so." She gave a wan half smile. "But give him credit, Juliet. I'm sure the music is sublime—all those instruments: flutes, cellos, trumpets, violins—music to break your heart, I expect. But I want—I want something quieter, smaller." She gave a tiny resigned gesture. "Just a sextet. A quartet. A trio . . ." She gave Juliet a small glance. "Who knows? I expect I'd settle for a duet."

"All of those can be exquisite," Juliet said, in a measured way, hearing in Natasha's tones something that might have been anger, or irony, or regret.

"Yes, yes," Natasha said.

"You're an artist too," Juliet continued, after a pause, and with some sharpness. "He doesn't have a monopoly on art, Natasha."

"No, no. I'm a good actor, I know that. But I'm better when he's directing me, and I'm better still when he's written the script."

"I'm not listening to this." Juliet moved away to the dressing table, and looked at herself in the glass. She adjusted the jacket of her chic, dark suit, smoothed back her short, sleek, dark hair, and reapplied an angry red color to her lips.

"I love you," she said, looking at Natasha's reflection in the glass and frowning.

"I'm beginning to love you." Natasha paused. "You give me strength."

"I'd give you more if you'd let me," Juliet replied, turning and kissing her gently. "Now I'm going to take myself off. I'll leave you with that sacred monster of yours. Call me in the morning. Will he be staying late?"

"I'm not sure. He wants to talk about Joseph King again."

Natasha gave a weary gesture. "He thinks he knows who he is. He went on and on about it for hours, last night. It makes me so miserable and afraid. . . . Shall I tell you something, Juliet?"

"What, darling?"

"I used to think—there was a time, just before I left Tomas. . . . No, I can't say this."

"Darling, tell me."

"I thought Tomas *was* King. I thought he was sending those letters, making those calls. I don't know why I thought that; it wasn't rational. Sometimes King would call when Tomas was in the room with me. It wasn't Tomas's voice, it wasn't Tomas's writing, and Tomas would never make threats against Jonathan—but I came to associate them, somehow." She gave a small sigh. "I was very close to going mad, then, I think. I can't tell you what it was like. I always felt watched, over-heard. . . ." She glanced over her shoulder. "I thought I'd escape from that once I was here. But Tomas comes, and talks and talks—and he's brought it all in here too. . . ."

"Darling, don't cry. Don't get upset—look, do you want me to stay? I will. The hell with him and what he thinks—"

"No. No." Natasha gently pushed her away. "I'll be fine. Angelica will be back by midnight. That nice Maria girl's coming to sit with Jonathan. . . ."

"Does Tomas know that?"

"Of course not. He'd say I was smothering Jonathan—pandering to his fears. He usually says that; he says there are too many women around his son. But Jonathan wakes up and he gets frightened, so it's better if she's here. She has the key to the little door upstairs. Tomas need never know. . . ."

Juliet smiled and raised an eyebrow.

"It's *easier* that way," Natasha said, with a wry look. "We avoid another scene. I learned the advantages of stealth two months into my marriage. . . ."

"Darling. Most women do," Juliet said.

"Catullus?" Colin said, looking down at the book of poems that Lindsay had just presented him as a gift. He frowned; there was a narrow silk marker to the book, so it fell open at a particular page. On that page was the love poem he had quoted to

Lindsay in one of his Montana faxes. Colin gave a sigh; one diabolic eyebrow rose.

"You evil woman," he said. "You evil, devious, wicked woman."

Lindsay, who was wearing her red dress and her new Tiffany earrings, hid her smile; she gave him a meek look.

"Ah yes, Latin," she said. "I can read it. I had it rather dinned into me at school. . . . For eight years, in fact."

"You lied, in other words."

"Colin, I did."

" 'Et al.—I realized I do know some Latin after all'?" Colin began to smile. "Catullus. I knew you were a paragon."

"You can quote from my letters, Colin?"

"Why not? You've just quoted mine. Which makes me suspect you read it more than once. . . ."

"A couple of times, I admit. Nothing excessive . . ."

"I am *immoderately* happy," Colin said, putting the book against his heart, and discovering it fit the inside breast pocket of his suit.

"I love you to distraction," he continued, moving forward in a purposeful way. "What's more, that dress is having a very strong effect on me. . . ."

"This dress? Pixie hates it—"

"What does Pixie know? From a man's point of view, my darling . . ."

"Colin, no. Don't even *think* about it. We're more than five minutes late already. I—"

"Dear God, what's happening to me?" Colin said, five minutes after that. He detached himself from Lindsay. "Is it happening to you too?"

"It is. Can't you tell?"

"Oh God. Yes I can." Colin looked into her eyes. "And I can't go downstairs like this. Quick, think of something detumescent, and say it."

"Five hours at least until we get back to this room?"

"No good. No good. That makes it worse."

"What are nine eights? Twelve fifteens? What's six and a half percent of three hundred and twenty-nine? Why is the universe receding? What did Plato see on the walls of the cave?

What was the name of Rochester's first wife? How many states in America? This must be working, Colin. . . ."

"It's not. It's not. Stand further off."

"What's the capital of Mozambique? Chad? Who killed Cassandra? Why? Which is the highest mountain range in Canada? What's the longest river in the world? The deepest lake? Why do I like you so much, Colin?"

"Now *that's* a truly interesting question," Colin replied, leading her from the room to the stairs and taking her hand in his.

"Do you know all the answers to those questions?" he asked, as they began to descend to the lobby.

"Some of them. Certainly not all." Lindsay gave him a sidelong glance. "I can answer the final one though."

"Can you?"

Halfway down the stairs, Colin came to a halt. Below them, the lobby teemed with Thanksgiving celebrants. Oblivious to them, Colin turned her to face him. "Tell me," he said. "Answer that question. We're not going downstairs until you do. Not if we have to stay here all night."

Lindsay considered: lifting her hand, she laid it against his cheek; she began to speak in a low voice, hesitantly at first, then with growing conviction. Colin listened with absolute attention.

"Then?" he said. "Is that true of most women? Why? You're sure? But I thought—Oh God. *God.* I can't think for happiness. Darling, listen to me—"

Colin began to speak in his turn, with no sign of hesitation, and a conviction that matched Lindsay's own. Having spoken, he leaned her back against the wall; he looked into her eyes for a long time; Lindsay laced her arms about his neck. Then, with a small sigh on her part, and a marked determination on his, he began to kiss her. This embrace, chaste, rapturous, sweet, and prolonged, caused heads to turn. It was witnessed with indulgence, with envy, with nostalgia, annoyance, and amusement by various guests—either because they were themselves in a similar state or because they could remember the joys and perils of being so.

It was also witnessed by Rowland McGuire who, as chance would have it, entered the lobby at that precise moment. It took him an instant to realize who this couple was; then he recognized the dress Lindsay was wearing. He turned away at once, and with some presence of mind, attempted to lose himself in the crush of people. He had almost reached the exit, when his height and his haste betrayed him. Colin glimpsed him from the vantage point of the stairs, called his name, and hurried toward him, reaching his side before Rowland could escape.

He clasped Rowland's hands and began questioning him, his face bright. Rowland looked from him to Lindsay, who had slowly approached; he found their expressions dazed, secretive, radiant, and unbearable. Mustering his self-possession, he managed an explanation so unnaturally precise he felt it could convince no one; Colin, who had scarcely listened to it, accepted it at once.

"But that's great," he said. "I'm so *glad*. How lucky! You spoke to Markov? I expect he's already here. We're—well, we're a bit late. Why don't you go on through with Lindsay? You must join us for dinner, Rowland. We're going to Emily's. Frobisher always cooks enough for an army—Emily would never forgive me if you didn't come. . . . No, no, don't be ridiculous. Stop *arguing*. You can't possibly spend Thanksgiving on your own. Lindsay, you tell him, darling. I'll just give Emily a quick call, so she can organize an extra place. You two go on through—I won't be two seconds. . . ."

With which, Colin turned and darted away through the crowds. He had noticed neither Lindsay's expression, nor his friend's—but then, Colin was an innocent, as Emily had said.

A short while later, Lindsay found herself standing just outside the entrance to the Oak Room. She had no recollection of walking there, and she was almost certain that nothing had been said. All she could hear and see was the enormity of what was happening and the urgency of preventing it. People ebbed back and forth, separating her from Rowland, then tossing her back toward him again. Fighting her way past a crowd of gaudily dressed women, she made it back to his side and laid her hand on the sleeve of his black coat.

"What are you doing here? Oh, what are you *doing* here?" she began. "You have to go away—at once. At *once*."

"I'm joining you for a drink. I've just explained why I'm here."

"Oh God, why didn't you *call* me?"

"I've been trying to call you. For two days. I didn't know where you were."

"Rowland—please leave. It's much better if you leave. . . ."

"I won't leave. Not now."

"Rowland—didn't Markov tell you who else was coming tonight?"

"No, why? Does it matter?"

"I think it might, yes. Rowland, listen—"

"I don't give a damn who's here," Rowland said. "I want to talk to you. I have to talk to you. . . ."

"Now? You're mad. Rowland, let go of me. *Please* go away. . . ."

Jerking his hand aside, Lindsay darted past him. She looked across the room beyond; she saw Markov and Jippy; she saw Gini and her husband. She was about to dart back out of sight, when Gini looked up and saw her. She began to smile a greeting, then the smile froze; she stared across the crowded room, her face blank with shock. Lindsay swung around to find Rowland at her side. Her agitation increasing, she began to speak; she attempted to push him back out of sight; she tugged at his sleeve; a small, frantic, and undignified tussle took place.

The struggle was all on Lindsay's part; she had a confused sense of her hands plucking at his coat, and fluttering back and forth in a useless way, for Lindsay, a foot shorter than Rowland, was not particularly strong, whereas Rowland was. He did not move by so much as an inch; Lindsay thought he was unaware of her pushings and tuggings; when he did suddenly become aware of them, he caught hold of her two wrists.

"What's the *matter* with you?" Lindsay began. "Let go of me, for heaven's sake. . . ."

She looked up. She knew then what was the matter, for the expression on his face, and in his eyes could not be misconstrued. For one fleeting second, she thought that he had seen Gini; then she realized that he had *not* seen her, that he had not looked around once, that he was blind and deaf to his surroundings and that the expression on his face was caused by herself.

"I don't care," he said, in a low voice. "I don't care that this is the wrong time and the worst possible place. I'm not leaving until I've said this—and I'm going to say it before Colin returns—"

Lindsay heard herself make a sound of disbelief; the noisy space filled with a tumultuous silence. Her heart began to beat fast. She looked up, met Rowland's green intent gaze, and had a brief rushing sensation of how unfairly, how impossibly handsome this man was. A figure from a romance she had been listening to since her earliest childhood. All the pain and hope and obsession of the past three years swirled in her head, and she realized that she was angry—so angry she could scarcely speak.

"Don't you dare say anything," she said, in a low furious tone. "Not before Colin returns. Not after. Don't you dare to say one single *word*. . . ."

She saw Rowland flinch, as if she had just struck him, and angrily she shook her wrists free.

"Go *away*," she said. "Gini is here, and her husband is here. Colin is your *friend*. He trusts you. He's just . . . Oh, how can you do this? It's unforgivable, *unforgivable*. . . ."

"Will you listen to me? I can explain—" Rowland began, reaching for her hand again, but Lindsay had already dodged past him. She began to weave her way through the crush of people to their table, certain that Rowland would not follow her. She could still hear some sound, some rushing, crashing sound, like waves beating in on a beach, as she reached the table, and three men rose to their feet. She could feel the group was petrified with some collective embarrassment; she began flurried greetings; she embraced Gini, then Markov, then Jippy. Turning to Pascal, whom she both admired and liked, she realized that he was not looking at her, but at someone else, his face hardening in an expression of anger and disbelief.

She began to turn, seeing as she did so, that Jippy looked ill, and that Markov's face wore an expression of startled delight—an expression with which he always greeted incipient social disaster. Rowland McGuire was standing immediately behind her, she found, and next to him was Colin. Colin was pale with agitation; he looked as if he had just witnessed a car accident. He began to speak with great rapidity, a hunted, desperate look on his face.

"Oh God, *God*," he said, "this is terrible. We have to move.

We can't stay here. There isn't time to explain. This is a crisis, this is an *emergency*, oh, bloody *hell*. . . ."

"Col, dear heart, *there* you are!" said a famous and melodious voice. Colin looked at the table in a panic-stricken way, as if considering diving under it. "Too late. Oh *shit*." He made a moaning sound, as an arm fastened itself around his shoulders. Lindsay found herself looking into a cadaverous, arresting, and very famous face.

"Col, I've been chasing you all over New York—where have you been *hiding* yourself? I've just come from the Thanksgiving bash at Tina's and Harry's. Thousands of scribes, Hollywood out in force . . . Marty was there, and Michelle sent her love. . . . Col, how tremendously *well* you're looking. Fit, lean, tanned. Waiter, waiter—we'll need some more champagne over here. At your earliest convenience, if you'd be so good. Col, *great* to see you. I'm not butting in, I hope? Aren't you going to introduce me?"

The speaker paused, secure in the knowledge that he needed no introduction himself. His gaze scanned the group in an expert way; singling out Gini as the only person of any significance, an expression of homage to a beautiful woman came upon his face. He held out his hand.

"Nic Hicks," he said, unnecessarily, pronouncing his own name with humility and reverent conceit.

Lindsay, who could now hear bombs, mines, and howitzers going off, sat down abruptly. Jippy stole out a hand and pressed hers in a comforting way. Lindsay looked around the table as the various introductions and greetings took place. Pascal Lamartine and Rowland McGuire exchanged a curt nod; Rowland selected a seat as far as possible from Gini and as close as possible to Lindsay. Seeing this, Gini frowned and gave Lindsay a searching look. Lindsay could see barbed wire snaking in every direction; she could see vast bomb craters opening up. Through this blasted landscape, Nic Hicks drove the tank of his ego, its gun turret aimed at Gini, and its tracks flattening everyone else.

"Good news, Col," he announced, glancing away from Gini for a second. "I've been onto that maid of Emily's, what's her name? The dragon woman . . ."

"Frobisher. And she isn't a maid. She—"

"Dear heart, I'm joining you for dinner—isn't that splendid? Can't wait. Ah, the champagne. Waiter, well *done*. . . . Who wants my autograph? What, that young woman over there? Of course. Tell her I'll be delighted. I'll pop over in a second and have a word. Fans!" He gave the silent group a look of humble resignation. "*Can't* escape them, I'm afraid. Terrible *nuisance*—still, grin and bear it, eh? What was I saying, Gini? Oh yes, your piece on Natasha—*awfully* good. You lady journalists terrify me. . . . What? Yes, we start filming any day now. . . . No, not the husband, rather a dreary role, the husband, I think . . . I'm playing Gilbert Markham—the lover. *Fascinating* character. Difficult. Tremendous challenge. Rather dark. Sensitive. Immensely *complex*, of course. I wasn't too sure it was *me*, but Tomas twisted my arm. . . ."

From across the table, Colin caught Lindsay's eye. He put his hands around his own throat, stuck his tongue out, rolled his eyes, and gave a graphic impression of a man dangling from the end of a hangman's noose. Nic Hicks, revving up into overdrive, with his name-dropping rate up to three a minute and accelerating, did not notice this. Markov shot Colin a look of sly amusement; Rowland gave a chilly smile, and Lindsay, who wanted to scream or cry, began to laugh instead.

It was Jippy who finally procured Lindsay's release. He had remained silent since Lindsay's arrival, his anxious gaze moving slowly around the group, a sickly greenish pallor settling upon his face. Markov, attuned to his responses, could sense his growing agitation. He saw him look from Rowland to Pascal, and then, fixedly, at a space to the right of Pascal's chair, where nobody stood. Jippy looked at this space for some time, his expression sad; then, as if following the movements of some invisible person, his gaze traveled around the group, coming to rest upon Lindsay. Markov saw his lips move and leaned closer to him, taking his hand.

"What is it, Jippy?" he whispered. "Try and tell me. . . ."

Jippy fixed him with a beseeching gaze. His lips and tongue fought the word, and the word would not be said. It began with a "p," Markov could hear that much; Jippy struggled.

"P-p-para—" he whispered. Markov squeezed his hand,

trying to decode this. Paranormal? Paratrooper? Parasol? Parasite? Parapet? Paradox? He could think of nothing that made the least sense. He looked at Pascal Lamartine's tense figure; he too had said virtually nothing; his cool gray gaze rested on the figure of Rowland McGuire, seated next to Lindsay. Rowland, who appeared blind and deaf, looked as if he were standing on the edge of some cliff, undecided whether to leap from it or step back. Next to him, Lindsay was making a frantic and nervous attempt to prevent conversation from flagging. She had been discussing the weather for the last five minutes, in the desperate manner of one who, if need be, could discuss its minutiae for the rest of the night. Jippy's hand gave a small jerk.

"Paracetemol," he said, to Markov, in a low clear voice. Markov gave him a startled look, then, interpreting this as best he could he leaned across to Lindsay.

"Darling," he said, "I think I'm going to whisk Jippy away. He has a migraine—and it's getting worse. . . ."

Lindsay embraced Jippy, to whom she had never felt more grateful, and sprang to her feet.

"We should go too," she said hastily, looking at Gini.

"Colin, I'll just fetch my coat. . . ."

Gini also rose. "I'll come with you," she said.

They left before anyone else could argue or intervene; crossing the crowded room, Lindsay glanced back once. She saw Rowland McGuire rise and then, in a deliberate way, move across and sit down next to Pascal Lamartine. Gini also saw this, and came to a halt in the entrance; Lindsay, agitated and distressed, caught hold of her by the wrist and pulled her into the lobby.

"Let Rowland speak to him," she said. "Gini, don't go back. Rowland will explain—he'll tell him he had no idea you were going to be here tonight. Oh, Gini, I'm so sorry. I'm so terribly sorry. I didn't know Rowland was coming—I promise you. I'd never have let this happen. . . . Quick, let's go upstairs. My coat's in my room anyway. . . ."

Lindsay ran up the stairs to the first floor, Gini followed her more slowly. Entering her room, Lindsay saw with relief that the maids had been in during her absence; the tumbled bed was remade, at least. It had been turned down for the night, but two chocolates had been laid out on the two pillows, Colin's shirt was draped across the back of a chair, and a pair of Lindsay's stockings was dangling from the back of another. The room still sang of intimacy, and Lindsay began to blush.

Gini followed her into the room, her manner tense. She looked at the ridiculous chocolates, the pillows, the bed. Without saying a word, she moved across to the windows, parted the curtains, and looked out.

"It's still snowing," she said, in a flat voice. She drew in her breath and turned around. Lindsay saw that her hands were unsteady and her eyes unnaturally bright.

"So—Rowland must have told you about Paris then?" she said.

"No, of course not." Lindsay's color deepened. "He would never do that, Gini. I was *there*. It was obvious."

"Was it?"

"Oh, Gini, you know how it is. One look at his face; one look at yours. Don't let's talk about this. It's none of my business. It was a long time ago. . . ."

"I loved Rowland. In a way, I did. I haven't seen him since then—not once." Gini gave a helpless gesture of the hands. "And now—Pascal will be so furious. He's never really forgiven me, you see. It was all so *fraught*. Pascal found out—did you realize? He walked in on us in our room at that hotel. . . ." She hesitated. "There was this terrible scene; I thought they were going to fight one another. It was I who had to decide in the end. *I* broke it off, not Rowland. Rowland was devastated. *Devastated*. And now, tonight—he scarcely said one word to me. . . ."

"Please, Gini. I don't want to hear this. I—Look, I'm just going to try Tom in Oxford once more. I've been trying to get him all evening. Then I'll have to go. . . ." She moved past her friend and began dialing. She listened to the number ringing in Oxford—it was one o'clock in the morning in Oxford now. She let it ring and ring, then gently replaced the receiver.

"It was all so complicated. And so *painful*. The worst moment of my whole life . . ." Gini said, as if there had been no interruption. Tears had come to her eyes; Lindsay looked at her uncertainly, wishing she could have reached Tom, knowing that just the sound of her son's voice could have eased her confusion and distress.

"Oh, what am I going to do now? What am I going to say to Pascal?" Gini covered her face with her hands. "He can be so jealous, Lindsay. . . ."

"Just tell him the truth," Lindsay said. "There's a simple explanation, Gini. He'll understand. Look, I'm sorry, but I must go—"

"I still don't know why I let any of it happen," Gini continued, as Lindsay opened the closet and took out her funereal coat. "I look back, and I can't understand—I must have made a decision, there must have been a moment when I thought 'Yes. . . .' But why? It caused so much harm. Was it just because he was there at that particular time? Maybe it was just his appearance. . . ." She paused. "I hope it wasn't that. But he is so—I'd forgotten how handsome he is. . . ."

"It isn't just his looks." Lindsay turned away. "You know that as well as I do. Gini, don't pursue this—"

"I think I could have loved him. I said that to him once." Her face now wet with tears, she sat down on the bed. "But sometimes I think that wasn't true, that it was just my excuse. I might have been *using* him. . . ."

"Gini, I'm sure that's not so. You wouldn't do that."

"It could be true." Gini's pale face became set. "You see, I wanted Pascal to give me a baby, and he was resisting and resisting. That hurt me so much. . . ."

She made a small choking sound. Lindsay, distressed, sat down beside her and put an arm around her shoulders.

"Gini, don't, please don't," she said. "You'd been *ill* then. These things can happen. Loving one person doesn't prevent your being attracted to someone else."

"Maybe it was that simple." Gini gave her a doubting look. "I wish I could be sure, but Pascal changed his mind after I had the affair with Rowland. He was afraid of losing me then, so he gave way about the baby. Perhaps I just used Rowland to manipulate Pascal. . . ." She gave a small anxious gesture of the hands. "Oh, I hope that wasn't so. I can't bear to think I did that. Maybe Pascal sees it that way now. He might. Tonight— you know what he said to me tonight? He said I was tenacious, that I always get my own way in the end. . . ."

"He said that? Gini, don't cry." Lindsay took her hand. "Why did he say that?"

"Because I asked him to stop covering wars." Gini turned her face away. "I always promised myself I'd never do that. But I did—after Lucien was born. I was so afraid then. I had these terrible dreams—about snipers, mines, bombs. . . . I wanted Pascal to be safe. I wanted to believe he'd be there when Lucien was growing up."

"That's understandable. Any woman would want that," Lindsay said gently. "You shouldn't blame yourself for feeling that way. Even if you'd said nothing, Pascal must have known he'd have to make a choice. . . ."

"I coerced him—"

"That's ridiculous."

"That's how *he* sees it. His first wife made the very same demands, and now I'm doing it. I'm turning into a second Helen. I was always afraid that would happen. . . ." Bending her head, she began to cry again. "Oh, Lindsay—I feel afraid. I was sitting downstairs tonight and I just felt afraid. I looked at Rowland, and I thought about all the decisions I'd made, and it seemed to me . . ." She hesitated. "It seemed as if I couldn't be sure of anything. Not my own motives, not the choices I made. Nothing. I was looking at my own life story, and it seemed so *arbitrary*. Maybe I could have written it differently."

"You regretted Rowland?" Lindsay said quietly.

"Perhaps. In passing." Gini rose and turned away. "And I felt guilty for that. I have a son now. I love Pascal. But . . ." She hesitated, then shrugged. "Love, love, love. I've always cared about it too much perhaps. My father made sure of that."

There was a silence. Lindsay looked at her friend with affection, with pity, and with a certain fear.

"Is that wrong?" she began slowly. "Love matters more than anything, surely?"

"Count the crimes committed in its name," Gini replied, her manner resigned and her tone hardening.

"You don't mean that," Lindsay said.

"Probably not. I'm a woman." Gini's tone became dry. "All for love—which might be a strength, or a weakness. Tell me . . ." She hesitated, wiping the last tears from her face, then turned back to Lindsay. "Tell me, Lindsay. Do you love Rowland? Does he love you? Is that what that scene was about tonight?"

"I don't want to answer that. I don't want to talk about it at all. . . ." Lindsay rose, and began to put on her black coat. "Please, Gini. Leave it. I'm late and I have to go. . . ."

"He's not right for you." Gini made the statement in a flat way; she gave a small sigh. "Lindsay—I have to say this. I *know* Rowland. I know him through and through, and I wish him well. I wish you well. But whatever's happened between you, you're wrong for each other. You do know that?"

"Do I?" Lindsay turned to face her friend; she felt her heartbeat quicken, as the room became unnaturally quiet. "Why do you say that?"

"For a hundred reasons—every one of which you know yourself." Gini paused, then lowered her gaze. "Not least, he'd damage you. He'd try to be faithful to you, and then he wouldn't be. . . ."

"I see. Thanks. Well, that's clear, at any rate—"

"Lindsay, I don't mean to hurt you. . . ." Gini's face became troubled. "But someone has to tell you the truth. Just look at it from the most obvious point of view of all—Rowland should marry. He should have children. He needs a woman who can give him children. . . . Not someone your age, Lindsay." She hesitated again. "I know that's hard, but you have to consider it—in Rowland's case and in Colin's."

"I'd rather you didn't discuss Colin, if you don't mind." Lindsay turned sharply away. "Gini, please, don't say any more. . . ."

"I liked Colin." Gini frowned. "He seems sweet-natured, witty, great charm. . . . A bit feckless, perhaps—"

"Don't you *dare*." Lindsay swung around, white-faced. "Don't you dare to presume you know him. Leave him alone, Gini. What gives you the right to lecture and interfere? I'll make my own decisions—"

"Then think before you make them," Gini replied, her tone also sharpening. "Have an affair with Colin, by all means; have an affair with Rowland, if you don't mind getting hurt in his case, but just remember—for any man who wants a family, needs a family, you're too *old*. You can't start having babies again at forty-one. Lindsay, you're nearly forty-two—you might not be *able* to have children now. You already have a son, and I know how much he means to you. . . ." She broke off, her troubled gaze resting on Lindsay's face. "Rowland wants children, I know that. Does Colin?"

"I don't know." Lindsay averted her gaze.

"How old is he? He's never been married? He's never had children?"

"He's my age. And no, no marriage, no children—"

"Ah, Lindsay." With a sigh and an expression of concern, Gini moved forward and rested her hand on Lindsay's arm. "Then *think*. Whatever you may feel about Rowland or Colin, you can't be selfish here; you must surely see that?"

The words were quietly said, and firmly, for all their tone of regret. After Gini had finished speaking, Lindsay could still hear them echoing and re-echoing in her head. The words shocked her, though indeed, as Gini said, the sentiments expressed were obvious enough. She felt herself give some small, numbed gesture, as if warding the words off.

"Selfish?" she heard herself say, in a low voice.

"You can hurt someone by loving them," Gini replied, her eyes becoming sad. She put her arms around Lindsay, and for a while the two women stood together quietly in this embrace.

It was hard to hear such an unpalatable truth from a friend, Lindsay thought, turning toward the door when she was sure that she had composed herself. She walked along the corridor, Gini following more slowly. Reaching the stairs, Lindsay looked down at the lobby, where the rest of their group was now awaiting them. With a dazed disbelief, she saw that Rowland McGuire and Pascal Lamartine were now deep in conversation, as if they had put aside their past enmity. Markov and Jippy were waiting to say good-bye, Jippy's face still white, pained, and anxious. The actor, Nic Hicks, was signing autographs, and there at the foot of the stairs, waiting for her, was Colin.

Seeing his face light up as he caught sight of her, Lindsay felt a surge of misery and distress. Colin could not hide his feelings for her, and had no wish to do so. Lindsay, looking at the openness of his gaze and the transparency of his affection, felt ashamed. The last thing she would have wished to do was injure him, yet now she saw injury was inevitable—and for that, she blamed no one but herself.

Her farewell to Gini took place outside, on the sidewalk, and Lindsay felt, as she kissed her, that it was in some ways a final farewell. She pressed her cold lips against her friend's cold cheek, and she knew it would be a long time before she could forgive her for what she had said. Plain speaking should not, but did, cause rifts; nor was she entirely sure that Gini's reasons for speaking out were as pure as she claimed. Perhaps her motives were altruistic, but perhaps also jealousy had played a part, she thought, as she watched Gini briefly clasp Rowland's hand, then turn away without a backward look. It made no difference—she saw that with a pained clarity. Whatever had prompted Gini to speak, her arguments concerning Lindsay's age were unanswerable. However much that particular truth hurt—and it hurt very deeply—it was one that could neither be argued away, nor escaped.

Chapter 15

How long had this truth lain in wait for her? Lindsay asked herself, approaching the stairs at the Conrad. She looked at the red-carpeted stairs, with their sentinel slaves, holding up torches that gave insufficient light. She followed the flights of stairs with her eyes, as they wound up and up, and doubled back. Gini's arguments had a remorseless logic, and she could not understand how, afflicted with a peculiar blindness, she could not have seen this. Or had she seen it—and merely turned away her face, refusing to confront the issue, as she had in the past refused to confront other issues of equal seriousness in her life?

Am I infertile? I might not be infertile, she thought, looking at the red tide of that staircase. She brushed the last of the snow from her black coat; beside her, a radiator sighed; it murmured of biology and bad timing; of statistics and birth defects. She looked at Colin, at the silent figure of Rowland, at the terrible actor, who was bounding up the stairs, still with an endless, irrepressible, meaningless flow of words on his lips. These men were her own age. Any one of them could hope, even expect, to be able to father a child for the next twenty years and beyond; she herself did not share this uncircumscribed fecundity, and it had never occurred to her how much that might matter until now. Redundant yet again, she thought, and although she could smile at that, the pain and rebellion in her heart were acute. She glanced over her shoulder, feeling an instinct to leave, a longing to leave; but the evening, of importance to others, had to be endured, she knew that. Disguising her feelings with some remark, she crossed to the stairs and began to mount them. At the first landing, she heard a sound that sent a pang of recognition straight to her heart; she stopped.

"What was that?" She swung around, looking along the shadowy galleries. "I can hear a child crying. . . ."

Above her, Nic Hicks continued to mount the stairs; both Colin, who was next to her, and Rowland, who was behind her, came to a halt. They listened.

"I can't hear anything—can you, Rowland?"

"No, nothing."

"You *can*. Listen—there it is again. . . ."

Colin hesitated, then with a glance at Rowland, took her hand in his. "Darling, I really can't hear anything. . . ."

"Neither can I. Lindsay, are you all right? Colin, she looks terribly pale. . . ."

"Lindsay? Darling? Darling—look at me. Christ, Rowland, I think she's going to faint."

Lindsay heard this exchange from a great distance. The words were fuzzy and obscure, receding from her fast. A small serene catastrophe occurred: she watched placidly as the banisters tilted, the stairs somersaulted, and the dome above her head moved in a slow and beautiful arc, coming to rest beneath her feet.

Someone caught her, as she commenced a slow, obedient, dizzying trajectory; when the world reassembled itself and recognized its usual rules once more, she found she was sitting on the top stair of the first flight, with her head between her knees. From this antipodean viewpoint, she discerned that the man on her left had his arms around her, and the man on her right was holding her hand. The man on the right was somewhat calmer than the man on her left.

"Oh God, God, *God*," said the man on the left. "She's ill. I *thought* she didn't look well at the Plaza."

"Let her breathe. She's coming round. She'll be fine in a minute. Lindsay, keep your head *down*," said the man on the right.

"Stop *pushing* her. You'll hurt her—"

"I won't. For God's sake—"

"Go and get her some water. Frobisher will give you some water, and ice. Or a key—I remember now—that's what you do. Something cold down the back of the neck. Or is that for a nosebleed? Oh, Lindsay, Lindsay . . ."

The man on her right sighed and rose to his feet. Lindsay listened to his footsteps mounting the stairs to the next landing. There was a jingling sound. The man on her left began fumbling with her collar. Something small, cold, and metallic was inserted against the back of her neck.

To her surprise, upside-down Lindsay found this object produced a discernible effect. Its small chill cleared her vision; she looked down at the red stairs, and seeing they were no longer playing tricks, slowly raised her head. She found herself looking into a pair of blue eyes, alight with anxiety and concern. As she raised her head, a transformation came upon this face.

"Oh, it's worked. Thank God. I only had a Yale—this stupid little Yale. Lindsay—look at me. Can you hear me? Are you all right?"

Lindsay found she could hear him. It seemed to her astonishing and marvelous, that without a muscle moving, the expression in these eyes could alter with such eloquence. She saw anxiety become relief, relief become joy, and joy modulate to love; the love, which moved her very deeply, struck in her some chord, for she recognized the quality of this emotion at once. It was in this way that she looked at her son; this love, unqualified, poignant, and direct was always powerful—and she could sense its power at this moment. The last residual skewing of her vision ceased: the walls stood upright, at right angles to the floor; the last hissings and whisperings she had been hearing, which might have come from the radiators, although she thought not, also ceased. She had a sense that something in this interior shielded its eyes from the powers here and scurried off.

"A Yale key?" She gave a low sigh. "Oh, Colin."

"I know, but it was all I could find." He paused. "It's the key to my apartment in England. I have this sort of apartment in my father's house. The house is terribly large. It's called Shute Court, but everyone just calls it Shute. . . ."

There was a silence. "Shute?" Lindsay said. "Colin, I don't understand. . . ."

"That farmhouse belongs to it as well. It's—well, it's part of the estate, and the estate's enormous. My family has had it for four hundred years. It will all be mine one day. Lindsay, I'm rich."

There was another silence. Colin had spoken in the tones of one confessing some mortal disease. His blue eyes were fixed steadily on hers and his face had become very pale. Lindsay wanted to weep and to laugh. She took his hand in hers.

"I think now might be the moment to faint again," she said.

This reply appeared to delight Colin; his face lit up. He drew in a deep breath, as if about to dive into icy water from some great height, and clasped both her hands in his.

"I want you to marry me," he said. "I want you to overlook everything I've just told you and marry me." He paused. "I know I proposed before, and I think I meant it then, but there's always the possibility you didn't believe me, considering a few minor factors. . . . I'd never met you; I was blind drunk."

"I'm not narrow-minded," Lindsay said, in a reproachful way, her vision beginning to blur. "Colin—"

"I'm not very good at proposing." Colin gave an agitated gesture. "On the telephone. On the stairs. I was going to do it in two days' time, by moonlight. I thought if I did it by moonlight, you might accept."

"I'm glad you did it here, on the stairs. I'm so—"

"Lindsay, why are you crying?"

"I'm not really crying. Well, I am a bit. I'm—taken aback. Colin, I'm touched, more than touched, and I'm honored. . . ."

Colin, who could hear the "but" coming, lifted his hand and quickly laid his fingers against her lips. He looked into her eyes intently. "Don't give me your answer now. I was incapacitated the first time I asked you, and you're incapacitated now. It's not really fair to propose to someone who's just fainted. No, don't say anything." His expression became tender; he frowned. "Now keep still. I'm going to fish that key out."

The process of retrieving the key was complicated and took some time. Having finally extricated it, Colin held it up and looked at it somewhat sadly.

"This is yours," he said, in a quiet voice. "It's all yours. I'm yours. I tried to tell you that in my fax from Montana. Did you notice?"

"Ah, Colin—yes, I did." A tear fell onto her knee. "I wasn't sure that was what you meant."

"If I didn't mean it, I would never say it." He paused and gave her a sad, steady look. "I believe I could make you happy, Lindsay. I don't have any illusions about my failings—but I know I could do that. I could make you happy tomorrow and next year and thirty years from now. And thirty years from now, if you were my wife, I'd know I'd achieved something worthwhile in my life, and I'd be completely content. That doesn't sound very romantic, perhaps, but it's my best qualification. I would never alter, Lindsay, I promise you that."

"Ah, Colin," she said, turning her face away to hide her tears. "People do alter. They alter very swiftly, despite all their best intentions. . . ."

"No," Colin said with great firmness. "I give you my word. *Semper fidelis,* in my case. And I know I won't have to translate that, my darling." He paused. "Look at me, Lindsay. And when you're considering your answer, just remember: I am not going to miss this particular bus, not if I have to go on chasing it for the next ten years. And I give you fair warning of that."

Taking her hands in his, he drew her gently to her feet and turned her to look at him. "You look so beautiful. The color's come back to your cheeks. Your eyes—well, I won't ask you why you have tears in them; I know you'll tell me in due course. Meanwhile, I'm going to kiss you." His manner became sterner. "So don't argue, don't faint again, and don't move an inch."

He did so. Rowland, returning with the water, and with ice Frobisher had taken an age to provide, saw that these aids were not needed. He looked at the embracing couple, at the sweep of the stairs with its sentinel slaves, and quietly turned back.

He returned to Emily's apartment. There, he was introduced to a small, melancholy man called Henry Foxe, and to three ancient women whose identities he at once confused, and remained unsure of ever afterward. Hearing the trickle of dropping names from Nic Hicks threaten to become a flood, knowing he would insult him if he stayed a second longer, he withdrew to the kitchen with some muttered and inadequate excuse.

Frobisher, as fond of him as Emily, took one look at his face and gruffly put him to work. Things not being what they had once been in this household, she informed him, he could make himself useful. He could open that wine; he could hold that tureen steady while she decanted her Alice B. Toklas Algonquin soup. Finally, he could light the candles through there in the dining room, but she gave him warning—the room was drafty and the candles temperamental, so they kept going out.

Rowland went through to the dining room, a shadowy place. It was chilly; he draped the curtains more tightly closed, then began to light the array of candles one by one. They made the corners of the room more suggestive. In the glimmering polished surface of the table, Rowland found he could see some pale and insubstantial reflection, which he assumed was his own. In the still of the room, he found he felt haunted and uneasy; if he turned, he felt, he might encounter some other self.

The last of the candles refused to light. Patiently, Rowland struck another match; as it again guttered out, with the candle still unlit, he became aware of the noises for the first time. He tensed, then swung around, sensing someone behind him as close as a shadow; he found he was looking at empty space.

The voices emanated from the floor, he was almost certain of that, but the acoustics here had an odd quality, so the voices shifted their position—now they came from his right, now from his left. He was no sooner certain that they issued up from beneath the parquet, when they seemed to come from the walls, or the corridor beyond instead.

He burned his fingers, dropped the match, and again tensed. The shadows bent upon the walls; the voices, a man's and a woman's, he was almost sure, whispered of past losses and future loneliness. He could hear a sound like water; then, as he leaned against the table, head bent, the tenor of the voices changed. A new sound began, mounting above these miserable whisperings and drowning them out.

Rowland, less quick to identify the sound of a child crying than Lindsay, finally recognized it. Something brushed against his hand, and he drew back sharply, his heart full of inexplicable grief. He found he was now listening to silence, to a thick, hushed expectant silence. He found he was no longer certain whether he had identified that last cry correctly. It unnerved him, for he had been sure, so sure, that he had heard the impossible: the calling to him of a son he did not possess.

"Jonathan, try to eat your dinner," Natasha Lawrence said. "Please try, darling. Angelica went to a lot of trouble. . . ."

Her son speared a tiny fragment of turkey on his fork, put it in his mouth, and chewed. Eventually, he swallowed; he bent his head over his plate.

"Natasha, there's no point in forcing him," Tomas Court said, in a quiet voice. "Angelica's out. She's not going to see whether he eats it or not."

"That's not the point." His wife gave a small nervous gesture. "This is our first Thanksgiving here. I planned it all so carefully. I wanted . . ."

"The sweet potatoes are certainly very good," Court interrupted, in a pacifying voice. "Are there any more?"

"There's heaps." His wife rose in an eager way. "They're in the kitchen, keeping warm. I'll get them. . . ."

As soon as she left the room, the eyes of Court and his son intersected. Court laid his finger against his lips, picked up Jonathan's plate, and scooped most of its contents onto his own. By the time Natasha returned, both were eating, at a steady pace.

Court, who had no appetite whatsoever, forced himself to eat everything put in front of him. He tried to fix his mind on the scene with Natasha that had to take place after dinner, when his son was safely in bed. All the while, Natasha kept up a steady flow of conversation, to which he responded with a polite murmur whenever appropriate. Both of them, he thought, could sense Jonathan's mute distress; both of them, helpless in the face of it, tried to conceal their knowledge. Court began to wish they were not alone, and that Natasha, accepting that his presence was unavoidable, had not canceled the invitations to her other guests.

He looked around the dining room from time to time with a sense of dazed incomprehension. No invitation to see the apartment had been extended by his wife on either of his visits since his return from Montana; he had, as yet, seen only a few of its many rooms. He had seen a whitish hall and a white-on-white living room where he and Natasha had quarreled, the previous

night. Now he saw this appalling dining room, where, as
Natasha had informed him, the decorator recommended by
Jules McKechnie had been given his head.

The dining-room walls, at this man's behest, had been lac-
quered a deep and not unsubtle red. The furniture, old, heavy,
and acquired from God knew where, was black. Court faced
his wife across a blackened expanse of oak; his view of his son
was half obscured by the ranks of ecclesiastic candlesticks.
At intervals around the room were modish arrangements of
plants: a white orchid reared up at him from a side table; one of
Natasha's mother's orchid paintings cried out at him, open-
throated, from above the mantelpiece; in the grate burned a
recalcitrant, smoky, obstinate fire, which gave, and needed to
give, no heat.

The temperature in the apartment was in the high seventies,
he would have guessed. The air, dry and scented by candles,
smelled of pine needles; it had an acrid quality that caught at
his throat. He was breathing with caution and with irritation,
and trying to disguise this.

He found the apartment uneasy, a little schizoid and desperate. He pitied Natasha for the desperation he could read
here, and he pitied his son, who had to make a home in this vast
mausoleum of a place. He thought of the small, ugly frame
house where he himself had grown up, a place he had not loved
at the time, and from which a drive-in movie theater two miles
away had provided, in his youth, the only means of escape.
Poor and cramped his childhood home might have been, but it
seemed to him a thousand times preferable to this. He half listened to Natasha, as she coaxed replies from their son, and the
air began to whisper to him, and he allowed his mind to start
traveling, to drift back.

That drive-in, that drive-in, with its lousy sound system, old
scratched prints, and an audience who rarely bothered to watch
the movie because they were too busy making out. That drive-
in, with its output of old B movies and violent cartoons; with
its terse private eyes and taciturn cowboys; with its vampires,
zombies, and supermen. That drive-in, where all the slurry of
the movie industry was dredged up night after night. A sudden
longing rose up in his heart for those gangsters and their molls,
for those Apaches gathering on the horizon, for the trench-

coats, tough dialogue, and slouch hats. He saw himself as a boy, not much older than his son was now, sitting there entranced, eyes fixed on the screen, lips moving to dialogue he knew by heart, watching the camera angles, watching the lighting, learning the grammar of this rough magic, the grammar of kisses, weapons, buddies, and baddies; of cross-fades, close-ups, reverse shots, two-shots, and cuts.

Ah, the terrible beauty of film, he thought—and he had been so confident of mastering it once. It was only now, when he was practiced in his art, when his health was poor and his life disrupted, that he was beginning to learn just how ravenous the appetite of this art was. It ate him alive—and what was the result? Approximations merely, he thought, as the ghosts of his past and future work moved in his mind; into this maw he poured all his energy, all his acquired skill—and it was never enough.

One of his sins—and he now thought of it as a sin, as well as a gift—was that these ghosts of his work were more real to him than anything else; they drained the blood from all his other concerns, including his concern for his son and his wife. Much of the time, as his wife had often accused him, he lived in that other parallel world; even now, the air teemed with its spirits; their hands plucked at his sleeve, begging him to give them expression and thus release. He could hear two men's voices now, arguing some issue back and forth; he could hear a woman's footsteps, pattering between them. It was in this spectral way that his movies always first came to him: the next movie but one, he thought. He looked up and returned to the red room. His wife had just risen to her feet.

"It's time for Jonathan to go to bed," she said. "I'll just see him up. You go through to the living room, Tomas. I won't be long. Darling, kiss your father good night."

Court hesitated, wondering whether he should suggest accompanying them. Seeing the suggestion would be refused, he rose and held out his arms to his son. Jonathan held back, his face tense and pale. He glanced toward his mother, then cannoned into his father's arms, clinging to him as he was hoisted aloft.

"Will you be here in the morning, Daddy? Will you be here when I wake up?"

"Darling, no." Court concealed his reaction and evaded the question. "I start work again tomorrow. I'll be leaving for work long before you wake up. We'll all be off to England soon, remember. Now—off to bed." He embraced his son tightly, then passed him across to his mother, and listened to their footsteps retreat. He returned to the white living room, where another stubborn fire smoldered; he kicked at its graying embers and it flared briefly into life.

He picked up the briefcase he had brought with him, with its faxes and photographs, with the documentation that had been pouring in now for a day and a half, and which had to be shown, and explained, to Natasha that night. Where should they sit when he embarked on this explanation? This question, a trivial one, refused to be dislodged. He looked at the room as if it were a set; he adjusted the lighting; he moved an irritating feminine cushion; he rehearsed evasive sentences, and calming ones—after all, the important thing was that the mystery attached to Joseph King was now solved; it was out of his hands and in those of the proper authorities. An arrest must now be imminent. What he must stress, he told himself, was that the stalking was now over; he must emphasize that he and Natasha and Jonathan were now safe.

He did not feel safe, however, but he blamed that reaction on the long years of unease and the atmosphere in this apartment. He blamed too the devices of the movies with which his mind was saturated: at that drive-in in his mind, evil was always reluctant to die; up from the floor rose the dead body of the enemy; from out of the grave came the snatching hand; just as hero embraced heroine, the lights flickered and a door creaked.

A door *had* creaked. He turned and crossed to the hall, frowning. He looked along the pale corridor that led, as those plans of the Conrad had informed him, to that inner and elusive staircase, and those rooms on the upper level where he supposed his wife, and perhaps his son, now slept.

Those plans had disappeared with the rest of the detritus that had been littering the floor of his Tribeca loft on the night he had entered it and someone unseen had attacked. His memory of that night was fragmentary; he supposed that Thalia had destroyed the architectural plans with the rest of the papers and tapes. It was of little moment, since he could remember their details with precision—and he could also see that these spaces here, and those plans, did not fit.

The apartment might appear unaltered and in its original state—indeed Natasha had claimed, with pride, that that was the case. Yet that could not be so, he realized, looking along the corridor, looking from the doorway on his right to that on his left. They did not *match*, and this perhaps accounted for his feeling, intense since he first entered this place the previous day, that his perceptions were skewed. It was not his perceptions that were to blame, he told himself, what was wrong here was the *space*.

On Hillyard White's drawings, this corridor had run through the center of the apartment like an artery; now he could see that the corridor, although arterial, was neither centered, nor straight. It angled around a corner that should not have been there; to his immediate right was a wall where there should have been a room—could that room have been bricked up?

He looked at the wall in question, and at the odd sweaty sheen achieved by some specialist paint effect; hung upon it was a picture by Natasha's mother he had always greatly disliked, in which a man's hand grasped the stem of some white and repugnant flower. The picture was askew; irritably, he moved to straighten it, then drew back, with a low exclamation and a sense of dread. A sound was coming from behind the wall, a dry, persistent scratching sound, as if something were clawing at the plaster, desperate to get through, desperate to get out. Court, who had grown up in a farming community, recognized the sound instantly as that of rats.

As a boy, he had shot rats for his uncle in one of his barns; he was paid a nickel a dozen, and the task was one he disliked. It was not easy to shoot the rats, for they were fast and agile; their death throes, prolonged, acrobatic, and squirming, were vile yet fascinating to watch. It was difficult too, to collect up the bodies: he had a superstitious fear that one rat might be faking, that it would rise up and bite him as he stooped. Also, he discovered, the live rats retrieved the dead bodies of their fellows, and did so in a bold, knowing way, even as he approached. He had never been able to decide, nor could his uncle inform him, why they did this: did they give their rat brothers honorable burials—or did they eat them?

He stared at the wall, sweat breaking out on his brow, and all
the fears of his childhood rising up; the scratching continued
for a while; then, abruptly, it stopped.

"Would you like me to read to you, Jonathan, or shall I tell
you a story?" Maria said, as Natasha's footsteps retreated into
the distance. A door closed. Maria, plump, bespectacled,
and familiar, switched on the night-light. Jonathan found her
comforting—not as comforting as his parents or Angelica, but
comforting nonetheless.

Maria's speciality was fairy stories, of which she had a vast
repertoire. In the past, she had told him the story of Hansel and
Gretel, and the Babes in the Wood; of Red Riding Hood, of
Rapunzel, Cinderella, and a Sleeping Beauty cursed in her
cradle by a wicked godmother who was also, Maria said, a
witch.

Maria's witch performances were convincing, and Jonathan
had enjoyed them at the Carlyle, in company with Angelica.
He felt less sure he would enjoy them here. He was discovering
that the Conrad was never quiet; there was always some
alarming sound, some creaking or inexplicable slithering, just
as he was about to fall asleep.

"We could look at my new animal book," he said, a little
uncertainly. "Daddy gave it to me tonight." He paused. "Daddy's
downstairs now, with Mommy. He may come here to live with
us, I think."

"Well now, wouldn't that be cozy," Maria said.

She plumped up his pillows, smoothed back his hair, picked
up the book, and made herself comfortable on the duvet next to
him. "My oh my," she said, flicking the pages with great
rapidity, "will you look at that."

Jonathan looked at her curiously. Maria did not seem very
interested in the pictures, although she had removed her
glasses—the better to see them, she said. Jonathan had never
seen her without thick and unflattering lenses and now that he
did, he found her eyes odd. They were set too close together
and they had a yellowish glint. He thought Maria's eyes had
always been brown—dark brown; he said this.

"Brown, blue, green . . ." Maria shut the book. "Contact

lenses. All the colors of the rainbow. You can buy eyes in a store, these days. Any color you like. Didn't you know that?"

"I guess so. . . ."

"Fat, thin, dark, fair, pale, tanned . . ." Maria laughed. "These days it's easy. A woman can be anyone she wants. Magic, Mr. Sharp Eyes." She gave Jonathan's arm a sharp pinch.

Jonathan did not like the way she said that, and the pinch hurt. He gave her a doubtful look. It would not have surprised him if Maria were capable of magic; he thought of her turning up at the Carlyle to give his mother her pretheater massage, with all her little bottles of special oils. These oils were magic, she had told him once, and when he had told his mother, she had smiled. "Well, magic in a way, maybe," she had said. "They smell nice, and they make me relax."

He sniffed. Maria smelled faintly of her own oils now, he thought, and he could recognize some of them, all the herby scents, lavender and rosemary; beneath them, though, and not quite masked by them, was another, less pleasant odor, that might have been blood or sweat. Maria smelt nervy, twitchy; he laid his hand on her dark sleeve.

"Are your special oils magic, Maria? Do you make them up yourself?"

"I surely do. Mix, mix, mix."

"What do you put in them?"

"Eye of newt and toe of frog. Slugs and snails and puppy dogs' tails—that's what little boys are made of. Sugar and spice and all things nice . . ." She made a coughing sound. "I had a little boy once. You know what happened to him? He was growing away in my tummy—you know babies do that?"

She turned a yellowish eye toward him; Jonathan gave her a scornful look. "Of course I know that. It's in all my books. Human babies stay there for nine months. With small animals, it's much shorter, and with big ones, like elephants, it's . . ."

"Well my little boy didn't stay there nine months, Mr. Smart-Ass." She pinched him again. "My little boy was in there *three* months." She prodded her stomach. "He just had time to grow all his fingers and toes and his ears and eyes—and then you know what? Some doctor came along and sucked him out, scraped him out, vacuumed him out. Then they put him in a bucket, because he was just so much *mush*. Red mush. And I wanted to hold him, but they said I couldn't do that. . . ."

Jonathan had frozen still as a mouse. Something was badly wrong with Maria tonight; it was not just the horrible things she was saying, it was the *way* in which she said them. She kept opening and closing her mouth like a fish, and gasping for breath; her mouth was an ugly, jagged shape. She had now started to cry, but she did not cry as his mother did, quietly, making no sound, the tears coursing down her cheeks; Maria cried noisily, with her face all twisted up. Jonathan did not really want to touch her, but he knelt up in bed and put his arm around her shoulders.

"Maria, don't cry. Please don't cry." He put his hands over his ears, and tried not to think about red mush and a bucket.

"Maria, shall I get Mommy?"

"No, don't do that." She stopped crying as suddenly as she had started; she smiled instead. "I'm okay. It's just I miss him sometimes, my little boy. He'd be five years old today. You could have played with him, like a little brother—you'd have liked that. Now lie down, I'm going to tuck you in."

Jonathan wanted to argue, but found he was too afraid. He climbed back beneath the covers and lay very straight.

"Now you go to sleep, you hear me?" She leaned over him very close, so her yellowish eyes had a squinty look, and he could smell something sour and pepperminty on her breath.

"I will, I will," Jonathan said. He tried not to think about peeing, because he found he wanted to pee, urgently and badly, but he was afraid to tell Maria this. He made a small wriggling movement, then lay still. Maria took his hand in hers; one by one, so it hurt a little, but not too much, she started bending his fingers back.

"And I want you to stay nice and quiet. No calling out when I'm watching TV. I'm going to watch TV now, and I don't want my program interrupted. You know what I'll do if you give me any trouble?"

Jonathan shook his head.

"I'll open that closet door in the hall. And I'll let the bogeyman out. His name's Joseph, and I'll send him in to deal with you. You won't like that. You know what he does to naughty boys, little know-it-alls like you?" She gave him a long, still, yellowish look. Leaning over, she yanked the bed-covers off. "He eats them up. He eats their fingers and their toes and their ears, all the bits that stick out—they're his favorite bits. Then he bites off their little wee-wees, so there's a big hole, and he sucks and sucks, and all their insides come out, all their heart and lungs and liver, and he swallows them up like soup. Slurp slurp." She laughed. "Sleep tight, precious," she added, and switched out the light.

Jonathan lay there in the dark, too afraid to move. He wanted to pee very badly now. He told himself there was no such thing as the bogeyman, and there was nothing in the hall closet except sheets. Then he found he could hear footsteps dragging along the corridor; he could hear the TV and he could hear footsteps. . . . He peered into the dark, clutching at his bear, and the dark moved like eyes. He made a small whimpering sound, and the warm urine came gushing out in a flood. It felt comforting at first, but then it began to feel cold; he listened and listened, but the footsteps seemed to have stopped.

He wondered if Maria was really watching TV, the way she said. If she was, she would have her back to the door and her back to the corridor. He thought if he was very very quiet, and avoided the floorboards that squeaked, he could creep past her and she would never know. Then he could run downstairs to Mommy and Daddy, and they'd be angry with Maria and she'd never come back.

Very slowly, he inched the bedcovers aside. Clasping his bear, he crept to the door and looked out. He could hear the TV again, but the door to that room was closed. He inched past it, pressing himself against the wall. His pajama bottoms were wet and clingy, and he felt cold and shivery; he inched a little bit more and a little bit more: past the sitting room, past the bathrooms; he could see the light was on in his mother's bedroom, and the light was spilling out through the open door into the corridor ahead.

He crept toward the patch of light and then stopped, too afraid to go on and too afraid to go back. Maria was in his mother's room, where she had no right to be. He could hear her muttering and talking to herself; she was doing something to his mother's bed; he could hear some horrible ripping, grunting sounds. He could just see Maria's upraised arm and something bright and sharp in her hand, then she bent and grunted and disappeared round the edge of the door.

Sweat ran down into his eyes; he opened his mouth to cry out, but he only made a little sound, some dry squeaking sort of sound. Maria was panting now and groaning, and that made him more afraid. He had heard noises like that before, a long time before, coming from his mother's room, and when he had gone to help her, there were his parents, naked in bed. His mother's head was tilted back over its edge, her hair rippling down like water, and his father was on top of her, gripping her wrists, moving to her cries, rising and falling, rising and falling, his face sharp and gleaming, rhythmic as an ax.

"Daddy?" he said in a low voice. "Daddy are you there?" The door instantly swung back. His father was not there, and when he saw what Maria had done to his mother's room, he started to cry. He slid down the wall in a little pool of misery and fear, not daring to look up.

"Just in time, just in time," said Maria, crouching down beside him. She jerked his head up. "Now we can really have some fun, precious," and she showed him the knife.

"Are you worrying about the time for some reason, Natasha?" Tomas Court said, catching his wife in the act of easing back her sleeve and checking her watch.

"No, no," Natasha replied, "I'm listening, Tomas. It's just— I thought I heard something. I was wondering if Angelica had come back early. . . ."

That possibility did not please her husband. His face tight with annoyance, he crossed the room and went out into the corridor. His wife folded her hands on her lap. It was ten-thirty; Angelica was not due back for another hour and a half. She looked at the briefcase on the table, and the mass of papers inside it that her husband had been about to take out. She knew the subject of Joseph King could be put off no longer, and the effect, as she had predicted to Juliet McKechnie, was to heighten her nervousness.

The slightest sound now made her tense. For the past thirty minutes, in a hopeless way, she had been trying to think of some pretext to leave the room, go upstairs, and check that Jonathan was safe. She knew this was unnecessary; Maria knew about his nightmares; if any problems arose that she could not cope with, Maria would summon her. All the same, she longed to be in the same room as her son, to see with her own eyes that he was at peace and soundly asleep.

It angered her that she could not bring herself to leave the room and risk her husband's certain irritation if she did. She knew she was still subject to the tyranny of her husband's moods, but she also knew that if she risked angering him, he would stay even longer. He might pick a fight with her again, as he had done that previous night, and if angry, or desperate, he might then attempt to make love to her. He had been very close to doing so yesterday, but Angelica's presence in the apartment had, finally, inhibited him. The knowledge that her guardian was not there to protect her tonight, made Natasha excited and fearful. If Tomas began to touch her, or to kiss her, she might begin to want him again. What would the consequences then be? Then she would be admitting Tomas, and all the chaos he brought with him, back into her life.

"This precious apartment building of yours is infested with rats, do you know that?" he said, returning to the room and picking up the briefcase. "If you stand in the hall, you can hear them scratching. What's behind that wall? Heating ducts? You should talk to the super—"

"I don't think it's rats, Tomas," she said, in a quiet voice. "There's some service area for the elevator behind there. It opens through into the elevator shaft. It's just machinery noises, cables, drafts. . . . I'll mention it to Giancarlo though, just in case."

"Fine. Then let's continue. You need to hear this." In a weary way, he drew out a sheaf of papers. "Most of this came through yesterday and today from the investigation agency. If I'd waited for the police to make those checks it would have been six months before we got the results. As it is, once the agency had something solid to go on, they made progress." He paused, looking at her as she sat huddled at one end of the white sofa. "I once knew Joseph King, Natasha, and so did you. Do you want to see a picture of how King looked then, when we first met?"

He tossed a photograph toward her. In silence, Natasha examined it. The picture, in black-and-white, showed a group of people eating lunch around a table; the setting appeared to be a movie location. She examined the picture, recognizing no one in it.

"The third from the left. Fair hair."

Natasha swallowed nervously. "But that's a woman, Tomas," she said.

"A woman. Precisely." He crossed to the sofa and sat down next to her. Natasha, looking at his white set face, realized that he was exhausted; she could hear now that his breathing was stressed. Quietly, she held out her hand to him and he took it in his own.

"Her name then was Tina Costello," he continued. "She's had a great many names since. That's some of the crew on *The Soloist*. She worked in makeup. Assistant to an assistant to an assistant. So when I say you knew her, I'm exaggerating. You'd have passed her, maybe said good morning—no more than that. She was twenty years old then, and studying film at UCLA. I hired her as a favor to the third assistant director, who said she was his cousin. I spoke to him today, at length. It turns out she wasn't his cousin. He denies it, but he was screwing her, I suppose." He paused, looking away. "I fired her—or someone fired her on my behalf, six weeks into the shoot. There'd been complaints from the makeup department: time-keeping problems, general incompetence. I've never given her a second thought until she turned up yesterday at the door of my loft in Tribeca."

His wife bent her head over the photograph. From upstairs, in Emily Lancaster's apartment, came the sound of voices; a chair scraped back.

"Tomas," she began, "this isn't possible. Those telephone calls weren't made by a woman. . . ."

"No. She didn't make them—but she scripted them, I'd guess. Someone else had to be recruited to make the calls—and I think I know who that was." He gave a sigh. "She has a brother, to whom, by all accounts, she's very close—unnaturally close, you could say since according to several sources, he is also her lover. Let me tell you about the brother, and listen carefully. Both of them have a history of psychiatric problems, as you might expect. She's worked all over the States. She worked, among other places, at that photographic lab in California—you remember? She's been able to hold down a job; the brother has not. He likes to think of himself as an artist, a painter—or so that assistant director says. According to the agency, he's done small-time building work now and then: decorating, plumbing, wiring. He's a jack of all trades, master of none, and his name actually is Joseph, oddly enough. Now listen to these dates, Natasha. . . .

"Last July, within one week of my trip to Glacier with Jonathan, and almost certainly just after that Australian tourist was killed there, the brother's mental condition deteriorated. He was admitted to one of the psychiatric wards here in New York, in Bellevue. His sister took a room in the East Village, and she visited him in Bellevue twice a week. He finally came out, Natasha, exactly two weeks ago, on Thursday November twelfth. My loft was broken into in the early hours the next day—Friday the thirteenth. The calls began again the same day. The choice of date is characteristic, of course. It's not too difficult to work out, is it, why we had nearly five months' respite?"

"But we had no letters either. . . ." She turned to him, her face shocked and white. "And here, there's been nothing here for a week. Just that flurry of calls when the decorators were here. . . . Nothing since. You saw her *yesterday*. You *met* her? Did you recognize her?"

"No, of course not. She looks totally different now. I wouldn't have remembered her, in any case."

"And yesterday she told you that she'd worked for you in the past?" Panic had come into his wife's eyes and her hands had begun to tremble. "Tomas—I don't understand. No woman would do this. All those years; all the *work* she put into it. She'd have to be so obsessed to do that. Did she have a grudge against you because you fired her? Is that it?"

"Who knows?" He looked away. "She's obsessed with my work. She isn't sane. Her motives don't interest me, I just want her and her brother found. I want them locked up, and I want them out of my life. That's it."

"I can't bear this." With a sudden despairing gesture, his wife rose and turned to face him. "You're lying, Tomas. Why do you do that? I know you so well. I can tell when you're lying—something happens to your eyes and your voice. . . ."

"Natasha, don't pursue this. Let it be. It's irrelevant now."

"Irrelevant? I don't think so. You'd better tell me, Tomas. Which of them was it? The girl, or her brother? It could have been either, we both know that."

"The girl."

"You slept with her? When we were making that movie? Then? But Jonathan was only a baby then. I thought—"

"Then. At my apartment yesterday also. And sleeping wasn't involved. Natasha. . . ."

"Ah, dear God, I'm still jealous." She turned away, covering her face. "I still can't bear it, even now. In your apartment? Some woman who'd turned up out of nowhere? Some woman you didn't even *know*?"

"Natasha—not knowing them, before or after, is always the point." He gave a sigh, rose to his feet, and crossed toward her. In an awkward way, he laid his arm across her shoulders.

"Natasha, *don't*. We've been over this and over this a thousand times. She's unimportant. They're all utterly unimportant. They have something I want for five minutes, ten—and then it's over. Done with."

"*Done* with? Not for her. Tomas, we've suffered for five years because of this. You put our son at risk—"

"I know that now. I couldn't foresee it then. Natasha, listen to me. I have always loved you—and I'll go on loving you for the rest of my life. You're everything I want, and you always have been—"

"No, I'm not." She rounded on him, tears springing to her eyes, and her face white with distress. "I used to believe you when you said that; I don't anymore. You want me and you want my opposite as well. You always have."

"Briefly I can want that. I'm not unique in that respect," he replied, with a slight edge. He looked at her carefully.

There was a small tense silence, then, breaking his gaze, his wife moved away. "I'm not listening to this," she said. "I want to see her picture. I want to see what she looks like *now*. I want to see what it is you needed yesterday, when you love me so much and I give you everything you want. . . ."

She pushed past him and picked up the sheaf of papers, scattering them in all directions. "Show me, Tomas. I know how thorough you are. I know there'll be more pictures. You won't have been satisfied with one that's nearly six years out of date. . . ."

"No, you're right. There's a picture of her taken when she renewed her driver's license, about two months ago. The agency found it. It's in that pile there. Look at that if you must. It will tell you nothing."

She snatched at the pile of papers he had indicated, tossing aside sheets of print. Coming upon the right picture at last, he saw her face change. She gave a sharp intake of breath.

"Is this a joke?" She stared at him. "There must be some mistake. . . ."

"No. No mistake."

"But I know this woman. Tomas—you met her one day at the Carlyle with Angelica."

"I never met her. What are you talking about?"

"Glasses. She wears glasses usually. Maria. The one who used to give me a massage before I went to the theater—once a week, twice a week sometimes—"

Under her left breast, Court heard; he stared at his wife.

"Oh, dear merciful God. She's upstairs," she said in a low voice. "She's upstairs, with Jonathan, tonight." He saw her face become blank with fear, then she turned and ran from the room. Court followed. Halfway along that narrow artery of a corridor, pain tightened in his chest. He slumped back against the wall, fumbling for his inhaler. When the pain eased, he began opening doors, calling his wife's name. He found himself in a kitchen, where a machine threshed, then in a laundry room, where a tap dripped in a white sink. He opened another door and brooms fell out at him. Then he saw the right door, the only possible door—a jib door, small, wallpapered, disguised, and practically invisible.

He forced it back and began to mount the stairs. His wife began screaming before he was halfway up.

"They locked her up," Frobisher said, coming toward the end of a ghost story familiar to everyone present except Rowland McGuire and Nic Hicks. She produced some mince pies, dusted with sugar and fragrant with spice, placing them in the center of the table.

"That's why she still *walks*!" Emily put in. "Confinement!

She couldn't be confined then—and she *still* can't." She shivered. "That woman had a lust for blood."

"Em, please. *I* am telling this story. We will tell it *my* way, if you please. Now, shall I continue?"

Everyone at the table except Lindsay gave some form of assent.

"As I was saying . . . The Conrad brothers locked their sister up—for her own safety, or so they told the staff. The room they kept her in is just under this one." She glanced down. "That apartment is a duplex—the only one in this building. The room was tucked away up some stairs, so on one could hear her if she cried out. The Conrad brothers told everyone that Anne had left for Europe on a visit, and all of their friends accepted that. . . ." She paused. "Although there was gossip, wasn't there, Emily?"

"Indeed yes. Tongues wagged. The Conrad brothers were rich—and strange. So there had *always* been talk."

"Be that as it may," Frobisher continued, lowering her voice, "their precautions were to no avail. Every night, one of the brothers would stay with her; they took it in turns to do that. And one night, one of the brothers got careless. . . ."

"*I* heard," said one of the ancient women whose identities Rowland confused, "*I* heard that the brothers quarreled and one of them let her out. . . ."

"Possible. In the circumstances, even probable." Emily glanced around the table. "They were all so very *close*. . . ."

"Either way," Frobisher continued, doggedly, "a fatal error was made. Her door was left unlocked. She ran down to that great drawing room, in a white muslin dress. . . ."

"*Blue,* Froby. I always heard it was blue."

"*White,* Em. A white dress—in fact, a kind of nightgown—and her black hair all loose. She was a very beautiful young woman, no dispute about *that.* It was a summer's morning. The shades were down against the heat, but the windows were wide open. There was a struggle—the brothers tried to subdue her, or so they later said. She broke free of them, gave one last terrible cry, and she jumped. Or . . ." Frobisher paused, giving the assembled company a dark glance. "Or, she was *pushed.* That possibility was whispered at the time. . . . But pushed by whom? Which twin? Both? History does not relate, alas. And naturally, the whole matter was hushed up afterward. Though people did say—"

"She was with child?" Another of the ancient women asked, on a gentle, interrogative note.

"Six months gone," Emily said, in a brisk way. "Six months gone, my dears. And her skull cracked open on the sidewalk right outside the entrance. Cracked open like an egg."

Lindsay made a small sound. "Poor, poor child," said the third of the old women, glancing toward her. "Such a terrible thing. Tell me, Emily—was she truly mad, do you think?"

"North northwest," quoted Emily in a sage way. "When the wind was southerly . . . And at what point did she *become* mad, if she did? One cannot be sure, since it was the brothers who took charge of the story afterward. As is generally the way, of course."

A silence fell in the room; a candle guttered; Lindsay felt Colin's hand reach for her own under the table. Rowland stared fixedly at his plate. Nic Hicks, having been silenced by Frobisher's story for the first time that evening, passed the mince pies, then took one himself.

"A rat, a rat . . ." he said, taking his cue from Emily's quotation, and acknowledging this with a charming glance. "So, who was the secret lover? One of the brothers? Does history relate that?"

"No, it does *not*," Emily replied in a huffy tone.

Nic Hicks never noticed when his knuckles were rapped; he pursued his point. "But what *happened* to the incestuous brothers? I'll bet they came to unpleasant ends. . . ."

"You are correct."

"Fascinating." Hicks sighed. "You know, Emily, it reminds me of the first production of *Hamlet* I acted in. At Stratford—a million years ago now, of course. My salad days. I was straight out of drama school, playing Osric. . . ."

"Excellent casting," said Colin, under his breath.

"Sir Peter directing, wonderful Hal in the title role, Gwen as Ophelia. She played her pregnant! Visibly so by the mad scene, and when she was brought in on the bier—well! Unmistakably *enceinte*. This very, very round belly—a *huge* gasp from the stalls. *Ruined* the graveyard scene—such a scandal! A *cause célèbre*, overnight! Letters to the *Times* . . ."

"Let me out," said Colin in a low voice only Lindsay could hear. "Please God, let me out *now*. I can't stand any more of this."

As he spoke, he suddenly remembered an intention disclosed in one of his Montana faxes. Unspeakable things! Gently, he released Lindsay's hand. Turning to Nic Hicks with an expression of profound interest, he slipped his freed hand beneath the folds of Lindsay's red skirt. He began to move it gently upward. He could feel the top of her stocking, then the skin of her inner thigh, which was astonishingly smooth and soft. He sighed. Lindsay, who had spent the dinner shuttling between dismay and despair, became aware of the intent, thoughtful gaze of Rowland, seated immediately opposite her. She gave the straying hand a caress, then a small and desperate pinch.

"I gave my daughter a Shakespearean name," said the quiet and melancholy voice of Henry Foxe, seated to her immediate left. "Marina. I called her Marina. Such a lovely name, I always thought."

"A beautiful name," Lindsay said gently, feeling pity wash into her heart. Henry Foxe had shown her a picture of his daughter before they came in to dinner. His daughter, dead a decade, was tonight much in his thoughts, he had said.

"It's a pun on 'mariner,'" Rowland said, making Lindsay jump. "In the play, that is."

"Is that so? I didn't know that." Henry Foxe gave a small sigh. "Well, that would make sense. It's from *Pericles*, my dear." He turned back to Lindsay. "Very rarely performed. I'd never seen the play, never read it. I did read it finally, when she was a little girl. . . ." He gave a small dry sigh. "Of course, as Mr. McGuire will know, in the play, there is a happy ending. The daughter is not dead, as her father has believed. She has been rescued from the sea by pirates. So she returns from the dead."

He paused. "It is a very moving scene, when the father and daughter are reunited, when they recognize one another at last. Such a beautiful scene." Henry Foxe said, shaking his head. "Such language! One is robbed, in the modern world, of such language. That scene was my mother's favorite in the entire canon. An unconventional choice. Perhaps that's why I chose

the name for my daughter. How odd. I'd never thought of that
possibility until tonight."

He gave another little dry sigh. Lindsay, pitying him, found
she could think of no adequate reply. She felt her eyes swim
with tears. She laid her hand quietly on his arm, and Henry
Foxe, not looking at her, patted it. Lindsay rose, and with a few
whispered words to Colin, left the table, finding she could
no longer bear to be in this room with its eddying under-
currents, its ghosts, and its griefs.

"Hi, it's Tom," said her son's familiar voice. "Katya and I can't
take your call right now. But leave a message after the tone,
and we'll call back."

Lindsay, sitting on the bed in one of Emily's guest rooms,
stared at the wallpaper. It was yellowish, old, and formal in pattern. She had received no reply from Tom's room when she
called from the Plaza at eight; she had received the answering
machine, less than an hour later, when she had called from this
room before they went in to dinner. This fact had refused to lie
still in her mind ever since; all through Frobisher's meal, she
had felt an irrational and mounting anxiety—and the turn
the conversation had taken had made that anxiety worse.

"Tom, it's me," she said, into the phone, trying to deaden the
panic in her voice. "I left a message earlier. Darling, are you all
right? I'm—I've been worrying about your flight. Tom, if
you're there, will you pick up? I know it's late but . . ."

The machine cut her off. Lindsay replaced the receiver. To
hear her son's voice, yet be unable to speak to him, made the
panic much worse. She rose and began to pace, then sat down
on the bed again, trying to calm herself.

Frobisher had piled everyone's coats on the bed as they
arrived. Lindsay could see her own new black coat, a scarlet
scarf that belonged to Nic Hicks, a moleskin cape affair that
one of the three ancient friends had been wearing, and lying
side by side, virtually identical, the two dark overcoats
belonging to Colin and to Rowland. Lindsay looked at these
coats and heard herself make a strange sound, half gasp and
half sob.

Oh, what am I going to *do*? What am I going to *do*? she
thought, rising again, and again pacing. She looked at her

watch; it was almost half past ten. She tried to work out what time that meant it must be in Oxford, but her mind refused to do the math. It kept washing back and forth in a mad futile way, seeing pain and problems at every turn. Oh why did Colin propose on the *stairs*? she thought, then, telling herself that the location was unimportant, her mind went rushing off in another direction. No matter what she did now, thanks to her past actions, others were going to be hurt. Was there some way of preventing that? She could see no such way, no route out. There would be some damage to Rowland, she was not sure how much, and there would be considerable damage to Colin. I must *extricate* myself, she thought. I must take action and I must *plan*. But she found she could not plan, because she had looked at the telephone; her anxiety for Tom had come surging back, and all she could think of now was the necessity, the *urgency* of hearing his voice.

Be calm, don't be so *stupid*, she said to herself, these wild fears for her son, to which she had been subject often when he was a child, were absurd now. He was a man; he was grown-up; there were a hundred ordinary sensible reasons why he should not be answering his phone. Tomorrow, this fear would seem ridiculous, and thinking this, she went into the bathroom beyond, walked across its checkerboard floor of black and white tiles, and seeing in the mirror how white and odd she looked, splashed water on her face.

She looked down at the tiles and thought of how, when he was seven, she had taught Tom to play chess. He had been good at the game and he had been able to beat her, consistently, by the age of eight. Hopeless, hopeless, Lindsay thought, leaning against the basin; she had not been gifted with an analytic intelligence, and she conducted a chess game with the same foolhardy incompetence with which she conducted her life. Precipitate in attack, devoid of defense, she thought, and a slow tide of misery rose up in her heart; she did not mind losing the game—she had never minded that—but this was not a game, and as a result of her foolishness, her lack of foresight, others would be hurt.

For that, she could not forgive herself. I must go back to the dinner, she thought, returning to the bedroom. She turned toward the door, turned back toward the telephone, then bent, and on a sudden impulse, picked up one of those near-identical coats from the bed, and buried her face in it.

Swimming into her mind came a vision of her future: she saw herself, despite her best resolutions, continuing as before, her life a series of ill-planned expeditions. There she was, as she had always been—a poor helmsman, charting a desperate, erratic course across an interminable ocean, always believing that land would be sighted soon. At sea: the story of my life, she thought.

A sound came from the doorway behind. "I'm sorry. I didn't realize you were in here," said Rowland McGuire's voice.

Lindsay dropped the coat guiltily and stepped back.

"I didn't mean to interrupt. I just came for my coat, Lindsay. I have to leave now."

"You're not interrupting. I was just trying to call Tom. I've been worrying about Tom for some stupid reason. . . ."

"You weren't calling Tom then."

"No. I was—thinking."

This remark met with a silence—a silence that clamored to Lindsay. Rowland picked up his overcoat and slowly put it on. Lindsay, afraid to look at him, could feel the tension radiating from him. She hoped he would remain silent; she hoped he would speak.

"I went to Oxford to see Tom yesterday," he said, finally, turning to look at her. He hesitated. "He'd left for Scotland, so I missed him. I—Lindsay, I went there because I had this fixed idea in my head that I had to ask Tom's blessing before I spoke to you." He gave a sigh, looking away. "Now, I don't even know why I felt that. I went as soon as I received your letter. Your letter was delayed, you see. At the time, it seemed important to do that. Now it seems obtuse."

"Rowland, no—" Lindsay took a step toward him. "You mustn't think that. *Not* obtuse . . ."

"I really couldn't have borne it in that dining room for another second," he went on, in a quiet voice. He glanced toward the door, then rested his green eyes sadly upon her face.

"I couldn't hear what anyone was saying. I was trying to understand how much all of this was simply a matter of chance, accident—mistimings, especially on my part. I kept trying to convince myself that if I stayed, the timing might suddenly come right. Then—something someone was saying—I realized: better absent myself. I shouldn't have been here. I shouldn't have come to New York. My presence has already caused enough trouble for one evening, and I don't want it to cause any more, especially for you. . . ."

He hesitated, then moved into the doorway. Lindsay watched the light from the corridor glance across his face. She could see the strength of emotion he was struggling to conceal, and her heart went out to him. A great surge of words rose up within her; she said his name and began to move quickly toward him. Reaching his side, she realized that none of those words could be said.

"I wanted to know—" He broke off, taking her hand. "Did you understand my letter, Lindsay?"

"I didn't then, but I do now. Rowland, I'm so sorry. I'm so desperately sorry—"

"My love." He caught her against him, cradling her head in his hands. He began to kiss her hair, then pressed her tight against his chest. Lindsay listened to the beating of his heart. Everything she had never said to him, and everything she had ever hoped he might say to her, were expressed then, she felt, in the confusion and flurry of that brief embrace.

Gripping her by the arms, he drew back and looked down at her face.

"Yes or no, Lindsay—just tell me that."

The question had been torn from him. Lindsay could see that he had not intended to ask it, and perhaps regretted it the instant the words were said. Loyalty and fear of disloyalty could be read in his face. To his question there was a rich fund of answers; she could feel them stored in her heart. Three years of answers and explanations and revelations never made; she consigned them to oblivion.

"No," she replied, in a low voice—and she admired him then as much as she ever had, for although the recovery was not instant, it was courageous and it was swift.

"Ah, I feared you would say that." He stopped, fought to control his voice, then continued. "Lindsay you will always be very dear to me, and I wish you nothing but joy. I want you to know that."

He embraced her gently as he said this, drawing her into his arms in a quiet protective way. Lindsay found she could not see for sudden tears. As once before in Oxford, she was encircled by his arms, and her face was resting against his chest.

"If you were wearing that green sweater," she said, in a shaky voice, "I'd kiss it now, Rowland. . . ."

"Never mind. You can kiss my tie instead."

Lindsay kissed his tie. She was just thinking how much she liked the patterns of this tie, how sensible and orderly they were, and how calm she felt, when someone began screaming. It was a woman, and the sound was painfully close. The cry was repeated, then repeated again, on a mounting note of terror and distress.

Colin was halfway along the corridor when he too heard this cry. The corridor in Emily's apartment, as in that of Natasha Lawrence's below, ran like an artery from the reception rooms at the front of the building to the bedrooms at the back.

In the dining room, halfway along this corridor, there had, for some time before, been sounds that indicated disturbance, trouble, and distress.

For a while, still seated at the table, Colin had been deaf to them. To his right, some interminable conversation between Emily and her three ancient female friends had begun; it concerned the current vagaries of the elevator. Colin had been deaf to that too; the whole of his mind dwelt upon Lindsay—to such an extent that he scarcely noticed Rowland rise and speak to Emily in a quiet voice. It was only when Rowland came around the table to him that he had realized he was leaving; he half rose, but Rowland immediately pushed him back toward his seat.

"No, really, Colin. I'd rather see myself out. I don't want to break things up, and I have to go—"

"Don't be absurd. Let me see you out. . . ."

"Really." Rowland's expression did not encourage argument. "I'd rather slip away. I have an early plane to catch. My thanks for this evening."

He turned and left. Colin settled into his chair thoughtfully, puzzled by Rowland's expression, tone, and haste.

"The *override* switch, Emily dear," one of the ancient women was saying, and Colin, scarcely hearing her, began to feel a sick unease. Something was happening, he felt; something *had* been happening, and he had been blind and deaf to it. But what was it? What was it?

He could sense some dark and shapeless idea at the back of his mind, and he knew he had been given clues, that he could see this thing if he concentrated, if he dragged it forward into the light. But the thing would not move, and was almost instantly occluded by another, more pressing thought. Colin began to realize that Lindsay's telephone call was taking too long, that she had been absent too long. Could she have felt faint again? And why had Rowland chosen that moment to leave? It was then that the sounds from below, apparent for a while, finally registered. He heard the running footsteps, the slamming doors, the woman's voice calling, at exactly the same moment that anxiety for Lindsay gripped.

"Is something *wrong*, Emily?" one of the ancient women suddenly asked. "My hearing is not perfect, but . . ."

"I can hear someone crying," said Henry Foxe, becoming very pale and rising to his feet. "Emily, it sounds like a child crying. . . ."

"What's that *banging*?" Frobisher rose with a look of alarm. "It's coming from the stairs. Is some door being forced? Colin, I think you should—"

Colin was already running from the room as she spoke. As he reached the main corridor, he heard the scream, rising up from below his feet. He froze, feeling the cry reverberate up through his body. His heart had started hammering; he glanced along the corridor, to his right and to his left. To his right, he saw nothing; to his left, he half saw in a bedroom doorway some shape that should not be there, that could not be there, and that he knew he had to be imagining. From beyond the front door, straight ahead of him, a renewed, confused clamor broke out. He could hear a frantic, metallic, banging sound, some broken protest, the cries of a child in obvious distress, then the sound of a man's voice—a voice he recognized at once. No, dear God, please no, said this voice, and Colin found he was across the hall, through the door, and out in the shadows of the landing.

It was of the utmost urgency and importance to be there, he knew that, even as he also knew that it was of the utmost urgency and importance to remain in Emily's apartment, where he could look again at the two people—yes, it had been two people—who had been standing together in that doorway to his left.

He peered along the galleried landing, trying to see past its riot of pillars, trying to make sense of its shapes. Ahead of him, that red carpet poured itself down the stairs; above him, other galleries whispered and cried out alarm. He could hear doors opening and closing; he could sense a terrible, gathering collective fear: something had been let loose in this building—but Colin's mind refused to tell him what it was. He heard Emily's voice from the corridor behind him, then a cry from one of the old women. He fixed his eyes on the landing, and found he could see some haunting white shape, moving beyond the pillars; the shape was the size of a child; it was airborn; it had too many arms, and there was something that appalled him about its face.

"Lindsay, stay *there*. Colin, what's happening?" Rowland said, from behind him, and that banging and crashing and anarchy burst out again. Of course he was not surprised to hear Rowland's voice, Colin thought; of course he already knew that Rowland had not left; of course he also knew why Rowland had remained. He had seen him with his arms around Lindsay. He had been shown the unthinkable, the unimaginable, and the impossible just now, in that bedroom doorway to his left.

How stupid of me, he thought. How unbelievably stupid. How could I not have seen something so obvious? A dull pain settled itself inside him; looking along the galleries now, he found the pain steadied his vision and comprehension had come. He saw a simple tableau—father, abductor, child—that made clear and immediate sense.

"Oh, my heart—let me sit down. I can't breathe," said a voice from the hall behind him. Glancing back, he saw Emily being helped to a chair, Rowland bending over her with a look of concern, and Lindsay running toward him.

It seemed to take her an immense time to approach. Years passed while he looked at her pale uplifted face. He knew she was saying something, but her words would not transmit their sense. He said something to her—he was never sure afterward what it was, but it was probably something about the police, about calling the police. He thought maybe he told her to keep the door *closed*; he certainly slammed it, and he thought he said that.

As soon as it *was* shut it was very clear to him what he had to do next. None of this was really happening, but even so he had to help the child—so he began to run along the gallery toward the child, and the man grasping the child, and the figure slumped against the banister, breathing painfully, who, he realized, was Tomas Court.

As soon as he moved—and only seconds had passed, but they felt like years—the man holding the child stopped scrabbling and banging at the elevator doors and ran off. He was still clutching the child, like some pale bulky parcel, and he still had his hand clamped across the child's mouth. Colin could see the child's hands plucking at air, and he felt outrage and incomprehension at this. He paused only for a moment by Tomas Court. Then, seeing he could scarcely breathe, let alone pursue, set off in pursuit himself. He expected the man to run down the stairs toward the entrance hall; but, since nothing was obeying the usual rules, he did the opposite and started to run up. Colin followed, running at speed, stumbling, then running again. His heart was now pounding; the man had a head start of almost two flights, and as he ran Colin had a clear sense that this was all a dream, and at any moment he would wake up.

"Stop, stop, stop," he heard himself shout in this dream, and it struck him how absurd this was. Even so, he cried "Stop" several times more. He changed it to "Please, stop" on the sixth landing, which was even more absurd, and "Don't, please, *don't*" on the eighth. He found he was saying something garbled and incoherent to a tiny, frightened, wizened, ancient face that popped out from behind a door on the ninth floor, but the door then slammed, and the bolts were drawn across. In his dream, Colin could then concentrate on what really mattered, which was making his legs move faster, and getting the air into his lungs, which were starting to seize up.

Reaching the top floor at last, he had a glassy sense that it was not a dream, after all, but that everything was now going to calm down; normality was about to prevail, no one was going to get hurt, and the child—he realized the child must be Tomas Court's son—was going to be safe.

He had a *reason* for thinking this, he saw, stepping onto the landing and slowing his pace. The abductor, he could now see, was not a man, but a woman. He could see why he had made that mistake: the woman was wearing trousers and her hair was hacked raggedly short. He could also see that she was holding a knife—but he found he was not alarmed by the knife. A woman must be as incapable of hurting a child as he was of hurting a woman: this creed it did not occur to him to doubt. He felt totally sure that the instant the woman saw he did not intend to hurt her, she would give him the child and surrender the knife. Fighting to steady his breathing, he began to walk toward her.

"You're frightening him," he began. "He's only a little boy and he's terrified. Please, put him down. You can't want to hurt him. Give me the knife. . . ."

The woman had been scratching and banging at the elevator doors. As soon as he spoke, she made a panting, grunting sound. She darted away, across the landing, which was large, and backed up against the banister. Colin hesitated; there was a sheer ten-story drop behind her. He felt a vertiginous fear then; his shocked calm began to fragment; the floor began to move, and the dome tilted above his head.

"Precious, precious," the woman said, and cut the child's face.

Blood welled; Colin looked at the blood welling up in disbelief. She had cut the boy just below the eye, very close to the eye; blood welled up and dripped down over her fingers, which remained clamped over the boy's mouth. Colin saw the child give one terrified convulsive movement, then fall limp. He could both see and smell his terror now; he could also see that the knife, a long, thin switchblade, was pressed up against the child's bare throat.

"Oh, dear God, what are you doing? What are you *doing*? You *cut* him." He stared at the woman. "You—how can you do that? You can't want to hurt a child. It's so wicked, *wicked*. Please—give him to me. I'm not going to touch you, or hurt you. Let him go. Let him go *at once*. . . ."

"He stinks. Filthy little know-it-all." The woman spoke in a low rapid voice, eyeing him. "You take one more step and I'll jump." She frowned. "I'll cut his throat."

"You can't do *both*. What are you *saying*? Look, please—listen to me. Why are you doing this? What's the *point*? You can't get away from here now. That elevator isn't working. Every resident in this building will have been calling the police. . . . Please, give him to me."

He stopped. He could hear just how stupid and fatally inadequate he sounded. He could not understand why these arguments, so true and so obvious, would not be properly expressed. He tried to look at the woman; think, *think*, said some irritating, confusing voice in his head. He began to see that the woman was very afraid; her face had a twitchy, jittery look; she was breathing in and out very fast and beginning to shake. Colin took another step forward. He wanted to make a rush at her, a grab at her—but the knife was just under the boy's ear, and that ten-story emptiness lay in wait.

"Precious. Precious baby," said the woman, in a low crooning voice. She looked down at the boy; Colin risked another silent step forward. Her head jerked up and the white of her face flared at him.

"Do *you* have a baby?"

"No, not yet. Look—*please*. Let me help you. You need help. . . ."

"Call the elevator. Tell Joe to bring the elevator *up*. . . ." Colin was afraid to move away to the elevator. If he did, he would be at a greater distance. She might jump.

"The elevator isn't working," he began. "I told you—it won't come. It's broken down. Listen—"

"I had a baby once." Her eyes flashed at him. "Didn't I, Jonathan? Where's my baby now? Flushed down some drain. Tossed out with the trash." Her mouth moved. "Get the elevator. Get the fucking elevator, right now, or I'll jump."

She made a jerking movement and the child gave a moan of fear. Colin's heart leaped. He started to move toward her fast, because he suddenly saw with absolute clarity that if he did not act now, and act quickly, the unthinkable was going to happen right in front of his eyes, and fifteen seconds from now the boy would be dead. I'm going to *kill* her, Colin thought, moving, propelled on sudden violent rage, and realizing that he *could* kill her, if only he could get hold of her before she used the knife.

"Get the elevator, Colin," said Tomas Court's voice. "Get the elevator now. Do what she says."

Colin stopped dead. Tomas Court had spoken sharply; he was standing on the far side of the landing, at the top of the last flight of stairs. Colin stared at his white face. He decided he was going mad; surely there was no way in which Court could have recovered and made it up those stairs? Yet there Court was, breathing quietly, if with obvious pain. He paused for only a second, looking at the woman and his son, then he began to walk toward them, his hand held out.

"Jonathan, don't move," he said in a quiet voice. "Just stay still. Colin, get the elevator, please. Now, Maria—do you want me to call you Maria? I don't think of you by that name. I think of you as Tina. I always will, and always have—if you'd said yesterday that your name was Tina, it would have made all the difference. Didn't you realize that?"

The use of this name had a magical effect. The woman became still; she stared at Court and made an odd gentle sound in her throat. Colin found he could breathe again. He darted across to the elevator and summoned it in the certain knowledge it would not come. Hope winged through him; he knew this was the correct thing to do, because Tomas Court had instructed him. Court knew this woman; he could *reach* her in a way Colin could not. Disaster was about to be averted, Colin thought. Two men against one woman was no contest, in any case. He could now see every frame of this movie playing itself out; it was a movie he'd seen a million times; it had a kindly director, who ensured that the hero disarmed the assailant, or, failing that, resolved everything quickly, without bloodshed, after a brief and well-choreographed fight.

At any moment, Tomas Court would give him a *signal*, Colin thought. He'd stop talking and give him a signal, and the two of them would launch some effective, concerted male attack. He moved back toward Court, who was still speaking. The scene in front of him would not stay still, but kept jerking about; Tomas Court was not only ignoring his presence and failing to give him any signal, but saying things that made very little *sense*.

"Didn't you get my messages?" he was saying, in a quiet, puzzled way. "All those messages I sent? I don't understand why you're doing this. You must see—I can't talk to you now, not with the boy here; he's in the way. Look at me. Tell me you got those messages, Tina. Tell me you understood."

The woman's grip on the boy slackened for a second. Her mouth moved. "Messages?" She stared at Court in a mesmerized way. "I sometimes thought—when I was alone . . ."

"I can understand that." Court had finally come to a halt a few feet in front of her. Colin edged his way to Court's side. He could see that Court was looking at the woman with tenderness and with regret.

"Don't be afraid," he went on, in a quiet voice. "Trust me. I'm not going to touch you—though I want to very much. All this time . . ." He gave a sigh. "You know not one day has gone past without my thinking of you? I've read your letters a thousand times. I know them by heart. There's one you wrote—" He hesitated. "And I keep it next to my heart." He sighed. "How is it you know me so well? You're closer to me than anyone I've ever known. I can talk to you without any fear of being misunderstood—and you can talk to me the same way. That's how close we are." He held out his hand to her. "Put the boy down, Tina. He's in the way. You're so very dear to me. Give me the knife."

The woman began to cry. She cried in a heartrending way, Colin thought, making ugly, gulping sounds, and twisting her face. Colin found he pitied her, and that Court's quiet words, for all their obvious effectiveness, made him uneasy. They were familiar to him, but he could not place them; recently, he felt, he had heard, seen, or used words that were very similar himself. He shifted his weight from his right foot to his left; he had a vague, nasty sensation of evil, breathing quietly, standing close.

"Hate you," said the woman, glancing down. "Hate you, hate you, hate you . . ."

"Of course." Court glanced toward the knife; it had moved a little, but not, Colin thought, enough.

"Don't *always* hate you," she added, in a low voice. An expression of irritation passed across Tomas Court's face. As soon as the woman saw it, she made a low, moaning, anxious sound. Hope, and fear, flickered across her face.

"You know what I want, Tina?" Court fixed his pale gaze on her. "I want you in my arms—and at this moment I want that more than anything else on this earth."

"Lies." The woman's eyes flashed at him. "Lies, lies, lies, *lies.*"

"No. The absolute truth." Court's pale gaze did not waver, but again that expression of irritation passed across his face. "I'm not arguing with you, Tina. If you want to hurt me there are more imaginative ways of doing it than this. When I tell you to put him down, I mean it. Now do it."

"Won't." She stared at him. Court, to Colin's alarm, gave a sudden shrug and a look of dismissal.

"Fine," he said coldly. "Fine. You're boring me. Jump."

Colin stared at him in stupefaction. He heard himself make a low sound of fear and protest. "Oh *Christ*," he said, starting to move forward, because he could see the woman's expression altering, and he could see her starting to turn toward that ten-story drop. She lifted the boy high in her arms, and Colin knew that she was about to throw him. The child gave one terrified cry; Court did not move, and as Colin lurched forward, the woman dropped the boy at his feet.

Colin made a grab for him; he got his arms around him and started to scoop him up. Neither Court nor the woman had moved, Colin thought, and he could sense that they were looking at each other, that their gaze, which he could feel rather than see, was interlocked. He gripped Jonathan tightly, and the instant he touched him, the boy began to fight. He was half crazed with fear, and the fear gave him strength. Colin was straightening up with the boy in his arms, trying to back away, to get him out of the woman's reach, and the boy was *fighting* him. He thrashed and squirmed; he rained down punches and slaps on Colin's head and face. He sank his teeth into Colin's hand, and as Colin tried to catch hold of his arms, he began to kick and scream. He caught hold of Colin's hair, and tugged at it. "Jonathan, Jonathan," Colin said, trying to calm him, trying to get him out of the woman's reach and away from that ten-story drop. The boy rose up in his arms, arching and yelping.

For a moment Colin could see nothing but his flailing arms, and that moment was all it took.

Darkness moved; something clattered to the floor, and somewhere to the side of him, something bunched. Over the boy's shoulder, past his white face, Colin saw Tomas Court enfold the woman in his arms. He knew that was all right, because he had heard her drop the knife. He started to tell Jonathan this, that it was all right, that he was safe, that it was over—but Jonathan was still yelping and screaming and trying to scratch his face.

Colin ducked his head away; he heard a crunching sound, then a sharp exhalation of breath, and he began to realize that some blow had been struck. He started to run, and heard himself make a sound, of fear, of protest. "Daddy, Daddy, Daddy," Jonathan cried, and Colin froze in horrified disbelief.

He watched the woman move upward and over the banister with a gymnast's grace. She went over backward, head first, in a beautiful dive; he saw her eyes widen and her hands grasp space. She seemed to hang there, supported by air, for an immensely long time, then she disappeared from sight. Tomas Court stepped back from the banister. He brushed at his jacket—one sleeve was torn; he stood listening, white-faced.

There was a silence, then a faint, thin cry, then a thud. Colin, shocked, appalled, unable to move, did not need to look over the banister to know what had happened; he knew she was ten floors down on a stone floor, and she was dead. He began to tremble violently; he had begun to weep. The little boy, sensing a change, made a whimpering sound, lay still, and covered his face. Colin cradled him tightly against him and stared at Tomas Court, whom he could scarcely see for distress.

"Why? Oh, dear God, *why?* Tomas—she'd let him *go.* He was *safe.* Tomas—she was this poor, mad, pathetic thing. Oh, *Christ.* You hit her. I heard you hit her. . . ."

"I did not hit her. Colin, I tried to take the knife from her. She was struggling—I don't know what happened. One second I had hold of her, the next she was toppling over. These banisters are deadly; they're not even waist high."

"Ah, dear God, you *pushed* her. You lifted her up and pushed her over. . . . I can't believe—Christ, *Christ* . . ." There was a silence; this silence, to Colin, was very loud. It was filled with clamor and movement and cryings out. He buried his wet face against the boy's hair. Tomas Court put his hand on his arm; Colin flinched and held the boy tight.

"Colin," Court began, in a quiet voice. "Colin, you're in shock. Wait until you're calmer before you speak. It doesn't matter what you say to me, I understand—but what you say matters very much when you talk to the police."

"She believed you." Colin raised his eyes to Court's. "All those things you said to her—all those *lies*. She believed them. This awful mad *hope*. Tomas, she'd given me the boy, she wasn't dangerous anymore. Oh, why did you touch her? Why did you *lie*? It was horrible—"

"Much of what I said was true as it happens." A spasm of pain passed across Court's face. "Colin, you're not thinking clearly. I told her what I knew she wanted to hear. What else was I supposed to do?" His voice had begun to break; Colin saw that he too was now beginning to tremble, that his face was drained of color, and that the love he felt for his son was naked in his face. "Colin. I'm grateful to you for what you did, you're a good man, but—just give me my son, Colin."

Colin looked down at the boy, now curled in his arms in a fetal position. He kissed his hair, then lifted him into his father's arms. Court clasped the boy tight against his heart, and began to say his name over and over again, in a low voice. Colin saw the boy slowly begin to move. He made a small mewing sound, and scrabbled at his father's jacket, then stole his arms about his neck.

Colin's vision blurred. He found he was blinded by tears, and by the force of his own emotions. He rejoiced that the boy was safe, but his rejoicings were shot through with fear and with doubt. He thought: I heard the knife *fall*; I heard it fall *before* he touched her. The knife fell and *then* there was that embrace.

The knife was lying on the floor, he realized; it lay several feet away from the banister, and its position told him nothing. He stared at it, and as he stared, the sequence of events, so clear to him only seconds before, began to shift. He found he was not certain of sequence, of cause and effect. Had the knife really been dropped *before* the embrace? And why did he think of it as an embrace anyway? It might, as Court claimed, have been a struggle of some kind, a contest for a weapon. He stared at the area of the landing where these glimpsed events had occurred. He found they were now receding from him fast; they were as fragmentary as the details of a dream, forgotten on waking. The harder he struggled to recall them, the ghostlier and more insubstantial they became. They were impressions only, and Tomas Court was correct: a muddle of impressions should not be imparted to the police.

He swung around to Court, suddenly wanting to ask him again why he had put his arms around the woman and what that embrace *meant*. Court was now huddled against the far wall, stroking his son's hair and speaking to him in a low, soothing voice. He did not look like a murderer; an embrace could mean so many things, Colin thought.

He turned away; he was beginning to see why this one question so preoccupied him. He was still almost sure that he had seen Court embrace the woman, and he was absolutely sure that he had seen his friend Rowland with his arms around Lindsay in a bedroom doorway—and now, with his whole heart, he wished to believe that both embraces were innocent. Concentrate, concentrate, he thought. He looked at his watch and found an impossibly short length of time had passed since he had slammed the door of Emily's apartment. He looked up at the dome, then down at the floor. Neither were securely themselves. I understand *nothing*. I am certain of *nothing*, he thought.

He moved toward the banister, gripping it tightly, and looked down. The air came rushing up at him. He began to understand that, for some time now, the Conrad had been stirring, and coming back to life.

He could sense its pulse now, and its intakes of breath. He found he could see a shape on the floor below, arms flung out, and a stain spreading. A man he knew was bending over that shape, and he could see people, emerging, merging, and milling back and forth. He could see a woman in a red dress, standing to one side at the foot of the stairs; his heart, in whose promptings he retained faith, told him this was the woman he loved and wished to make his wife.

He watched the man bending over the body rise to his feet

with a shake of his head; he watched this woman he loved turn away and cover her face with her hands.

This is happening and it is not happening, Colin thought, as he watched Rowland gently put his arms around Lindsay, and hold her against him for the second time that night.

Chapter 16

At four the following morning, Colin and Lindsay were finally able to leave the Conrad. They stepped out of the building into a hushed, near-silent Manhattan. The snow on the sidewalks was unbroken; there was a serene high moon, and each limb of the trees in Central Park was frosted silver.

"Oh, let's walk, Colin." Lindsay took his hand. "Let's walk. How quiet it is. . . ."

"You won't be too cold?"

"No. I need air and silence. And you must need them far more than I do."

Colin was indeed desperate for both. He took her arm in his; they crossed to the far side of the avenue, and began to walk south. Colin listened to the crunch of their footsteps; he glanced back at the trail they left in the fresh snow. Snow was continuing to fall, gently, as they walked, and it was already beginning to fur and obliterate the marks of their feet. Much preoccupied with death that evening, Colin thought of death as he walked. He and Lindsay were the same age—how many years or decades had they left? It was so important that they should waste none of this future time, he thought. He hoped they would be granted many years, but for all either of them knew, the time allotted might be short.

He could hear the wheels of Time's winged chariot very clearly tonight, but he heard them, he found, without fear. They concentrated the mind wonderfully; he drew Lindsay's small cold hand into the warmth of his overcoat pocket and clasped it tightly. He wondered if Lindsay could sense his thoughts, if she felt something similar. Looking at her quiet face, he felt that she might.

As they walked, the unusual quietness of the city began to calm him; he allowed his mind to consider the events of that long strange night. He thought of his still-unanswered proposal, of a death he had now decided *was* accidental, of the labor of his interviews with the police; the more accurate and factual his replies to their questions had been, the less accurate they felt. He still was not sure of the dead woman's name, he realized. He had still been trying to piece together her story and her connection to Tomas Court, when he had learned that she had an accomplice, and that this accomplice had been found when, at Tomas Court's suggestion, the tiny service room off the elevator shaft on the first floor had been searched.

A man—perhaps her brother; the police had seemed as uncertain as Colin—had been found. According to one of Colin's informants, he had been in a delusional state. According to another, the man, freaking out, had finally been yanked out of the tiny room gibbering about ghosts.

"So—was *he* Joseph King?" Colin had asked Tomas Court, as they sat together between police interviews.

"No." Court had given him one of his still, pale looks. "No, he was just her medium, if you like. He killed that tourist in Glacier. It was he who attacked me at my loft that time but his sister planned it, I think. Colin, don't worry about the details; they're not important, and they don't concern you. Let it go. Just tell the police what you saw and heard tonight."

Colin looked around the room where they were waiting. Its light was too bright. There was a clock on the wall, which Colin refused to look at. He had a strong sense that he and Court were outside time, outside place. Here, he found, he could ask Court anything, and Court would reply without evasion or deceit.

"Do you feel free, Tomas?" Colin had looked at his white, strained face with concern. "Do you feel free—now that she's dead?"

"Free?" Court considered; the concept of freedom seemed unfamiliar to him. "No, not really. I had hoped I might, but I can't erase the tapes, or forget those letters she wrote. I listened to those tapes once too often."

"I heard a bit of them." Colin colored. "That night with

Thalia, at your loft. They were still playing—and I couldn't find the off switch. . . ."

"Really? I usually used a remote."

"In the end, I couldn't bear it anymore. I just ripped the tape out of the machine. That stopped it."

"Did it?" Court gave a half smile. "And do you still remember what was said?"

"No, not really. I did for a bit, but it's worn off now. It was just pornography anyway. . . ."

"*Just* pornography?"

"All pornography's the same." Colin colored more deeply. "It's repetitious. I hate things like that."

" 'The road of excess leads to the palace of wisdom—' "

"What?"

"William Blake." Court gave a sigh. "It was one of King's favorite quotations, that. There were a lot of quotations. . . ." He turned and gave Colin a still, tired, and affectionate glance. "What a good decision I made when I hired you, Colin."

"I don't see why." Colin sank his head in his hands. "I've been a fucking disaster as far as I can see. I couldn't find you the right Wildfell Hall. I spent weeks sitting around saying 'but.' And tonight, I tried reasoning with a madwoman. I kept saying 'please' and 'don't do that.' It was the most fucking pathetic thing I've ever heard in my life."

"I wouldn't agree." Court frowned. "I could hear what you were saying as I came up the stairs. I knew it wouldn't work, but that wasn't the point. To the pure in heart, all things are pure—and besides, I think it had some effect. After all, she didn't stab Jonathan; she didn't jump; so maybe she did listen to you after all. . . ." His pale eyes rested on the wall opposite. He sighed. "You used the word 'wicked.' It's years since I've heard anyone use that word in its proper sense. Ah well." He touched Colin's arm briefly. "You're a very good location manager, Colin. Let's leave it at that."

Court had said nothing more. Colin had completed his police interviews, but had not seen Court again that night. In a state of glassy and unnatural calm, he had returned to Emily's apartment. There, he found Lindsay and Rowland waiting for him. Nic Hicks, to his relief, had already left; Henry Foxe had returned to his own apartment, it seemed, once he was sure that

Emily's collapse in her hallway was not, as had been feared, a heart attack.

Emily, Frobisher informed him, had been put to bed and was now asleep. Her three ancient indistinguishable friends, meanwhile, were preparing to depart. They had wanted to wait, it seemed, until Colin came back. Why they should have wished to do this, Colin could not conceive, since they seemed remarkably unconcerned as to that night's events. The eldest and frailest of the three was virtually blind, Colin realized, as she kissed him good night; all three lingered, and all three were *still* twittering on about the elevator. Finally, they wrapped themselves in their ancient moleskins and glided out. And Colin, finding himself alone with Lindsay and Rowland, had discovered that he knew what he had to do next.

"Rowland, could I have a word with you alone?" he said.

Lindsay at once rose, consternation on her face. She had been about to protest, Colin feared—but perhaps his determination communicated itself to her. She glanced from one man to the other, then, saying she would fetch her coat, quietly left.

The door closed behind her. As if from a great distance, Colin considered his friend. Rowland had risen, and his discomfiture was evident. Colin saw he was finding it difficult to meet his gaze, and this puzzled him for a second. He was not angry with Rowland, he realized. He did not feel angry, or jealous, or confused, or betrayed. He simply felt calm—and armed. Excalibur was in his hands, he thought.

"I have to say this, Rowland, and I have to say it now," he began, in a quiet voice. "There's been enough confusion and uncertainty tonight—"

"I wouldn't argue with that."

"I didn't realize until just before I saw you together in that doorway." Colin sighed. "That must seem stupid to you—but it wasn't stupidity. It wasn't even that I trusted you, so it never occurred to me you might lie. It was just that I was so happy, I couldn't see beyond the happiness—I think it was that."

"Colin, I regret this more than I can say. I want to explain— I'm entirely at fault here. . . ."

"Rowland, you're my friend." He paused. "I know you won't have done this lightly."

"No, I did not."

"You had three years, Rowland. You've known Lindsay three years. You could have acted at any point in those three years—and you didn't. Tell me why not. Was it her age?"

"Partly." Rowland looked away. "Also—"

"Tell me."

"Colin, I wasn't in love with her. I looked on her as a companion, a colleague, a friend. I came to love her—and that process, well, it had never happened to me before. I wasn't sure it was enough. I was very afraid of making a mistake and hurting her. I wasn't sure of her feelings either. Colin, I'm sorry. I can't discuss this."

"So when did it change? In Oxford—that lunch?"

"No, before. When she spoke to you on the telephone in Yorkshire; maybe before that. I thought of her, when I was away in Scotland. Colin, I don't *know*. . . ."

"You wouldn't make her happy, Rowland." Colin gave him an anxious look. "I think you'd end up making her very *un*happy. If I thought you'd make her happy, and go on doing so, I'd walk away from this myself—I promise you that. I'd remove myself from the scene with as much grace as I could muster and I'd go off and lick my wounds in private. I'd hate you for a bit, obviously, but that would wear off." He paused, his blue eyes resting on Rowland's troubled face. "But I would do it, Rowland. You see, I love her very much."

"I can see that." Rowland's expression hardened. "And now I'm supposed to act in a similarly noble way, is that the idea?"

"It's not noble. It's sensible."

"Since when has sense had anything to do with love?"

"It's the right thing to do." Colin's gaze also hardened. "I'm asking you, Rowland, to walk away from this. If you won't . . ." He sighed. "If you won't, I'll fight you every inch of the way, with every weapon at my disposal. But that would be the end of our friendship, and I'd like to avoid that."

There was a silence. Rowland turned away, with a sudden dismissive gesture.

"Your request is immaterial, as it happens," he said, "as Lindsay made very clear to me tonight."

As always, Colin thought, he disguised pain and uncertainty with curtness, with coldness; even when making an admission of defeat, Rowland could sound arrogant. The reply, which ought to have given Colin joy, did not. Looking at his friend, his calm and certitude began to ebb away. He could not believe in Rowland's rejection, he realized. Why would any woman turn Rowland down? In Colin's experience, no woman did— and this had never really surprised him, since he loved his friend, and admired him without reservation himself.

He looked at Rowland, so gifted in so many ways, not least in his looks, and suddenly he saw the hopelessness of his own case. Whatever Lindsay might have said to Rowland, it seemed inevitable to him that, faced with a choice between the two of them, she would choose Rowland. He himself had no weaponry at all, he thought, except love—and now, it seemed, Rowland could also give her that.

But for how long? Colin thought. Not—and of this he remained utterly certain—not for long enough.

"Rowland," he said, "please leave her be. Let her love me. I believe she could."

"Are you totally blind?" Rowland gave him an angry glance. "Use your *eyes*, Colin. She already does."

"What?" Colin said, staring at him, unable to believe his ears, feeling the beginnings of joy, of a most wonderful hope. He felt himself begin to blush—an affliction he had never been able to cure.

"Oh God, *God*," he heard himself say, discovering he was beginning to pace about. "Do you mean that? You really think that's true? Could it be? Why? Why? Rowland, you can't possibly be right—what could she see in me?"

"God alone knows," Rowland replied, frowning, then beginning to smile, as if despite himself. "You're bloody impossible, but presumably it can't be that. According to Markov, it's your hyacinthine hair. Oh, and your Apollonian body. That famous way you have with women. . . ."

"What? What are you talking about? I don't have a way with women—I never did. What's an Apollonian body, for God's sake?"

"I'm not too sure. Maybe it's your vast wealth. Have you told her about Shute?"

"Yes, yes—but it won't be that. It has to be something else. No, I think you've got it wrong, Rowland . . . Oh God, *God*. I'm going *mad*. I was just starting to *hope*. . . ."

Rowland hesitated. He gave Colin a long and considering look. With a sigh, he put his arm around his shoulders and pushed him toward the door.

"Colin, I wouldn't keep her waiting any longer if I were you. You'll find out the answers to your questions in due course, no doubt." He paused. "Are you sure you haven't been given them already?" His voice became dry. "As you may imagine, I was paying close attention. I'd have thought you'd been given your answers, Colin—judging from the way Lindsay was looking at you tonight."

Colin turned to look at him. Their eyes met, and Colin, who had never felt more grateful to Rowland than he did then, gave him a troubled look.

"I think that sometimes," he said, in a quiet voice, "sometimes—I have no doubts. She knows that I love her, of course. . . ."

"Colin—"

"And I know that she likes me. Tonight, she said such extraordinary things to me. And I felt so happy—but she said 'like.' She was very definite about it. And liking isn't enough."

"Colin, listen to me. I know Lindsay very well, and she's rather more careful with words than she appears to be. If that's what she said, there will have been a reason. She's impetuous *and* hesitant, you know. Give it *time*, Colin. Trust your instincts. I would—" He broke off. "What am I doing? I appear to be encouraging you. Why I should be doing that, in these circumstances, God alone knows. . . ."

"It's because we're friends," Colin said. "You like me even as a rival, and I like you even as a rival. You know that."

"I admire your ability to get your own way." Rowland gave him a considering look. "In fact, I sometimes think you're the most ruthless man I've ever known. As to liking . . ." He repressed a smile. "Go away, Colin, and don't push your luck."

Colin advanced as far as the door. He stopped and turned back.

"Advice," he said. "Rowland, I need *advice*. I mustn't mess this up. I have to get this *right*. . . ."

"Dear God, you are *unbelievable*." Rowland gave a groan. "You want *my* advice? *Now?*" He paused. "Very well, Colin, I'll give you my advice—and much good it may do you. Bear in mind my own record. Bear in mind the fact that I obviously don't understand women and never have. . . ."

"I'm sure that's not true, Rowland."

"Just don't waste any time, Colin, trying to work out their motivation, that's all. Don't assume that they are ever rational—they're not. Remember, they change their minds every five seconds. Remember, their requirements from a man tend to vary, so one moment they want a tyrant, and the next a Galahad. Remember they're quite keen on priests, father substitutes, son substitutes, brother substitutes, and grandfather substitutes for all I know. Remember their penchant for princes, and heroes. . . ."

"Hell. Rowland, are you sure about this? That rules me out then. . . ."

"And remember that quite a lot of the time, Colin," Rowland cast a suspicious eye upon him, "quite a lot of the time, I think they'd just settle for a man who was very very good in bed. . . ."

"No, no, no," Colin said, in a somewhat evasive way. "I'm sure you're wrong there, Rowland." He paused delicately. "Of course, I admit it would probably *help*. . . ."

"Who knows?" Rowland pushed him toward the door again. "I most certainly don't. Nor do I care anymore. As of now, I'm giving up the quest. I shall remain celibate. Solitude has always suited me. I shall live like a monk. . . ."

"I *slightly* doubt that, Rowland . . ." Colin had said. He had looked carefully at his friend. Rowland had other ways besides arrogance of disguising pain, he thought. And so, knowing how much it cost Rowland to turn the conversation in this way, and knowing why he did so, he had left.

Walking beside Lindsay now, with the Plaza in sight, Colin's heart lifted. He had known Rowland wished them to part without animosity or resentment; he had never seen better evidence of his acting ability, or his generosity, than he had then—and if that generosity came about only as a result of a rejection, well, he could forgive Rowland that. The question was, when Rowland spoke of Lindsay, had he been right?

He came to a halt at the corner of the park and turned Lindsay to face him. He watched the moonlight work its magic upon her face. It made her skin silver, it gave brilliancy and depth to her eyes; tiny crystals of snow clung to her hair and to her lashes. Looking at her, Colin felt a wash of desire and helpless love. Bending down to her, he kissed her lips, which felt warm, and which opened in a sweet, familiar way under his.

A thousand questions and hopes thronged in his mind, yet the instant he touched her they became immaterial. Who could define or explain love, he felt, looking down at her. If he had to say why he loved her, he could give a million answers, none sufficient and none exact.

He loved her because she made a day bright; because she made him laugh, and think; because she was truthful. He loved her because she was often muddled and confused, as he was; he loved her because, when he kissed her, her mouth was the way it was.

Lindsay, looking up at him, wished he would kiss her again, because when he kissed or touched her, she remembered who she was. As they had walked quietly together through the snow, it had come to her that she had made one decision correctly tonight, and that a second was easily made. Navigating here was less difficult than she imagined; there were reefs, it was true, but there might be a way of avoiding them—a way that had stolen into her mind in this quiet moonlit city as they walked.

"Can you wish on a full moon, or only on a new one, do you think, Colin?" she said, unfastening her coat and his, then moving inside it, so the warmth of her body was pressed against his.

"I'm sure you can," he replied. "I'm sure you can wish on the moon at any point in its cycle. It's a powerful planet."

Lindsay wished. She wished a momentous wish—but being practical, as well as superstitious, she had no intention of relying solely on supernatural forces. She rested her head against his chest and—the decision made—found herself at peace.

"I want you to know something," she said. "I know you saw me in that doorway with Rowland tonight. Did you ask him about that?"

"No. Not directly." He hesitated. "I would ask you, but I'm afraid to, I think."

"You have no reason to be afraid. I give you my word, Colin."

"Then I have no questions; they're all answered."

"I was saying good-bye to Rowland, and he to me. We were both leaving behind something that didn't happen. I can't explain it any other way. Can you understand that?"

"Of course."

"It was a final good-bye, Colin. Truly." Her eyes rested on his, then a glint of amusement came into them. "And it was a very *quiet* good-bye too, you should know. Marked by English understatement and English restraint."

Colin's face lit up. "I'm very glad about the restraint," he said, in a dry way. "If it had been unrestrained, I should have found it very hard to bear." He paused. "Just don't try saying good-bye to me, because I won't let you. Are you clear about that?"

"You sound very determined."

"I am very determined. I've learned a lot tonight. Never waste time—you might have very little left. Besides . . ." He took her hand and they began walking again. "Don't forget all those ancestors of mine. English and American. I have centuries of ruthless self-interest in my veins, Lindsay. Never forget that."

"Ah, yes, those ancestors," Lindsay said, as they were about to cross Central Park South. "I'd forgotten about them and all those riches of yours. Ah well, I forgive you for them. I can love you despite them, I expect. . . ."

Colin stopped dead in the middle of the road. He went white. "What did you just say? What did you just say?"

"I used a four-letter word," Lindsay replied. "I'm sorry about that. . . ."

"Say it again!" Colin made a grab at her. "Say it again, loudly, at once, without equivocation. . . ."

"I shall whisper it," Lindsay said, pulling him toward the hotel entrance. "First we have to go upstairs, then I have to call my son, then I have to wash and undress. . . ."

Colin groaned.

"Then maybe I'll admit it. I'll slip it into the conversation . . . when we're in bed."

They were in their room, and in their bed, with great speed.

The call to Oxford was made, but it was brief. There was no conversation—or need for it. Lindsay's confession, which Colin extracted with some ruthlessness, was made, she later claimed, *in extremis*—this being a phrase, she added, that she knew Colin would not need her to translate.

As Colin and Lindsay, that morning, finally slept, Jippy got up. He tiptoed out of the bedroom, where Markov lay dreaming, and crept into the living room beyond. He had spent a night without sleep, watching the flux of future events. This process, Jippy felt, was akin to the processing of photographs. When he helped Markov develop his film, and in particular when he worked with the delicate techniques needed for silver prints, it delighted him that an image could be stored, invisible to the human eye, on paper. He loved to watch the pictures-to-be as they lay in the baths of developing fluid. He loved watching them slowly emerge, as mere shapes and outlines at first, then, gradually, as shapes that had content and could be read.

Sometimes if errors had been made, this process remained incomplete—and sometimes Jippy would deliberately lift the picture from the developing fluid too soon, because he liked suggestions and hints better than exactitude. To glimpse the future, he felt, was like this. He was rarely, virtually never, shown a clear image—although, in the Plaza the previous night, he had been shown just that.

For this Jippy was grateful. To see the future, even a suggestion of the future, was terrifying. Few could live their lives with any tranquillity, he believed, if they could see what lay ahead.

Today, seeing the possible future and hating it, he had decided on a spell. Jippy had only intermittent faith in his spells, most of which had been taught him as a child by his Armenian grandmother. He suspected she had muddled the spells in the first place, and that his own memory of them was imperfect at best. Nevertheless, he intended to try. For Pascal Lamartine, he could do nothing; for Lindsay, whom he knew well, intervention might be possible, and since he loved Lindsay and could see the urgency of intervention, he had decided to do the spell now, at dawn—a powerful moment, his grandmother always said.

He decided to do it on the kitchen table, which was next to a window facing east. On the empty surface of this wooden table, he assembled the objects he needed. He laid down a hair, which he had removed from Lindsay's coat when he kissed her good-bye the previous night. Next to the hair, and for want of anything else, he placed a postcard Lindsay had sent him some time before, when she and Markov were away in Thailand on a fashion shoot. The postcard showed a glittery pagoda, and the message was brief: "Today Markov and I came here and were given a lotus flower. It is like an artichoke, only prettier. Markov misses you badly. I send love."

This, if characteristic, was less than ideal, but it would have to suffice. He rummaged around in the pantry, and eventually settled for a packet of muesli—again, less than ideal, but it contained nuts and grains, and they had some powers, of course. Jippy sprinkled the muesli in a lopsided circle, centered the hair and the postcard inside it, and then, after further consideration, placed next to them an orange and an egg. The egg kept rolling around, so eventually he put it in an eggcup and surveyed his handiwork. It was not impressive, and its lack of symmetry offended him. He decided to add a second egg, also in an eggcup, and resisted the impulse to arrange these objects in the vague shape of a face.

He glanced toward the window; the sky was lightening and he knew he had to be quick. The orange kept rolling around in an unstable way, and this made his hands start to shake. "Stay s-s-*still*," he whispered, as the orange threatened to roll out of the circle. The orange obeyed and Jippy felt a little happier.

From the pocket of his neat striped pajamas, he took out the small bent coin his grandmother had once given him—a rare coin, this—and placed it in the circle, between the orange and the eggs.

Then he knelt down, rested his forehead against the edge of the table, and waited. He muttered under his breath. He watched thin sharp winter sun strike the edge of the window frame and the edge of the sink. As it slowly began to reach the table, and his circle of objects grew bright, Jippy began on his special prayer of benevolence.

Jippy prayed this prayer with absolute concentration. He gave it every ounce of his energy. When he was on line, the sweat began to run down his body, and his feet and hands began to twitch like a dog dreaming. Halfway through the spell, finding he was afraid, he left out one vital phrase and had to go back. He asked the spirits—politely; his grandmother had always emphasized the importance of politeness—to avoid the certain evil he had glimpsed the previous night; to make the unlikely, likely; to bend, twist, distort and reassemble events, and having done so, to reorganize them so they were sweet to the eye and the heart. Jippy knew this was well within the powers of these spirits; they did that sort of thing a hundred times a day, on a whim, on a flick of the wrist.

In a humble way—humility was also a wise tactic, his grandmother said—Jippy asked these spirits to employ their artistry. He said this several times, emphasizing the point, because the spirits, on occasion, could be tired or bored, and could simply botch the job, then walk away from it. Jippy did not want botching here—he feared it. He wanted perfect joinery; he wanted a seamless finish. The capricious spirits appeared to listen to this.

To listen, however, was not enough. Jippy redoubled his efforts. He lapsed; he went down, down, down into some strange liquid, swirling space, where he swam back and forth, back and forth. In this space, his spell came to an end. All the words were used up. There, Jippy found he was very afraid; it was so hot it was cold; he started shivering and panting—and it was in this state that Markov found him.

Markov stared at him in panic; Jippy was lying on the kitchen floor, twitching. An epileptic fit, Markov thought. Jippy's eyes were shut tight and there was foam on his lips. Giving a cry, Markov fell to his knees and put his arms around him. He lifted him up, then found Jippy was too heavy to move. He almost fell over; he started shouting Jippy's name and kissing his face. He tried to remember what you did if someone had a fit—but was this a fit? "Darling, darling, darling," he said, clasping Jippy's hands. He tried to find a pulse and could not find one. Jippy seemed not to be breathing. Frantic now, he laid him back down on the floor, and in the wrong way, at the wrong angle, placed his mouth on Jippy's mouth. He breathed air into him. He started counting, realized he did not know why he was counting, and breathed again. He had begun to cry, and his tears ran down onto Jippy's white face. "Please, please, please, please," he said. He breathed a third breath and Jippy's eyes opened.

"W-what are you d-doing?" he said, and sprang to his feet. He made a grab at the table, which Markov was about to knock over, and Markov, feeling foolish, slowly rose to his feet. He looked at the table, at a ring of muesli, a postcard, a human hair, a coin, two eggs and an orange. Jippy was looking at this orange in consternation. The eggs were fine; the hair and the postcard and the coin were fine; the orange, probably thanks to Markov's ministrations, and kickings out, was inside the circle still—but only just.

"I thought you were dead," Markov said. "I was giving you mouth-to-mouth."

"W-well, you n-nearly ruined the whole th-thing," Jippy said, somewhat crossly. "It's very d-delicate."

Markov was hurt. "Jippy," he said, "these goddamn spells of yours do not work. They have never worked and they are never *going* to work. Those spells are a load of *baloney*."

Jippy, who did not agree with him in this case, gave him a calm look.

"Th-this is for Lindsay," he said, "and it *is* going to work."

"For Lindsay?" Markov looked at the assemblage with more interest. "Explain," he said.

Jippy explained. Markov paled, then nodded, then frowned, then, smiling, raised his eyebrows.

"Well, well, *well!*" he said. "Stranger than fiction! Who'd have believed it?"

Markov himself did not believe it, but he did not want to hurt Jippy, so he kissed him. "Now come and look at the news on TV," he added. "You were certainly right about the Conrad, darling. Updates every half hour, and paparazzi positively crawling all over the place. . . ."

The Conrad, Juliet McKechnie discovered, was crawling with paparazzi, and with police. Arriving there at seven in the morning, having failed to get through to Natasha on the telephone, she then experienced considerable difficulty in gaining admission to the building. When she finally did, she found the elevator was back in service.

"You can't see her," Angelica said to Juliet, in a sullen way, opening the door to Natasha's apartment. "She's sedated. She's not seeing anybody."

"Then I shall wait until she is ready to see me."

Juliet, who disliked Angelica intensely, and who knew her dislike was returned, gave her a dismissive glance and walked past her. She went through into the white living room, and sat down.

"Angelica, I know perfectly well that Natasha *won't* be sedated. It's difficult to persuade her to take aspirin. So don't waste my time, please."

"She's upset. Distraught." Angelica glowered at her. "Most people wouldn't need to be told that."

"That's precisely why I'm here. She will need me."

"What she *needs* is sleep, rest, and peace and quiet."

Juliet gave her a cold glance; she was not a woman who wasted time arguing with those she disliked, and her upbringing had taught her that under no circumstances did one argue with servants.

"I do *not* understand . . ." she said, frowning around the room, "how any of this could have happened. It's appalling. Is Jonathan all right?"

"He's better now." Angelica's face softened. "He was frightened out of his wits. But the doctor came. He quieted down eventually. . . ."

"Where's his father?"

"I wouldn't know," Angelica replied, her tone suggesting she did not greatly care either. Her face became set. "He had to talk to the police—him and that Englishman who was with him when she fell. He took off for Tribeca. Knowing him, he'll be working."

"At a time like this?"

"At any time. He's like that."

Juliet considered this information, and her dislike for Tomas Court deepened.

"If I'd been here," Angelica said suddenly, her face reddening, "it would never have happened. She wouldn't have got past *me*. I'd have cut her throat for her. Strangled her with my bare hands. That's what I'd have done."

Juliet looked at her heavy bulk, at her small black eyes, and the hate in her face; she could well believe this flat and definite statement.

"I don't understand . . ." she said, "how she managed any of it. Where were the bodyguards? What in hell was that stupid Texan doing?"

"Natasha gave him the night off." Angelica's expression became evasive. "She didn't want anyone here, not him, not me. I said I'd stay, but no, she wasn't having it. . . . She didn't want people around—you know, when *he's* here. She doesn't like people to see—it upsets her, the way he talks to her."

Juliet digested this interesting information also. She might have liked to question Angelica further on that subject; unfortunately her upbringing had taught her not to listen to servants' gossip, either. She considered the hulking, handsome Texan bodyguard, whose blond, muscled good looks and constant presence had always annoyed her.

"So where's that ridiculous Texan now?" she said. "I blame him for this. It was a rank dereliction of his duties. No matter what Natasha said, he should have *insisted*. What's he doing now? Running around shutting the stable door after the horse has bolted?"

Angelica shot her a small black glance. She smiled. "*Maybe* he's busy shutting doors," she said, an odd gloating note entering her voice. "I wouldn't know. He's around here somewhere. I saw him talking to the police. . . ." She paused. "Mind you, that was hours ago. . . ."

"Well, I hope Natasha dispenses with his services. She won't need them now in any case. . . ."

"You think so?" Angelica smiled again. "You could be right. Natasha might want him to stay around though. She's been very satisfied with him—the way he performs his duties. Always vigilant. Never lets up . . ." She paused, her small black eyes resting on Juliet's face with detectable malice. "You really want me to tell Natasha you're here? You want me to do it right now?"

"Yes, I do." Juliet gave her a cold look. "And when you've done that, you can bring me some strong black coffee, please. And while you're about it, an ashtray."

The eyes of the two women intersected. Angelica left the room. She was frightened of Juliet McKechnie—but she had additional reasons now for obeying her. She made a brief call on the internal line from the kitchen, replacing the receiver after the telephone in Natasha's room upstairs had rung only twice. She began to prepare coffee; she watched the percolator begin to bubble. Then, despite explicit instructions to the contrary from Natasha, instructions given her only a few hours previously, she opened the jib door as she had been longing to do, and in a state of mounting excitement, began to climb the staircase.

She padded silently along the upper corridor, pausing by the sheet closets. The door to Natasha's bedroom was closed; she listened to silence. She then padded quietly to the end of the corridor, and Jonathan's room. He had received a mild sedative, even if his mother had not; he was now sleeping peacefully. Angelica looked down at him with pride and love; she tucked the duvet more securely around him, kissed his flushed cheek, and touched the dressing that had been applied to the knife cut.

Love and fear for him rose up in her heart with such force that she felt almost dizzy. She straightened up, pressing her hand against her chest, as her heart began to hammer painfully. Angelica had never carried a child, but this boy, whom she had nursed from birth, she loved with a mother's intensity. Tears came to her black eyes. Making a small crooning sound, she tucked his favorite bear more securely in his arms and padded from the room. Bitch, bitch, bitch, she muttered to herself. *Dead* bitch, she corrected herself, thinking of the sheeted shape she had seen on her return to the Conrad. Well, my curses surely worked, she said to herself, and feeling a dark exultation, her breath coming faster now, she padded through into the small sitting room.

This room, as she had expected, had been used. She looked at the crumpled cushions on the couch; she looked at the two glasses on the nearby table. Natasha drank wine; the Texan bodyguard favored tequila. She picked up the glasses in turn and sniffed them. One smelled of red wine; the other—and she tasted it to make sure—contained a few droplets of water.

She stared at this glass, the blood rising up and darkening her face. She looked at the other clues here: a pair of Natasha's pretty shoes lay kicked aside near the couch; on the carpet next to them, she saw, was a string of pearls. Stooping to pick them up—they were valuable—she saw their clasp was broken and the pearls were unraveling. A cascade of seed pearls fell from the end of the silk stringing. She weighed the fatter pearls in her palm; she rubbed them back and forth between her fingers. Making a small grunting sound, she bent and groped for the lost pearls and found them secreted in a fold in the couch's upholstery. Her breathing had become shallow and rapid; the clasp to these pearls had not been broken when she helped fasten them around Natasha's neck the previous evening.

Dropping the pearls, she pressed her hands over her mouth. She felt dizzy again, and she had never felt heavier, bulkier, slower. Her heart was now pounding and her head was swimming with blood. "No, no, no," she said, under her breath, rocking back and forth. She looked at the scattered pearls, and then turned, clumsily, knocking over one of the glasses. She stumbled across the room, then, slowing, crept along the corridor. She stopped at Natasha's door, her heart thumping, and pressed her ear against its panels.

She could not hear properly. Her heart was banging too loudly, and there was another noise, a sighing and a susurration, a tidal sound, like waves beating upon a beach. She shook her head, as if to clear her ears of water, and the sound increased in volume. It began to beat on her with a mounting rhythmic insistence. She pressed her hands against her hot face, and then over her mouth, to stop herself from crying out. She knew what she was hearing now: she was hearing a mystery, a rite to which she had herself never been admitted. Of its details, she was ignorant, since she had never had a lover, male or female. Even so, she knew what was happening on the other side of that door. She knew who these lovers were, and she could see and hear what they did with the hot clarity of a vision: the moistness of it; the touchings and whisperings; the mounting urgency; the seeking mouths; the desperation. She began to tremble violently; a low sound of rage escaped her lips as she heard the groan and the cry that marked the crucial moment of union.

She backed away from the door and pressed herself back against the wall, covering her ears with her hands. She turned her face to the wall; through the wall she could sense violence, secrets and pleasure; she trembled at the force of this *thing*, this force, which excited, shamed, and angered her, and which she thought of as a violation. It went on and on, for a longer time than she would have believed possible. It was like listening to a killing; then, with some guttural extreme sound from the man, and some strange drowning yet victorious cry from the woman, it was over.

Angelica waited. Gentler sounds came from beyond the door now. She wiped away her tears. She wiped the envy, outrage, and anger from her face; she waited until her breathing quieted and the hot flush of excited shame subsided, then she crossed to the door and rapped on its panels. She gave the message she had been told to give, and after a delay—an insolent, careless delay—the door opened a fraction.

Angelica was given a tiny glimpse of the devastation wrought to the room the previous night, a devastation that Natasha and her partner were blind to, she presumed—unless, she realized, it suited them. Then Natasha Lawrence interposed her body. She stood there, wrapped in a loose, thin, white robe, the door open only a crack, looking at Angelica. As Angelica well knew, Natasha Lawrence, though gentle, could be cruel—and this capacity in her had always intensified Angelica's devotion. There was cruelty now in the way she flaunted her state, Angelica found. The expression in her eyes, dreamy, sated, yet faintly amused, cut Angelica to the heart. She knew at once that, while her position in this household was safe, that look was a form of dismissal.

Natasha made no attempt to disguise the fact that this was an unwelcome interruption. Her black hair, loose on her shoulders, was damp with sweat. There were vivid marks on her pale throat; she was breathing rapidly, her lips parted as if in expectation of more kisses. Color stained her cheeks, and her eyes, liquid, brilliant, seemed to rest on Angelica, yet look beyond her to further pleasures. The thin robe, carelessly clasped at the waist, was neither properly wrapped around her, nor fastened. Angelica could see the roundness of her breasts and the hard points of her nipples; she could see her slender bare feet and glimpse her pale slender thighs. Her thighs were wet, Angelica saw, and the thin material of the robe adhered to this seeping, spreading dampness.

She was being shown sex, Angelica realized. With pain, she also realized that Natasha enjoyed showing her this, and that the demonstration was both deliberate and careless. It seemed to her that Natasha wished to exult, yet was ultimately indifferent to her reaction. She wondered if this exhibition was intended to evoke desire—as it certainly did—or whether it could be a warning, an instruction to observe her place from now on, and accept her exclusion from these precincts. Whatever the reason for this manifestation, Natasha's beauty, at that moment, burned her. To Angelica she looked like a goddess.

"Tomas will come down," she said, giving a small sigh. "Angelica, tell Juliet that Tomas will be down directly."

This information proved inexact; Tomas Court did come downstairs—but he did so one hour later.

"Would you mind not smoking?" he said in a polite way to Juliet, moving across the white room and opening the window. "Angelica brought you coffee? Good. Now—how can I help you?"

Juliet slowly turned her azure eyes upon him. Angelica had said nothing of his presence in the apartment—her motive no doubt malice. Tomas Court's arrival came as a complete surprise to her. Having met him in person only once before, at the Foxe party the previous evening, Juliet now saw the necessity for examining him a great deal more closely. She measured his height and build; she noted that he had calculated—and she was sure of the calculation—that his appearance would impart its own message. His demeanor was that of the husband, at ease in a familiar home; it was also—and markedly so—that of the lover.

He was dressed in the manner of a man who had thrown on his clothes in haste. He was unshaven, and as he moved past her, she realized he was also unwashed. A faint but unmistakable scent reached her nostrils; she understood that he had been careful to come downstairs with the smell of sex still on his body.

She felt jealousy and pain at once. Seeing he was watching her face for just such a reaction, she gave him none.

"You can't help me," she replied coldly. "I want to see Natasha. Does she know I'm here?"

"Yes, I'm afraid she does."

"Well, *I'm* afraid I'll just have to wait until she's ready to see me."

"As you wish," he replied quietly.

Juliet's mouth tightened. That brief exchange told her a great deal—not least that Tomas Court now knew of her relationship with Natasha. It had not taken him long to extract that confession, she thought; then she realized that, in a polite way, he had also rebuked her.

"I came when I saw the news on TV," she said at once. "I wanted to say—I am very sorry for you both. It was a terrible thing. . . ."

"Terrible things happen."

"Is your son recovering?"

"I hope so. He is sleeping now. The doctor will be calling in again later. He wasn't physically harmed, apart from a small cut. But the shock—you can imagine. . . ."

He paused, then, as if coming to a decision, sat down opposite her on the white couch; Juliet wondered if he knew it was a couch she had chosen.

"I think it will be very good for Jonathan to get away from this place," he continued, in a deliberate way. "I'm sure it will help him to spend the next three months in England. Natasha too, obviously . . ."

Not a man who wasted time, Juliet thought—and that remark had been a throwing down of the gauntlet.

"I'm sure," she replied, in a cool way. "You've decided not to postpone then?"

"I won't alter my plans."

"Really? I'd have thought Natasha might need time to recover."

"Natasha is resilient. Very."

Juliet flushed. She could hear the warning in that quiet remark; it was meant to suggest a more intimate knowledge of Natasha than her own, and that angered her. Meeting his gaze squarely, she said, "Are you flaunting something? It isn't necessary. I always knew that Natasha would be away with you for three months while you made this movie. I'm prepared for that."

"Are you?"

His expression, to her surprise, became one of sympathy. He

rose and began to move about the room. He reached out and straightened a picture. His manner, Juliet noted, remained calm and considering.

"It's a very good part for Natasha," he remarked, after some minutes of silence. "Tell me, did she show you my script?"

"No," Juliet replied, knowing he would see this as an admission of weakness. "I have read the novel, however, and I wouldn't share your view about Natasha's part. I disliked this Helen Huntingdon she's going to play. A pious, possessive, masochistic woman."

"I agree, particularly as the novel progresses. There's an irresolution on the author's part, I feel. She gives us glimpses of a far more interesting woman. She placates the conventions of her time, while also challenging them." He gave her a somewhat bored glance. "In any case, the novel is an irrelevance really. I do not make adaptations. I dislike the Brontë output on the whole, with the exception of one novel—not this one, as it happens—and I have never subscribed to all that hysterical Brontë worship. Emily excepted, the Brontës wrote women's novels."

"I certainly hope so," said Juliet.

"My script bears little relation to the novel, in any case. I've made drastic changes. I've altered the end completely. . . ."

"Have you also altered the husband's part?" Juliet put in, coldly. "I'm sure you'll have made that a great deal more sympathetic."

"I've insured it's played by a great actor." He gave a shrug. "That will make a difference, of course. And yes, the character is certainly changed. As to sympathy—I'm not interested in evoking sympathy. That is always easy to do—quickly and cheaply."

"How very arrogant you are." Juliet rose. "I knew you would be, of course. I detest men like you. Why didn't you bother to wash before you came downstairs? I don't smell victory, if that's what you're hoping. Conquest, possibly. I'd rather wait here alone, if you don't mind."

"That is your prerogative."

He turned his pale steady gaze upon her. Again Juliet had the disconcerting feeling that the only emotions he felt for her

were curiosity and sympathy. His refusal to betray the least
indication of anger, uncertainty, or jealousy enraged her.

"May I say something, though, before I go? You may feel
that you know my wife—"

"I know that I know her, and she is not your wife; you
should remember that she's your *ex*-wife."

"I never think of her in that way. If you asked Natasha, I suspect she would tell you that she never thinks of me as her ex-
husband, either. Never mind that. Were you ever married?"

"Yes, once."

"Then you will know, every marriage is a secret shared by
two people. It's unwise for any outsider to assume they know
that secret. I'd prefer you to be spared the ordeal of a long
humiliating wait, so I'd suggest, for your own sake, that you
leave here now."

"I'll wait until Natasha asks me to leave. This is her apartment, not yours."

"As you wish." He gave a sigh. "She won't come down, you
know."

"I don't believe that. She wouldn't do that—"

"I think you'll find that she will."

He spoke quietly and with total certainty. So authoritative
was his tone that Juliet, for the first time, felt doubt. Instantly,
she was less composed; her voice rose as she replied, and she
regretted this, but could not prevent it.

"If Natasha does not come down," she said, "it will be
because you are here. You're obsessed with controlling her.
You aren't satisfied with controlling her work, you have to control her life as well. She's frightened of you. You bully her."

"Is that what you think?" He looked surprised. "I thought
you were more intelligent. Don't you find that scenario a little
glib? Simplistic? Is Natasha really such a poor thing? I don't
believe so." He paused. "I begin to see—you don't really know
her at all, do you? Have you ever seen Natasha when she's
working?"

"I've seen her onstage, yes. Many times."

"That wasn't really what I meant; then you're watching a
finished performance. If you had watched Natasha put that performance together, piece by piece . . ." He gave her a steady
look. "Working with my wife is a very interesting process. Her

approach is the very opposite of my own. She is oblique, timid, instinctual, and emotional; I am none of those things. She swerves in on her target, whereas I track it in a controlled, planned way. Yet she hits that target, time after time after time. . . ." He paused. "So I have come to see, Natasha's attack is every bit as carefully planned as my own—but being a woman, she prefers to disguise that. On set, obviously, I give Natasha direction. I can assure you, on set and off, she submits to direction only if she wants to do so. And sometimes she contrives it so that the direction I give her is the direction she has been secretly desiring."

There was a silence. Juliet met that pale gaze. She did not like the information he was giving her, and she did not like that word "submit," either. She suspected he had intended it to cause a specific unease—and if so, he had succeeded.

As she stood looking at him, weighing the implications of his words, she became aware, for the first time, of the background noises in the room, the clickings, creakings, and shiftings that, in her experience, were always to be sensed at the Conrad. A radiator made a faint sound; a voice filtered into the room from the stairs. It was brought home to her, with sudden force, that a woman had been killed in this building the previous night.

She found herself looking at Tomas Court's hands; her throat had become dry; he had strong square hands, of some beauty. Suddenly, information rushed at her. She had been telling herself that Court's presence here could be explained, that if he had been admitted to Natasha's room now, it was because, after the night's events, she was afraid and desperate for consolation or protection. Now she saw that supposition was wrong; she knew it with every instinct in her body. Court's sexual reunion with his wife had another explanation—and it was one she had no wish to examine.

"It's a little hot in here, don't you find?" he said.

"A little, yes," Juliet replied, moving farther away from him. "I'll ask Angelica to turn down the thermostat."

He removed his jacket as he said this, and rolled back his shirtsleeves. Juliet saw—and knew he intended her to see—that he had a scratch on his inner arm. He had read her mind,

Juliet thought, and he was now answering an unspoken question. She looked at the scratch, which ran from elbow to wrist. Since she had a similar scratch on her own back, she knew precisely who had made it and in exactly what circumstances.

"You've injured yourself," she said.

"The injury was not self-inflicted."

"Your marriage is *over*," she said, paling with anger. "It was over before you divorced. It's *finished*."

"You would want to believe that, of course." He paused; for the first and only time she saw his equilibrium threatened. "I wouldn't deny there's been pain in my marriage. Considerable pain is involved—and that pain is mutual."

"I'm not discussing pain—of any sort—with you," Juliet said sharply. She moved farther away. "I'm aware of your interest in the subject. It's apparent—only too apparent—in every one of your damned movies."

"True, true." He gave her a pale glance. "But I do at least avoid the banalities of pain, you know. Give me credit for that. You won't find whips or masks in any of my movies. That kind of tawdry game doesn't interest me remotely. . . ." He paused. "Nor, in case you're wondering, does it interest Natasha."

He bent and picked up his jacket. Juliet, uneasy and distressed, looked at him with loathing. He was intensely male, she found; the fact that even she was aware of his sexuality made her violently angry. She was beginning to see that Natasha might desire and fear this man—or desire him *because* she feared him. That idea sickened her; of that need, Natasha could be cured, she told herself. Giving Court a glance of defiance, she returned to her chair and sat down again. This, she was glad to see, annoyed him.

"Shall I tell you why you're wasting your time here?" he said. "And why my wife will not come down to see you, however long you wait?"

"Natasha will come down. She loves me."

"Perhaps, to an extent. There is one requirement, however— and in your case, it's missing."

Juliet gave him a look of disbelief and scorn.

"Oh, please," she said, "don't tell me you're *that* stupid. Believe me, that particular lack is an advantage, as Natasha has often told me."

"Has she? Well, my wife will always try to be gentle, but I'm afraid you misunderstand." He paused. "There is one difference between you and me, and it has nothing to do with gender. You cannot hurt Natasha, you see, whereas I can. And my wife retains the ability to hurt me. She is the only woman who has ever had that ability—and don't smile, no man has it either."

"I wasn't smiling. I don't view the ability to cause pain as a distinction."

"Then we differ." He gave her a quiet glance. "And now, if you'll forgive me, I have to work. I'm going down to my loft in Tribeca. You're sure you won't let me see you out, drop you off somewhere?"

"No. And I find it astonishing you can even consider working at such a time—"

"Oh, I can always work." His pale eyes rested steadily on her face. "No matter the circumstances. The work, ultimately, is the only thing of any importance."

"Another male boast." Juliet returned his look coldly. "If your son had died last night, would you be working this morning?"

"No." His gaze moved away from hers and came to rest on the blank wall opposite. "But next week I should have worked, or the week after."

His tone reproached Juliet, who at once regretted her remark.

"That wouldn't be true of Natasha," she said slowly, considering him. "If anything happened to Jonathan it would destroy her."

"I think so too. I believe that is the one difference between us." He paused. "Now I must go. I'm glad to have met you."

With that—and Juliet sensed he meant his final remark—he left. Still angry and discomposed, she remained in the room. She sat there for four hours, trying to understand the information she had been given, and the information she was certain he had withheld.

Several times she rose to her feet, intent on going upstairs and confronting Natasha. Each time, realizing that such a confrontation at such a moment was unthinkable, she sat down again. As Tomas Court had predicted, she began to feel a pained humiliation. When she could endure that no longer, she left.

She called many times over the following weekend, to find all calls fielded by a machine or a surly Angelica. Not one of her calls was returned and, subsequently, not one of her letters was answered.

She suffered, but less than she would have when younger, she told herself. Refusing to speculate any further on the nature of the bond that held Court and Natasha together, it came to be her view that Natasha had accepted her husband's aegis—an error fatal in its consequences, she believed, and one made by too many women. She wrote no more letters, and in this way, with many questions left unresolved, she came to accept that the Conrad chapters of her life, as she now thought of them, were over.

Being a resilient woman, she determined not to look back, but to close the book on the entire episode; in her experience, such ends were always best viewed as a new beginning.

Part Seven

ADVENT

Chapter 17

"I'm going to show you the south front first," said Colin.

"Where is it? Where is it?" said Lindsay.

"You can't see it yet. Wait until we come out of the wood. You'll see it clearly from the deer park. . . ." Colin hesitated. "That is, well, it's not much of a park. More a sort of field, really."

It was going to be a *park*; Lindsay knew that immediately. She could hear the anxiety and hope in Colin's voice; she now knew what to expect when Colin began on qualifications and understatements. It was going to be a park, a huge park, a *demesne*, a place of appalling perfection. She had encountered this park in innumerable films and novels, and in her mind's eye, she could see it already.

It had been landscaped by Capability Brown, or some similar man of genius. It would declare at a glance the mastery of his vision, his gift for disguising artifice, and his sublime use of asymmetry.

There would be *oaks*. She could see these oaks now, in their venerable majesty; she could see not grass but ancestral greensward, descending from the brink of the house to the brink of some lake, a lake created two hundred years before (or thereabouts; she was not too sure of the exact dates here), a lake that now looked as if the hand of God had put it there.

She was sure that, on the far side of that lake, there would be some quaint temple, the vista toward which, and from which, would have been contrived with eighteenth-century grace, wit, and decorum. She was afraid of this temple, this lake, these oaks, and this greensward. She was afraid of any property large enough to boast a park, and she was terrified of the house at the heart of it. The reason for this fear was simple: she feared temple, lake, greensward, oaks, park, house, because they belonged to Colin.

For the past two days, she had been trying to persuade Colin to describe his house—forewarned is forearmed, she had told herself. She had tried on the long overnight flight from New York, which they had taken that Friday; she had tried in her London apartment, to which they had returned from the airport in Colin's extraordinary car, the most powerful she had ever driven in. She had tried on the highway down here, and when they finally arrived—not at some country inn, that plan had changed, but at Shute Farm—she had tried again.

Not at first. She had been so entranced by the farmhouse, which proved even lovelier than it had seemed in photographs, that for some time she had forgotten Shute Court altogether. Colin had somehow ensured that the farmhouse had been made ready for them; they could spend this night there, he had suggested. Some fairy had been in, Lindsay felt, forgetting the magic wand of money. This benevolent personage had lit the fires, polished and cleaned, made up the brass bed with lavender-scented sheets, and left food and wine for them. Even the lights had been left on, so, as Colin's great car purred and bumped its way up a rutted track, and she saw the house for the first time through the gathering dusk of a winter's afternoon, its lighted windows seemed to welcome them.

With excitement and delight, Lindsay had rushed from room to room, while Colin pointed out to her its various architectural features. Lindsay loved its wide-boarded, uneven oak floors, which reminded her of the deck of a ship. She loved its beams and low doorways, which meant Colin constantly had to duck his head. She loved its old and twisting stairs, the soft honey stone of its lintels, and the kitchen, with its scrubbed floor, warm range, rag rugs, dresser, and array of blue-and-white china dishes.

Such was her delight that it was a while before she noticed that Colin was becoming quieter and quieter. The more she exclaimed and praised, the unhappier he became—and Lindsay, realizing the reason for this, blushed guiltily at her own stupidity and was silenced. Colin, after all, did not want her to live here. He wanted her to live in Shute Court, and—although that issue remained unresolved between them, Lindsay not answering his proposal and Colin not pressing her—she could understand that he now felt it was a mistake to have brought her here. He had not foreseen the extent to which this place, small and humble no doubt by his standards, would please her.

Later that evening, still feeling an unaccountable residual anxiety for Tom, she telephoned him at his Oxford lodgings. But Tom, deep in an essay on Nietzsche, claimed he was too busy to talk, and too busy to see her for the next few days. Lindsay, who had been longing to see him, resigned herself to this; over dinner, she began on her questions about Shute again. Colin could not be persuaded to describe his house, however; he admitted it was large—well, quite large; beyond that, not one word could she prize from him.

As the hour grew later, and outside, owls called to each other, she began to suspect that Colin had further plans for that night, which he had not disclosed to her. Lindsay was drawn to that brass bed, in that blue painted bedroom; for once, Colin showed no haste to be there. They sat in front of the wood fire, in the small beamed living room, drinking a delicious wine that Colin said was a Bordeaux, and Lindsay kept calling a burgundy. As midnight approached, Colin grew more and more tense; his face became pale and fixed and his replies increasingly distracted.

Eventually, as midnight struck, he rose to his feet, and taking her hand, pulled her upright.

"It's Sunday now," he said. "It's the first Sunday in Advent. I'm going to show you Shute now. I want—I'd like you to see it by moonlight."

Lindsay was moved by his expression and by the fact that he had evidently planned this. Had she ever doubted how much this meant to him, those doubts would have vanished now. She had never seen him more serious; she could sense his agitation and she could see his determination to conceal it.

It was cold outside; the air was fresh and still, and a light rain was falling. They put on coats and boots and scarves. Colin took her hand in his and, as before, held it inside his coat pocket. They set off down the track from the house, Colin refusing to use a flashlight. Her eyes would grow used to the darkness, he said, and Lindsay, unused to walking in the dark anywhere, and certainly unused to walking in the dark in the country, found this was so. The moon, high, round, and seeming to be in constant motion as small clouds moved across its face, gave easily enough light. There was no color; it was like walking through a negative. The moon silvered the track ahead of them and gave to the familiar—a hedge, a post—a fleeting, fluctuating shape she found restful. Above them, there was a myriad of stars; the only sound was their footsteps and the calling of the owls. The air smelled of earth, of the rain, and of woodsmoke. Lindsay felt tranquillity steal into her mind; the world of cities, planes, cars, appointments, and people fell away from her. Clasping Colin's hand and looking at him with love, she felt they breathed in truth and breathed out contentment.

Then Colin, taking her hand more tightly, drew her away from the track and into a small wood. There, Lindsay's moonlit confidence began to desert her. In part, this was because, used to cities, the wood itself unnerved her. Here, there was less light, the moon shining through the branches and illuminating the ground only in patches. The undergrowth was thick; from all sides came tiny sounds she could not identify. The rain dripped and pooled the path; there were constant rustling, scurrying noises, and she had to keep telling herself that these were caused by the harmless nocturnal activities of small animals. Rabbits, weasels, she said to herself, and then acknowledged the truth: these sounds were not causing her fears; her fear was for Colin. She was afraid, very afraid, that when she finally saw this house of his, she would betray a reaction that would hurt and disappoint him.

This is his *home*, she kept saying to herself; he cannot help his home. It is the place where he grew up; he loves it; it is as cruel and wrong to shun it as it would be if he had grown up in some slum tenement.

Yet this argument did not altogether convince her. She must try to imagine this house, she thought, then she would be prepared, and could, if need be, feign her reaction. By then, her mind had already laid out that park, the terrible perfection of that park; now she must try to face the house itself. She knew it would not be quite large, but very large; she immediately made that adjustment to Colin's statement. She found she could begin to see this very large house, this mansion. It was perched up, she discovered, on some eminence. It was gray, austere, grand; its architectural style was both classical and assertive. She felt this house might well resemble Mansfield Park, or perhaps that great edifice, Mr. Darcy's Pemberley. On the other hand, it might look, dear God, like Brideshead, or Thrushcross Grange, or Manderley. It would be like *all* of those places, she thought, in that it exacted a charge from interlopers such as herself who crossed its threshold. That charge was a male child, a son for the son, an heir for the heir; this hidden aspect of his house, Colin had not mentioned once. She wondered now, for she could feel how tense and anxious he was, whether he would ever be able to bring himself to mention it. She looked toward him; she knew he loved her; with pain, she accepted that on this subject he would remain utterly silent.

"Through here," Colin said. He held out his hand to her. "Let me help you over the stile."

They had reached the edge of the wood at last. The moon, veiled by a ragged scrap of cloud, was revealing nothing. Ahead of her, Lindsay thought she could glimpse something still—and something moving. She gave Colin her hand and climbed over. She stepped down onto soft grass, cropped by animals. Colin put his arm around her shoulders and turned her a little. He raised his fingers to his lips; Lindsay peered into shadows and tried to make substance of shadows. A light gust of wind washed soft rain against her face; the cloud stayed still and the moon moved, bestowing radiance.

At first, Lindsay did not see the house. She saw that there was a river, wide and swift-flowing, curving along a valley. Ahead of her, beneath the spreading branches of a tree, a group of roe deer were grazing. She could see the females, heads bent to the grass, the moonlight graying the lovely curves of their necks and flanks. A little apart, head lifted and alert, there was a stag; she just glimpsed the branching of his antlers, then he scented their presence, and with one accord, moving at speed like a single creature, the herd ran off. She listened to the soft drumming of deer hooves; following the deer's passage with her eyes, she found she was looking at Shute.

It was not as she had expected. It was not set up upon an eminence, but lay against the side of the hill, as if it had gradually grown up from the ground over the centuries. There was, at one end of its irregular outline, an attempt at a fortification, for there was some form of tower or gatehouse there. Leading away from this was a long quiet frontage, which had a collegiate or monastic look. It had glorious ranked windows, which the moon made silver and mercurial; she could see square bays; she glimpsed curved gables, gentle stone embrasures, clustering and fantastic chimney pots; and, seeing a house built not for display, but for the quiet delights of domesticity, she gave a low cry of unfeigned pleasure.

"Oh, it's beautiful," she said. "Colin, I never imagined it would be this beautiful. . . ."

Colin, who had been watching her face with the utmost intentness, gave a sigh. All the tension left his body. His heart, which he was sure had stopped beating, now began to beat strongly.

"It's the most romantic house in England," he said, looking at it with love. "At least, so it's been said. . . ."

"Who said that?" Lindsay asked, still staring at the house. "They were right; it *is* romantic. It's wildly romantic. . . ."

"I think it was William Morris," Colin said, "or it might have been Ruskin."

One of them, Colin thought, had said something roughly similar. He hesitated; oversell, he knew, could be fatal.

"Oh, what's that glorious tower thing at the end, Colin?"

"Well, it's a gatehouse really. A tower-shaped sort of gatehouse."

"I *love* towers. I *love* gatehouses."

"That's medieval." Colin was beginning to feel more encouraged. "It's the only part of the original house that's left. Various Lascelleses kept adding bits. They had this compulsion to *build*. Apart from the gatehouse, what you're looking at now is mostly late Tudor and partly Jacobean."

"Oh." Lindsay gave a long sigh. "It was there at the time of the Armada. When Shakespeare was writing his plays. Mary,

Queen of Scots was alive then. Raleigh was discovering his New World. . . ."

"Yes," said Colin, feeling this was a fairly accurate summation.

"It has a Wars of the Roses sort of look too," Lindsay went on. "And I can just imagine Crusaders riding off to fight the Saracens . . . from the gatehouse, that is."

"Definitely," said Colin, who by then was inclined to agree to anything.

"I shouldn't be in the least surprised if Henry the Eighth didn't stay here, with Anne Boleyn." Lindsay gave a deeper sigh. "While he was still in love with her, of course. Some years before he chopped off her head."

Colin hesitated then. To this, the purist in him could not consent. Anne Boleyn, executed in 1536, was, strictly speaking, unlikely to have visited a house the construction of which commenced some fifty years later. On reflection, he felt he could stretch a point.

"More than possible," he said. "Maybe he composed "Greensleeves" for her here. . . . You never know."

"Colin, my dates aren't that bad. I'm teasing you." Lindsay turned to look at him. He saw she had tears in her eyes. "I'm teasing you and I'm not teasing you. And it's lovely—so very lovely." She paused. "I don't think it frightens me, after all. I thought it might, you see. I thought it might be, you know, grand. Regimented. Marble halls. Great staircases . . ."

"I love you," said Colin, realizing the wisdom of showing her the house from this side and at night. He need not mention the large eighteenth-century wing, invisible from here, until the morning, he decided. William Kent's contributions to the house, he felt, were better approached with circumspection. Lindsay would cope with Kent, he was sure, in time. After all, she was prepared to forgive his money and his ancestors. If he could ensure that his careful plans for the rest of the night, and for the following day, went as well as this, his opening move, then success might be his.

Accordingly, and with deep emotion, he kissed her. When this long kiss finally ended, and Lindsay drew back from his arms with a blind, urgent look, Colin, who felt equally urgent, but determined, caught her by the hand and began to draw her toward the house. He was having difficulties with his voice, which had dropped and kept catching.

"I want to—show you the inside. Introduce you to my dogs. My father will have gone to bed, but I want you to meet my dogs. I have these two old dogs, and—Lindsay, quickly. Darling, this house is *nearer*. . . ."

Lindsay, not inclined to argue, allowed herself to be drawn up the slope toward the walls of the house. The moon lit it and hid it. Reaching a dark porch, Colin drew her inside it and began to kiss her again. Then, suddenly remembering another aspect to his plan—a key aspect—he drew her out again into the moonlight, where, as resolved, he again proposed to her. He watched the moonlight move upon her face and brighten her eyes. Lindsay took his hand in hers and kissed it. In a halting way, beginning the sentence, breaking off, then beginning again, she said that she needed more time to consider—but so sweet and so gentle was her expression as she said this that conclusions leaped into Colin's brain. He could see she was anxious to cause him no pain by this answer; he felt at once a soaring conviction that progress had been made. An advance on silence, he thought, drawing her toward the studded oak door deep in the porch. He must persevere; he would soon—it must surely be soon—be rewarded with acceptance.

Colin had left his father very explicit directions; as a result, his home looked as it usually did, which was untidy and idiosyncratic. As he had foreseen, Lindsay did not notice the Gainsborough portrait in the entrance hall, partly because it was badly lit—in fact, unlit—and partly because she was distracted by the room's very noticeable oddities. These included a line of walking boots, sturdy shoes, and rubber boots sufficient in number to have shod the feet of a small army; a mountain of binoculars, field glasses, and small telescopes; a baby owl, one eye open and one shut, perched on the back of a chair by the fireplace, and, in a cardboard box lined with newspaper, a small hedgehog, which smelled pungently.

"My father has a bit of a thing about wildlife," said Colin, looking at her with hope. "When he's not watching birds, which he does most of the time, he's *rescuing* things. Like that hedgehog. The gardener—someone found him the other day. He should be hibernating. Daddy's been making him a new hibernating nest; he goes back in it tomorrow."

Lindsay was undone. Afterward, she was never sure whether to blame the hedgehog, or Colin's use of the word "Daddy," which had slipped past his guard and caused him to blush crimson. Hiding her face, she bent over the hedgehog box. The hedgehog, not fully grown, was curled up in a ball, and was slowly beginning to bristle. Lindsay, who knew herself to be a sentimentalist, with a weakness for all animals, particularly small ones, looked at the beauty of its spines. They were darker at the tip, paler at the base. Touching them with one finger, she found they felt soft and vulnerable, except at the tip. If Colin does not say anything about fleas, she thought—most people, in her experience, could not mention hedgehogs without mentioning fleas in the next breath—it will be a *sign*: I shall know I am right about Colin.

Colin, watching her with a tender expression, said nothing about fleas. Lindsay waited. Minutes ticked. He still said nothing about fleas. The hedgehog, having decided the possible threat had retreated, lowered its spines and uncurled; Lindsay saw its sharply pointed snout, its black nostrils. It made a snuffling noise, retreated the snout, and went back to sleep. Lindsay acknowledged the truth; not that she loved Colin, she had known that for some time, but that she loved him in the right way—that being, as she felt any woman would know, a nice but vital distinction.

Now there was nothing to do but hope, she thought, straightening. She looked at Colin across the entrance hall. She was aware, dimly, that it was paved with a checkerboard of worn black and white flagstones. She vaguely perceived that it contained furniture and paintings, that there was an owl on the back of a chair, and that two rough-haired dogs, stretching, a little arthritic, had now appeared, and were greeting their master.

She watched them lick his hands; their tails thumped; they gave small yelps and barks of canine pleasure. She could not even see these dogs clearly, she realized; the rest of the room blurred as she looked toward Colin. He was bending down to his dogs, his hair falling forward across his face, his hand extended. He was wearing an old tweed overcoat, which was muddy. She had a muddled sense that he was good—she knew him to be good—that he was strong, and that he was deserving. Straightening up from his dogs, he met her gaze, his face becoming serious and quiet as he read her expression. With love, her eyes rested on his hair and the beauty of its coloration; they rested on his blue unwavering gaze, and it seemed to her extraordinary that she could once have been blind to this face's distinctions.

She might have liked, perhaps, to accept him as a husband then, but since she could not, she went across to him, greeted his dogs, then took his hand and went upstairs with him to his bedroom.

Colin was careful to take a route to this room that led away from the larger and grander rooms here; the great hall, he felt, with its bristling displays of ancient weaponry, and the long gallery, flanked with too many portraits of too many ancestors, a *surfeit* of ancestors, could safely wait until the morning. So he took her up to his rooms by a winding back stair, pointing out to her only those small things he felt would please her—the old pane of glass on which, in 1672, a lover had scratched with a diamond the initials of his mistress; the bedcurtains in his room, which had been embroidered and stitched with consummate skill by some latter-day Lascelles wife who had had the patience of a Penelope.

Lindsay, entering his bedroom and admiring the bedcurtains *en passant*—she herself hated to sew—saw that the room was at the very top of the house and was open to the roof, with the rafters exposed and the great structure of its beams and king posts visible. This delighted her. Colin, thankful that his windows faced south, thus giving no view of the more dangerous classical wing of his home, told her that when she woke in the morning, she would look out at the river.

Lindsay, who had not taken her contraceptive pills for two nights, not since that walk back through the snow from the Conrad, was pleased by this. She had no intention of taking those powerful chemicals again and, feeling that she was giving herself up to the equally powerful forces of nature, she liked the idea that the first thing she would see from these windows was the flow and currents of water.

She was aware that this strategy—like most of her strategies—was unreliable and could not be continued indefinitely. If she conceived, well and good; she would then be in no doubt as to her next action. If she did not conceive, and Gini's predictions proved true, then she would have to find a way to leave Colin. So she would have to determine a time limit, she thought, as Colin drew her down beside him on the bed. Six months? A year? No, a year was too long, she thought; a year with Colin and she was afraid she would never have the willpower to disengage from him. Six months then, she thought, as Colin kissed her. Perhaps seven, she thought a minute later. Here, of course, was the right and perfect place to conceive his child, she thought a minute after that, though, in truth, this idea had first occurred to her somewhat earlier.

Moving against him, she began to say and do some of the marvelous things that Colin, alone in Emily's apartment all those weeks before, had hoped for and imagined. And Lindsay, who had always believed in those forces to which Jippy, in New York, had addressed his prayers and his spell, conjured them in her mind now, as, after delays sweet to both of them, Colin came into her body.

The following day was bright, cold, and clear. Lindsay was introduced to Colin's father, whom she found brusque, possibly kindly, and certainly intimidating. With Colin, she attended church—in her case for the first time in many years—where, to a congregation of eight, in freezing conditions, a sermon was preached on the subject and significance of Advent, and Colin's father, mustache bristling, read the lesson with considerable bravura.

After Sunday lunch was completed, father and son exchanged a glance that Lindsay failed to notice. Colin announced, in a somewhat mysterious, evasive way, that he had one or two people he ought to see. Lindsay was never sure how the two men contrived this, but five minutes later, she was sitting talking to his father, and trying to think of some possible subject of conversation with this brisk, alarming, soldierly man, while Colin, unbeknownst to Lindsay, was steering his fast and exquisitely engineered car in the direction of Oxford.

As he drove, at speed, with skill, Colin rehearsed sentences. These sentences proved less easy to handle than his demanding car; he was getting sentence wheel spin, drift, and skid; the results were unfortunate. "Tom," he muttered, "it is your mother whom I wish to marry. Tom, your mother and I . . ." No good, no good, Colin thought. Try again; concentrate. "Tom, for some time now, it has been my hope to . . ."

No good either, Colin thought, becoming desperate. Why had this appalling pomposity descended on him? He was starting to sound like some ghastly suitor in a nineteenth-century novel. Loosen up, he thought; be cool and relaxed, modern and casual. "Hi, Tom, how's things? Just thought I'd let you know. I've asked Lindsay to . . . Lindsay and I are . . ." Asked Lindsay to what? Colin was now sweating. He could not think of any appropriately cool, relaxed modern usage. Shack up with me? Get hitched? Tie the knot? Worse and worse, Colin thought; either he sounded like an aging hippie or like Bertie Wooster.

Start again, he thought, zipping around the Headington traffic circle. Keep it simple. "Tom, I want to marry your mother. Tom, I have asked Lindsay to marry me. Tom, I am deeply in love with your mother, otherwise known as Lindsay, and I want to marry her. I want you to give us your blessing, and tell me what in hell I can do to get her to accept me."

This was an improvement, Colin thought. At least it was honest. He could refine this, bang it about a bit, get it into some sort of shape. "Tom, I am very deeply in love . . ." Very, very deeply in love? Fathoms deep in love?

Get ahold of yourself, Colin thought, swerving violently. He realized that he was now in Tom's street, and his nerve had entirely failed him. He slowed to a crawl. The words jammed in his brain. He began to see that this expedition was the most foolish of mistakes. It was an error of judgment of colossal proportions. On the last occasion he had seen Tom, the *only* occasion he had seen Tom, he had been drunk . . . face facts, *paralytic*. Tom was unlikely to have forgotten this. Supposing Tom turned around and said he had never heard a worse, a more fatuous suggestion in his life? What was he supposed to do then? Ignore Tom, or just crawl away and die somewhere?

He stopped the car outside Tom's house, but did not turn off the engine; he sat there for several minutes in a state of indecision and panic. He told himself this meeting was better postponed. Tom, according to the telephone call with Lindsay the previous night, was working flat out on an essay on the philosophical background to Fascism. He was toiling through *Also Sprach Zarathustra* and tackling Nietzsche's concept of *Übermensch*. For this reason, Tom had put off Lindsay's suggestion of meeting. *Übermensch?* This essay now seemed to Colin a most excellent reason for driving away again. He was just about to release the brake, engage the gears, and go, when he had the sensation—the very odd sensation—that someone had just tapped him on the shoulder.

So precise was this sensation that he actually glanced around. There was, of course, no one behind him. He hesitated. The someone who had tapped his shoulder was now drawing his hand toward the ignition keys. Colin turned the engine off. The invisible someone, he found, was now urging him to get out of the car. Realizing that this invisible person must be his conscience, telling him not to plan something, then mess it up, Colin did get out of the car. He found himself encouraged up the path; in an encouraging way, just as he was about to ring Tom's doorbell, the door was opened for him. A young woman—it was Cressida-from-upstairs—paused in the doorway.

On learning that this tall, anxious-looking, handsome man wanted to see Tom, she let him in, started to leave herself, then paused.

"The thing is . . ." She gave a frown. "He's in a bit of a state. Did you know? Are you a friend of his?"

"I'm a friend of his mother's. A state?" Colin also frowned. "That's odd. She spoke to him last night—she said he sounded fine then. . . ."

"Well, I guess he would—to his mother. You know how it is." She made a face. "He doesn't want people to know, but he and Katya had this horrible fight—last Thursday, when he got back from Edinburgh. In fact, they've split up, and Tom's pretty miserable. I'm worried about him. I tried to talk to him last night, but he wouldn't say a word. I tried this morning, but he wouldn't even open his door. So, like, take it easy with him. . . ."

She went out, closing the door behind her. Colin saw that now was not the moment to start discussing Lindsay and proposals. The best thing to do, he decided, was to go back to Shute, collect Lindsay, and bring her over here. He turned toward the front door, and again felt that discernible tug from that invisible hand. The hand seemed to propel him to the stairs. After more hesitation, Colin went up them.

He paused on Tom's landing. He could hear music coming from rooms on the upper floors; he thought he recognized a Mozart opera, just discernible beneath the heavy beat of some rock group. Then he realized that from beyond Tom's door came the sound of a man crying.

"Tom?" he said, in a low voice. "Tom? Are you in there?"

There was no reply. Colin felt a mounting concern. He knocked on the door. "Tom, I know you're in there," he said. "It's Colin Lascelles. I need to see you urgently. . . ." He tried the door, which was locked. "Tom, could you open this door, please?"

There was silence, then the sound of a chair moving. "Go away," Tom said indistinctly. "Just go away, okay?"

Colin hesitated. He thought he ought to go away; he also thought he ought to stay. The more he thought about it, the more important it seemed to remain and get into the room. Tom, virtually fatherless, had struck him as volatile when he met him; he thought of how he himself had been at Tom's age, in the wake of his brother's death. He thought of how he, at this age, had swung wildly from one extreme to another, and how, on bright mornings like this one, he had got up, looked at the day, and started drinking.

He knocked on the door again. "Tom, I'm not leaving. I must talk to you. Now open this door. . . ."

"Fuck off." There was a painful sound. "Just fuck off and leave me alone. . . ."

Colin considered. Three days ago, had this happened, he would either have left to fetch Lindsay, or gone in search of a landlady and a key, or made foolish threats about breaking down the door. He had been shown, however, that there were quicker approaches—and speed mattered; he could now sense urgency.

Blushing scarlet, he said, "Tom, there's been an accident. Now open this door at once."

There was a brief silence, then footsteps, then the sound of a key turning. Colin took one quick look at Tom's face and pushed past him before he could shut the door. He glanced around the room, which was in a state of chaos. The cerise sofa was without its Indian throw, which was crumpled in a corner. The bed in the alcove was unmade. There were papers and books all over the floor—and there was something else, something that caught his eye as he turned back to Tom, but he was too distressed by Tom's appearance to take in its significance.

Tom might be his own height, but he now looked like a boy rather than a man, Colin thought. He was unshaven; his eyes were swollen, and his face was white and tear stained. He was looking at Colin with an expression of fear and bewilderment.

"What's happened?" he said. "What's happened? Is Mum all right? I only spoke to her last night. . . . Oh, *Christ*."

"Nothing's wrong," Colin replied quickly. "There was no accident. I couldn't think of any other way to get you to open the door, and—"

He broke off, seeing a furtive ashamed look cross Tom's face. Slowly, he turned and reexamined those objects that had caught his eye on the table. There was no mistaking their purpose. He turned back sharply to Tom and the boy's face crumpled. He gave Colin a blind, miserable look and drew in an unsteady breath.

"It's okay," he said. "I wanted to, but I couldn't even fucking well do that." He began to cry again.

"Katya said I was useless—and she's right. I bought the fucking drink and the fucking pills, and then I couldn't do it. I've sat here for three hours looking at them—and I couldn't take them. . . ." He pushed past Colin, fumbled for a chair, and sat down on it. "You know where she's gone? She's taken the train to London. She's gone to see fucking Rowland McGuire. She thinks she's in love with him. . . ."

Quietly, Colin moved across to the table. On it was a notebook with some penciled message and numerous crossings-out. "Dear Mum," Colin read. He passed his hand across his face. Next to the notebook was a full bottle of vodka, and laid out in rows, very neatly, was a large number of white pills. The boxes they had been taken from were stacked neatly to one side.

Colin was very afraid; he looked at the pills, then at Tom.

"This is paracetamol," he said. "Paracetamol, not aspirin. Have you taken any?"

"No. I told you—"

"You're sure? Look at me, Tom. If you've taken any, I have to know—"

"I haven't. Not one." Tom gave him a frightened look. "Count them if you like. They're all there. . . ."

Colin counted them; they were all there. He found he was not only afraid, but very angry.

"Do you know what happens to people who take a paracetamol overdose?" he said. "They die. It doesn't work, using a stomach pump on them, as it can do with aspirin. It's irrevocable. Paracetamol causes irrevocable liver damage. You could kill yourself with a quarter of that dosage, but you wouldn't die now; you'd die in a week's time. Did you know that?"

"No. I didn't."

"Did you think of your mother? Tom, how could you do this? Did you think what it would do to her?"

"Look, I didn't take them. I didn't take *any*. . . ."

"You thought about it. You sat here and you wrote a note. 'Dear Mum.' How could you? *How?* You're her only child. She loves you so much. . . ." He looked around the room. "Where's the phone? I'm calling your mother right now. . . ."

"No, don't do that." Tom sprang to his feet. "Please, don't do that. I don't want her to know. . . ."

"Too bad. You should have thought of that before. I'm not hiding this from her."

"Please—*please*." Tom caught at his arm. "Don't do that. Let me explain—I wouldn't have done it. Really, I just—I couldn't *think*. I've been walking round Oxford for two days, trying to think, and I couldn't. Nothing made *sense*. It was just all this fucking awful horrible *mess*. Katya said all these horrible things—and I couldn't believe she'd said them. I kept thinking, it's all a dream. I'm going to wake up in a minute.

And this morning—I went around to her college this morning. She told me to get lost. She had this *mad* look on her face. She went on and on about him, Rowland this, Rowland that—I could kill him. She's been writing to him. I *know* he's been writing back . . . and I thought, I'll show her. . . ."

He rubbed at his eyes and began to cry again. "I kept thinking she'd come in, and see all that stuff—and then she'd *see* how much I loved her. Only she didn't come, and I'd locked the door anyway. Oh *shit* . . ."

Colin hesitated; it seemed to him that he ought to call Lindsay, and at once. But he could feel it again, that small odd tug at his sleeve. With a sigh, he did what it seemed most natural and useful to do: he put his arms around a boy he scarcely knew, as if he had known him all his life. Gently, he steered him to the sofa and sat down next to him. He looked anxiously at Tom.

"You give me your word you didn't touch any pills? There aren't any other boxes hidden away?"

"None. I swear. It was just an idea; a *gesture*. That's all I'm capable of—fucking *gestures*. . . ."

"I don't believe that," Colin replied in a quiet way. "Not taking that amount of paracetamol shows remarkable good sense. Now why don't you tell me what's happened? Go back to the beginning, and when you've finished, I'll call Rowland." He paused. "I know you need have no worries on that score, Tom. Whatever mad idea Katya may have got into her head, Rowland won't have encouraged her. . . ."

"You're sure?"

Colin was *not* sure. True, he could not imagine Rowland leading Katya on, but if she had actually gone to see him, if she turned up on his doorstep? Katya was young; she was noticeably attractive. Thinking of Rowland's past, he felt doubts, and knew it was vital to conceal them. "Has she gone to his house, Tom?"

"That's what she said she was going to do. Oh, *Christ*. She'll be there now. You don't know Katya—you don't know what she's like. She reads all these fucking books. She thinks she's *in* a book half the time. . . ."

"I'm sure Rowland will cope with that. I know exactly what

he'll do. He'll give her one of his ticking-offs—and they're not pleasant, I can tell you. Then he'll put her on a train and send her packing, which will almost certainly bring her to her senses. . . ."

"It won't make her love me again though, will it?" Tom bent his head. He wiped the back of his hand angrily across his eyes. "She doesn't fucking care anymore. She said. . . ."

He glanced toward the bed and began crying again. Colin put his arm around Tom's shoulders. He produced one of his Thalia-scorned handkerchiefs and handed it over.

"Start at the beginning," he said, "and remember, people don't always mean what they say in these circumstances."

"They don't?"

"I certainly hope not," Colin replied. "Considering some of the things that have been said to me in the past. Now, how did this begin, Tom?"

"When I got back from Edinburgh, she just went mad— totally *mad*. She'd written this mad note. . . ." He blew his nose. Looking at Colin fiercely, he drew in a steadying breath.

"I'll never love anyone else, you know," he said. *"Never."*

Colin was careful not to disagree. "Of course that's how you feel," he said. "Now, you talk and I'll just sit here and listen. And then we'll find a way to sort this out, I promise you."

"Rowland, I love you," Katya said. She cleared her throat. "I want you to be very clear about this. Of course, I still love Tom. In many ways, I shall *always* love Tom, but I love Tom in a quiet, peaceful, everyday sort of way, whereas, with you . . ."

Katya paused. She had been rehearsing this difficult speech the whole way to London on the train. Now that she was actually here, in Rowland McGuire's strange, spartan house, it seemed more difficult to say. She had hoped that, by this point in her speech, Rowland might have *done* something.

He had done and said nothing. She had been admitted into the house with considerable reluctance, and only after she had burst into tears on the front step. She had been shown up to this cold, unwelcoming room with these photographs of ugly mountains. She had been in it less than five minutes before she realized that unless she embarked on her speech, she was going to find herself out on the pavement again. Rowland was now leaning up against the mantelpiece, his arms folded; his green eyes rested on her face in a manner that was not encouraging. Katya flushed.

"With you," she continued, "it's *different*. It came to me very suddenly. It was that day I met you in Oxford. It was something Miriam Stark said. Learn to *read*, she said. So, after you left, I started reading this novel." She paused again, half hoping Rowland would ask her which novel; he did not.

"I found I could read it—and I could also read myself. And you. I know what you *need*, Rowland. I know what you *want*."

"Really? You have an advantage over me there."

"I want to go to bed with you, Rowland." Katya's color deepened. "You may not realize that you want to go to bed with me yet, but you will. I want you to understand. . . ." She paused, trying to recall her script. "I know it won't be *permanent*; it will just be an affair. And when it's over, I'll go away quietly; I won't pester you, or anything like that. I know that in your case it will be just—you know—*sex*, but from my point of view, it's something I *need*—at this moment in my life."

Katya paused again. Rowland, she felt, must surely now speak. There was a second part to her speech, much concerned with the nature of love, its dynamics, and Katya's theories on these dynamics—which were numerous. There was a coda to this speech that dealt with such questions as twin souls, fate, sudden attraction, and the consequences thereof: looking at Rowland's green eyes, Katya decided to skip this section. While it had made great sense on the train to tell Rowland that she had realized he was the love of her life, it now did not.

She looked more closely at the expression in those eyes, which might have been lazily amused.

"Are you laughing at me?" she said. "This isn't funny. It's not easy, you know, doing this."

"I agree it's not funny, and I'm certainly not laughing at you. Have you finished? I did say I'd hear you out."

"Look." Katya struggled. "Look—I know you're a lot older than I am. I know you won't be used to this kind of thing, but I think a woman should say what she *feels*. What's the point of going through life covering everything up? I *love* you. I came up today to tell you that. If you like, we can go to bed now, and then I'll go back to Oxford. You'll never hear from me again. I've got a day return ticket, just in case."

Rowland gave a sigh. He wondered if Katya could possibly imagine the number of times this had happened to him before. The women were different; the words were different; the intention was the same. This, of course, was the very last thing to mention.

He looked at Katya. She was wearing the workman's jacket again, a man's shirt, jeans, and a pair of Dr. Martens boots. He found himself both moved and amused by this. He was moved and amused by the combination of posturing and sincerity in her expression and voice. She was now examining him closely with her large, blue, short-sighted eyes. Her hair, which was beautiful, the color of a fox, was loose on her shoulders. She had freckles on her nose and cheekbones; her hands, he saw, were unsteady. He could see that what she said she both meant and did not mean.

He glanced away toward the windows. It was midafternoon, and the light was already beginning to fade. Three nights ago, he had been at the Conrad; he had spent most of the following day, Friday, on a plane, and the whole of the following day, yesterday, seeing his newspaper to press. He felt as if he had not slept in a month, and he had realized, shortly before Katya's unannounced arrival, that, without doubt, a Sunday was the cruelest day of the week. Most people spent Sundays with their families. In the past, he had often spent this day, or part of it, with Lindsay. Such meetings would now cease. This prospect pained him; he found himself at a loss. In a familiar city, in his own home, he felt as if he were distanced and disoriented; whatever planet this was, its atmosphere was alien.

On this planet, it seemed, anything could happen at any moment; its rules were arbitrary. Temptation could turn up at three in the afternoon, in the shape of a girl wearing Dr. Martens boots, a girl with a round-trip ticket and a wish to seduce him. This apparition, he found, made him feel very tired. He had the sensation that, if he turned away, then looked back, Katya would vanish in a twinkling. He looked back; she had not vanished; speech was necessary.

"Katya, I'm sorry," he began. "I'm touched by what you say,

and flattered, obviously, but you must know—it's out of the question. . . ."

"Why?" Katya became pale. Before Rowland could answer, she undid the man's shirt she was wearing and began crying. She hesitated, then parted the shirt to reveal a black, lacy, seductive bra.

"You won't *look* at me," she cried, tears welling. "You never do. Well, I'm going to *make* you look at me, Rowland. Oh, God, I'm so bloody miserable. I can't work. I can't *think*. Tom said I looked mad. I *feel* mad. I might as well go just jump in the Thames. I nearly did, this afternoon. I went and stared at the Thames for *hours*, but I couldn't find the right place to jump, and it was low tide and there was all this *mud*. . . ."

She made a wailing sound; large tears fell down her face. Rowland found that somehow—he was never sure how it happened—he had put an arm around her. The next thing he knew, Katya's tears were being wept against his shoulder.

"I want to *die*," she said, indistinctly. "I could die of *shame*. You don't fancy me, do you? I'm fat. I'm undesirable. I've made an idiot of myself. Oh, this is horrible. Why did I come here? Why was I so horrible to Tom? I threw all these books around. We stayed up all night, arguing and arguing, and I drank all this wine and said these horrible, cruel things. . . . Rowland, I could feel this *storm*—there wasn't a storm, but I could hear *thunder*. I kept seeing these flashes of *lightning*. . . ."

Rowland made a sympathetic noise. In an awkward way, he patted, then stroked, her back. He found himself in a quandary. He was in no doubt as to how he should now behave: he should calm Katya down, talk to her in a kind, fatherly way, and, with the utmost firmness and tact, get her out of his house and back to Oxford. This course of action was totally clear to him; however, on this planet he was presently visiting, other factors seemed to be influencing him. He was finding himself distracted by the warmth and proximity of Katya's body, by her tears, and—not least—by her breasts. He couldn't quite forget that glimpse of the black, lacy bra. Katya was neither fat, nor undesirable; the bared skin of her chest had proved to be pale, beautiful, and dusted with freckles. She had a slim waist, a strong young back, and her skin had a faint, pleasant nostalgic scent to it, which Rowland thought might come from talcum powder.

Despite her words, she had contrived to put her arms around his neck, and her breasts were pressing against his chest. It had been a while since Rowland had slept with a woman; the misery of the day was acute, and he was, he thought, only human. Katya had truly beautiful hair, he realized, laying his hand against it, hesitating, then beginning to stroke it.

He was just about to tilt Katya's face up to his when he had the sensation—the very odd sensation—that someone had just tugged his sleeve. So strong was this sensation that he looked down; but no, as he had known they were, Katya's arms were clasped about his neck. There was, of course, no one else in the room and no one standing next to him.

He found he was now looking down at Katya. She had stopped wailing and crying as suddenly as she had begun, and was now regarding him in an alert, desperate way. Her eyes were lovely, Rowland thought; her mouth was lovely.

"I wish you'd kiss me, Rowland," she said. "Just a very *brief* kiss. Just *once* . . ."

It seemed to Rowland that, indeed, one brief kiss could do no harm. He hesitated. The telephone began ringing. On its third ring, understanding that he had been rescued, Rowland gently released Katya, told her to do up her blouse, crossed the room, and answered this timely call. The caller proved to be Colin Lascelles. He did not mention alcohol or pills, but he explained where he was; he spoke for some time, and he spoke with emphasis.

"Quite," Rowland said, several times. He glanced across at Katya, who was buttoning up her shirt. "No. She got here about half an hour ago, Colin. We're just leaving now. I agree. Yes, she is rather upset. I'll drive her back to Oxford. I think that would be best."

Rowland replaced the receiver. He looked at himself and disliked what he saw. "That was Colin," he said, "calling from Tom's room."

Katya blushed scarlet again. There was a silence. Katya, who as Rowland well knew, was by no means unintelligent, gave him a look that gradually became considering.

"I do love Tom, you know."

"Then learn to behave accordingly."

Katya's color deepened. "Okay, okay. I deserved that. I'll go. You don't have to drive me."

"No, I will. I don't want any detours to the Thames."

"I'm not really the suicidal type." She paused. "One question—how close, Rowland?"

"Too close for comfort."

"I thought so." Katya's face lit up in a brilliant smile. "Well, that's *some* consolation."

"Not for me it isn't."

"So what do we do now, Rowland?"

"Now, Katya, you come downstairs, and you get in my car, and I drive you back to Oxford—which is an interruption I could well do without. While we're on the motorway, I'll give you a sensible fatherly talk. And you will behave yourself."

"All right." Katya frowned. "I did mean what I said to you, Rowland."

"No, Katya. I don't think you did mean it."

"I shall feel awful tomorrow. I'll want to die of embarrassment and humiliation."

"Don't. I'd concentrate on Tom, if I were you. That's rather more important. Now get your coat. And Katya, be more careful which books you read in the future."

"All right, Rowland. I'll stick to Trollope." Katya gave a small smile. "All those clergymen. I should think that would be safe. . . ."

"Out. *Now*," said Rowland.

In his car, true to his word, Rowland provided sensible fatherly advice. He produced Kleenex from the glove compartment when Katya hit another weeping phase. He drove at exactly the speed limit for the entire route—not his usual practice—and by the time he dropped Katya off at her college, he realized he had never felt so hypocritical and so ancient.

"Do you think I ought to go and see Tom now, Rowland?"

"No, I don't. I think you should give it a few days, Katya. Colin's taking him back to his place, anyway. Lindsay's there. Give yourselves a few days to think, and calm down a little. . . ."

Katya gave him a sidelong glance; she departed.

Rowland drove around Oxford, feeling a curious reluctance to leave the city. He thought of how easy it was to give advice to others in such matters and how peculiarly difficult it was to act on such advice oneself. He thought of the time he had spent in this city, and of what he had done—and left undone—since he had lived here. He tried not to think of the fact that Lindsay was close by, yet out of his reach.

He drove around the one-way circuit six times. There were no tourists in Oxford at this time of the year; the semester was ending, undergraduates were departing. The darkness of a winter's evening gave to these beautiful college buildings a sweet melancholy. It came to him that he had no reason to hurry back to London, since no one awaited him there. About to go around the one-way system for the seventh time, he changed his mind, parked the car with surprising lack of difficulty, and began walking. He walked through Christ Church meadows, and along the riverbank, and found himself alone, the river swollen by rain, and dead leaves drifting. He walked for some way, then, hearing the chapel bells begin to ring, and the church bells start to toll the hour, a long process, for as Tom had noticed, none of these clocks synchronized, he turned back.

Again he had the sensation—the very odd sensation—that he was being guided. This time, no invisible person tugged at his sleeve, but his feet seemed to know in which direction to take him. They led him back to Katya's college. Once he was in the porters' lodge, he found he had decided that, since he was in Oxford, it might be sensible, even prudent, to have a word concerning Katya with her tutor, Dr. Miriam Stark, a cool woman of sound sense, of good judgment, whose books he had always admired; a woman he had once liked, but with whom he had lost touch all those years ago.

The porter informed him that Dr. Stark did not live in college, but might be in her rooms. A call was put through to these rooms. Dr. Stark, it seemed, was there working, but was prepared to see him briefly. Rowland was given directions. Wondering why Dr. Stark would have elected to become a fellow of a women's college, when Balliol or Christ Church or Magdalen would surely have welcomed her, and wondering how to broach the difficult subject of Katya, Rowland set off across the quad, reaching her ground-floor rooms as the chapel bells stopped tolling.

Dr. Stark's room was lit by lamplight and its curtains were not drawn. From the quad outside, Rowland glimpsed her, framed by the window. She was seated at a desk, in profile to him, her face hidden by her dark hair, which fell forward as she bent over her work. The quietness of her room communicated itself to Rowland; he could see she had books piled upon her desk and a book open before her. He found himself very curious to know what she was reading.

Three days later, Lindsay's tenancy began. Colin left to begin work in Yorkshire and Tom went with him.

"Don't worry about a *thing*," Colin said to Lindsay for the tenth time that morning, drawing her back into the hallway of Shute Farm and kissing her. "Darling, I promise you—I need another assistant. It's the vacation; he can be my runner. He's mad about films. Work and a change of scene are just what he needs. Once he realizes there's a world elsewhere and a universe beyond Katya, he'll recover very quickly. I won't let him out of my sight—and I won't let him notice that, either. Besides, it's been good for him here. He's better already. He'll never consider anything that foolish again, I'm sure of that. . . ."

"I don't know that. He promised me, but I still—"

"Trust me."

"Colin, I want him *near* me. I feel so afraid for him—"

"I know you want him near you," Colin said quietly, "but you have to know when he wants and needs something else. Let him have the chance to prove something to himself, Lindsay. That stupid girl hurt his confidence badly."

"I mustn't even fuss, you mean?" Lindsay gave her new landlord a wry look.

"You can fuss a bit, but don't overdo it."

Lindsay took this advice. Going out with Colin to his great car, which Tom was admiring, she saw her son's face tighten with apprehension. Guiltily, Lindsay realized that she was responsible for this. Tom was now expecting one of the endless epic motherly recitals that delayed all his departures. For the first time in his life, Tom was spared them; Lindsay abjured all the talismanic sentences that she had come to believe ensured her son's safety. She did not tell him to get enough sleep, to eat properly, avoid illness and accident, and call if there was the least problem. These, and many other imprecations, she said silently to herself; to him, she said only to take care, work hard, and enjoy himself.

This so astonished Tom that it silenced him completely. He and Colin were five miles down the road before he felt able to speak.

"How did you *do* that?" he said, looking at Colin, who, he noticed, drove fast and with great skill. "How on *earth* did you do that?"

"I didn't do anything. Lindsay's getting used to the idea that you're a man now, that's all."

"You're kidding."

"Tom, don't be hard on her." Colin hesitated. "It's because she had to bring you up alone. If she was anxious, well, she had no one to share those anxieties with, so they got worse. . . ."

"You reckon?"

"Oh, definitely. Anyway, all women are a bit like that. It's a strength as well as a weakness. I promise you, Tom, my mother was exactly the same. She used to cry when she saw me off to school—I boarded when I was seven."

"Seven? Jesus."

"It's only because she loves you. And, maybe, she hadn't realized the effect it had on you. She . . . she—" Colin struggled. "She has a very warm heart, Tom, and she can't always disguise her feelings. And—"

"And you love her, right?" Tom grinned. "It's okay, Colin. I kind of noticed."

"I want her to marry me. I want her to marry me *desperately*. . . ." Colin slowed. He looked toward Tom, his expression both desperate and woeful. "That's why I came over to Oxford on Sunday. I wanted to—actually I'm not sure what I wanted to do. Ask your blessing . . ."

"That's cool. You've got it."

"Ask your *advice*." Colin groaned. "She won't say yes, and if she doesn't say yes soon, I'll go mad. . . ."

"You want *my* advice?" Tom blushed with pleasure. "Really? Wow!" He gave a smile. "Well, with a normal woman the car alone would do it. I mean, if I was a woman and a man drove up in this, I'd say yes before he got out of it. . . ."

"That's because you're a man. Think female."

"Okay, okay. Well, the house ought to help—but Mum's not normal there either. She likes your dad, I can tell, and that's a plus factor. Hang on, I'm thinking. . . ." He frowned. "I mean, it's weird—but then she is a bit weird. I can see she's mad about you. Something happens to her face when she looks at you. I've never seen that happen before."

"Never? You're sure?"

"Well, a bit, once or twice. She was keen on Rowland for a time. . . ."

"I know, I know. Don't mention him, it doesn't improve my driving."

"Oh, you don't have to worry about *that*," Tom said in a negligent, dismissive tone. "Rowland's all wrong for her. She knew that really. I mean, Rowland's fine as a friend, but can you imagine *living* with him? If she'd actually gone to bed with him, she'd have gotten over that in about a *week*, but she didn't. Rowland never fancied her anyway."

"You're sure?" Colin looked at Tom in astonishment. "More fool him."

"Oh, he *liked* her," Tom said in an airy way, "and Rowland's getting a bit desperate—his age and still unmarried—so maybe he persuaded himself it was more than that—I did think that, once or twice. When we had that lunch in Oxford, for instance." He gave Colin a shrewd glance. "But that was partly rivalry. I mean, he could see how you felt about Mum. Everyone at the table could except her. It stuck out a mile. . . ."

"Did it?" Colin asked, "Oh God. *God.*"

"But you don't have to worry about Rowland. She never looked at him the way she does at you. So if you really want to marry her . . ."

"If? *If?*" Colin overtook three cars superbly. "There are no 'if's' here, Tom. Advise me."

Tom looked at Colin and considered. He now felt ten years

older than when he'd gotten into this car. He was realizing how much he liked this somewhat eccentric man. He was wondering if this man would be eccentric enough ever to let him drive the Aston Martin. He was wondering why he had not thought of Katya for over twenty hours, and whether that could be seen as a falling off or as progress.

Deciding that, as stepfathers went, Colin might prove an exceptionally nice one, he sighed.

"Are you any good at chess?" he said.

"Not bad. Why?"

"Mum's appalling. I mean, so bad it's *awesome*. But there's something she does when she plays; it's just given me an idea. . . ."

Tom spoke rapidly, for some minutes. Colin's eyes widened. "You think so? You're sure? When?"

Tom frowned and considered again.

"When does this movie finish? End of February? Three months from now? That's about right. Go for March first. . . ."

"Three months? I can't stand it. . . ."

"Festina lente," Tom said, surprising Colin. "Trust me—the first of March is perfect."

A week later, in mid-December, Lindsay went up to London to help Pixie move into her own once much-loved apartment. This process did not take long, since Pixie's belongings consisted of a hi-fi system, some CDs, a budgerigar, and a suitcase.

"Don't you have anything *else*, Pixie?" Lindsay said, as they deposited these in her former sitting room. "What about books? Clothes? Where are all your clothes?"

"Oxfam," said Pixie.

She yawned, stretched, rearranged her red hair, and executed a small jig.

"I'm beginning a new life. New apartment. New hair color. New job. New clothes. New future."

"How's the job working out?" Lindsay said, looking around her and feeling despondent.

"Brilliantly. Max says I'm the best fashion editor he's ever had. Except for you, obviously."

"Oh, great. Terrific. Thanks a million."

"And this place is a *big* improvement on that horrible hole I had . . . I might repaint it. Do you mind?"

"Feel free," said Lindsay.

. "You sure you want me to just rent? I'll buy it if you like. I'm getting into mortgages. *Gearing.*"

"No, you can't bloody well buy it." Lindsay sat down. "I may need it."

"Is something the matter with you?"

"Yes. I'm postmenstrual."

"Post?"

"That's what I said."

"You're joking." Pixie stared at her hard and long. "Tell me I'm not hearing this."

"I'm not joking. I was never more serious in my life. I love him. I love him desperately. I want his babies."

Pixie opened her mouth to protest, argue, and expostulate. She looked at Lindsay's face and closed it again.

"Plural?" she said, being nothing if not practical.

"If possible. One would make me so happy, but if the one was female . . ."

Pixie felt she wanted to scream—loudly. Since she was fond of Lindsay, she did not. She sat down beside her and took her hands.

"Lindsay. Look at me," she said with great sternness. "Now tell me, is this for him or for you?"

"Both." She gave Pixie a look of misery. "I can't help it, Pixie—I'm just like that. I always was. There's this direct line between my heart and my womb. I'm a throwback, Pixie. I'm *primitive.*"

Pixie agreed with this view, but held off saying so, since Lindsay had now begun crying.

"Oh, Pixie, I love him so much," she said, "I love him with all my heart. He's the most wonderful man. He'd be such a wonderful father. I know he needs an heir—but it isn't that really. . . ."

"I should hope *not*," said Pixie, who disapproved of primogeniture and found this a very nineteenth-century predicament.

"He should have children. I know he wants them, but he won't say so—he's afraid of hurting me. He's afraid I'm too old—and so am I. Oh, what am I going to *do*? What am I going to *do*?"

Pixie thought for a while.

"Give me your dates," she said. "Right, now let's make the calculations here. . . . When's he next down from Yorkshire?"

"Tomorrow. But only for about half a day . . ."

"Tomorrow's perfect. Half a day? What's the matter with you? You can fix this inside ten minutes."

Pixie rose. She opened her suitcase, rummaged around inside, and brought out a small white jar.

"Right," she said. "Now, you rub this stuff into your skin about half an hour *before*, okay? It's unbelievably expensive and it never fails. Believe me, Lindsay, this would fix it for an *eighty*-year-old woman. . . ."

"What are you doing with it?"

"Sample," Pixie said briskly. "It came into the beauty department the other day. I thought I could use it. It's an aphrodisiac as well. . . ."

"I don't *need* an aphrodisiac. That's not the problem."

"Lindsay, with this cream and no Pill, you *conceive*. Believe me."

"I don't believe you. It's so much quackery."

"You put this on. You also wear an amber necklace—do you have an amber necklace? No? Well, buy one on your way home and *wear* it. Throughout. Don't take it off under any circumstances. Promise me now."

"All right. I promise." Lindsay smiled.

"That's better. Now—let's have a drink and I'll tell you all the gossip. You go first. . . ."

"I don't *have* any gossip." Lindsay sighed. "I sit alone with all these books and papers and I do *research*. What else? I go to see Colin's father sometimes, or he comes to see me. I like him very much. He talks in this antique way. He says 'by Jove.' Yesterday, he brought me a puppy—it's the sweetest thing, Pixie. It has this brown fluffy fur, and these deep brown eyes. I may call it Jippy. . . ."

Pixie smothered a yawn.

"Tom's much better. He's having a wonderful time in Yorkshire. He and Colin are working an eighteen-hour day. I miss

Tom. I miss Colin." She hesitated. "I live from phone call to phone call, Pixie. From letter to letter. I love him so much—I dream my life away." She gave a small sigh. "I know you don't approve, but you'll understand one day. . . ."

Pixie was very determined not to do so. She was, however, not as unaffected as she might have liked to be by the expression in Lindsay's eyes and by the way in which she spoke. She decided to change the subject quickly.

"Well, I can do better than that. . . ." She poured two glasses of some terrible wine she had brought with her. She sat down on a cushion on the floor, stretched out her legs, and made herself comfortable.

"First of all," she began, "you, Lindsay, are *dead*—did you know that? I met some terrible crazed PR woman, Lulu something, yesterday, and—"

"Lulu Sabatier? I don't *believe* it. That bloody woman hounded me for *months*. *I* told her I was dead. . . . You actually *met* her? What does she look like?"

"Weird. Tall. Long white hair. About forty. Rabbity teeth."

"No!" Lindsay stared at her, recognizing the woman from that corridor at that party. "But I met her! She gave me some other name. Why would she do that?"

"I tell you, she's *weird*. She kept rabbitting on about how much she'd liked you, how you'd gone down to her garden, or some crap. You know why she was hounding you? She represents that gruesome actor—what's his name? The one that looks like a recently deceased choirboy . . ."

"Nic Hicks? I don't *believe* this."

"That's the one. She thought you might want to use him in some male fashion feature, and now she thinks I might. Can he be that desperate for exposure?"

"Oh, yes. Without doubt." Lindsay frowned. She thought back to Halloween, to Lulu Sabatier's party, to that aircraft-carrier loft, and its magical garden.

"How odd," she said. "When she'd called thirty-five times, it did cross my mind it might have been important. The party was important—I see that now."

"What?"

"Nothing. Go on."

"Secondly—guess who Rowland and Max have signed up—exclusively? Pascal Lamartine, no less. Max says he's working on some book, but next year, once that's done, it's off to war zones again. . . ." Pixie paused. "I thought you said he'd given all that up for good. . . ."

"He has. He's agreed to work for Rowland? That's not possible. It's totally *im*possible."

"Wrong. It's signed and sealed. Apparently, Rowland approached him and Max clinched it. . . ."

"Which war? I can't believe this. . . ."

"Oh, there's always a war," Pixie said airily. "And now for the *really* interesting news: Rowland McGuire himself. Knock that back, Lindsay, you're going to need it. You may not believe this, but *I* hear . . ."

Lindsay listened. A sadness crept upon her. She looked at the sofa on which she was sitting, the sofa where she and Rowland had sat talking, late at night, on their return from that lunch in Oxford. She thought of what they had both said then—and what they had not said. She could see now that it was one of many past moments when she, and also perhaps Rowland, had been haunted by a future that might have been, and to which, briefly, they were close. It was just the other side of a door, just around a corner—and now, vestigial, imprecise, perhaps imagined, it would remain there. She bent her head, she found she could hear Rowland McGuire's voice, describing his Hebrides, or Hesperides.

"I wish him well," she said quietly, when Pixie had finished. "I hope it's true. And oddly enough, Pixie, I have no trouble believing it."

"Are you wearing a new scent? Darling, you smell wonderful," Colin said, burrowing beneath the bedclothes in the brass bed, in the blue bedroom at Shute Farm. He drew the blankets and the patchwork quilt over them.

"Mmmm," said Lindsay. "It's something Pixie gave me."

"I like the necklace too. I like you wearing a necklace and nothing else. . . . Is it the necklace? Or the scent? Or absence? Something's having a very powerful effect on me."

"It's the necklace, I expect," Lindsay replied, in a dreamy

way. "I bought it yesterday. It's that lovely *dark* amber. It's the color of your hair, Colin. I wonder . . ."

Colin burrowed down farther in the bed. With love, he kissed her thighs, and the triangle of springy hair between them, and her stomach, and her near-invisible stretch marks, and her breasts, and her mouth. These stations of her body were all dear to him.

"Ah, I can't bear this," he said. "Darling—it's nearly five; it will be getting light. I'll have to leave soon."

"Oh, don't go, don't go yet. I can't bear it either. It's still dark. It can't be twelve hours yet. . . ."

"It's twelve and a half. Lindsay, marry me—"

"Colin, I—Give me a little more time. I'm—it's a very serious step. . . . Darling, if you—oh, *yes*. Just like that. Oh, that feels so *right*. If you move just the smallest amount . . . Oh, that is the most miraculous thing when that happens to you. But we mustn't; not *again*. You'll be late. . . ."

"Frankly, I don't give a damn," said Colin.

"Happy New Year, Lindsay," said Rowland McGuire, climbing out of his car and walking around to its passenger door. "Can I say that, considering it's nearly the end of January? We made it—just. The roads from Oxford were very icy, and that track . . . Did you have a good Christmas?"

He kissed Lindsay, who had ventured out to meet the car, wrapped in several sweaters, a jacket, and Colin's overcoat. Rowland stared at her. "You're looking wonderful. You look— This place is obviously suiting you." He paused as his passenger climbed from the car. "Lindsay, this is Miriam. Miriam, this is Lindsay."

The two women shook hands. It was Miriam Stark's impression that this small woman, with her untidy hair, scarcely saw her. Her face was lit with an astonishing radiance. The cold air had made her cheeks pink; her eyes shone with an infectious happiness. Gesturing with small hands in red woolen gloves, and talking away rapidly, she led them into the farmhouse.

With an obvious pride and delight in it, she settled Miriam and Rowland by a great fire, and began to rush back and forth fetching tea things. She had made a cake, she said, in their honor—but she wasn't very good at cakes, so this one was a little lopsided. . . . It was a while before she paused for breath; by then, she had removed the layers of outer clothing and was standing by the fireplace, looking at them.

She was wearing flat leather boots, with a pair of claret-colored trousers tucked into them like breeches. She was wearing a careless vivid shirt and what might have been a man's tweed jacket. Around her throat was a dark amber necklace.

Miriam Stark, looking at her quietly, found her beautiful. She looked, Miriam thought, a little like a boy, a boy in drag, and she reminded Miriam, who was steeped in Shakespeare, of a Viola, or a Rosalind. Every second sentence she uttered, Miriam noted, began with the name "Colin." When she pronounced this name, she would color a little and the light in her eyes would intensify. "Holla your name to the reverberate hills," thought Miriam, taking a piece of the lopsided cake, which proved excellent.

Then, as the afternoon wore on and the light outside faded, her impressions of this woman began to shift a little. She was older than she appeared, Miriam realized, and probably, given her son's age, older than Miriam herself. Though in this light she looked, with her short hair, impulsive manner, and velveteen breeches, like some Elizabethan boy actor, there was another quality to her joy that proclaimed the woman in her. Miriam could sense an uncertainty, a hope qualified by wistfulness, which she found moving. She wondered what might be the cause of this, and had the opportunity to continue these speculations, for she was a woman of few words herself, and in the company of strangers always said little.

She noticed that this Lindsay appeared hungry, yet ate little. She noticed that, from time to time, she rested her small hands across her stomach, just below her breasts. She was very slim and seemed unconscious of making the gesture, but to Miriam, who had once carried a child herself, the movement, half protective, half superstitious, was unmistakable.

She glanced at Rowland, wondering if he too would recognize it. He did not, she thought; he had become increasingly silent as the afternoon wore on, and seeing him avert his eyes from the radiance in Lindsay's face, she realized suddenly that he was finding it virtually unbearable to be here. Pitying him, she rose to her feet and quietly suggested that they leave now.

"So, did you like her? I hope you did," Rowland said, breaking a long silence in the car, when they were halfway between the farmhouse and Oxford.

"Very much. She is—transparent." Miriam paused. "I envy her that." She paused again. "I think she will not write her book however."

"Probably not." Rowland kept his eyes on the road. "But I think she'll abandon it without regret—in the circumstances."

"That cannot have been easy for you, Rowland," Miriam ventured, after a further pause, turning her cool gaze toward him as he drove.

"No, but it will get easier eventually. I am still very . . ." He paused at an intersection. "I am very fond of her, and I'm equally fond of Colin."

"Describe this Colin. I look forward to meeting Colin."

"He's excitable. He says 'oh God, God, *God*' very often. And sometimes . . ." Rowland hesitated. "Sometimes I have the sensation that God listens—which is strange, considering I'm an atheist. Colin—well, Colin has a good heart, apparent naivete, and an instinct for the jugular. As you'd expect," he added, in a dry way, "considering his background."

"And will she really marry him?" Miriam frowned. "That vast house? All that money? Those possessions?" She gave an involuntary shiver. "She must surely fear . . ."

"You saw her face. She's afraid of nothing."

The interruption was curt; Rowland's tone, Miriam felt, could not disguise an emotion that might have been regret, but that she suspected came close to anguish. That tone, she found, affected her deeply. She said nothing.

They had reached the Headington traffic circle and the outskirts of the city; Rowland turned into Oxford. He could sense Miriam Stark's increase in tension before he had driven a hundred yards.

"Where shall I drop you, Miriam?"

"At the college, please, Rowland."

Rowland slowed the car.

"Why won't you let me come to your house?" he asked, in a quiet voice. "Miriam, is there some reason for excluding me?"

"I exclude all men from my house. That is my policy."

"That wasn't always the case. It wasn't the case fifteen years ago."

"No." She looked away. "I was younger then. Now—I write my books at home. I prefer to keep that part of my life separate. I value that purity."

"Very well. The college then."

They drove on in silence. Miriam Stark looked at Rowland's dark hair and at his profile. Knowing that she was being influenced by the joy seen in another woman's face, and knowing that she was breaking a resolution made several weeks earlier, she said, "Rowland, I will come with you to a hotel, if you like. . . ."

"I do like."

"Then turn left here. We can go to the Randolph."

"Lindsay, I want you to listen to me very carefully," said Colin.

He was speaking to her on a mobile telephone, from one of the upstairs rooms of the perfect Wildfell Hall Rowland had found him. From this room, where he knew he was safe from interruption, he could see across the moorland that surrounded the house to the path that led down to the beach below. From this vantage point, he could just glimpse the far end of the beach; he looked at a crescent of pale sand and a still, calm sea. It had been his practice, these last months, whenever he could escape from the demands of filming, to walk on this beach and think of Lindsay. He had grown used to the hours of its tides; thinking of her, always with love, sometimes with impatience to be with her, and sometimes simply with yearning, he had found the regularity of these tides soothing. The tide was now coming in fast; the day was fine, with a scent of spring, and a sharp, late winter's sun was shining.

"Can you hear me, darling?" he said.

"I can hear you absolutely clearly, as if you were standing next to me."

"What date is it today, Lindsay?"

"It's the twenty-eighth of February, Colin." Her voice, Colin thought, sounded a little unsteady. "And it's the last day of filming—unless Tomas Court has decided to go over. . . ."

"He never goes over."

"Then you're a free man in about—what? Two hours? Three hours?"

"Ten minutes," said Colin. "He says he's going to do this in one take—and I believe him. That means I'll be with you before dark. They're shooting the first scene of the movie now, then I'm leaving."

"Why do they *do* that? Shoot inside out and back to front? It's confusing. . . ."

"Not when you're used to it." Colin drew in a deep breath. "Darling, I'm going to ask you something that I first asked you on the telephone in a cottage not far from here. Lindsay, tell me—and by my calculations, this is the thirty-fourth time I'm asking, are you going to marry me, yes or no, because in my pocket, at this moment . . ."

"Yes," said Lindsay.

"I have—somewhere—ah, here it is, this special license, which means that tomorrow, in Oxford, whether you consent or not, I'm taking you to . . . What did you just say?"

"I said yes," said Lindsay.

Colin then became incoherent. She became incoherent. She decided to wait until he was with her before telling him that this would be, in effect, a shotgun wedding.

"Ten weeks," said Lindsay, coming to the end of her confused, halting, hesitant explanation.

They were standing in the kitchen at Shute Farm, where Colin, having driven at fearless speed, but with the caution of a prospective bridegroom, had arrived half an hour earlier.

Listening to her explanation, Colin had blushed one of his agonizing blushes. His face was now white. He was hearing a tremendous rushing sound in the quiet of this room. Its power astonished him; it came to him, very slowly, that this sound indicated profound joy, a joy so overwhelmingly intense, it left him speechless. Moving toward Lindsay and taking her in his arms, he found speech did gradually return to him, so he could express, by word and by touch, the fears, hopes, desires, and plans that sprang into his mind now—and that she, similarly gifted, could reply to them.

Later, a father-to-be's panic came upon him. He felt that Lindsay should not be standing. He felt she might need to lie down; he felt she might need to eat—or possibly *not* to eat. He felt perhaps she needed fruit, or milk; he certainly felt—though he kept this to himself—that Lindsay must, at the earliest opportunity, be seen by Harley Street's most expensive, wise, and infallible obstetrician. Was she sleeping? Could she rest? Did she have cravings? Colin hoped, with a fond, wild hope, that she had the most impossible of cravings—whatever she craved, he would obtain for her.

"Oh God, God, *God*," he said, striding up and down the kitchen, hitting his head on the beams several times, and scarcely noticing. "Darling, you must sit down. Put your feet up. Do you need a rug? Are you warm enough? You shouldn't have been *alone*. If I'd known, if I'd even *suspected*, I'd never have left you. Sod the movie. Sod Tomas Court. I'd have *been* here. Oh God, *God*. Can we still get married tomorrow? It might be too much. All that stress. Women get stressed on their wedding days. Clothes! Flowers! They worry about things like that. I *told* Tom. Christ! Tom! Tom has the ring. I'll have to call him now. . . ."

"*Tom* has the ring?" Lindsay said slowly.

"*Of course* Tom has the ring. Tom's going to be the best man. We fixed it all, *weeks* ago. The Ulanov Maneuver—you pin the queen with a bishop and a knight—he *said* your game always collapsed immediately. What am I going to *do*? The honeymoon—I'd forgotten about a honeymoon. Oh *God*, I'm so happy. This is a disaster. What's my father going to think? He'll never forgive me for this. He adores you. He'll think I've behaved appallingly. *Appallingly* . . ."

"Why don't we go and see?" Lindsay said, rising. "Why don't we go and tell him? And yes, I can walk there, dearest Colin, and yes, I might even be strong enough to marry you tomorrow. I feel amazingly strong, and well. Pregnancy isn't an *illness*, Colin."

"Pregnancy! Pregnancy! Oh, what a wonderful glorious word," cried Colin, hitting his head on the beam again. "With child. My child. I love you so much. Let me get your coat, and a scarf, you'd better wear a scarf. Lindsay, I can see for a thousand miles. I can move mountains. I can perform wonders. . . ."

"Well, yes. So it would seem. . . ." Lindsay smiled.

"I'm frightened. I'm happier than I've ever been in my life, and I'm afraid." Colin fell to his knees and pressed his face gently against her stomach. He began to kiss her woolly skirt, the waistband of which Lindsay, with pride and excitement, had let out for the first time that morning. She rested her hands on his hair, her heart full with the love she felt for him. Then, gently, she drew him to his feet.

She allowed herself to be wrapped up like a parcel in layers and layers of unnecessary but loving protective clothing, then they set off for Shute. On the track Colin was armed with a glorious optimism; by the time they reached the wood, he felt he might not be worthy; crossing the deer park, he felt he might be, if Lindsay could help him.

Colin went into his father's study alone to break the news to him. His expression was anxious; Lindsay waited and communed with Colin's dogs, stroking their rough fur and their elegant muzzles.

Colin came out after considerable time, his expression astonished. It seemed that Colin's father, so soldierly, so old school, so imbued with a lifetime's belief that a man under no circumstances showed emotion, had behaved in a way Colin could never have foreseen. He had said "by Jove"—his only oath—several times; several times he had remarked that he was so surprised that Colin could have knocked him down with a feather. He had begun on a few terse remarks about man's estate and his son's future responsibilities, frowning fiercely, his mustache bristling. Then, breaking off, he had embraced his son; much coughing, turning away, and blowing of his nose had not been able to disguise the fact that he was weeping.

It was bad enough that Colin should witness this weakness; for Lindsay to witness it was unthinkable. He would be coming out to her, Colin said, in a few moments, when he had regained his composure. His parting shot to Colin had been, "Damn good thing you're making an honest woman of her tomorrow. Left it a bit late by *my* standards. Luckily for you, she's an honest woman already. Knew it straight off. First second I laid eyes on her."

Colin's father regarded this remark as a witticism of Wildean elegance. So pleased with it was he that he was to repeat it to Colin, at intervals, for some years to come. Being of the old school, it was not a witticism, needless to say, that he would have dreamed of expressing to Lindsay. To his daughter-in-law-to-be, he said in a gruff way that she was a good woman for taking this son of his off his hands. "By Jove," he added, coughing again, "thought I'd never get shot of him. . . ."

Lindsay smiled and kissed the old man, the kiss causing him to suffer severe bronchial disturbance; he bolted from the room immediately.

Lindsay was very touched by this. A sojourn here was teaching her, she felt, the value of certain conventions.

So the wedding went off the next day, happily, and without untoward incident, at a small registry office in Oxford. Tom remembered the ring and attended the ceremony with Cressida-from-upstairs on his arm, having discovered that Cressida, a sensible girl, had a way of making Katya forgettable. This discovery he had made with a little assistance from Colin, who had suggested one day in Yorkshire that this friend of Tom's might like to come up to watch a day's filming; of this assistance, Tom remained unaware, for Colin was subtle.

Colin's father attended, and—while not disgracing himself with tears—blew his nose loudly and continuously throughout the ceremony. Pixie attended, looking formidable and smiling pityingly. Lindsay's difficult mother arrived late, but was there, and remarked only a few times, as she clasped her headmaster husband's arm, that she was glad to see her daughter at last following her own example. Rowland McGuire, unable to attend because of work commitments, sent excellent champagne, his love, and a telegram that, when read out by Tom, was agreed by everyone to be very dry, very witty, rather *risqué*, but very Rowland.

Lindsay wore a whitish ensemble bought in a great rush that morning, a blue garter borrowed from Pixie, and a ring—and *old* ring, Colin's father assured her—that had once belonged to Colin's mother. It was a beautiful ring, and although Lindsay believed Colin when he said its stones were very ordinary garnets, she also knew beyond a doubt that they were rubies.

Markov telephoned at intervals throughout the day, requiring updates on everyone's precise degree of happiness; he contrived to conceal his deep affection for Lindsay beneath remarks that as usual, were both affected and waspish.

Mellowing slightly by the time of his final call to Shute, he announced he had decided it was time he made an honest man of Jippy. He was starting to plan a marriage ceremony somewhere suitably charming, such as Big Sur, or Las Vegas. Signing off, he informed both Colin and Lindsay that they had his lover to thank for their present state of bliss. Jippy, he added, sent them both—or, rather, sent them *all*—his blessings.

It was that night in New York, much affected by that day's events in England, which he had watched from afar, that Jippy began dreaming.

These dreams, which first came to him that night, and continued for some nights afterward, came to him when he was lying restlessly beside Markov, in a state between waking and sleeping. In these dreams, he discovered, he watched present and future with a steady tranquillity. This form of precognition had never happened to him before and he much preferred it to those flashes and flickerings that had previously constituted his clairvoyance.

In these dreams, he found, he could watch over those he loved, such as Lindsay and Colin; he could watch them and others, with engagement, yet with distance. He could feel, as he watched, pity, fear, and compassion, yet he no longer wished to intervene; he no longer had that painful need to seek to spare and protect; he no longer attempted to pull the invisible strings he saw manipulating this universe. He watched and accepted these inevitabilities.

And so he saw, in these nights of dreaming, that the outcome for others was less benevolent than it had been for Lindsay and Colin. He watched the director Tomas Court complete a movie that, from start date to final cut, was almost the same length of time in gestation as a baby. Nine months, and the visions Court had seen in his mind, those ghosts, were fixed upon celluloid. Tomas Court, with whom Jippy felt a certain fellowship, moved on to his next movie. Jippy could see that ultimately his health would fail him; he could see, meanwhile, that the loving war—or warring love—with his wife was still continuing.

Jippy watched this man and this woman and their son at a ranch in Montana, near Glacier National Park. Then, with some reluctance, he scanned away from them, moving off on his dream thermals, to look at another man, woman, and son, whose future lay, clear as a lake, spread out to his view below him. He watched Pascal Lamartine meet a fate that had dogged his footsteps for many years, and that Jippy had seen plucking at his sleeve that Thanksgiving night at the Plaza.

It could only have gone one way, the dreaming Jippy felt, and he sensed that this person, who had been waiting for Lamartine so long, was someone Lamartine himself had been seeking. He might have taken many forms, this person, and he might have issued forth in the course of almost any war, in any country. It could have been Beirut, or Mozambique, or Bosnia: it proved to be a small town of little importance in Sri Lanka. The instrument was not a mine or a bomb, as it might have been, but a boy—a frightened boy, toting a scavenged rifle, who fired out of panic and confusion, as Lamartine raised his camera.

The boy, horrified to see the realities of guns for the first time, bent over the body and touched the blood with a wondering finger. He had not quite believed, until that moment, how easy it was to kill a man, and he had not foreseen that a killing could happen so quickly. He looked at the eyes of this stranger, which were glazing, then ran away, hid, prayed to his gods, and vomited. Later, astonished that this event had been so simple and that he had survived it, the boy came to boast of his feat. He added embellishments; he fictionalized it. And dreaming Jippy, sorrowing for the dead man, sorrowing for the boy, saw that this fictionalizing, like the death, was inevitable and unremarkable. Similar things happened every second of every day and, sensing their clamor, dreaming Jippy moved onward.

He watched the consequences of this event, which he had only been able to glimpse before, and now saw through his dark glass clearly. Lamartine's wife was graceful in her widowhood, assiduous regarding her son's welfare, and assiduous in preserving her dead husband's memory. Some years later, she married an American—a man old enough to be her father,

her friends said—whom she had first encountered at her father's funeral.

Was she happy then? Jippy did not stay to watch over her future happiness or lack of it. He moved off again on his thermals, which were swifter and more powerful than a jet plane. He could have paused in his dreams in a thousand places; traveling on, he could feel their stories rising up at him. Sorrows drifted up like smoke as he passed, but Jippy, a kind man, wanted benevolence, so he moved on and on, pausing only when he was in its vicinity.

So it was that Jippy saw Dr. Miriam Stark return home one day from her women's college, her mind preoccupied with thoughts of Rowland. She was a woman who lived her life by rules, and one of those rules—to let no man come close to her—she was beginning to fear she had broken.

On a summer's evening, heavy with the scent of roses, she let herself into the small house to which she had refused Rowland admittance. It was situated in that part of Oxford where a confluence of rivers and a canal create small packages of land; her house, looking out over water, filled with the sounds of water, was virtually moated. This house, quiet, scholarly, calming, and familiar, she found both unchanged and changed that evening. Its rooms, as always, were orderly, but she could not look at them, as she usually did, with serenity.

She had done *wrong*, she felt; she had done *wrong* to create this cool, quiet, virginal enclave. She walked through its peaceful rooms with a sense of mounting perturbation; in her living room, with its books and its French windows opening onto the garden, she found her son; he had fallen asleep on a couch. He was still wearing his tennis clothes—he had been playing tennis with friends all afternoon—and his racket lay beside him. He had a book on his knees, and in front of him, switched off, was a television bought by Miriam and rarely watched by either of them.

This boy was fourteen, now approaching his fifteenth birthday. When awake, he had the clumsiness and awkwardness of any adolescent, but asleep, he was beautiful. Miriam stood there for some time, looking down at him. He was sprawled full-length, his long golden limbs stretched out, with the easy grace of an Adonis in a Renaissance painting. His head was tilted back, exposing the line of his throat; his face was flushed from the sun and from sleep, and his dark hair, in need of cutting, curled with a girlish grace around his neck and forehead.

He was going to be as tall as his father was; he had his father's hair, his father's features, and his father's extraordinary eyes; this beauty was inherited. In the past, watching it form, Miriam had regretted this and tried to make herself blind to it. She had wanted this child as her child only, and she had wanted to deny the part his father had played in his making. It was, after all, the most minimal possible—the fatherhood here came about as a result of chance, a miscalculation, a copulation neither partner had intended to take place, which, afterward, had dismayed both of them.

The Rowland McGuire of that time was a very different man from the one she had remet recently: he had been more markedly arrogant, less scrupulous, and more impatient. He was making a career for himself, as she was, and shortly after their one night together, he left to take up the first of his assignments in America. She, glad he had left, glad he need not threaten her equilibrium, had continued to write her book. When, two months later, having heard nothing from Rowland McGuire in the interim, she discovered she was pregnant, she had felt a fierce angry pride rise up in her; she would have died sooner than inform him.

So she had brought up her boy alone, without male aid, and this too she took pride in. She felt scorn at the need other women seemed to have for male companionship, finance, and protection. She needed none of it. This scorn, and this shrinking from the male sex, from men who conquered and colonized females with such ease and such carelessness, remained with her. She wanted a lover only occasionally, and she hated the idea of a husband.

So she did not regret her past actions; she did not for one instant believe in, or wish for, any future for herself and Rowland. Certainly not; yet still there was that sense, that perturbing sense of her own wrongdoing. Rowland McGuire now mourned his single state and mourned his childlessness; this boy, she saw, was not solely her possession.

And so, later that night, when her son was in bed and asleep, she paced her room, then, with reluctance, breaking off then starting over, began to write a letter. Words, words, words. It was late, very late, before she finished the letter.

Did she send it? Jippy saw her carry it as far as the front door of her house; he watched her hesitate. Then his air thermals lifted him away, to a house in London, a house overlooking a Hawksmoor church, the spire of which could be seen from its main bedroom. Rowland McGuire did not sleep, he saw; watching him, Jippy felt he might act, or he might not act. He might receive the letter, or, not receiving it, be told its contents in some other fashion, on some other occasion. In his dreamings, Jippy, who was softhearted and given to optimism, bestowed on this scholarly woman and this solitary man, a wish for a benign resolution. He stayed to see Rowland McGuire open his shutters to the morning and pick up the telephone—then he moved on for the last of his visitations.

High summer still and he found himself in—ah yes, a hospital. There, his Lindsay, his dear Lindsay, and his good Colin, were watching on a black-and-white ultrasound screen, for the small fist, the fetal shape of their unborn baby.

The ultrasound operator, a young woman used to the emotionalism of these moments, kept her eyes on the screen as she moved her magical device across Lindsay's bared stomach. Lindsay, as she never stopped telling everyone, was very large, was hugely pregnant, was carrying a giant of a baby. This baby, limbering up for birth, gave her permanent and acute indigestion. He or she never appeared to sleep, but was ceaselessly and exhaustingly active. He or she liked to calm down a little in the evenings, and wait for the moment when Lindsay hauled herself into bed with Colin. Then, just when they were curved together like two spoons, in a state of the most peaceful contentment, this baby would remind them of its presence. It would punch, kick, roll, somersault, perform uterine headstands. This baby was a wrestler, a boxer, a gymnast; this baby was a judo black belt, and it was working on its fetal karate.

Both Colin and Lindsay, needless to say, were immensely proud of these feats. They would complain, and they did complain, but they did so while exchanging glances of marital and parental complicity. Both were clear that their baby was unique; no other baby in the history of the world had ever manifested such prowess, such interesting characteristics. Colin, desperate for sleep, drugged with exhaustion, could still roll over at three in the morning and, with an expression of wonderment, rest his face or his hands against his wife's stomach, so that he could feel the miracle of these kickings and strugglings.

Now, holding Lindsay's hand very tightly, Colin fixed his eyes on the screen. Science took him on an odyssey into the interior of the womb—and he found it was the strangest of journeys. He had expected this interior world to resemble the diagrams in the pregnancy textbooks he now consulted twenty times a day. But this world, he found, resembled none of the maps and sketches in those textbooks. What he saw resembled a canyon, a moonscape, or some deep trench under the ocean. He could see shapes that might have been rivers, rocks, or chasms, but none of these shapes was fixed; there was constant flux and movement; there were blips, as the operator, frowning, made some adjustment. Here, somewhere, floating in that mysterious amniotic sac, was their child, their fully formed child, whose small heartbeats he could feel at night when he touched Lindsay.

He found tears had come to his eyes, for what he was seeing was so ordinary and so miraculous. Ah, dear God, let this child be well, he thought; let this child be whole and unharmed and born safely. Let Lindsay and me know how best to care for, console, guide, and protect it from now on.

The screen gave one of its blips; the landscape, or seascape, reformed. His wife gave a low cry, and the operator a nod of satisfaction. Colin saw his child. He could see the curve of his spine, the outline of his skull, and a tiny clenched hand; this child flexed its fingers.

"Goodness me," said the operator. "I think—just one second . . ."

Colin's heart stopped; Lindsay's face drained of color.

"No, no, don't worry," said the woman. "Everything's fine; everything's normal. It's just that I thought . . . one moment." She gave a bright professional smile. "Have to adjust. This is a bit tricky. . . . Ah yes. *There*. The cunning little . . ." She blushed. "Sorry. Congratulations. There are two of them."

"*Two?*" said Lindsay.

"Twins?" she and Colin said in unison.

"Absolutely. No doubt about it. Look . . ." She pointed. "There's one, and there's the other. Shall I tell you the sex?"

"No," said Lindsay.

"Yes," said Colin.

"You're right. Yes, yes, yes, tell us."

"A boy. And—wait a second. . . . A girl."

"Oh God, God, *God.* Darling, you're so clever. . . ."

"I don't *believe* it. I *told* that doctor. I *knew* I couldn't be this big with just one in there. Oh, Colin . . ."

"The girl's the smaller—as is usually the way," the operator continued, frowning at the screen. "She has a powerful kick though—look at that. And she's been hiding herself away behind her brother. They do that sometimes. Well now, Mrs. Lascelles, are we excited? *Isn't* that a lovely surprise? I—Mrs. Lascelles, is your husband all right? He looks rather pale. . . ."

Colin heard these words from a great distance. They were small fuzzy words, receding from him fast. The room, beginning to tilt, was not recognizing the usual rules of the universe. Intent on not disgracing himself, he sat down on a small hard chair, and stared at the wall. He was a father now—no more tears, he told himself, and certainly no fainting.

He looked at the joy in the room. He could sense a cluster, a *preponderance* of angels. He wanted to embrace Lindsay and the operator who had been the harbinger here. He wanted to cry aloud, to voice some great, thankful cry of hope, promise, and jubilation. He sprang to his feet and embraced his wife, who was struggling to sit up and weeping.

The operator, with a quiet tact, left them alone together. Colin, holding his wife in his arms, seeing her tears, rested his hands over the tautness and stretch of his wife's stomach. Feeling his karate babies kick out, he knew beyond question, knew without a second's doubt, that grace existed, and grace had been bestowed on them.

Their silent watcher, Jippy, cocooned in his dreams, knew this too. He watched a little longer and a little longer, until he was sure these babies were safely born. They were. He found he could relinquish his dreams now. Recalling his spell, that orange and those two eggs, he sighed. His powers were greater than he had realized, he thought; in the future, he would have to be more careful. He yawned; then, reassured to have seen the good, forgetting the bad, he let his dreams go.

He closed his clairvoyant eyes. Hearing his lover make a small sound, he clasped his hand, then lay down and fell asleep beside him.

"A delicious stew of crime, passion,
high fashion, and tragic love."
—*Affaire de Coeur*

From Sally Beauman,
the bestselling author of *Lovers and Liars*,
comes a tale of international intrigue
and fatal passion.

DANGER ZONES

A reclusive designer of originality and passion, Maria
Cazarès is a legend shrouded in mystery. When the
fashion glitterati assemble in Paris to breathlessly
await the new Cazarès collection, a long-buried secret
resurfaces and tragedy strikes. Two journalists,
Rowland McGuire and Gini Hunter, pick up the scent
of an unfolding scandal that will converge with the
desperate search for an innocent girl who has disappeared. And at last, some blood red truths will be
revealed....

**Published by Fawcett Books.
Available wherever books are sold.**

More international suspense
and erotic adventures in

LOVERS & LIARS

by bestselling author
Sally Beauman

Assigned to expose the story of a lifetime, photographer Pascal Lamartine and reporter Gini Hunter penetrate the perfect facade of John Hawthorne, the charismatic U.S. Ambassador to Great Britain, a man who is not what he seems. As they penetrate the web of betrayal and deceit surrounding Hawthorne, Gini and Pascal must also confront the love they shared twelve years before, a passionate liaison that ended explosively.

Lovers & Liars is a romantic and thrilling journey into the deepest reaches of the heart, where love can sustain the soul—or twist it cruelly....

Published by Fawcett Books.
Available wherever books are sold.

Look for these exciting novels
of romantic suspense
by *New York Times* bestselling author

SALLY BEAUMAN.

Available in bookstores everywhere.
Published by Fawcett Books.

Call toll free 1-800-793-BOOK (2665) to order by phone and use your
major credit card. Or use this coupon to order by mail.

__LOVERS & LIARS	449-22368-X	$6.99
__DANGER ZONES	449-22561-5	$6.99
__DECEPTION & DESIRE	449-00248-9	$6.99

Name_____
Address_____
City_____State_____Zip _____

Please send me the FAWCETT BOOKS I have checked above.
I am enclosing $_____
plus
Postage & handling* $_____
Sales tax (where applicable) $_____
Total amount enclosed $_____

*Add $4 for the first book and $1 for each additional book.

Send check or money order (no cash or CODs) to:
Fawcett Mail Sales, 400 Hahn Road, Westminster, MD 21157.

Prices and numbers subject to change without notice.
Valid in the U.S. only.
All orders subject to availability.   BEAUMAN

Want to know a secret?
It's sexy, informative, fun, and FREE!!!

❧ PILLOW TALK ❧

Join Pillow Talk and get advance information and sneak peeks at the best in romance coming from Ballantine. All you have to do is fill out the information below!

♥ My top five favorite authors are: _____

_____

_____

_____

_____

♥ Number of books I buy per month: ❏ 0-2 ❏ 3-5 ❏ 6 or more

♥ Preference: ❏ Regency Romance ❏ Historical Romance
❏ Contemporary Romance ❏ Other

♥ I read books by new authors: ❏ frequently ❏ sometimes ❏ rarely

Please print clearly:
Name _____

Address_____

City/State/Zip_____

Don't forget to visit us at
www.randomhouse.com/BB/loveletters

beauman

**PLEASE SEND TO: PILLOW TALK/
BALLANTINE BOOKS, CN/9-2
201 EAST 50TH STREET
NEW YORK, NY 10022
OR FAX TO PILLOW TALK, 212/940-7539**